GEOFF RYMAN is the extraordinarily talented author
of hugely praised novels like *The Child Garden* and
Was and, most recently, *253*, the world's first internet novel published to tremendous acclaim in 1998.

By Geoff Ryman:

253
THE CHILD GARDEN
WAS
UNCONQUERED COUNTRIES

Lust

or

No Harm Done

Geoff Ryman

Flamingo
An Imprint of HarperCollinsPublishers

This novel is entirely a work of fiction.
The names, characters and incidents portrayed in it are
the work of the author's imagination. Any resemblance to
actual persons, living or dead, events or localities is
entirely coincidental.

Flamingo
An Imprint of HarperCollins*Publishers*
77–85 Fulham Palace Road,
Hammersmith, London W6 8JB

www.**fire**and**water**.com

Published by Flamingo 2001
1 3 5 7 9 8 6 4 2

The Author asserts the moral right to
be identified as the author of this work

A catalogue record for this book
is available from the British Library

ISBN 0 00 225987 7

Set in Slimbach with Helvetica Neue display by
Rowland Phototypesetting Ltd,
Bury St Edmunds, Suffolk

Printed and bound in Great Britain by
Clays Ltd, St Ives plc

para o meu Txay

Um livro dedicado a ti deveria ser intitulado *Amor*,
ou no mínimo: *Sem Escândalo*. Eu prometi que nele
tu não te encontrarias, mas tu estais em todo lugar.

'In the bend God created the hen and the education. And the education was without founder, and void; and death was upon the falsehood of the demand. And the sport of God moved upon the falsehood of the wealth. And God said, Let there be limit; and there was limit.'

A text produced from the Book of Genesis using a method invented by Jean Lescure in which each noun is replaced with the seventh noun following it in a dictionary.

As reported in *Oulipo Compendium* edited by Harry Matthews and Alastair Brotchie

Acknowledgement:
The experiment with chicks described in this novel is loosely based on a real experiment described in *The Making of Memory* by Steven P. Rose.

Part I

So how does it start?

Michael was happy. It was the first day of his research project. His team waited for him outside the gates of the lab, in the March chill. Ebru, Emilio and Hugh all smiled when they saw him.

It was a new lab, in rooms within arches under a railway. Michael had the keys, leading his team into one beautiful new room after another. They moved their desks and wired up their computers. They arranged staplers, pens and envelopes in drawers, determined that everything would stay tidy.

Ebru had brought flowers and a traditional Turkish shepherd's cloak to hang on the wall. She was one of Michael's students, doing a doctorate of her own, and had been hired to help administer the project. Ebru had bet Emilio a bottle of champagne that his new network would crash. Instead, the network came triumphantly to life, and they exchanged chiding e-mails, and raised glasses of champagne to the start of their brave new project.

'To continued funding,' toasted Michael. They all laughed.

The first shipment of eggs arrived in a box marked FRAGILE COMPUTERS. This was to fox the animal rights activists. The eggs were packed in grey foam like recording equipment. Ebru and Michael laid them out in the darkroom, on straw, to hatch. Everything was in place.

'This is going to work,' said Michael.

In the evening Michael went to his gym. He saw Tony. Tony

3

was a trainer and Michael had a crush on him. Tony was tall and sleek and so innocent in his manner that Michael's nickname for him was the Cherub. Tony had a radiant announcement to make.

'I decided to take the plunge,' Tony said. 'Jacqui and I are going to get married.' He had the eyes of a happy schoolboy.

'Aw, that's fantastic. Well done!' said Michael and they did an old-fashioned hand slap. Tony's hair was cut short and dressed in spikes. Everything about him took Michael back to his youth. Tony talked a little bit about how he had realized he didn't want anyone else. 'It'll mean moving up north, but hey, she's worth it.'

That's what I want, thought Michael. I want a beautiful love.

Inspired in his heart and in his belly, Michael decided to visit the sauna in Alaska Street.

The smell of the place – hot pinewood, steam and bodies – produced an undertow of excitement as if something were pulling insistently downwards on his stomach. Naked men circulated in the steam in early evening.

Stripped of his glasses and lab coat, Michael was tall and athletic. A young Sikh with his hair tied at the top of his head in a bun saw Michael and did an almost comic double take. He was hairy and running slightly to fat, but the face, Michael suddenly saw, was smooth as marble. This was a young man with a fatherly body.

Michael followed the Sikh into the steam room with its benches. The Sikh looked at him with a teasing smile. They moved towards each other.

Michael didn't trust kissing. He knew people often brushed their teeth before cruising. Brushing teeth always produced blood; blood carried the virus. When the boy leaned towards him, Michael turned his head away and pressed his cheek against his. Michael gave him quick, dishonest pecks on the lips, pretending to be romantic and playful instead of merely safe.

Even this was enough for the young man. They sat down and Michael leaned back on the bench as they embraced. Briefly

4

they made a shape together like a poster for *Gone with the Wind*. Then the Sikh slipped lower and went to work (work was the only word for it) on Michael's cock.

Michael's cock stayed dead. All the young man's ministrations only made it worse. It retreated further, back up and away. Not again, thought Michael, not again. It always happened, and it was always worse than Michael remembered. It was always worse with someone he liked. Most especially it happened with people he liked. The Sikh stopped, and looked up. He turned down his mouth in a show of childish disappointment.

Michael asked, 'Are you too hot? Would you like something to drink?'

It was a way of saving face.

On the mezzanine, there were free drinks in the fridge and smelly beanbags on the floor. Michael poured them each a glass of spring water. Perched on a beanbag like a Buddha, the boy shook down his long glossy hair and began to retie it. Michael wanted to take him home and watch him wind it in his turban.

Michael passed him the water and the young man gave him a sharp little smile of thanks. When Michael lay down next to him, the Sikh stayed seated upright. In his heart, Michael knew what that meant, but yearning and hope persisted.

The young man talked politely. He was a medical doctor, a specialist in tropical diseases. He had been working in Africa and was back home to see his family. His name was Deep.

Michael asked him: did he work for Médecins sans Frontières?

'No, I don't like those organizations. They are too Western. They go there thinking they will show the natives how to do it. But, you know, they have no experience of infectious disease. I apply for the same jobs as the local doctors. I learn more that way.'

He was pleased to talk about his time there. The lack of roads, the digging of wells. Suddenly Deep lay back and let Michael rest his head on his fatherly bosom. Deep's breath smelled of liquorice. 'You know, I was working in a hospital in Malawi, by a lake. I was sitting out by myself drinking a beer. And I could see the animals come down to drink. The deer and the lions. And I could watch the deer as they kept watch. They kept flicking their ears. There was a moon on the lake.'

I'd go there with you, thought Michael. For just a moment he glimpsed another life. He was by that lake with Deep and they were together and Michael was doing . . . what? Michael was binding an antelope's broken shin.

Michael ventured forth. 'I, uh, have a boyfriend, but he won't be there now. I don't live very far from here.'

Despite his size, Dr Deep's face was thin, slightly cynical, and it did not respond to the suggestion.

Michael endeavoured. 'Would you like to come back with me?'

Dr Deep shook his head. 'I'm not what you're looking for.'

Oh, oh, but you are, thought Michael. 'You're sure?' he asked and tried to engineer a winning smile.

Dr Deep was sure. 'You know, I have been very tired and tense coming back here to see my family. I'm about to change countries again. So I just came here for the sex.'

They kissed and parted company. Deep was one of those perennial boys who only like older men. Over the next 45 minutes Michael watched Dr Deep kneel in front of one middle-aged man after another, his head bobbing away and then abruptly withdrawing, like a bee gathering honey. A medically trained bee who must know the risks.

The last Michael saw of Dr Deep, he was standing utterly alone, having sucked off every older man who wanted sucking. Dr Deep held up his towel, masturbating on show. Only one person was watching, but Dr Deep was looking pointedly away from Michael.

It's all you want, Michael thought in disappointment. And if I'd been able to give you that, would you have talked to me? Gone out to a movie with me? Become friends? Do you want to die that badly, that you can't even take time to talk? No one ever even talks. No one ever rings back. Is a hard dick really that important to you faggots?

How could I be stupid enough to get emotional? I know the

score; I can't get it up, so I either put up or dry up. I know what will happen, it always happens and I always forget. I always keep thinking it's not that bad. But it is that bad. It's like I think it will clear up by itself if I leave it alone. Like a sock that loses its other half. You put it back in the drawer, hoping it'll find the other half by itself.

Well, I'm sorry. I'm sorry that I look like such a big butch man who'll slap you and then fuck you silly. I'm sorry that I got a bit romantic. I won't do it again. I keep forgetting what you guys are like.

Michael dragged his ass back into his underwear and out to Waterloo station, and on the underground platform. He cursed sex. He cursed the need for it, and how men wanted it. He cursed being gay. He cursed all other gay men. He cursed his dick and he cursed himself. As all the day's happiness crushed around him like ruins in an aftershock, he prayed, or came as close to praying as he could get.

Michael pleaded for all the weary dead weight of his sexual desire to be taken from him. 'Look, just castrate me, get rid of it, please, please just take it all away!'

Was a train coming? Wind blew along the platform; a newspaper rose up by itself into the air.

And Michael noticed that his gym instructor was standing a few feet away. Oh Jesus, not now, thought Michael. He didn't want to see happiness; he didn't want to see joy. He looked at Tony and thought: all I want to do is see your dick.

There on the platform, with fifteen other people, Tony pulled down first his tracksuit bottoms and then his clean white briefs. The Cherub stood still and exposed, his bovine thighs and brown pubic hair on display. His stare was as blank and disconnected as a sleepwalker's.

The people on the platform looked disconnected as well. A greying man in a tan checked jacket glanced sideways and began to edge closer, eyes flickering. A woman searched her purse with immense concentration.

Then Tony sat down on the platform, and rolled onto his back, sticking the perfect bottom into the air, like an animal about to be spayed.

Oh, Jesus, thought Michael. So much for innocence. Bitterness and rage were countered by another thought: Tony must be in trouble.

Michael walked towards him. He saw the chords of muscle on the inside leg, and the head of the reasonably sized uncircumcised cock. Michael looked and then was sorry for looking. Tony gazed up at him, eyes unfocussed, dim with a half-formed question.

'Fancy a portion?' the Cherub asked.

Drugs, Michael decided. He doesn't normally do drugs, so he's gone and got what he thought was E only it was speed, plaster of Paris and battery acid.

'Tony. What are you doing on the ground?' Michael felt the eyes of the other people on the platform. His ears burned. He wanted them to know his intentions were honourable. The Cherub blinked, his head haloed by the grey and white patterns of the platform paving.

'Stand up, come on.'

Michael didn't want to touch him in public. Tony rolled to his feet. He stood without adjusting his clothes, facing the woman with the handbag. She looked like she might pull it down over her head.

Pull your trousers up! thought Michael, and immediately, the Cherub bent down and nipped both layers of clothing back into place.

'Did you take anything? Do you remember what it was?'

The mouth hung open, the lips fatter when they were not smiling. Tony's brows clenched, trying to find an answer. 'I didn't take anything.'

'Are you sure? Try to think. What was it called?'

Tony nodded his head solemnly, yes. 'Diclofenac,' he said. 'For my knee.'

Michael was a biologist. Diclofenac was a powerful anti-inflammation drug. Did it have side effects?

'Have you taken it before?'

Tony nodded yes again, like a child.

The wind blew. Like a friend showing up, the train rumbled out of the tunnel. 'This is my train,' said Michael, trying to keep the tone conversational. 'Where are you going, Tony?'

The Cherub replied as if the answer were obvious. 'With you.'

It wouldn't be right to leave him. Michael looked up at the handbag lady and she looked away hastily. The greying man looked miffed that Michael had got there first. Michael pushed his way onto the train as others were getting off, and Tony followed him. Michael clenched the handrail almost as hard as he was clenching his teeth, and looked around him.

Two teenage Indian boys were talking about cars or computers in a jargon he didn't understand. A woman turned over a page of her crinkly newspaper as if toasting its other side, and sniffed delicately. None of them had seen the banquet of Cherub laid out on the platform. Very suddenly, normality closed over them. The doors rolled shut. The noise of the train provided an excuse not to talk, as if it were embarrassed for them.

Tony simply stared, the flesh on his face slack, like old Hush Puppy shoes. There was definitely something wrong with him; he squinted up at the advertising, looking as if ads for Blistex were beyond his mental age. As the train approached Goodge Street, Michael wondered what on earth to do.

'Look, Tony. I get off here. Will you be OK?'

Tony nodded yes. The train stopped and the doors opened. Michael got off. Tony followed him.

'Do you want to see a doctor?'

Tony shook his head, no. Michael could think of nothing else to do, so he headed for the WAY OUT sign and the lift. Tony started to whistle, in a kind of deranged echoing drawl.

I don't like this, Michael thought. He said airily, 'So. Do you live around here, Tony?'

'I live in Theydon Bois.' Theydon Bois was at the end of the Central Line. This was the Northern.

'So,' Michael ventured. 'You're meeting someone?' A coldness gathered around his heart.

'No,' said the Cherub in the same numb, faraway voice.

'So where are you going?' Why, Michael thought, does the underground always smell of asbestos and urine?

'I don't know. I don't even have a ticket.'

They had reached the lifts. The windows in the metal doors looked like empty eye sockets. This was getting weird. 'Look,' Michael asked him, 'if there's something wrong, I'm not sure I can help you. Do have a phone with you?'

'I don't think so.' Tony patted his tracksuit pockets.

Michael began to be afraid. This guy can bench-press 130 kilos. The elevator arrived filling the two windows with light as if they were eyes that had opened. The doors beeped and gaped but Michael did not get in.

'You don't want to go this way,' said Michael. 'You want to go back that direction.'

'What I want doesn't count,' said Tony.

My God, thought Michael. He hasn't blinked, not once.

Stand clear of the doors please said a cool, controlling voice. Michael decided it was best to get upstairs where there were people. He got in, Tony followed, and the doors trundled shut. They were alone.

Tony slipped his fingers under the spandex waistband, and pulled down both trousers and underwear, businesslike, as if finishing a warm-up.

Stop! thought Michael. Tony stopped. 'Pull them up!' said Michael. Tony did. The Cherub looked back at him, scowling slightly as if he couldn't quite hear what was being said.

Jesus, thought Michael, this is what you get for fancying some guy at the gym: you chat away, you're nice to him, and suddenly you've got a psychopath following you home. There was sweat on Michael's upper lip. The lift did a little bounce and stopped, mimicking the sick sensation in Michael's stomach.

The doors opened and Michael swept through them, fumbling to pull his season ticket out of his jacket pocket. He strode to the barriers, slipping his card into the slot like a kiss, nipped it free and pushed his way out and away. He could feel Tony's eyes on his back as he escaped.

Michael thought and then stopped: you know he's in trouble. It might be an insulin reaction, something like that. You can't just leave him. He turned around. Tony was standing dazed behind the ticket barriers. What if he's too ill to even know his way home? Michael sighed and walked back.

'Is this something that happens to you sometimes? Are you diabetic, are you on any kind of medication?' Michael was thinking schizophrenia. The ticket barriers were hunched between them like a line of American football players.

'No,' said Tony, as if from the bottom of a well.

'Well look, the Central Line is back that way,' Michael said. 'Go back down and change at Tottenham Court Road.' Michael glanced sideways; the guard was listening.

The guard was a young, handsome, burly man whom Michael had once halfway fancied, except for his unpleasant sneer. The guard was looking the other way, but his ears were pricked.

Tony said, mildly surprised. 'Don't you want to fuck me?'

Michael said, 'No. I don't.'

The guard covered his smile with an index finger.

Tony looked bruised. 'You do,' he insisted.

Michael began to talk for the benefit of the guard. 'I'm sorry if you got that idea. Look, you're in a bit of a state. My advice is to try to get back home and sort yourself out.'

The guard suddenly trooped forward, his smile broadening to a leer. 'Bit off a bit more than we can chew, did we, sir?'

'I think he's on something and he's been following me,' said Michael.

'Must be your lucky day,' said the guard. He began to hustle Tony back from the barriers. 'Come on, let the Professor be. He probably can't afford you anyway.' The guard had the cheek to turn and grin at Michael like he'd said something funny.

'He's not well,' said Michael. Gosh, did he dislike that guard. But he needed him. The guard herded Tony back towards the lifts. Michael saw Tony look at him, with a suddenly stricken face. It was that panic that frightened Michael more than anything else. The panic meant that Tony needed Michael. For what? Something was out of whack.

Michael fled. He turned and walked as quickly as he could, away. He doesn't know where I live, Michael thought, relieved. If I get away, I find another gym, and that's the end of it.

11

Michael's stomach was shuddering as if he had run out of petrol. The tip of his penis was wet.

It had been raining, and the pavements were glossy like satin. A woman bearing four heavy bags from Tesco was looking at her boots; Michael scurried to make the lights and bashed into the bags, spinning them around in her grasp.

There was a shout from behind him. 'Oi!'

Michael spun around, and saw the Cherub sprinting towards him. Michael knew, from the way his athlete's stride suspended him in mid-air, that Tony had jumped the barriers.

Michael backed away, raising his arms against attack, terror bubbling up like yeast.

Keep away from me! Get back, go away!

And the street was empty. Tony was gone.

Michael blinked and looked around him, up and down the pavement. When he looked back, he saw the guard hobbling towards him, pressing a handkerchief to his face. He'd been hit.

'Where did he go?' the guard shouted at Michael, strands of spit between his lips. 'Where the fuck did he go?'

'I don't know!'

'Bastard!'

Michael tried to look at the guard's lip.

The guard ducked away from Michael's tender touch. He demanded, snarling, 'What's his name, where's he from?'

Michael did not even have to think. 'I've no idea. He just followed me.'

'Oh yeah. Just followed you, did he? If I press charges, mate, you'll bloody well have to remember.'

The guard pulled the handkerchief away and looked as if expecting to see something. He blinked. The handkerchief was clean, white and spotless.

This seemed to mollify him. 'You better watch the kind of person you pick up, mate.'

Then the guard turned and proudly, plumply, walked away. For all your arrogance, Michael thought, in five years' time you'll be bald and fat-arsed.

Michael stood in the rain for a few moments, catching his

breath. What, he thought, was that all about? Finally he turned and walked up Chenies Street, mostly because he had no place else to go, and he began to cry, from a mix of fear, frustration, boredom. Christ! All he did was go to the sauna. He didn't need this, he really didn't. He looked up at the yellow London sky. There were no stars overhead, just light pollution, a million lamps drowning out signals from alien intelligences.

Michael lived in what estate agents called a mansion block: an old apartment house. It was covered in scaffolding, being repaired. He looked up at his flat and saw that no lights were on. Phil wasn't there again. So it would be round to Gigs again for a takeaway kebab and an evening alone. Involuntarily, Michael saw Tony's naked thighs, the ridges of muscle.

He clunked his keys into the front door of his flat. The door was heavy and fireproofed and it made noises like an old man. Michael dumped his briefcase on the hall table and snapped on the living-room light.

The Cherub was sitting on the sofa.

'Bloody hell!' exclaimed Michael, and stumbled backwards. 'What are you doing here?'

Tony sat with both hands placed on his knees. 'I don't know,' he said in a mild voice.

'How did you get in!' The central light was bare and bleak.

'I don't know,' Tony said. He still hadn't moved.

The scaffolding, thought Michael. He climbed up the bloody scaffolding. 'Get out of here!' Michael shouted.

The eyes narrowed and the head tilted sideways.

And then, Oh God, he was gone. The air roiled, as if from tarmac on a hot day. It poured into the space Tony had suddenly vacated. There was no imprint left on the cushions.

The Cherub simply disappeared. Not even a flutter of wings.

Michael stood and stared. He kept staring at the sofa. What had happened was not possible. Or rather it made a host of other things suddenly possible: magic, madness, ghosts.

Michael sat down with a bump and slowly unwound his scarf. He stood up and poured himself a whiskey, swirling it around in the glass and inspecting it, yellow and toxic. Whiskey had destroyed his father.

In a funny kind of way, it felt as if Tony was his father's ghost come back to haunt him.

Michael took a swig and then sat down with his notebook and Pilot pencil to answer every question except the most important.

Who indeed is Michael?

In a very few photographs, Michael was beautiful.

Most photographs of him were short-circuited by a grimace of embarrassment or a dazzled nervous grin that gave him the teeth of a rodent. If someone short stood next to him, Michael would stoop and twist and force himself lower.

In other photographs, Michael looked all right. In those, he would have taken off his wire-rimmed spectacles and combed his hair and stood up straight. By hazard, he would be wearing a shirt that someone had ironed, and he would have left the pens out of the top pocket. It would be a period in which Michael was not experimenting with beards to hide his face, or pony tails to control his runaway, curly hair.

The best photographs of all would be on a beach, on holiday, with something to occupy his awkward hands. It would be apparent then that Michael had the body of an athlete. He was a big, broad-shouldered man. Because of the flattening of his broken nose, his face was rugged, like a boxer's. Michael could look unbelievably butch.

There was one photograph from Michael's youth.

It was hidden away, unsorted. Michael would not be able to find it now. He didn't need to. Michael carried it around with him in memory. He could always see it, even when he didn't want to.

His father had taken it from a riverboat in California, during their last summer together. In the photograph, Michael is sixteen

15

years old and is quite possibly the best-looking person on the planet. He is certainly one of the happiest.

In the photograph Michael sits in a dinghy. He's laughing and holding up a poor pooch of a dog. She was called Peaches the Pooch. Peaches gazes miserably out from under a thick coating of river-bottom mud. Michael's thighs and calves are also covered in mud. Even then he was a big lad, with wide shoulders and lines of muscle on his forearm. His black eyes are fixed directly on whoever is taking the photograph and they are wide with delight. His face is nut brown, like an Indian's, and his smile is blue-white in contrast. His black hair has reddish-brown streaks from constant sunlight. Sunlight glints all around him on the slick, brown water and onto his face, which is indisputably happy.

If you look closely, the nose isn't broken.

By the time that photograph had been developed and posted back to England, it was winter. That summer Michael on the Sacramento River was already history. Michael remembered opening the envelope. There was no letter inside from his father, just photographs, that photograph.

It should have been the moment when Michael learned to love himself. Like every teenager he had been gawky and spotty. It should have been the moment he left doubt behind, and finally accepted that he was beautiful.

Instead, all Michael could do was regret. The beauty, he felt, was a mask. He'd been hiding behind it. It was better now, being ugly. It was closer to the truth. Michael made himself ugly.

The photograph was the last thing he ever had from his father. He knew what his father was saying: this is who you could have been.

Everything changed without Michael noticing at the time. In the summer, he had been determined to be a vet. Now he was a scientist, who experimented on animals.

The summer Michael had enjoyed acting; had been in a drama class for fun, and took the lead role in all the plays. He had a way of conjuring up old ladies, terrified spivs and policemen out of his own body.

In winter, Michael seemed dispossessed of his own body.

This made him mostly harmless. Women liked him; his students liked him. He always kept a distance from them. It was not that he was afraid of women or students, exactly. He was afraid of how he became around them. He knew he could be waywardly funny, exact, truthful. But then something would happen, and power would withdraw from Michael like the tide. Beached and helpless, he would fumble and make mistakes and let himself down. He would forget things, like appointments or his glasses. Uncomfortable, he would grin and grin and grin.

Michael was impotent. If this were symptom or cause he could not distinguish. He didn't care. Impotency meant that only the most brutal and depersonalized of sexual episodes were safe enough for him. Only parks or toilets or saunas could hide him.

If his partners had no idea who he was, how could they hurt him? If they could hardly see him in the dark and didn't know his name, there could be no embarrassment when he didn't get it up. They didn't care if Michael got it up. They were too terrified of police to notice and too desperate to come quickly. It all stayed hidden and detached.

But it relieved the pressure. It relieved the pressure of living with someone who gave him no sexual satisfaction. It relieved a kind of erotic itch, which he could never satisfy, and had not been satisfied for more than twenty years. Michael was 38 and his very skin crawled with lust.

A quick jerk off in a car park, a slap on the ass in bushes in a park provided cessation and a masturbatory climax but no satisfaction. So he would have to go back again, to a sauna or a cottage. And then, again. This is addiction. Michael was a nice man who was addicted to speedy, functional sex. He kept this shut away from the rest of his life.

In the rest of his life, he offered the world sweetness, integrity and intelligence. He placated life. He worked himself nearly to death.

Michael had a contract to teach biology two afternoons a week. He prepared his lectures and marked papers, just as if he were full-time, only he was paid less.

He joined academic committees and fought for new IT networks. He joined Boards that recruited new teachers and exposed his bitter elders when they said, untruthfully, that a candidate for a post had been fired from her previous position.

Michael lifted weights and read all the journals in his field and did desk research. He became a rising star in his field, producing publishable papers in biology from scanning work in two fields and bringing them together. Somehow this still resulted in very little extra money.

The two fields were neurology and philosophy, the grey area where biology was helping philosophers answer questions such as: do we have a soul? What is the self?

Michael understood how we see. Images are formed from millions of separate stimulations in the brain: one area responds only to vertical lines; others to angles; others to oncoming movement. Others are tickled by symmetry of any kind, or by green or pink. Still others react to shadow; whole other areas bring together the slightly different angles provided by two eyes.

The brain responds to verbs of movement, adjectives of colour, and nouns of space and shape. We spend our first six months learning to read these complex sentences.

Could the grammar of language have its origins in the grammar of sight? If so, then how could people blind from birth learn to talk? What if grammar came before both vision and speech? Michael wrote papers on the subject. They were influential. People were surprised that he was not a professor.

In the spiritual space where ideas were formed, Michael had power. He found power in snatching those ideas out of air and putting them to paper with rattling keystrokes. Michael wrote all weekend long.

In order to answer those people who insisted on modelling the living brain on circuit diagrams, Michael was taking a conversion degree in Computer Science.

So, as if he did not have enough to do, Michael was learning how to program in C and studying how the registers of computer memory worked. He had to turn in programs to a colleague who opposed his views on what networks the students needed.

The programming module alone took ten extra hours a week.

When major coursework was due it would be twenty extra hours a week. Having worked all day, he would work all night, and when finally the program worked, he would weep from joy, as if he had climbed Mount Everest. That was the payoff. He had a blazing moment of joy. Two hours later, he crawled out of bed, and it all began again.

Sometimes, Michael saw friends. He would arrive late at their houses, streaming cold air and apologies and feeling awful because he hadn't been able to organize buying a bottle of wine. His boyfriend Philip would be there waiting for him in worn silence. Perhaps everyone had already begun the first course.

'Michael's always late – we told you he would be!' his hosts would exclaim, laughing and admonishing. Michael's smile would flick like a switchblade with annoyance. The blade cut both ways: himself and his friends.

Michael spent some of his time in a haze of either petulance, or depressed exhaustion, elated only by his studies and his flashes of inspiration into who we are and how we think. These were brilliant enough and expressed clearly enough to make most guests sit up and listen. They found themselves asking intelligent questions, to which Michael could give simple replies. For the time that they were with him they found themselves in love with learning and with science, and so a little more in love with themselves. Which is why even now, from time to time, Philip's eyes would shine with pride, if not exactly love. And why, curiously, Michael left the dinner parties even more drained and exhausted than when he arrived. Sometimes he cried without knowing why.

He really couldn't think why he should be crying. He had a good job, didn't he? He had a flat in London's prosperous West End. He had a sensible relationship that had lasted nearly thirteen years. His papers had helped earn his ex-polytechnic a 5 from the Higher Research Board. Who was he, to be unhappy? Who, indeed, was Michael?

So where is Philip?

Out, as always. Michael had no idea where.

It hadn't always been like that. There was a time when they did things together and regularly cooked meals for each other. There was a time when he and Phil regularly attempted to make love.

They'd met more than twelve years before. Michael had been 26 and had his father's athletic build. His beard outlined a smooth and doleful face, but in doleful repose it was rather beautiful. His hair, for once, was cut short. Michael at 26 was many people's cup of tea, if not exactly his own.

They met at First Out, a gay coffee shop. Phil was trying to find copies of the free newspapers. Michael gave him his, and Phil sat next to him in the window.

Phil had been skinny, intense and spotty. His cheeks were pitted, but that only increased the craggy drama of his face. He was all a-quiver, in his first week of art school, nineteen, terrified, anxious, and aggressive, like a stray terrier needing a home. It is perhaps to Michael's credit that he found this touching, moving and beautiful in a way.

Their attachment was brusque. Halfway through the first lovemaking session, Michael had known it would work. Philip was hot to the touch and his ribcage showed pale and lean. His hands shivered like butterflies. The two men made a shape together – Michael's bulk against Philip's fragility – that seemed to tell a coherent story.

On their second date, Michael called Philip 'my love'. Phil hated his student roommates; they didn't wash their cutlery or themselves. He needed a place to crash, he said. Michael, full of hope, asked Phil to live with him. There was something suddenly erotic about being the older man, about offering a flat, an income, a routine, a home. Philip moved in two weeks later.

Domestication with its rituals over salt and spoons soothed them both. They took turns with the washing-up and shared expenses, and settled quickly into a life of tidal regularity. There was something soothing, too, about being with someone whom so few people would find attractive.

The age difference helped. Michael could play the role of protector and teacher; and Philip was insecure and young for his age and needed that. For a time it was charming that Philip's nickname for Michael was 'Father'. It sounded like an old-fashioned marriage. 'Hello, Father,' Philip would call out on Michael's arrival home, or when Michael showed up at the pub for a crawl.

Early on, before art school got to him, Phil painted Michael's portrait. This was before Philip stared to glue dirty carpet onto metal poles, so it was a perfectly conventional painting. Philip said that it was designed to fill a niche in the sitting room.

It portrayed Michael as ballast. The jacket, slightly crumpled, looked like a carved stone replica of clothing. The weight of his body was given a granite substance, and he stood feet well apart looking as immovable as the Earth. The painting was called 'Taurus'. At least in the beginning, Michael was an anchoring point.

Even then the sex didn't work. But it didn't work in a strange backward way that they both noted and were proud of. It seemed to confirm they were some kind of perfect match. They would allude to it lightly, discreetly to their very best friends.

Phil hated any male response from his partners at all. For all his fluttering, or perhaps because of it, he would not suck Michael's cock and found the idea of anal penetration repulsive. Which was just as well, considering Michael could not penetrate whipped cream.

It was no mystery to Michael why Philip was screwed up. A

21

year after they met, Philip finally summoned the nerve to take Michael home to meet his parents. Michael would not have believed Roland and Virginia if he had not met them. They were fake posh. They pretended to be from Surrey, where they now lived. Who in their right mind pretended to be posh these days?

Philip's father was some kind of retired manager from ICI. He had a worn moustache and some kind of dressing on his hair which rendered it flat and glossy. Roland wore navy blazers without the right to, and shirts whose thick blue stripes were still somehow garish. Virginia's hair was died orange and piled high like Margaret Thatcher's, and she had an air of studied, delicate refinement. She talked like an actress in a 1950s film.

They had made cucumber sandwiches. Their teapot had pink curlicues. Michael kept his eyes fixed on it as Philip's mother made efforts to persuade her son to go back to medical school. They didn't like the idea of art school at all. Roland was robust. 'Don't want people to think you hang around with a bunch of arty-farty people, Philip.' Arty-farty meant queer. Roland was supposed to have no idea about his son's sexuality. Only Philip's mother 'knew'.

The family had a best room that was kept under wraps, and of which Michael was vouchsafed a glimpse. The furniture was sealed in plastic and the carpets covered with protecting translucent treads. It was as if they wanted people to have safe sex with the sofa. The dresser proudly displayed the Wedgwood china, which was never used. 'This is for special events,' said Philip's mother, communicating with no effort that the first visit of her son's partner was not special enough.

When Philip's sister died unexpectedly, his mother rang to ask that Michael not come to the funeral, as it was 'a family occasion'. In any event, Michael was not 'to visit quite so often, as it might give rise to questions'.

'I'll make it easy,' said Michael. 'I won't go at all.'

'That's not what she wants, Michael,' said Philip, looking anguished.

'It's what I want,' said Michael. 'I don't like being treated like the mad aunt in the attic. It'll be easier for you too. You won't even have to mention me.'

Indeed, Michael was not mentioned in family conversation. Philip's family weekends were now just another period of absence.

Which Michael had been grateful for, as it made it easier to bring people back. It's how most gay marriages are supposed to work. You get tired of sex with each other, and being a man yourself you understand: it's fun to be let off your leash for a scamper.

But when does it cease to be that? When do you start hoping he won't be home so you can bring a trick back? When do you start saying: 'Got another arts do on tonight. You won't want to come, will you?' When do you start slipping sideways into bushes at Russell Square after every social engagement?

How long is it then before there is no sexual side to the marriage? What do you call the marriage then? Like other mainly financial arrangements, you might call it a partnership. They still both took a measure of pride in it.

'He's a scientist,' Phil said at a recent party, as if clearing the table for a specially cooked, nut-free dish. Philip at 31 was already beginning to look ragged and discontent. 'He's doing brain research. You're trying to prove we have a soul aren't you?'

'Do we have a soul then?' asked Jimmy Banter. He was a better-known artist than Philip. He had a merry smile and a watchful eye.

'What we have,' said Michael, feeling his weight, 'is more like a centre of gravity. You can't find a centre of gravity surgically. It's not an organ or an inner eye. You won't find a car part called the centre of gravity, but the car has one anyway. The self is like that. It's the centre of focus if you like, where all the stresses and strains of the brain come together.'

Jimmy Banter looked over his shoulder. 'Is that why you've got such a big ego then, Phil? All those stresses and strains?' Jimmy disliked weight and he disliked bald truth but he loved drama.

'At least my work doesn't involve killing chickens,' said Philip.

Thanks, Phil, for blowing my cover.

23

The room went cold and still. 'What was that?' a woman in a red dress asked, sitting up.

Michael sighed. 'Uh. I am about to start a research project that involves experimentation on animals.'

'And how,' the woman asked him, with the cautious determination of the righteous, 'do you justify that?'

With difficulty. It takes a long time. Most of the night, in fact. And the one thing I dread is some animal rights activist getting hold of it because my partner wants to score points at parties.

Michael glared at Philip who stared sullenly back. It was very difficult to see any love in his eyes now.

Some weeks before, Philip had come home at eleven o' clock. For Philip, that was early. Michael was still up, exhausted from marking phase tests. Philip came home elated rather than high. He came home seductive.

'How would *you*,' Philip said, sitting on the arm of the sofa, 'like to be photographed in the nude by *me*.'

'It depends on what it's for,' replied Michel.

'It's for my next and breakthrough show. It's called *Lust*.'

Ah.

'You're going to be the centre piece.'

'Am I, now?'

'Yup. I want your cock to be the anchor. I want it to look earth-bound. I want to adorn it with grass and soil and flowers. And I can tell people: it's my boyfriend, actually. It will all be terribly Gilbert-and-Georgeish.'

Philip. Phil, you are 31 years old. Shouldn't you be getting beyond this?

'Are you trying to get into advertising or something? It won't work, Phil. If advertising agencies like your stuff, they just steal it and call it a quote.'

'And that promotes you too. Just hear me out.' Philip shifted, smiling on the arm of the sofa. 'I haven't pitched it to you properly.'

Pitch? What are you, a filmmaker?

'Everything is a branch of pornography, including religion.'

'No, Phil, it's not.'

24

'In this sense. It uses the same techniques as pornography. Nothing to do with sex. Pornography is to do with keeping people comfortable and managing their disappointment. You cannot give someone sex except by giving them sex. But you can give them a substitute, and make sure it's barely just good enough. So they're not satisfied and have to come back for another fix. McDonald's hamburgers are pornography. Blockbuster movies are pornography. The key to their success is that they don't offend and never satisfy. The other thing is that nobody gets hurt. Or rather they get hurt, but there's no real pain. So, in *The English Patient* you can set people on fire and cut off their thumbs and everything still reads like a Fiat ad.'

'So. How are you going to demonstrate this intellectual point using craft skills? Which, as I understand it, is your definition of art.'

Philip was grinning. 'I'm going to photograph your cock in a McDonald's bun.'

Michael couldn't resist. 'It will certainly be an improvement on their usual fare.'

'I'm going to photograph you as Billy Graham preaching, but with your cock hanging out.'

See what an education in the arts can do for you? 'What about lawsuits?'

'You want lawsuits? I'm going to dress your member up as Monica Lewinsky.'

'How? How are you going to do that?'

'I'll put a beret on it, and stick it in a weight watchers ad. I'll wrap it up as a cigar. I dunno.'

'Phil. This is not art. These are ideas for joke greetings cards. You know, courgettes standing in for dicks. And why pick on poor Monica?'

'Because she got hurt. The Republicans got it wrong. They thought pornography meant sex rather than harmlessness. They wrecked a nice, modern girl's life and people hated it. I mean, would Republicans understand pornography? Politics is pornography. Will the Right Honourable Member for Finchley East please stand?' Phil flickered like a candle about to go out.

Michael was smiling. In many ways, this was the best

25

conversation they had had in years. 'Phil. You are not going to photograph my dick. Use someone else's, but not mine, OK?'

'Why not?'

Partly, Michael thought, because it's so ugly. 'Well aside from putting your audience off their dinner . . . I just don't want to. I'd be embarrassed. I'm a lecturer, I've got students. It might cause trouble at work. OK?'

'All right.' Philip stared at his knees. He looked genuinely disappointed. 'I just thought that for once you might like to share in my life.' His voice went even quieter and he muttered, 'Instead of me always having to share in yours.'

This was neither jovial nor seductive. 'I'm afraid I don't understand that last remark, Phil.'

Philip stood up, disconsolate. 'Look around you, then. The flat's yours, everything in it's yours.'

'You're perfectly welcome to buy something, Phil.'

Philip said very softly, 'I don't have any money.' And he went out to the kitchen.

Somewhere in there, Michael sensed, there had been a wasted opportunity.

Lovers come and lovers go. Usually they leave by the door. Sometimes, very occasionally, they just disappear.

Was the guard hit?

Philip did not come back until gone 2.00 AM.

All lights were out and Michael was nearly asleep when he heard the front door wheeze and grumble its way open. Phil let it swing back and slam. It took him forever to lay out his keys, undress, have a glass of water, pee, flush, belch. My God, how long can it take someone to get to bed? Perhaps he was just washing himself after sex.

When he finally lay down next to Michael, Philip fell instantly asleep. His breath rattled out of him like leaves blown along a sidewalk. He smelled of cheap red wine.

Michael was left awake, full of lust, but not for Phil.

He thought of the Cherub: the smooth pink arms, the smooth pink face, the ready smile. Michael saw him again, prone on the platform, undignified, head over heels and his face sad with questions, as if he had learned about death for the first time.

I won't sleep, thought Michael.

It is bad behaviour to wank in the same bed as your partner. Michael got up and went to the bathroom. Michael tried to ease the bathroom light on soundlessly, but it snapped anyway. It sounded as loud as a gunshot.

And there, standing in the shower-bath as Michael had really rather known he would be, was Tony.

The Cherub looked like he had been scanned in from a photograph and pasted onto another image. His back was towards Michael. He was drying himself with a white gym towel. Michael

27

did not own any white towels. His scientific mind clocked: towels are part of the deal.

So was the perfect, pink, hairless bottom, rounded muscle so lean that the cheeks were parted even standing up. The anus was visible, pouting as if for a kiss. Michael touched Tony's shoulder, and he turned around. His face had the same baffled expression. Michael wanted him to smile. Smile, he yearned.

The Cherub smiled in delight. Michael kissed his cheek. Tony's smile did not respond. It remained fixed and dazzling.

Michael sat down on the lid of the toilet. Tony's penis was still recognizably stale from being swaddled all day, even in the most evenly white, clean briefs. Michael checked that the head was dry, permitted it to enter his mouth once. The penis swelled, lengthened, and went bulbous at the head. Michael pulled back.

Michael touched Tony's body, started to masturbate and told Tony to do the same. Tony leaned back against the bathroom door, head thrown back, eyes closed, as he would have done if he were alone. Michael looked at his beautiful body as if it were a photograph in a magazine. The Cherub came arching into space.

Then the room cleared as if a mist had been burned off. Michael padded back into the darkened bedroom where Phil still snored. Michael had a moment's worry: he'll smell it on me. Then he realized the tastes and smells on his tongue and fingers had all evaporated. Leaving nothing.

In the morning, the mystery remained.

As always Philip slept on while Michael prepared instant coffee and granola. I must have dreamed it, thought Michael. He picked up his filofax and looked at his notes from the night before. There was hardly anything useful except for one clear question.

Was the guard hit?

He walked to Goodge Street tube. There must have been an unusual shift pattern, because the same guard was lurking behind the barriers. Or maybe he just needed the money. He was propped up against the wall and nodded a grim good morning at Michael.

Michael shuffled his apologies. 'Uh. I'm sorry about last night. Did he hit you?'

The guard looked up, bleary from lack of sleep, angry at first for being disturbed. Then he remembered to be civil. 'Sorry?'

'Um. Last night. That big bloke who was a bit woozy. You came running after me and I thought he'd hit you.'

The blue eyes were too pale; there was something frozen about them. 'You must want someone else, mate.'

Michael shook his head at his own mistake. 'Of course. You wouldn't get two shifts in a row would you?'

'I would. I need the money. I was here last night, but there was no big man. Sorry.'

Michael stood frozen. All right, Tony had not been real. 'But don't you remember talking to me?'

The guard wanted to read his paper. It was called *Loot* and sold houses and cars to people who had no money to buy them. He lowered the paper. 'There was something. You were standing there by the barriers.' He gestured towards them, scowling, looking as baffled as the Cherub had the night before. Michael saw that he needed a shave. 'That's it. You were drunk.' The guard's lip curled, and he lifted up his paper. He looked pretty and petulant and butch, all at once. 'You were right out of it, mate. So that explains it then. All right?' He stared stonily at his paper. Conversation over. They waited for the lifts to arrive.

I didn't drink anything. Michael reconstructed the entire night and day in his mind. He hadn't been to the pub. He hadn't drunk a thing.

The guard rocked himself away from the wall on which he was leaning, and punched big silver keys. The lift door opened.

I must be going nuts, Michael thought.

'Sleep tight,' said the guard and gave him a cheery, leery grin.

There were smiling Japanese tourists in the lift. You are bowing to a crazy man, Michael told them in his mind.

I made the whole thing up. I had a bad experience in the sauna, my life is shit, I've been depressed for years without doing anything about it, and now I've gone and broken my brain.

29

Christ. Michael remembered the feel of Tony's skin, its smell, its taste. It increases your respect for schizophrenics, really. They're not just a bit muddled. All those brain cells get tickled up, and they start making brand-new sentences of sight and sound and touch. The new sentences are lies, but they feel like the real thing.

You lose a certain kind of innocence when you go crazy. You used to take it for granted that your brain shows you what's actually out there. Now all you've got left is doubt, Michael.

But then, science is built on doubt.

The train bounced and rattled him, like life.

At the lab, Michael strolled through his normal routine as if sleepwalking.

He fed his smartcard into the reader at the front door. He said hello to the security guard Shafiq and showed him his pass. He went down the line of offices, one by one. None of them had windows.

Hello, Ebru! Hello boss! It amused Ebru to call him boss.

Hiya Emilio, how's the system? Why you ask? It's great like always!

He heard their voices, as if in his own head, as if no one were really speaking.

In his own office, Michael slipped into his entirely symbolic white lab coat. He asked Hugh to check the thermostat readings in the darkroom. 'If the temperature goes much under or over thirty-eight, give me a shout.'

And he sat down and he had no idea what to do. His desk stared back at him, as orderly as his notebooks. There were three new things in his in tray, and the out tray was empty. On his PC would be a timed list of things to do.

What the fuck do I do now?

Look in the *Yellow Pages* for psychotherapists? Do they section people right away? Should I be writing my letter of resignation? What do you do when you realize you're seeing things?

You might just try to see if it's going to happen again. Look, I'm still capable. I can say maybe it won't happen again, maybe it was just a one-off, something that only happened once. Maybe I'm better already.

Put another way: just how badly broken am I?

The door opened and the sound was as sudden and as loud as if he made it up, and Michael jumped up and turned around.

It was Ebru. 'First day post.' She always made English sound like something delicious to eat: post almost became pasta. She passed him five different coloured files – his sorted mail.

'Thank you, Ebru,' said Michael. He felt like a bad actor, awkward on the stage, with a fixed grin. She read him out a list of messages. He didn't really listen. He just kept smiling. Finally she left, bouncing and strong in blue jeans, a picture of wholeness.

Then Michael stood up, and looked from side to side as if there were someone watching. He padded carefully to the lab's one WC.

It was a single tiny room with sink and toilet crowded together. Michael locked the door.

OK, he said to the air. Come back.

Suddenly crowding against the edge of the sink, the Cherub ballooned into reality. Tony was jammed against Michael, forcing him to sit down or fall over. Michael felt the texture of the brick against his back. It seemed to push him insistently back into Tony's arms. Go on, the wall seemed to say.

Michael reached out and prodded Tony's collarbone. He could feel it solid under lean flesh. He could feel the green T-shirt slide away from it. The room was reflected in Tony's eyes, perfectly, the glint from the strip light, and Michael himself. In the fine-grained skin there was one clogged pore going slightly red.

Michael prodded him again. Dammit, he was solid. Michael picked up Tony's hand and saw ridges in the fingernails and flecks of white.

No. Hallucinations were foggy, you knew things were clouded, you felt confused. This did not feel like the product of a confused brain.

I am not making this up!

'Come on,' said Michael.

He took hold of Tony's hand and felt its palm, fleshy and armoured with weightlifter calluses.

Then Michael stuck his head out into the corridor. It really would not be a good idea to be seen coming out of the toilet with a strange man.

'OK. Come on.'

Tony followed him. 'I don't like this,' he said. 'Tony doesn't like this.'

So, Michael thought: he thinks of himself and Tony as being different.

'Does Tony know this is happening?'

The copy nodded. 'He saw last night in a dream.'

Michael kept his voice low. 'I need to know if anyone else can see you.'

They went into Ebru's office. Her back was turned and slightly hunched as she read personal e-mail from Turkey. Michael coughed.

She turned around. 'Sorry, Michael. My mother sends me e-mail here.' She looked embarrassed, her smile dipping and then she looked up straight at Tony. 'Hello,' she said.

'This is Tony.' Michael paused. He had not really expected Ebru to see Tony, so he had nothing ready to say. 'He's uh, my trainer at the gym.'

Ebru raised one eyebrow at Michael briefly, as if to say: and he's good-looking, what's going on here, Michael? She stood up and reached across the desk to shake Tony's hand. The meeting of the hands was perfect, like those moments when the CGI dinosaurs actually seem to touch the ground.

'Hello,' said Tony, in a soft, neutral voice.

Michael explained. 'Um. I hurt my elbow weightlifting, so Tony's here to give me some advice about it.'

'A handsome gym instructor who makes house calls.' Ebru's eyes glinted.

A certain adjustment was necessary. 'This isn't my house. Tony only makes office calls. We wouldn't want anyone to get the wrong idea.'

'Um,' said Ebru, as if to say, OK, I'll mind my own business.

'I guess that's about it,' Michael said to Tony. In the empty corridor, he sent Tony back. To wherever it was he came from. The air closed over him like surf and he was gone.

What the fuck is going on?

Michael got out his notebook and drew a line down the middle.

On one side he wrote 'Hallucination' and on the other he wrote 'Physical Presence'.

Under 'Hallucination' he wrote: my distressed mental state. He wrote: lack of reaction from people on platform. He wrote: guard did not remember Tony. He wrote: guard said I was drunk.

He stared at 'Physical Presence'. The page was blank. All he could write was: Ebru shook its hand.

So what was it? Hallucination was by far the simplest explanation, except that either Ebru was hallucinating too, or Michael had made her up at least temporarily. The physical presence would have to be some kind of physical copy of a human being.

Until recently, teleportation was supposed to be impossible. Then in 1998, the mathematics of quantum theory were revised, and it became, at least in theory, possible that objects could be completely read, and thus reliably re-created somewhere else. Or rather, duplicated. Michael had been searching for information on quantum computing and had accidentally ended up deep inside the IBM website, on the page describing IBM's teleportation project. The aim was successfully to transport an inanimate object by 2050. There was the usual team of delighted, slightly skuzzy-looking men, thrilled to be living in the dreams of their youth.

So who or what would be sending you copies of handsome young men, Michael? Who would devote the time and expense necessary? If you postulate that, you can postulate Descartes' evil genius, but an evil genius could just as easily be beaming hallucinations as well.

What we have is an anomaly. Something that does not fit with currently accepted theory, something we cannot explain. The first task, therefore, is to describe it accurately. Order and method seemed to dissolve like Pepto Bismal, calming Michael's stomach. He made a list of what he knew.

A physical copy
of someone I know
in train, tube and 2 x in my flat, 1 x in office
Can call up at will and banish
other people appear to interact
His behaviour, my behaviour both sexual
the real person is straight
copy says real person dreams what happens
So the next question is: what else don't I know about this?
In effect, the next question is: what question do I ask next?
Well, so far, all he had done is call up a copy of one person.

Can I call up a copy of
someone else?

Michael needed to limit variables. He needed to think of someone who shared as many characteristics as possible with Tony, someone known, someone whom he had seen and fancied, at least somewhat, in the gym.

The showers at Michael's gym were full of men. It was one of the things that kept Michael motivated to work out.

There was the tiny brown Englishman with a beautiful body and a hatchet face whom Michael nicknamed the English Thai. Michael knew he had a wife from Thailand, and imagined that she had married him because he looked so much like one of her own people: small, neat and brown. The English Thai wore fawn trousers with a spandex waist instead of a belt. Michael had decided he worked in a car repair workshop, but at the front desk, greeting customers and nervously mismanaging staff. Michael could imitate the way he moved, not quite relaxed, hopping instead of stretching to reach parts on the top shelf.

That's what Michael did now, back in the WC at the lab. Michael's arms sketched how the English Thai moved.

OK, he said. His mouth had gone dry. He was half-hoping nothing would happen. Come on.

The English Thai arrived, naked, streaming water from the showers. He blinked and rubbed the water from his eyes.

Well there we go, thought Michael. That's it. Reality's got a hole in it.

The English Thai stood five-foot-four and proportioned as if he were a taller athlete, brown all over, a beautiful swelling chest, slim belly, tiny circumcised dick. He had a face like Mr Punch, with designer stubble.

Turn around, Michael thought at him. He did. Hold your cheeks open. The English Thai did, and easily and effortlessly his anus also opened, and mouthed desire like a fish.

Michael could direct him.

You like being fucked, Michael realized. The English Thai turned back around and nodded yes, mournfully. Michael could imagine him in insalubrious surroundings, with that same expression. There was something in the hurt and ugliness that created in Michael a stirring of lust.

Michael asked him, murmuring, 'What does your wife think about this?'

'She don't know nothing,' said the English Thai.

'What do you think about it?'

He shrugged. 'It's just something I do, you know?' He smiled, embarrassed, his wounded animal eyes saying fuck me, hurt me. I'm ugly.

There was a knock on the bathroom door. A voice came beyond it. It was Emilio, sounding reluctant. Michael sliced the air with his hand, and the English Thai was gone, as if he were a shower that someone had turned off.

Someone spoke, Emilio, sounding reluctant. 'Uh, Michael. Do you have someone in there with you?' This is not a question many people like asking their boss.

'Uh,' Michael improvised. 'No, just talking to myself.'

My God, do they really think I'd have someone in here with me? Well, actually Michael, you did. He flushed quickly to explain why he was there and flung the door open.

Emilio was already halfway back down the corridor.

'I'm sorry Michael, I have to use the toilet.' Emilio smiled and shuffled. He wore yellow trousers and black sneakers, which emphasized the embarrassed digging of his feet.

'We need more than one, don't we?' Michael said.

Emilio nodded, embarrassed. Michael held out a generous arm. Go in. See? No one there.

Michael went back to his desk and tried to work. He liked to work and had certainly ensured that it would not be in short supply. He had e-mail to answer. He had tomorrow's lecture to prepare on nerve cells. He had a program to write for his MA Computer Science course. The assignment was to write a program that was supposed to convert any ordinary text to all capital letters. He knew how to do it principle . . . just add a fixed number to the ASCII code that would move it to upper case. He just couldn't make it work in practice. That morning, he could make nothing work.

All right, then! He surrendered as if in anger. Michael stopped working and went to the gym.

The gym was one more way of working himself to death. It also made up for a feeling he had of losing time. It was too soon to be exiled from the world of male beauty. Michael didn't question why he wanted to be beautiful or what the ultimate goal of that beauty would be. He did know that he could bench-press three sets of 100 kilos and do 80 crunch sit-ups.

Tony was there, filing work-out cards in a box.

'Hiya Tony,' said Michael, like an anxious parent trying to sound cool for his son's friends.

Tony's head jerked around almost in panic, and he glared at Michael, alarmed and hostile. With a snap, Tony mastered himself. He gave a brief and professional greeting. Michael's ears felt numb and he didn't hear it. Tony turned his back.

Fumbling slightly, Michael straddled himself onto an Exercycle. He pedalled for six minutes, and for six minutes he tried to catch Tony's eye. Like a compass needle pointing north, somehow the broad back in its green shirt was always turned towards Michael. It was like stalking a rare marsh bird. Michael finished his aerobics.

'Tony,' Michael asked him. 'Is there anything wrong?'

'No, mate, no,' said Tony, shaking his head.

'You had a bad dream last night,' said Michael. Tony's face fell, gathering a line of pale tissue either side of his mouth. 'So did I,' said Michael.

Without another word, Tony turned and walked into his tiny office, and firmly closed the door.

What if this isn't about sex?

The next day, the chicks hatched.

Ebru came into Michael's room looking slightly blue and pinched around the cheeks. 'I am hearing peeping from the darkroom.'

'OK. Make sure nobody goes in.'

They weren't set up yet. There was a small workroom with a sink, a draining board, and an interrogation lamp. Something that looked like it might be for stretching tyres over wheels was in fact a small centrifuge. There was a kitchen magimix. Setting out the instruments of the experiment brought home to their hearts and stomachs what they were about to do.

There were new garden secateurs, the blades a polished chrome. There was the cheese shave with its wire. There were the lined bins, with their black sacks wafting plastic odours.

Inside the darkroom, the new chicks were wet, warm, shivering. In the dull red light, their ancient heads looked outraged, as if they had been pulled back out of heaven after death. They demanded, mouths open.

Every other chick was lifted up and lowered into a trolley. They jolted with life in Michael's hands as if attached to live wires. The trolley was wheeled through the double set of doors that cut off all light, and into the workroom.

'OK, let's have some light,' said Michael. And as if the chicks were criminals, the workroom lamps were switched on, blazing.

For the first time in their lives, the chicks saw light. They blinked and squinted.

'They look so small,' said Ebru.

Michael knew he had to be first. He was the boss, he had designed the experiment, and he couldn't ask them to do anything that he himself ducked. Come on Michael, they wouldn't be here but for you; you have to take responsibility for their deaths as well.

Michael took a deep breath and picked up the first chick. It was no longer warm, but wet and chill and it went silent as he picked it up, and he knew it was because the chick was pre-programmed to treat large warm near objects as mothers.

He focussed, took the secateurs and as quickly as possible snipped into the little leathery skull, nosed in the secateurs, snipped quickly at the base of the brain.

'Let's start with the centrifuge,' he said. Ebru touched his arm. 'The trick is to do it quickly, so there's no pain.'

The first chicken brain was rolled carefully by Ebru into the palm of her gloved hand, and then dropped into the magimix.

The second was laid out in the tray.

One half of the brains would be reduced to their chemical components, which would be analysed. The other half would be stained and then frozen immediately in the cold room for slicing. The results would be compared with the control groups, who would die without ever seeing any light whatsoever. The bodies were thrown limp into the bags, which were then sealed.

Michael ran with the tray towards the cold room. The Fridge was a big white box, and it shivered to the touch, like Michael's slightly sick stomach. The tray was numbered and it was placed on a shelf space with a matching number.

When Michael returned, the centrifuge was humming, and the clean draining board was being dried, and the garbage bags were in hessian sacks stencilled with the words WATERLOO FEED COMPANY.

'Well done, gang,' he said. He had to go into his office and sit down.

Well, you knew it would be like this when you set up the

experiment, Michael. The same fate awaits every hen in Britain at some point, even free-range ones.

But they, at least, have some kind of life.

Did it make any difference that they were trying to provide answers to some truly big questions? Michael loved science and he loved life somewhat less, and he had faith that in the end the two would support each other. But he still felt sick.

He felt compromised. This affected his self-esteem in other areas. He had to go for a walk in the park to clear his lungs. He sat on a bench and ate his sandwiches, which fortunately were cheese and not chicken. Nevertheless, he found the sweaty taste of animal fat unappetizing. He crunched his way through his apple.

You know, Michael, it is not everyone who can call up simulations of people from thin air. This . . . this miracle . . . arrives. And what do you use it for? You use it to turn tricks. Which is what you always do. You can turn tricks in Alaska Street. What if this isn't about sex?

The more Michael thought, the more unlikely it seemed that the universe would change all its rules to keep him supplied with fancy men. Suppose I could clone Einstein and set him to work solving equations? What are the limits of this thing?

Michael wrote in his notebook.

Hypothesis: I can call up copies of people but I do not have to fancy them.

Method: Try to call up someone for whom you feel not a trace of lust and note the result.

Michael decided to call up Mother Theresa.

He admired her, he wanted to talk to her, perhaps about the morality of animal experimentation. And it was a certainty that he felt no lust whatsoever for her.

It was a brilliant diamond of a spring day. The light seemed to have edges and cut. Why not just do the show right here? What better church to call up Mother Theresa than Archbishop's Park?

He felt the sun on his face. It was as if the light was reflecting off the daffodils. He called out. With his eyes closed, it seemed to him, he reached out into darkness hidden behind the light.

Nothing happened.

He opened his eyes. A football team from a local office, in mismatched T-shirts and shorts, loped towards the red-grit soccer pitch. Michael closed his eyes, and asked again. The bench next to him remained stubbornly empty.

He got out his notebook, feeling disappointment. Just to be sure, he looked over his shoulder, and called up the Cherub. There was the faintest wuffling sound as the air seemed to fold itself into a green and pink origami. The Cherub sat next to him on the bench.

'Keep your clothes on,' whispered Michael.

So, thought Michael. This is about sex. He felt a further degree or two of increased disappointment.

'I don't suppose,' he whispered to the Cherub, 'you know how this works?'

The Cherub stared ahead like a starship captain gazing at a far galaxy. Michael suddenly saw how the real Tony would look when he was older: solid, pale and a bit blank. 'It goes all the way back,' the Cherub said. Then he turned and looked at Michael with a sudden urgency. 'The back of the head.' And he jerked it behind him.

'You wouldn't happen to know what part of the anatomy?'

'So far back it goes outside.'

Yes, well, it was possible that being copied induced mild brain damage. Michael gave him instructions. 'Stand up and walk away towards the alley between the two brick walls. If there's no one there, disappear.'

The Cherub stood up and more tamely than a Labrador walked towards his own oblivion.

Well Phil, Michael thought: there is one element you left out of pornography. Power. In pornography, you have the power to make people behave. Michael began to wonder how good this thing might be for what he still had to call his soul.

Michael's father had been a Marine. There was a plaque somewhere in Camp Pendleton that bore his name and a gravestone somewhere in Orange County that Michael had never seen. In America, everyone went to church, especially in the military. Every Sunday, he and his father would go to a bare and unvarnished Catholic church. Michael ate wafers, drank wine, and learned about sin, and then in the afternoon played touch football on the beach. The exposure was enough to make him feel regretful rather than indoctrinated.

Michael watched Tony's retreating back, wearing only a T-shirt on an icy spring day. The Cherub entered the funnel of brick between two high walls. There was a whisper in his head, and Michael knew the Cherub was gone.

So, he thought. I've learned I can't call up just anyone. It could be that I can't call up women. Or maybe I can only call up copies of people I've actually met. He stood up to go.

Or, it could be that they have to be alive. I'll have to go on asking question after question.

He left the green and the trees. Traffic and black brick made him feel English. God made him feel American. Michael would shift between American and English selves and accents without realizing it. His English self went back to work.

His American self thought of his messengers, how they came and went. Angels, Michael decided. Until I know them better, I will call them Angels.

Can Angels be dead?

When Michael was ten years old, he was sent to spend the summer with his father for the first time. He had cried alone in the airplane with his ticket pinned to his little grey dress jacket. He had to change in Chicago and everything looked like a Dirty Harry movie. Bleached blonde women wore denim suits and chewed gum and talked like gangsters' molls.

Michael knew his Dad was going to meet him at LA International. He arrived exhausted and trying not to cry and he looked at all the waiting people and he saw this huge man who looked like Burt Reynolds and wore a uniform. He carried a big sign with Michael's name on it.

'Hiya Mikey, howya doin'?' the man said in a mingled mouthful of words and chewing gum. He wore mirror shades.

Michael forgot to say anything. He gaped. This was his father? His father looked like something out of a movie too.

He chuckled. 'Come on, guy, we'll get you home.' Dad scooped up Michael's bag and threw it over his shoulder. Michael dragged his feet, walking behind. His father chuckled again, leaned over, and simply picked Michael up whole. His big arm folded into a kind of chair and Michael fell asleep being carried, his face resting warm against his father's chest.

After that, every two years Michael lived for the summer near San Diego with his Dad.

He loved it. Southern California is the perfect place in which to do nothing. Indeed, everything is so far apart, and it takes so long to drive anywhere, that it is very difficult to do anything other than nothing. You call it going to the beach.

On the beach at twelve years old, Michael felt he was immortal. He would take the big green bus out of Camp Pendleton, past the Rialto cinema with its delectable range of kung fu and horror movies. He would reach the cliffside park and the earthen cliffs of Oceanside, California. Once there, he would throw himself in front of a few waves and call it body surfing. Then he could do nothing but lie on his back for three hours, toasting. This was before skin cancer was invented. He went from lobster-red to California-brown in less than two weeks. His bright grin beamed from his newly darkened face – he felt like something from an American situation comedy: the young teenager part.

Resting on the beach, the idea came to him, that he could stay in America and become American. He could do it. After all, his father was American. He could stay in the sunshine with the movies and the skateboards and the long hikes in hills that Camp Pendleton protected from development.

The thought made something inside him flutter with fear. The part of him that fluttered spoke with an all-purpose London accent that was another layer of self. His mother spoke with a Sheffield bluntness. Michael felt himself stretched. Michael felt himself in danger of being torn.

'Whatcha do today?' his Dad would ask. Dad was trying to get to know his son. He had abandoned England and his wife when Michael was three.

'Went to the beach,' Michael said proudly.

'D'ja meet any girls?'

Michael did not say: Dad, I'm only twelve and um . . . but I have noticed that I'm not even looking at girls yet.

What he said was, 'No, Dad.' And he hung his head, feeling ashamed.

'Listen, there's a guy at work runs Little League. You wouldn't want to try your hand at baseball, would you?' His Dad looked hopeful, and made a swinging motion.

His father would have been shocked to discover that Michael didn't like sports. He didn't know then that he had a son who did nothing except cram for exams, and who now more than anything else just wanted to luxuriate on the beach or watch American TV.

American television was a miracle. There were about ten channels, so many that it made sense to flick round them until you found something you wanted.

What Michael found, luxuriating at 5.30 every Saturday afternoon, were old Tarzan movies starring Johnny Weissmüller. In the very first, Tarzan tore off Jane's clothes and threw her naked into a river. She swam deeper and deeper into the river, a glowing white against the darkness, shadows both covering and hinting at her nipples, her pubes.

His father called, 'Mike? Mikey? You wanna come outside and pitch a few balls?' Both father and son were exercising their American accents as if they were stiff muscles before a game.

Michael was staring bug-eyed at a naked woman.

Part of the luxury of California was having a TV of your own, in your own bedroom, to do what you liked.

'I can't Dad, it's time for the Tarzan movie.'

How many movie stars get officially called something as friendly as Johnny? How many of them are Olympic athletes who wear loincloths that let you see their naked haunches, thigh to stomach? How many of them are beautiful with a reassuring lopsided, chip-toothed face, and a high, light voice?

Under Michael's tan and athletic frame, his young and genuinely feminine heart would sit entranced by what his father thought were adventure movies.

'Mikey? We could go to the movies later if you wanna.' His father was big and athletic too, but his face was glum and disappointed. His son had been away all afternoon and they had only Saturdays and Sundays to do stuff together.

'Dad, I really want to watch this, OK?'

'OK, son. See ya later,' his Dad said. He left punching his baseball mitt. Michael felt bad. Michael had not meant to hurt his father's feelings. Michael's eyes were suspiciously heavy with deep feelings he had no name for. 'Dad. Why dontcha watch it with me? Dad?' He heard the back door slam.

His father had a rival.

Michael knew, even at twelve, what the MGM executives had known all along: they were selling a love story. A love story that promised, and delivered, a beautiful naked man. Michael's young heart would soar through the trees alongside Johnny Weissmüller. He dreamed of leaving the world behind, of living like a Boy Scout in a treehouse with a man as dumb and reliable and graceful as a horse. He dreamed of slipping the loincloth aside to see what lay underneath it. At twelve, that was as far as the dream went.

His father eventually nagged his son into joining a baseball team. It played on Sundays, which left Saturday for Tarzan and, in fact, gave Dad even less time with his son.

Summer wore on. Johnny got old. The series left MGM and went downmarket to RKO. It lost Jane and its love story. It gained Amazons in bikinis and cut-price Nazis. Johnny was no longer a sex symbol. He was a star of B-movies for kids. He got fat. A fat Tarzan is a great sadness. His last movie in the series, *Tarzan and the Mermaids*, was made in 1948, filmed in Mexico with beautiful Mexicans standing in for some kind of lost but completely unconvincing African tribe. Any one of the men could have made a more suitable Tarzan, except of course that Tarzan was supposed to be Anglo. Weissmüller was Romanian. He had been born near Timisoara and his real first name was Jonas.

Michael stayed in California long enough to see that sad ending and to experience something of a lover's sense of loss and longing as a partner ages.

Johnny Weissmüller died in Mexico in 1984, when Michael was 24 years old. Michael remembered reading about his death in the newspaper and thinking, Johnny Weissmüller? 1984? It was Michael's moment for realizing that we spend more of our lives being old than young.

In Michael's days of California sunlight, saltwater spray and young Americans in shorts, there had lived in that same state, an old bronzed man. He looked a little bit like a balloon from which the air had leaked. That man would have been able to tune in every Saturday at 5.30 as well, to see his sleek and catlike younger self pad lissomely through a studio jungle.

Maybe it was enough for him to remember the days when he had been a sex symbol, and it was possible that he could go on to be a real movie star. Maybe it was enough to have been the lover of Lupe Velez, the Mexican Spitfire, to have acted with Maureen O'Sullivan, to have people still call you Tarzan . . . once they recognized you. Maybe it was enough for him that he had won five Olympic gold medals and set 67 world records. In the encyclopaedias, it was those he was most remembered for, rather than a mere acting career. After all, sport is not fiction, is it? But Michael, even as an adult, would remember him for the heartbreaking climax of *Tarzan's New York Adventure*, when he leapt off the Brooklyn Bridge to almost certain death, yodelling backwards, for Jane, for Boy, for the jungle life.

Lust requires restitution. Even more frequently than love, lust goes unrequited.

Hypothesis: I can call up anyone that
- *I want sexually (confirmed)*
- *Who is alive or dead (not confirmed)*

Method: Try to call up someone I fancy who is dead and note result.

The Chez Nous Hotel near Vauxhall Bridge Road is a French franchise operation. To an Englishman, it looks Scandinavian: clean, spacious, bland and smelling faintly of the mildest possible cheese. Being near Vauxhall Bridge and south of the River Thames, it is actually nowhere, and no one wants to stay there. Even at lunchtime, its brasserie is empty. Michael could eat there in perfect anonymity, and go upstairs alone without the slightest fear of being seen by anyone he knew. How, otherwise, would you explain booking a room 500 yards from where you worked? He could enter his room at 12.30 PM in complete assurance that it would be comfortable, clean and looking exactly as it would look in Luxembourg or Shepherds Bush.

Michael sat on a bed so perfect it looked as if no one had ever slept in it. As this was the Chez Nous Vauxhall, it was perfectly possible that no one ever had. He disliked crumpling the mottled blue duvet. His breath came fast and shallow. He asked for his boyhood love.

As naturally as a light breeze through eucalyptus trees, Johnny Weissmüller was sitting next to him. Unlike most movie stars, he was bigger than Michael expected – huge, broad and smooth, wearing only the loincloth. A flop of silky brown hair tumbled into his eyes. He stared intently at Michael, half in fear, one hand on his knife.

'Tarzan,' he said, jabbing at his breasts.

'I'm Michael.'

'Tarzan. Mikey,' Weissmüller said, prodding Michael so hard that for a moment Michael thought he would fall backwards out of a tree. 'Mikey. Tarzan.'

Tarzan looked baffled by desire. Desire was something new that he had never felt. He leaned closer to Michael and sniffed his face.

'Mikey smell like flower.'

Tarzan smelt of Max Factor.

Michael said, 'That's my aftershave.'

'What shave?'

Michael stroked his smooth cheek. 'You know, shave. Beard.'

Tarzan looked even more baffled. He rubbed Michael's face and looked puzzled.

'Bee-arr-ddd,' he said.

'Yeah beard, you know, shave. You don't shave?'

Tarzan scowled. He rubbed his own perfect chin. 'How Tarzan shave? No razors.'

'I don't know. I guess I never thought about that. Yeah. Howcum Tarzan doesn't have a beard?'

'Not monkey,' said Tarzan, and grinned.

They hovered about six inches apart. Michael wanted to kiss him, except that Tarzan was covered in tan body make-up, head to toe. It would leave marks on Michael's shirt.

'Uh. Johnny. Could you drop the Tarzan talk? It's a little bit creepy. I want you, not Tarzan.'

Tarzan got that look of idiot firmness he got when mistaking the motives of white hunters. 'No,' he said firmly. 'Mikey want Tarzan.'

Tarzan was shaved all over. Everywhere Michael touched him there were little pinpricks of body hair, like mustard on ham. Michael leaned forward and tried to kiss him and Tarzan ducked away.

'It goes like this,' said Michael and brought their lips together.

Tarzan tasted like one of your mother's friends. He had that perfumed, powdery, clotted smell of face paint. Tarzan smiled and pressed Michael to him, rather as if he were Cheetah at the end of the film. Michael had to coax him out of the loincloth. Tarzan had no conception that it could be removed. He looked as surprised as Michael when it slipped aside to reveal handsome, Catholically uncircumcised genitals from which every trace of pubic hair had also been shaved. MGM couldn't have pubic hair leaking out over the edge of the loincloth.

And, having stripped Johnny/Tarzan, Michael discovered that, like his twelve-year-old self, he wanted to do nothing else.

So he lay next to Tarzan and was cradled. Protected like Jane by the Hays Code, Michael wallowed in the bed as Tarzan prodded him, tickled him, and examined his feet. He sniffed his chin.

As Michael lay there in his arms he wondered. Is this all I wanted all along? With all those other men? Just to be held, stroked and cuddled? Perhaps it is simply that I never wanted real sex at all.

In which case it is possible that I never grew up.

And he could choose to accept that. He could decide to stay a child. Who was anyone to tell him his sexuality was wrong? If this is what he really wanted, he could stay here, warm and sheltered. If this was some new sexual home, why leave it? Michael stroked the smooth firm backs of Tarzan's arms.

'Pee pee,' said Tarzan. He stood up and discovered with wonder that the toilet flushed. He roared at the gushing of clear water, knelt and began to drink from it, lapping like a lion. He looked up in delight.

It was nearly 2:00 PM. Time to go. Tarzan had no concept of time or work, and tried to keep Michael with him, holding his arm, stroking it. In the end, Michael had to disperse him.

He didn't want to see Tarzan dissolve like a TV channel.

Michael simply turned away and heard something like a gust of wind, and felt a sudden hollowness in the room behind him. Every trace of jungle was gone, including the smell of Max Factor.

At reception, he coughed and asked like an out-of-town guest about local restaurants. Tomorrow morning he would check out and pay his bill as if he had spent the night there.

Michael walked back through Archbishop's Park. It was a dull grey English spring, stark with no leaves on the trees. He thought of Tarzan's body, its pre-pubescent smoothness, of his tenderness and the caresses. The main sensation in the pit of his stomach was fear, as if he were still taking that first trip to California.

Circumstances meant that an unexpected question was answered next.

Can I make them do it
when I'm not there?

‘We've got an invitation,’ Philip said, opening their post. ‘It's from Zoltan Caparthi,’ he said. ‘You know, the glass artist? The one who does those fabulous piss-takes of beauty contests? He's invited us. Well, you me and whoever else we want to bring. He said everybody's lover has a lover, and they must come too. Do you want to come? Can you bring someone interesting?’

‘Oh,’ said Michael, ‘I think so.’

‘I'll meet you there,’ said Phil. ‘With mine.’

The house had a name: the Looking Glass. A sign said so, in a cluster of mirrors and neon and preserved feather boas high up, out of the reach of vandals. The walls were painted mauve covered with mirror stars along the top.

Michael arrived alone and rang the bell with a shiver of mingled anticipation and inadequacy. He held a John Lewis shopping bag full of his costume.

The door was opened by a young man dressed like Carmen Miranda. A Salvador Dali moustache was painted on his upper lip.

‘Hello, I'm Billy, welcome!’

Billy kissed him on the cheek and ushered him in. There was a kind of combination office, kitchen and reception area, covered in cork with photographs pinned to the walls. There was no one else. Michael had come on time, and was the first to arrive. ‘You want to change?’ Billy asked.

‘Yes indeed,’ said Michael, feeling dowdy. ‘I'm . . . I'm . . .’

51

He tried to think of the formula: somebody's amputated other half. He showed the invitation.

Billy completed the sentence. 'You're one of the optional extras. So am I. I'm the son of the woman who keeps Zoltan's books. You and I will have more fun than all these old slags because it's all new to us. Now, I want your drink ready when you come out looking fabulous. What do you fancy?'

Michael was scared of being boring so he said, 'A margarita.'

'I meant herbal tea,' said Billy.

Michael smiled at himself. 'I don't know anything about herbal tea. Choose the nicest.'

Billy smiled too. 'The nicest for the nicest,' he said.

Michael went into the bathroom as himself and came out with Tarzan. He wore Tarzan, Tarzan was his costume. Weissmüller loomed over him, loose-limbed, brown, sprawling, barefoot. Michael wore a concealing leopard skin that crossed his chest and hid his belly, as if he were plump. If anyone asked he would say he had come as Boy.

Billy looked a bit confused. 'Two herbal teas, then.'

'Yes, thank you.'

Tarzan approved. 'Tea good. Tea come from jungle.'

'This is . . . uh . . . Johnny,' Michael explained.

'Hello Johnny.' Billy was young enough that a beautiful body was nothing special. But he kept glancing back towards the front door. How did this person get in?

'Woman pretty,' said Tarzan. 'Nice moustache.'

There was a broad staircase leading upstairs. The host must have heard voices, for suddenly he descended. He was a huge man, big in every direction, with a pregnant potbelly and a devilish goatee. He wore a sari, and from out of his back, four extra blue papier-mâché arms.

Tarzan drew his hunting knife.

'Hello, hello, and welcome. I am Zoltan . . . and you?' He extended a hand towards the knife. He had style.

'Tarzan. Boy,' growled Johnny, hand on knife. Zoltan's smile thinned somewhat.

'Well, I am Kali. For the evening.' Hungarian was the lightest possible seasoning in the thick soup of his Oxbridge accent.

Michael said who he was and his name seemed to evaporate even as he said it. He didn't hear it himself. Tarzan was engaged in a traditional movie-monkey greeting, making Cheetah-like noises and sniffing Zoltan's extra blue arms.

'Will your friend keep this up all evening?'

'Day and night,' said Michael.

'You've sought help for him, I hope.'

Michael said without thinking, 'No, I love him just the way he is.'

'There are some trees upstairs,' said Zoltan, speaking to Tarzan as if to an idiot. 'Figs. On the trees. You'll like figs.' He turned back to Michael. 'Harry is the gardener, you'll have to talk to him not me. Perhaps your friend would like to swing in them.'

It was a cue. Michael said thank you, and walked upstairs without his host, both of them grateful to be spared more conversation.

The room was full of mythology and mirrors: a sphinx in gold foil with turquoise eyebrows, or a fourteen-foot-high statue of Liz, portraits of the famous on mirrors so you could see yourself as them. Much of it was beautiful. Michael wished he had managed to stay the distance with Zoltan, this far at least. He would have liked to know more about the glass buddhas, the holographic eyes. One whole wall was clear glass, and beyond it, huge-leafed plants.

'What a fantastic place,' he said and sipped tea. Fancy Philip knowing someone who lived in a place like this. Michael wondered what other places Philip had visited without him. What else, indeed, did he not know about Philip?

Tarzan was unimpressed. 'Crazy place,' he said. 'Boy go. Tarzan go.'

Why, wondered Michael, am I always playing somebody's father, or somebody's son?

'We'll stay for just a little while, OK?'

The room began to fill with people: ageing psychiatrists in beards; a filmmaker who had just done a documentary about Zoltan. As Michael approached them, summoning a smile, their eyes drifted off to his left or his right. A very nice woman from the corner shop wore a blue chiffon dress in folds and was far too butch to be intimidated by anything. Michael liked the look of her, and was grateful for fifteen minutes' conversation.

'Zoltan buys mangoes from me. They're hard to get this time of year, and he's very particular.' She shook her head as if to say: you know what I mean. Her eyes gleamed up at Johnny.

There was a roar of greeting from downstairs and a sound of cheeks being kissed. An actor who was one of the glass faces had arrived. Zoltan whisked him up the stairs, holding his arm. 'Everyone, Adam's here!'

'Oooh, Adam!' said the shop owner with enthusiasm. She turned back to Michael with narrowed eyes. 'He owes me money.' She joined the surge forward.

Michael stood alone. I am here because of Phil, he remembered, to show him.

Phil arrived an hour late. He was wearing bandages and a headdress hung with daisy chains of decapitated dolls' heads. He looked like a serial killer's chandelier. It's all right for me to try too hard, Michael thought: I'm a nerdy scientist out of my depth. But you are supposed to be an artist. You are supposed to be cool.

Michael met Phil's new friend. At very first glance, there was not much to see. He was a skinny young man wearing a brown sweater with holes in it. There was something familiar about his face; maybe he was an actor.

'This is Henry,' Philip announced, his eyes flicking back and forth between him and Tarzan. The dolls' heads kept clacking against each other.

Henry looked up. He had large brown eyes that engaged Michael directly with a pre-emptive warmth and kindness. The eyes seemed to say I know this can't be easy for you, but hi anyway. They shook hands, and Henry chuckled. God, he was handsome. His smile was sweet and broad and his skin was perfect, very pale but with flushed pink cheeks and a com-plexion as unblemished as shaving foam.

'Nice to meet you, Henry,' Michael said. 'Congratulations.'

'Why?' Henry asked. His voice was surprisingly resonant, rumbling.

'For not being bullied into thinking you've got to keep up with the rich and outrageous.'

'I don't have any money,' Henry said, and smiled and shrugged. Educated, Michael decided, old family, possibly dropped out. At a guess, I'd say you were the son of someone landed with a big farm in Norfolk, that you live in the country and possibly have a pair of tame jackdaws that sit on your shoulder.

Michael liked him. 'I don't think you're the type that would dress up anyway.'

Henry gave a very gentle bow of acknowledgement. 'Probably not, no.'

Michael fancied him. It was the same old mystery. Even Michael didn't think Philip was good-looking, but his boyfriends were always gorgeous. I'm forever fancying your boyfriends, Phil. Michael felt a thin strain of regret for his old marriage.

'Are you going to introduce me?' Phil asked, nodding towards Johnny.

'Him Tarzan,' said Michael. 'Me Boy.'

'Is Tarzan a paedophile then?'

'He's my lover, if that's what you're asking.' Michael kept his gaze steady and open. He found how little it mattered to him.

'Does he speak?' asked Phil, who suddenly looked frail.

'Not much. He's Romanian.'

Tarzan spoke. 'Tarzan loves Mikey.'

'I hope you and Mikey are very happy. Maybe you'll have a chimp together. Incidentally, Mikey, Henry is my lover too.'

'You couldn't find a nicer one,' said Michael. 'Really. Lucky old you.' Michael couldn't help reaching out and clasping Henry's arm. 'He's *very* nice.'

Philip stared back at him with the strangest expression in his eyes, ringed round with red: tense, resolved, heartstricken, angry. 'Henry is an animal rights activist, Michael.' He swept off.

Henry walked away backwards, holding out his arms as if to say sorry. Michael apologized to him. 'Sorry if we embarrassed you.' Henry shrugged his shoulders, which could have meant anything from nothing embarrasses me to sorry, I can't hear you.

'Tarzan not understand,' said Tarzan, standing alone.

'Angels wouldn't,' said Michael.

Well, he had come here in order to assist Phil in the wrecking of their marriage. If that was accomplished, was there any other reason for him to stay?

He worked his way slowly through the crowd to where the booze was being served. A woman in a beige dress, with beige hair and beige fingernails said, as he passed, 'I found the colour scheme of that film so irritating. All those reds.' Her eyes trailed off to Michael's left.

'But Monica, it was in black and white!'

'Oh, you know what I mean.'

It was strange. People looked distracted, even slightly out of balance, looking past him or around him. Michael began to be aware of something out of kilter, beyond his own unease.

The barman wore a turban and tossed the glass up in the air and caught it, like Tom Cruise, except that his eyes were fixed on something just to Michael's left. Michael followed the barman's gaze and finally understood.

People were staring past Michael at the same object. They were staring at Tarzan. The beige woman was intent, a cuddly woman carrying a tray kept turning in their direction, even the mango woman kept glancing through him. Michael himself was vapourware, but he was with the most overwhelming man in the room.

Right behind Johnny stood an old man. He was intent and pale and looked shaken as if he had seen a traffic accident. Cords of loose sinew hung down his neck. He wore a glass bow tie, blue with mirrors and a blue eye where the knot should be. He didn't move, transfixed.

'Hello,' Michel said to him.

The old man's face quavered like a flower in a breeze. Someone else out of balance. 'It's a miracle,' the man insisted, as if someone had contradicted him.

Michael felt careless. 'It is,' he agreed.

'It really is him,' the old man said, in the hushed voice of someone visiting Chartres.

'They're both Romanian,' said Michael. 'Family resemblance.' He realized he knew the old man from somewhere. Some old actor; some old impresario.

Very suddenly the old man wilted. He seemed to sink from the knees, and Michael had to catch him. There were further steps, a spiral staircase up to another floor. The old man shifted awkwardly like a collapsing ironing board. Michael lowered him down to sit on the steps. The old man took out an embroidered handkerchief.

'Do you want some water?' Michael asked.

'Please,' said the old man.

The turbaned bartender already had a glass of water ready. 'Is your friend OK?' he asked, American, concerned.

'I don't know. I think so,' said Michael.

The old man was sweaty, his elegance outraged. He mopped his brow. Elegance was what he had left.

He took the water and sipped it, and sighed. 'You keep thinking, you can just turn a corner, and you'll find us all there, like we were.' His rumpled old eyes suddenly went clear as if made out of glass. 'Beautiful and at the height of our powers. Like all of you now. Tuh. It seems more real to me than this.' He held up his hands. They were blue and crisp in patches and looked like melted candles. Eighty? Michael thought. Ninety?

The old eyes strayed back to Johnny. Johnny was standing tall, and still and distant, forgetful of himself. He was staring at the fig tree behind the glass wall.

'Did you know him?' Michael asked. 'I mean, the real one?'

The old man shook his head, without moving his eyes. 'Oh no. No. But I wanted to. People of my generation, you know we had never seen anything like it. For only a very few years, he was . . . It. A sensation. People don't remember that now.'

He closed his eyes and shuddered. 'The past is a chasm it's as well not to look down,' he said.

Michael sat next to him on the steps. 'How old were you then?'

The old man's eyes looked as if they ached. 'I was twenty-two when I saw the first of his films. Of course in those days you thought you were the only one in the world, and so you dreamed. You know what I mean, I don't have to spell it out. You lived in dreams, because you knew that you were a good person, or good enough, but you wanted things that everyone else said were evil. It was difficult. You ended up loving dreams.'

He shivered, gathering himself up. 'You've been very kind,' he said, and offered a hand. 'I'm so sorry to have a been a nuisance. I used not to be. But age hits you, you know.'

'Perhaps you'd like to meet him. His name is Johnny.'

A pause for about a beat. 'It won't embarrass him?'

'I think you'll find he is beyond embarrassment.'

Michael helped him stand up. The old man rose with a sudden fluidity that hinted at what he had been when young. 'The terrible thing,' he said, casually, as if making a general observation, 'is that we feel more as we get older. Not less. The heart really ought to diminish along with everything else. Don't you think?'

His eyes were ice-blue and not at all weak. At one time those eyes would have presided, gone flinty with the hard bargaining and constant politicking of putting on a show. He would have been cagey, cunning, enthusiastic, wise and probably indelibly handsome in an etiolated London theatrical way.

Without meaning to, Michael sketched with his own hands and eyes how the old man would have moved. In the joints of his hips, he embodied the way the old man moved now. Michael felt the bargain he had made with ageing, with the death of colleagues, the death of his world. Michael had seen that bargain collapse, because of him, because of the miracle.

Michael was moved by pity. He suddenly felt that something might be in his power. I know I can make them do what I want. Can I make them do it when I'm not there? With someone else? He stopped the old man and asked, in a low voice, 'Do you know this place?'

'Oh. Zoltan? He exhibits me as a piece of camp history, but it is good to receive invitations.'

'I mean, do you know if there's a bedroom. You can go there.'

The old face went limp, flesh as confused and blank as his understanding.

'I mean,' said Michael, 'you and he could go there.'

'What an extraordinary thing.'

Michael felt a full heart. Full of victory perhaps in part and also guilt for hurting Phil, but full of what . . . abundance, too. These episodes, wherever they came from, were an abundance, a superabundance that ached to be shared.

I create them, Michael thought. I make them. He told Johnny what he wanted him to do.

Tarzan turned and climbed the steps, perhaps without even knowing why. Michael hoisted the old man around and helped him up the steps. Outside the bedroom door, the old man turned still in disbelief, and Michael had to give him a gentle shove. Then Michael stood guard. He sat on the top step, looking over a party at which he did not belong. He wished that he smoked. At least smoking would have occupied his hands.

Someone dragged open the big glass doors to clear the air, and the party moved out into the sheltered garden. Suddenly you could hear air move in trees.

He gave them twenty minutes.

Then the old man blurted out of the bedroom doorway like a coltish teenager. His glass tie was askew; his smile was wet and broad. It was a grin. He looked foxed, as if a shaft of God-light had blazed its way back into his life.

Michael had time to feel happy for him.

Then he saw Tarzan's face. Tarzan was innocent no longer.

His face had curdled with disgust and outrage. His look said to Michael: I want to kill you.

He gave one animal growl and then hurled himself over the banister of the landing. People screamed. Tarzan landed catlike on his four padded feet. Then he jumped up onto the bar, bounded over the heads of the people.

Don't hurt anyone! Michael commanded.

Tarzan jumped up into the fig tree, and gave one long backward yodel, the Tarzan cry. He scampered up the branches.

The main trunk bent under his weight, then sprang back and he leapt up and over the brick wall. It was as if he were suspended for just one moment, against the stars.

Then he sank from view. Everyone in the room applauded.

Michael tried to leave.

'But he was magnificent! Who was he?' the beige woman asked. Michael thrust his way past her and through the crowd.

Billy stood back for him at the head of the stairs. He knew something was wrong. 'What happened?' he asked, walking with Michael down to the kitchen.

'I made him do something,' said Michael, and heard his own voice: shaken, sick at heart.

Billy's high heels made a sound like Carmen Miranda, as he ran on ahead to fetch Michael's coat.

'Does he have any other clothes?' Billy asked. 'He'll freeze out there.'

Michael stopped and turned and faced him. 'He's the real thing, OK? He's not in costume.'

Michael stumbled out the front door. In the brick street, he could hear the murmuring of the party. It was cold and he felt lumpen and foolish in his leopard skin. It was a bleak place of old brick warehouses and a single closed pub with lights on and street lamps throbbing yellow like the aftermath of a burglary.

Yes, I can make them do what I want. I can violate them.

'I'm sorry,' Michael said, to the shadows and street lights. 'Johnny? I'm sorry.'

'Not Johnny,' said a voice. It was fierce with pain, affirmation. 'Tarzan. Me Tarzan.'

Michael stood and waited. He could see nothing. He walked forward, out of the light, to the side of the house, in shadow. Tarzan stood there. He hugged his arms and shivered and the top of his head was pressed against the wall.

'I'm sorry,' Michael said again.

Tarzan threw off his hand. 'Tarzan want woman,' he said, accusing.

Michael had made Tarzan let himself be sucked off by an 88-year-old man. It would have been the first time he had had sex, the first time in his fictional universe that sex had ever been present. Love for him had been sexless: kindness, tickling and caresses. It had been the sensuality of childhood. Michael felt the full crushing weight of what he had done.

The physical reality of sex is always a jolt. How much worse if it is the wrong gender, with loose jaws and crumpled flesh.

'Sick. Old. Man,' said Tarzan. All three things were out of kilter.

'He loved you,' Michael tried to explain.

Tarzan snarled in rejection. That? That was not love.

'It wasn't his fault. He didn't know.'

Johnny glowered at him. 'You want that too.'

This was pushing certain buttons from Michael's past. Those buttons pushed deep. 'I didn't touch you. I left you as you were. Did . . . did you want to do anything with me?'

Johnny/Tarzan considered. 'I wanted what you wanted.' He made a cutting gesture with the edge of his hand. Only that. To hold and be held. Johnny's eyes, fixed on Michael, were now those of an adult. Michael had destroyed any trace of affection in them. That affection could only survive in innocence. Tarzan had grown up. He had wisdom.

Boy looked at Johnny. I don't know what you are, but you have feelings of your own and a mind of your own and you have a right to be happy. Michael thought of Jane swimming naked in darkness in the jungle of innocence. Maybe, he thought. Maybe I just fancy her enough.

Suddenly, there were many urgent questions to be answered.

Do they have to be male? Can I make more than one at once? Where do they go back to?

The answers came quickly one after another.

There was a blurring of flesh as if reality had been dipped in turpentine. Flesh smeared like paint. Something flowed sideways out of Tarzan's belly and ribs – skin and bone poured out of him onto the pavement.

Flesh sprouted like a plant in time-lapse photography, growing a leather skirt like leaves, long hair like flowers.

In the time it takes to pipe a musical scale, Jane had risen out of Tarzan. She stood beside him as if fresh from the depths of the river.

She was played by Maureen O'Sullivan. She was tiny, with a face as fragile as china under a mass of wiry hair.

Michael introduced them. 'Jane, Tarzan. Tarzan, Jane.'

Click. They fitted together. They had been married in spirit from the beginning.

Michael spoke quickly to Jane, who always spoke for both of them.

Michael asked, 'Can you go elsewhere?'

Jane's chin thrust out, and her voice was chilled. 'I'm afraid I don't know what you mean.' It was the voice she used with New York lawyers.

'Can you go back to your jungle?' he asked. 'I mean, does it exist somewhere?'

Jane's face softened. Her voice quickened. 'I think we can, yes.'

Back to the treehouse, with its Flintstone home conveniences, waterwheels driven by elephants. Back to a land where animals spoke and Tarzan could talk with them, where lions lived in forests, where chimps and gorillas mingled in the same tribes. A world where there was always another wonder, another lost tribe, another adventure.

Protectively, Jane took the arm of her innocent. 'Come, Tarzan,' she said, her voice cracking like an adolescent's on the love she felt for him. 'We're going home.'

And Michael felt the same ache of yearning he had felt as a feminine boy. He yearned for love, for that particular love between them. He heard the MGM strings, swelling like his heart, like his adolescent sexuality, for them both.

So Michael sent them home. He sent them to their monochrome jungle full of giant trees with conveniently placed trapeze swings. Tired old predators prowled slowly, but were speeded up when anyone was looking. Where love filled their days in pre-lapsarian innocence.

The pub lights rippled again, and the two of them evaporated into fiction, reels of film that had never been shot.

Hypothesis: Angels are a kind of fiction.
Method: call up an Angel who is entirely fictional.

Who killed Dumb Duck?

When Michael was sixteen years old there had been a hit movie called *Dumb Duck, Detective*. It combined live action with state-of-the-art animation, and it resurrected a great old cartoon character called Dumb Duck.

It was Michael's fourth trip to California and he saw it in floods of tears, to escape. He had to get out of the house. The television was barred to him, and his favourite records had been broken. Michael had fled, wanting never to return, wanting to die.

He sat trying to follow the plot while crawling inside his own skin with anxiety. Dumb Duck was a detective and his partner was a real live human gumshoe played by Clint Eastwood. Dumb Duck asks his partner to follow his wife, Taffy Duck. 'I'm too closssh to thisssh thing.' Dumb Duck sprays everybody every time he talks. Only Clint Eastwood can stand it. Eastwood follows the wife, but she keeps giving him the slip, and you keep on hearing things about her: like she's generous, like she's a good-time girl, like she keeps you guessing. You don't see her, so you assume she's a duck, like her name.

Then suddenly, Dumb Duck is found murdered. He's been partially erased. There are still crumbs of mingled eraser dust and ink on the floor. The wife shows up having spent the night elsewhere. She tells everybody she's innocent. She looks like a combination of Lana Turner and Rita Hayworth, shoehorned into a dress that clings to her like a kid's tongue to a lollipop.

She hunkers down over the corpse and cries and her heaving boobs make a sound like rubber balloons.

Eastwood goes to her nightclub. He sits in the dark and watches her sing. Taffy sings like Marlene Dietrich. She rasps every word. She sings like somebody's tickling your testicles. She's a sex bomb married to a duck.

Gay men can desire a woman if she is caked in enough artifice. Young Michael forgot his trauma. He found himself yearning to bury his face in those huge soft perfect breasts. And sleep. And wake up somewhere else, as someone else.

It was a comedy about being wrongly accused of murder. Ho, ho. The weapon, a giant eraser – stamped: the Philadelphia Rubber Company – is found in the trunk of Taffy's car. Tests confirm that the inkgroup is the same as Dumb Duck's.

For young Michael, Taffy's nightmare became his nightmare. At that age, he felt more affinity for fantasy than reality. When the film was over, it was back to reality, though in a curious way he felt the burden had been shared.

It was many years ago, but Michael still felt that affinity. The idea of calling up Taffy made Michael grin sideways. He didn't fancy Clint Eastwood at all. You aren't meant to fancy Clint Eastwood – you are meant to want to be Clint Eastwood. Eastwood had played the gumshoe like Humphrey Bogart. Michael went out to Jermyn Street and bought himself a trenchcoat and an old-fashioned fedora hat.

And then he wondered where you could go on a hot date with someone who was obviously an animated cartoon. It might cause comment at the Savoy.

A candlelight dinner *à deux* at home was the answer.

Phil, as always, was going to be out. Michael told him, I've got a hot date so come back late. Does this one jump out of trees as well, Phil asked. Ho ho.

Michael cooked a light meal of salmon with salad and cold Chablis. Light enough to assuage hunger, not heavy enough to weigh down desire.

Then Michael put on his trenchcoat and his 1940s hat and waited.

Go, he told the universe, at 6.00 PM.

At 6.00 PM the phone rang.

It was her.

'Oh, Mr Shamus,' she said breathlessly, helplessly. 'Thank you for returning my call. I need help so badly, and I don't know who I can turn to.'

'Well. We can talk in private here. How soon can you make it over? I took the liberty of preparing a meal.' Michael curled his upper lip inwards, talking American.

'Oh thank you. But I couldn't possibly eat. I'm too upset.'

'I got a good bottle of Chablis growing dew in the cooler.' It was like being in a role-playing game.

There was a pause. 'Mr Shamus. I'm sorry. I'm afraid cartoons can't drink wine. It dissolves the gouache.'

'Forgive me.'

'No, no. I know it's hard for you to imagine what it's like. I'm just so pleased that finally, finally, someone wants to listen to me.'

That damsel in distress routine. Standard forties stuff. The audience can read it like a peach, velvet skin and pit, and so can I. Under that svelte exterior pulses animal heat.

You spend most of the movie absolutely sure she did it and that she's playing Eastwood for a sucker. You see, Eastwood falls for her, and if Eastwood falls for somebody, you do too.

She was the kind of woman whose high heels you hear ten minutes before the doorbell rings. You're there waiting, trying to pretend you aren't hanging on like it's a liferaft. Where's the shipwreck? You've got sweaty palms and the fettuccine aren't cooked. The doorbell rings, you wipe your hands on your trousers, and you open the door. There should be a soundtrack, the kind with blowsy music played on a sax.

She's delicious. She's a cartoon, so her skin controls the light and shadow on her face. Right now she's dramatic, backlit, lots of shadows, and she looks up mournfully, helplessly. An unlit cigarette sticks to a white kid glove. The white kid glove goes up above her elbow. The gown is strapless, showing acres of shoulder and collarbone. The white fur stole has fallen back down to her elbows, like she's disrobing in public. Her red hair has a life of its own. It moves in a mass like a sexy octopus and there are no individual strands of hair.

Her way of saying hi is to hold out one long kid glove.

'Oh, Mr Shamus. I'm so glad we finally meet. Now I can put a face to that kind, kind voice.'

Never in real life could a pink dress be cut that low around mammary organs that large and stay in place.

'Come in, come in please.' Like the gumshoe is a priest offering sanctuary.

Michael reminds himself. This is an animated cartoon. It's walking across my hall carpet, and her stiletto heels leave no impression.

The white fur slips, trails. The assumption is that he will take it up, and hang it on (non-wire) hangers. He does.

Her head hangs down and she looks up coyly, the cigarette weighty on her lips. 'Could I trouble you for a light?'

No one in the household smokes, and all Michael can do is offer a rolled-up newspaper lit from the gas-stove pilot.

This kind of blows his cool gumshoe exterior. She looks stricken as he holds up the torching newspaper. 'I'm sorry, I should have asked if you smoked. How thoughtless of me.'

Michael reassures her, no, no, no problem, as he tries to put out the newspaper before it burns his fingers. Finally, he flips it into the toilet. The basin is still full of flame when he closes the bathroom door. He arrives back in time to slide the chair under her as she sits down.

'I can't tell you how awful it's been. People simply don't understand my relationship with Uncle Duck. Oh, I know he was older than I . . .'

He was also a duck, but then hey, you're both cartoons.

'People find it so hard to believe that you can love someone for their mind. Those terrible cheap parts the studio made him play . . .'

You mean the one where he keeps blowing off the top of the bald hunter's head? Or the one where he drops an anvil on it?

'This is a duck who dreamed of playing Hamlet, who read philosophy, who wrote poetry.'

Always tell an intelligent person that they're beautiful. Always tell a beautiful person they're intelligent. Tell a cartoon that they're both.

Michael says, 'It must have been wonderful for him to find a soulmate like you.'

Dreamily, she nods. 'Reading the classics by firelight together. It was all I ever wanted.'

Except for your boyfriend Bruno Bruiser.

Taffy bursts into Hollywood starlet tears. All coughing sobs, hankies and dry eyes. 'And to think that people could say that I am capable of . . . of . . . uh-huh uh-huh [sniffle]. Forgive me for carrying on like this.'

'It's understandable. Under the circumstances.' Michael lays his hand on top of hers, and she gives his a quick warm squeeze. She feels warm, human warm, but smoother too, slick, no creases or texture to the gloved and perfect hands.

Michael. Do you really want to have sex with a cartoon?

She looks up, determined now. 'We must find whoever killed my husband. I have money, Mr Shamus. I'll pay every last penny of it to find out who killed Uncle Duck.'

And to prove you didn't do it.

'I warn you. I don't exactly come cheap, Mrs Duck.'

She breathes heavily and leans forward. 'People say that you're the best in the business.' Appreciatively, she takes his hand again.

'Perhaps we can leave this difficult decision until later. Won't you eat something? Starving yourself won't help.'

Taffy looks wistful. She has a perfect tiny nose that is completely invisible except when she is in profile. 'No, thank you. Cartoons are different from people. We're fuelled only by our motivations.'

'Your motivations?'

'Our passions. They sometimes take us over. We like or don't like. We love, or don't love.'

OK, let's go for it.

'Then,' Shamus says, still steely in his old-fashioned, white knight/tough guy pose. 'Perhaps you know how I feel about you.'

Alarmed, she stands up. 'No! Don't say it.' She flees to the window on little high-heel steps, and frames her face between her kid gloves.

'Mrs Duck. Taffy. Kiss me.'

What does it mean when a homosexual wants to stick his face between two artificial breasts? It means that what he finds desirable about them is that men have thought of those breasts. Men imagined them and drew them and shaped them and shaded them. It means it is the male desire behind the image that draws him, the desire of other men.

'No. We must wait.'

'No one will know. It is our secret. Our love.'

'But the court case. People will talk. You don't know what it's been like.'

Oh, Taffy.

Her lips are not human lips. They are better than human lips. They are like Juicy Fruit chewing gum: thick delicious mobile wads that respond immediately to pressure, yielding and flowing but never too wet. They are the best lips Michael has ever kissed. And no moustache.

Over the tiny pinprick of her nose, her eyes go wide, wider, big as saucers.

'Oh. Oh, Michael. Hold me. Hold me close. Take away the fear.'

He cradles her. She has an invented nature and her invented nature is to respond in this way. Her mammoth breasts heave against him; the fabric of the pink dress stretches. She protests, but it is in the script, though normally after the fadeout. The breasts are unleashed from their pink constraints. They are Platonic breasts, breasts in the ideal. Large and firm, but also soft, peach-coloured with baby-bottle nipples. They are supported, protected by her crossed, fluid arms. She keeps changing shape, subtly, to embody the ideal.

Her nipple fills his mouth. She tastes tangy and slightly salty. He fondles a nipple with his tongue, and it engorges. Michael thinks of all those hairy arms that drew those breasts, the thick hands that outlined the nipples through the pink of the dress. Did they dream of supping where he now sups? Michael feels his lips move in unison with theirs. He lolls her in his mouth.

'Oh my love,' she gasps.

Her thighs are perfect and without pores. Her translucent panties shimmer their own way down. Michael sees pudenda as babyishly appealing and round-eyed as Bambi or Thumper. There is a button-cute clitoris under his tongue. Unlike the breasts, it tastes real.

A cartoon orgasm, as yet unfilmed, makes the cheeks of her face quake and ride up like a stocking. Her breasts not only heave, but swell. Her face is nearly the colour of tomatoes, and her eyes are huge and crossed. She looks like she's drowning, desperately holding her breath. Suddenly the nipples blow off steam, clouds of it. The breasts whistle in unison like two trains in a race.

Taffy settles back, crumpling. She goes fluid and pours down over the sofa onto the carpet, as flexible as a shadow, taking the shape of whatever supports her. She lies there panting for a moment, then sticks one of her fingers into her mouth, and reinflates herself, puffing, as if she were an air mattress.

Later, she dresses, in a lady-like fashion, smoothing down her hair and pulling straight the fingers of her gloves. She expertly cups the breasts back into their impossible fittings of pink.

'Michael, I want to tell you this. That was one of the finest moments of my life. You know so much about the needs of a woman. How to lift her up, away from the inelegant struggle to survive.'

No my dear, that's what you know.

What you know is what the men who embodied you want. Elegance.

Adjusting the perfect pink dress.

Need.

You turn your back for me to do up the zipper and I see the strong back, with two ridges of muscle down either side of the spine. You lift up the mass of your hair to show what every man dreams the back of a woman's neck is like.

Class.

What clumsy, sweaty, fat, balding men imagine they want

from women. They want to merge with elegance and delicacy, gain it by association.

She fiddles with what can only be called an evening bag. She extracts from it a tiny, flat silver case and takes out of it a single white address card.

'Call me. Please. I need to know I can rely on someone.'

The high heels clack, on a carpet. The high heels control their own sound. The dress swishes like someone shushing a child to sleep. The shoulders wait for their white furs, a hint of shoulder blade drawn onto the broad expanse of her back. He complies with the script, or perhaps his father's idea of how men should behave, and brings her wrap. She accepts it demurely, in a manner that can only be called gracious. As she walks away towards his front door, her bottom is shaped exactly like an upside-down heart under clouds of fur.

His door opens at the same moment as the neighbour's door across the hall.

In the doorway opposite stands a little girl. She gapes at Taffy.

A six-foot-tall animated cartoon fills the apartment corridor, and leans over, warm and giggling.

'Well, hello there,' says Taffy. 'Who are you?' She coos with a voice like melted ice cream.

'Mum, Mum come quick!' the little girl cries in panic and turns and lets the door close.

Taffy Duck turns to Michael and shrugs. She blows him a kiss, and as if disturbed by it, the air ripples and closes over her, just as the neighbour's front door opens again.

Perfect.

At the end of the movie, you find out that she didn't do the murder. Her boyfriend Bruno did. She really loved the duck and the detective after all. The last shot is a long kiss between realities. But no one ever shows what happens after the ending.

Twenty years before, at the end of the film, Michael stood up and drove back to the condo in Oceanside and told his father, 'I'm going back home tomorrow.' His father said nothing. He just stared up at him from the sofa. Michael still remembered his father's crew cut and his fathomless eyes, full of hatred.

Like the old actor said: the past is a chasm, don't look down.

Michael stood looking down in his own sitting room, wearing a trenchcoat and fedora. Fancy dress again.

Weeeellllllll, he thought. It was fun and I always was good at acting.

Uh-huh. And you didn't come and you didn't have a hard-on so the sex was acting too. She was about as far from the real as you can get. So when do you get real, Michael? How? You don't even know how, do you? You just keep repeating your youth. And it wasn't even a happy youth, Michael.

Do people I copy really know it?

Michael remembered Tony. The real Tony had some kind of sense of what his copy had done. It was one thing to hurt a fictional character. It was another thing to harm someone real. Michael had no business experimenting on people without being able to assess the extent of the trauma he might be inflicting.

But he couldn't test it first, because he couldn't call up anyone without being able to assess the damage, etc, etc. And it was not the sort of thing he could test on chickens, unless he was about to make the unwelcome discovery that he lusted after livestock. So how could he gauge what it was like to have a copy made of you? Michael spent a day in an experimental hall of mirrors, until that metaphor gave him his method.

He checked himself into the Hotel Chez Nous. He approached the front desk with some trepidation. He thought that Tarzan would have left the sheets covered in body makeup. Explaining that would be embarrassing.

The clerk was French and had irritating nostrils; they looked as if they were flaring in disgust at an unpleasant odour. He took Michael's card, and once he had come up on the screen said smoothly, 'Welcome back, Mr Blasco.' It seemed there was no record of Max Factor on the linen. The clerk asked the screen, 'Your usual room, sir?'

It was indeed the usual room. It was so usual Michael could not be sure if it really was the same room or not.

His stomach felt feathery, as if he had missed breakfast. He was, he realized, a little bit afraid of what he was going to do next. He started unbuttoning his shirt, knowing it was a delaying tactic. Every episode was a delaying tactic. He should just forget all of it, go to Alaska Street to get his rocks off and hope the whole thing would go away.

But then he would never know what this thing had come for.

Look, how can it hurt you? How can it hurt you, that is, any more than you have hurt yourself? Just do it and then you'll know, and that will help you decide to forget it, write it off. Just do it.

Michael called up a copy of himself.

The air wavered, parting to admit the newcomer. He was tall and stocky at the same time. You only noticed on the second glance that he was not fat, but really quite muscular: the hair on the arms disguised the definition.

Immediately, Michael felt sympathy for him. There was an air of caged and baffled decency about him, a slight scowl, a hopeful smile. In fact, he was not at all bad-looking, what Michael called a black Celt: slightly sallow skin, a heavy beard and black eyes.

Michael fancied himself. It's a well-known syndrome, and it had afflicted Michael far worse than most: daughters meeting their long-lost fathers for the first time; sisters and brothers separated at birth meeting on a course. There are two great triggers for sexual desire: extreme but complementary genetic difference, or extreme genetic similarity. You either find some-one completely different to complete the genetic puzzle, or someone who is kindred.

So here he was, dragged back to the seat of his neuroses: himself.

'Oh,' said Michael and Michael together.

Then they both chuckled shyly and looked down at their shoes in unison.

'Um,' they said in unison, embarrassed. They looked up at each other and two pairs of black eyes sunk into each other.

'Oops,' they said, understanding each other perfectly. They wanted to fuck themselves.

74

With that unspoken agreement, they both began to undress. Love finds faults endearing. For the first time ever, Michael saw that he only combed his rich black unruly hair in front. The back of his head was practically in dreadlocks. The back of one trouser leg was tucked into the top of his socks. He looked back around and it was true of him, too. Oh well, he was a bachelor.

The Angel turned back to face him, and viewed as a stranger, he stirred Michael's heart with forgiveness for what it means to be human. Here was a man of 38 winters, crepe paper around the corner of his eyes, and it was not until you held him that you realized all that flesh was solid. Somebody should tell him about his choice of knickers. And socks. The white Y-fronts were slipped to one side, and there was a penis that was in no way as tiny as Michael thought: it had a nice round head that was beginning to swell and weep.

'What . . .' they both began, and broke off, with a chuckle and a shrug. They were going to ask: what now? They didn't need to.

A lover who really understands you? Who really knows what you are thinking?

Michael had not felt such a surge of desire since he was sixteen years old: heedless and irresistible. With no discussion, they were pulled towards each other, to embrace, in the French sense of the term: to kiss.

Suddenly his copy jerked his head aside, lips pressed shut. He was frightened of AIDS. It was insulting, disappointing and childish.

The original Michael said, 'We can hardly give each other something we don't already have.'

And immediately there was a sense of parting, very slight like a tangerine being peeled. They were no longer exactly one. Their histories were now very slightly different.

'That's true,' said the copy, trying to look amused. He was stiff and awkward, and gave Michael a peck on the lips. Did Michael feel a slight echo somewhere, like a double image? Did he not very slightly feel his own lips peck someone else's, while they themselves were being kissed?

'Sorry,' the copy said and gave Michael a little cajoling shake.

'Old habits die hard.' He planted another chaste kiss on Michael's cheek. Michael felt a falling away. He let his own penis drop, and looked down and saw his copy, thrashing uselessly away at himself.

That was always the pattern. He'd start out well, with a promising swelling, gallons of lubricant, and then the sudden irretrievable collapse.

'We're not going to be much use to each other are we?' the original Michael said.

'We could just cuddle,' said his copy, hopefully. Michael had done enough cuddling. He looked at his own body and asked it: why? It's a beautiful body, everything else about it works.

'Shall we try again?' Michael asked himself.

'OK,' chuckled the copy, weakly. It was lie, Michael knew. He was ashamed and now simply wanted to escape. This Michael was an amazingly disheartening sexual partner. But Michael was determined to persevere, for both their sakes.

It is a very strange thing to kiss yourself. There is no change of taste, and you know exactly what the tongue will do, how it will respond. I'd never realized, thought Michael, how useful my lips are. I hated my fat lips. But they're great for kissing.

If only this Angel would move them.

Michael leaned back and looked at himself. He was surprised at how angry he felt. He had been moved, roused, and then let down. It felt like rejection, it felt personal. He made a soft fist and gave his partner a gentle, chiding thump. There was a distant disturbance in his own shoulder, as if someone had thrown a pebble into a pool some distance away.

'Now you know how other people feel,' said his copy, something dark and steely creeping into his own eyes.

'Oh, Jesus, let's sit down,' said Michael. They sat next to each other on the bed. His partner looked defeated, mournful. Michael put an arm around his shoulder to comfort him, and they lay side by side, comrades rather than lovers.

Michael changed the subject. 'You feel anything? From me?'

'A kind of a buzz.'

'It wouldn't hurt you, would it?'

The copy scowled. 'I don't think I would know what it was.'

'I just wanted to know if I could hurt people.'

The Angel sighed. 'It would give them a turn if they showed up at your flat and met themselves by mistake.'

'I'll remember that.'

They turned and looked into each other's faces, like brothers, like friends. They both had the same dark eyes, and his copy's eyes were black and sad. Do I always look this mournful having sex? Isn't sex supposed to be fun?

The Angel asked, 'Do you have any idea how we got this way?'

The focus of Michael's vision seemed to shift and he saw something in the face, and jumped up, and scuttled away. 'Jesus Christ, you look just like Dad!'

Michael turned back around, and the bed was empty. Even the baggy Y-fronts had gone.

Can Angels do work?

Back at work, Ebru asked Michael, 'Where do you go in the afternoons?'

Her smile was rueful, teasing, an evident *mise-en-scène*. Because her eyes were saying: you're supposed to be running this place.

'Lunch,' replied Michael. 'Why, was there a problem?'

She was leaning as if relaxed across her desk. She sprawled. It was a difficult posture to read, because it seemed friendly but was also disrespectful.

Her voice drawled; she sounded sleepy. 'The University called. You were supposed to be teaching a course today.'

Oh shit, oh no, of course, it's Thursday.

Ebru looked bored. 'What could I do? I told them you would call when you got back.'

'Oh, Jees, was it Professor Dennis? Oh darn. OK. I'll give her a call.'

'Could you leave me with your number please where you will be when you go out?'

'Yeah sure. I'll get a mobile, so you can call me.'

Michael jerked forward, wanting to escape. Ebru had more to say. 'The grant application forms have been on your desk for a week. I just wanted to make sure you knew they were there.' Michael had to apply for funds for the next stage of research; they were to teach the chicks tasks such as pushing buttons for food. The aim was to keep the facility going, so the

University could rent it out for other projects. The aim was that Michael would eventually make himself some kind of Director.

'Right, yes. I've been meaning to get to that.'

'Emilio was saying that he has not been told the file names for the control group slides. This means he has fallen behind on his data entry and filing.'

'Sorry,' said Michael. 'A lot on my plate.'

Ebru dismissed it, as if sleepy. 'I wasn't chasing you.'

Oh yes you were.

Alone in his windowless office, Michael told himself: you have been neglecting your job.

It had been just over three weeks since the episodes began. There had been five afternoons at the Chez Nous, four with Johnny and one with himself. They had moved from late winter into spring. How did he think people would not notice?

There was a Fridge full of frozen, unfiled slides. How could he ask people to work for him? People who were on short-term contracts, which meant they could not get a mortgage. How could he ask them to work punctiliously, perfectly, as science demanded?

And, oh shit, he was also supposed to be writing a phase paper on the difference between Windows NT and Unix for his MSc in Computer Science. It was due next Monday. He'd done nothing about it.

Michael hung his head, and then lowered it into his hands from shame.

God, he found himself asking, why have you done this to me?

God, in the form of the painted brick wall, could not answer, or rather, decided not to, or rather, couldn't be bothered.

Well, the wall seemed to say, on its own behalf if not God's, I'm just a wall and not very interesting, but I am the life you have chosen. You put yourself in this office with these slides and files and papers and coursework and you'd better get on with it.

Michael needed to talk to someone. He had no one to talk to, most especially not his staff, his lover, or their friends. All his friends were Phil's friends.

'Help,' he said in a small voice that was not meant to be heard.

'Hiya,' said a voice that poised somewhere in mid-Atlantic. Something white moved in the corner of his eye.

His Angel was sitting on the corner of the desk, wearing his white lab coat. His smile was mild and his eyes faded; he looked detached.

Michael saw himself. I have good feelings for people, but I don't connect. So they don't always know that.

'Hiya,' Michael said. 'I've been neglecting things.'

'You have a miracle to deal with. Ah. I think you'll find that most people who have one of those find it's a full-time job. I mean, Phil Dick just saw pink lights, and look how long that took to sort out.'

Michael's face shook itself with unexpected tears, like a dog getting out of water. He certainly didn't feel that unhappy. The reaction didn't seem to link to any emotion until he spoke, vehemently.

'I didn't *want* an extra full-time job. I didn't ask for this. What is it for, what I am supposed to do with it, and why, why me?'

The Angel looked back, big and kindly and powerless. 'I know less than you do.'

Michael apologized, his default mode. 'I'm sorry, this isn't easy for you either.'

'I don't matter. I'm not real.' The Angel managed to say that with a smile. 'Why don't you let me help?'

It took a while for the anger to be stilled. The Angel kept talking.

'I know what you know. I can do just as good a job as you can. We've got a backlog. Why don't you stay here and do the accounts or whatever? I'll go to the Fridge and do the slides.'

What a wonderful idea. Michael chuckled. 'It'll be like the Shoemaker and the Elves.'

'Let's wait until tonight,' said the Angel. 'That way no one will see you in two places at the same time. We don't want to give anyone a heart attack.'

'Can we talk afterwards?' Michael asked. He felt the same yearning he would for a lover.

'Sure, baby.'

That was what Michael always used to say to Phil. When they were young and in love.

So he filled in the form for the second stage of their research grant, and wrote the first draft of the accompanying business case. Michael's career plan was simple. He would keep using the lab for further research projects until his own reputation was established and then let out the secure facility for other projects. At 5.00 PM he was able to bustle into Ebru's office, fluttering papers.

'Well, here we go. This is the business case for the grant. First draft. Can you read it for me, make any comments. Oh. I also know nothing about the admin costs, so could you run off a 104 on the office expenses.'

Ebru was still watchful, languid. 'It's five o'clock. Do you need it this instant?'

'Not right now, of course. Close of play tomorrow for the comments. I'll need the 104 sometime tomorrow morning.'

'I can do that for you,' she said airily, gathering up her bag. No, she seemed to say, I am not working late to make up for your lost time. She smiled a hazy, hooded smile at him, and gave him a dinky little wave with the tips of her fingers. 'Good night. See you tomorrow.' Faultlessly polite. The draft was left on her desk.

He was left standing alone in the room. I have really pissed her off.

It was 5.03 and there was absolutely no one there. They had all gone home. Who would work late if the boss wasn't there?

The whole universe has burst its bonds in order to put you in this position. Impossible things are happening, and they are screwing up your life, and nothing in your intellectual or emotional history has prepared you for them.

And you have allowed yourself to become alone.

His only friend was literally himself.

Michael went into the cold room. There was his other self, big and happy, a cheerful anorak singing old Wham! songs.

'Bad boys . . .' The Angel was merry in his work. He turned around smiling, the smile coming from being usefully employed and suffering no doubts. When Michael smiled his eyes went tiny and narrow, almost closed, and that in turn made him look a bit like a Chinese Santa Claus.

'Just started,' said the Angel, cheerfully. His breath came out as vapour; frost settled on his eyebrows. 'Things really aren't that bad. Emilio's been good, he's using a temporary naming convention, which we might as well accept. And everything's been labelled, in boxes. It just needs to be put away properly.'

The Angel pulled open a drawer. There were the first of his slides, label side up and out, in neat rows. 'There's only about an hour's work.'

Things really weren't that bad. Relief was like a pillow. Michael settled into it. The work would be done, he would apologize to Emilio, and amends would be made. It would be all right.

'I'll be back then.' Michael kept the need out of his voice.

Back in his office, there were 37 e-mails needing answers. They were mostly from the University, agendas or minutes attached, or new curriculum proposals. He went through picking the most important first. His professor had written three days ago, asking if the project was progressing well.

Michael defaulted to apologies. Sorry, I've been in the grip of applying for grants. Wouldn't it be great if someone just said, fine, here's all the money you need in one go? We could put it in the bank and use the interest for the project as well. But the project is going fine, great. A lot of data to work through.

There was an invitation to speak at a conference, with a carefully worded guarantee of security. 'We realize your work is controversial. We will make sure that only nominated delegates can attend, so all questioning will be on the methodology and preliminary results.' This was exactly the kind of fallout Michael had wanted from the research: increased profile, keynote addresses, publications, and acknowledgement, if only from a very few people worldwide. Michael accepted the invitation, feeling suddenly that all was right with the world.

How delicious, he thought. I can pay my bills and iron shirts at the same time. I can stay late for one hour and do two hours' work. Everything will be perfect. My desk will finally be cleared; the flat will finally be clean. At last, I'll finally get everything done! He felt merry.

There were all kinds of admin he could feel virtuous about. There was his own personnel file that had been left blank. Let's get that out of the way. He had to fill in the name of the nearest relative to call in case of accident.

Once again, it would be his mother, miles away and untelephoned in Sheffield.

Was there anyone else for whom he was number one? It wasn't Phil.

Who loves ya baby?

'All done,' he heard himself say. Michael looked up at the big, reliable broken face. He felt himself smile with gratitude. 'So am I,' he said. 'Thanks.'

'You'd do the same for me,' said the Angel, and grinned. It was a Michael kind of joke.

He wouldn't be able to get a copy of himself past the security guard without telling some pointless story. Hi, this is my identical twin. 'I'm going to have to let you go,' Michael said quietly. His voice, he realized, was full of love.

'I understand.'

The whisper in the air, like a blown kiss. Papers on the desk rattled, lifted up, and sighed back into place, and Michael was left feeling a little lonelier. He packed up his bag, turned out the light, and decided in the corridor just to look at all the beautiful slides.

The cold room had a big white door and a big chrome handle. It was like a 1950s refrigerator you could walk into. Its surface trembled slightly from the chundering of the generator. It shook like Michael. You are in a bit of a state, mate. The door clunked open, the cold room breathing out refreshingly chill air. The temperature only sank into your bones and numbed your fingers once you were inside.

He switched on the light and pulled open a drawer, to admire the neat rows, to be grateful.

Instead there was a crumpled, much reused box, its red ink

finger-smeared, cluttered with a cross-hatch of piled slides. A whole week's work, neglected and growing.

It was as if someone had reached into him, and grabbed his heart and held it still.

He pulled open another drawer. It too simply stored an unsorted box.

All that beautiful work was gone.

But he had seen it! He'd seen it all being done, it was all just here!

In a panic he pulled open one icy drawer after another. The tips of his fingers stuck to the metal each time. One drawer was spread with unsorted slides. The next was empty. He pulled open another drawer. And ah! this one was full of ranked and ordered slides. There was a moment's relief, until he checked the dates. It was the first batch of slides from the learning group. Emilio had finished sorting that last week.

It was all undone, as if the Angel had never been. Michael clasped his own forehead in his hands. You may have seen it Michael, and you may be going nuts.

He called his Angel back. 'Where are your slides?' Michael whispered.

'What? What do you mean?'

'Well have a look!'

The copy pulled open the drawer. His face fell. His chin dropped and looked temporarily double. He turned his whole body as if his back was stiff, his chin still resting on his chest.

'Yes. Well,' the copy whispered. 'I'm not real, am I?' He did not manage to smile. He closed the drawer slowly, delicately with the tip of his finger. He stared at the drawer. 'I can't change anything.'

He looked back at Michael, and tried to smile. 'I can't write anything. When I go, so will all the marks on the page. I could do all your annual accounts and in the morning, you'd be back where you started. I can't father a child. I can't make a difference to anything.'

The two Michaels stared at each other.

'It really is a very peculiar sensation,' said the copy and

chuckled. 'I am completely and totally impotent.' The grin glazed. 'Can you send me back now, please?'

Afterwards, Michael went to the security room. The guard, Shafiq, sat there in slate-blue uniform, watching *EastEnders*.

'Shafiq, do you think we could look at the CCTV tapes, please?'

Shafiq was eating a Pot Noodle. His mouth stopped circulating for an instant and he froze in place. Then he swallowed and stood up.

'Why, Michael, is something wrong, has there been an intrusion?'

'No, no, no, Shafiq, nothing's wrong. I just want to check on something.'

Shafiq was upset. 'I have been here all the time, Michael. Watching, really.' The television was still talking, and his eyes listed guiltily towards it. 'I watch the television, you know, but I always keep one eye on the CCTV, too.'

'I know, Shafiq, you do an excellent job. I just want to check.'

In a more normal state, Michael would have been stricken with concern: Shafiq was a good man, a good father, who was proud of his work. Shafiq seemed to drop to his knees in prayer and began to open up the banks of secure tapes.

'What rooms do you think suffered? When?'

'About two hours ago. Let's try my office.'

'Your office.' Michael could hear the bottom drop out of Shafiq's stomach. 'With all your records, and papers!'

He really does care, thought Michael. Why does he care? What have I given him that he should give a tinker's?

Shafiq inserted the cassette and nervously punched rewind.

'But Ebru and everyone were here two hours ago. Michael, they would have heard something too.'

It wasn't fair to scare Shafiq like this. But looking at the security tapes would confirm something.

'There it is, sir.'

Michael's office. And there was Michael, turned around in his chair and plainly talking to empty air.

'Thank you, Shafiq, you can turn it off now.'

'Don't you want to wait until you leave the office?' Shafiq

was beginning to look baffled. 'How would there be an intruder, if you were there all along?'

'It's not an intruder, OK? Please Shafiq, don't be too concerned. Do you think you can show me the cold store interior at 5.03?'

Shafiq was going from baffled to slightly annoyed. 'What are we looking for, Michael? Perhaps I could suggest something else. The CCTV looks at all the doors and even the ventilation shafts.'

'I'm sorry to trouble you, Shafiq, but please show me.'

The cold room looked grey and indistinct and empty. It was hard to see; for a moment Michael thought he saw something move, as if through fog. He peered, but was finally sure beyond doubt. There was no one there.

The security video jumped between frames taken one second apart. Suddenly, the door was half-open. Suddenly it was wide open. Suddenly Michael himself stepped in in stages, lurching like Frankenstein's monster. He stayed alone and chatting to no one.

'OK, Shafiq. False alarm.'

Shafiq stood up straight and adjusted his blue shirt. 'But if there has been anything moved, surely it would be better to study tapes when you weren't there.'

Michael closed his eyes, to avoid Shafiq's face, and his voice was unnaturally quiet and precise. 'I was mistaken, Shafiq. I don't want to worry you further. Thank you for helping.'

He walked out of the room, his back held straight.

In the corridor he thought, I'm alone. I'm really alone.

Maybe I am just crazy.

But even if I'm not, they aren't real. My Angel said that. They are the universe breaking its own rules. If unreal people walked free to change the world, it would be a catastrophe. And so they come and work and love and when they leave, they leave no evidence or trace behind.

They can't sort slides; they can't be video taped.

The only evidence, the only scars, will be in my memory. I am the only thing they can change. Otherwise, poor Angels, when they go it is as if they never existed.

Michael felt sad for them. Because I know that when they

are here, they love and feel and want. When they're here, they're alive.

Michael sat at his desk and looked at the brick wall again, and heard his own voice rage, demanding, 'Why is the design of this experiment such crap!'

What is a sample of one going to tell you, God? Why bend all the rules of the universe just to do this terrible thing to me? Is it a joke, God? Does it amuse you to see people knocked sideways, their whole life go rotten like an apple? Do you like to see us hauled beyond our limits? Do you like to see us cry?

And why do this to an impotent man? What is it going to teach me, what are you going to learn from this except what we both know? I'm lousy in bed. What's the big deal about that, I live with it, I've learned to live with it.

Michael went back to the cold room. In a rage, sweating in the chill, he tore through the work. The glass edges of the slides cut his fingers.

It took an hour. When he was done he had a sudden moment of irrational fear that his own work would also disappear. He closed the drawer and opened it again, to check. The work remained.

So maybe I do just make them up, maybe I make up that other people see and hear them. Maybe I am just nuts.

Michael arrived back at the flat late, exhausted, chilled and sweaty. He must have looked a state. Phil glanced up at him from what looked like a plate of tomato sauce on cardboard. 'You didn't tell me when you would be home,' Phil said. 'So I went ahead with dinner.'

So when did Phil ever call to say when he'd be home? Michael sat down exhausted, shambolic. Today was a bad hair day: his scalp itched and he knew his hair tumbled down in dank, greasy curls. His five o'clock shadow had arrived on time, but now, at 8.30 PM, it was even thicker and coated with cold sweat. Phil wouldn't look at him.

'That's OK, I guess,' said Michael. 'You probably don't realize that I've been coming home on time lately. You're never in. It was my effort to be here in case you wanted to go to a movie or anything.'

Phil's eyes were shuttered like windows. In the silence, Michael had the opportunity to examine Phil's newly vegetarian food. There was no table fat on his bread.

Phil asked in a light voice, 'Where exactly is your work?'

It was a question that produced an automatic prickling sensation of suspicion, even fear. Hold on, thought Michael. This is Phil. Then he thought, hold on, this is Phil.

He stalled. 'What do you mean?'

'Oh. It's just that you've never told me, that's all. It can't be that long a trip. Waterloo, isn't it?'

'Waterloo? No! No, no, the Elephant and Castle.'

Phil shrugged elaborately and his eyes didn't move from the plate. 'I thought it was Waterloo.' His tiny mouth had to stretch to take a bite out of a chunk of bread that was the colour of brown shoes. 'In an old warehouse or something.'

Michael began to trace the criss-cross patterns of green on the waterproof tablecloth. I've never said in an old warehouse or anything else. Certainly not in the arches underneath an elevated railway.

'Yeah, an old warehouse. Near the Old Kent Road.'

Phil nodded now, very carefully, very slowly.

Michael pressed together his thick veined hands.

My boyfriend is pumping me for my work address so he can give it to animal rights demonstrators. My boyfriend of thirteen years wants to betray me. Henry has such a nice smile, doesn't he?

'So how *is* the gorgeous Henry?' The emphasis on the 'is' somehow made it plain that Michael had been reminded of Henry by the previous topic, that there was a connection between them.

'He's fine, thank you,' said Phil, coolly.

He doesn't even care that I've guessed.

Michael struck back. It was a bit like playing tennis. 'You know many couples in our situation would be busy reassuring each other that they practised safe sex with their lovers. They'd talk about whether they should be using condoms with each other. But . . .'

Michael considered letting his voice trail delicately away, but you play tennis to win. 'But we don't have to, do we Phil? We don't make love.'

It was only then, finally, that Michael realized he needed a new life.

Can they give me Aids?

After California, Michael spent the next ten years missing sexual opportunities. As these years were 1976 to 1986, missing opportunities probably saved his life.

Everyone else was going at it like ferrets, not knowing there was something brand-new in the world. By the time Michael emerged from purdah, he and the world knew things had changed, and were taking precautions.

But it was already too late for several dear friends. They rolled on all unknowing for many years, all through the eighties into the nineties, though they were, like Shrödinger's cat, already dead mathematically. They had the virus. Or rather, it had them.

If you can have sex with anyone in the world, you need to know as a matter of urgency, if they can make you ill. Answering this question presented Michael with several interesting methodological difficulties.

If he experimented on himself and it made him ill, that would indeed be a result, but it would rather defeat the purpose. On the other hand, experimenting on someone else did raise certain ethical questions.

It was also methodologically suspect. Michael would first have to ensure that whoever was being tested was HIV negative to begin with. Proving HIV negative status is extremely difficult. Antibodies take three months to show up after infection. That means a second test is necessary three months after the first.

During those three months, you have to know absolutely that the person has avoided all risk of exposure to the virus. That means no kissing. If there are any doubts, you have to test again three months after that.

If the subject was, say, a nun who never had sex with anyone, Michael would first have to find the one Angel in the world who could seduce her, and then persuade her that she needed an HIV test. This scenario seemed unlikely.

Perhaps his own Angel could sleep with another Angel with Aids. And then be tested twice, once while the infected Angel was still in the world, and again, once he had left it to see if the virus remained behind.

But that meant the slate would be cleaned whenever the carrying Angel disappeared. And even perhaps when his own experimental Angel dipped in and out of existence.

Both the infecting Angel and his victim would have to remain in the world for an uninterrupted three months.

Well, Michael could rent a house somewhere out of the way, Scotland maybe, and have them live there under iron orders to sleep with no one else. It was a little bit like keeping experimental dogs in kennels. There was no doubt that science was easier when you did it to animals.

But Angels are not people. What if their immune systems worked differently? Suppose Angels could infect people but not each other?

Michael considered testing with a less serious virus. He could conjure up an Angel with a severe cold, sleep with him, and see if he caught anything. Or call up a copy with diphtheria on his moustache and swab his own lips and grow a culture.

But HIV was a retrovirus. It copied itself into the RNA of your cells, and took over their reproductive function. It becomes you, and you are real. Suppose over the three months it worked its magic, the virus became so entwined with your non-miraculous body that it gained a real life?

The more he thought, the more difficult and absurd it all became.

Then he remembered that one of his many lost opportunities had grown up to be an expert on Aids. Her name was Margaret

White, but Michael had known her in school as Bottles. They had been friends during Michael's brief period of popularity before his last trip to California.

At sixteen, Michael was just American enough to find it easier to meet strangers and stay sunny and positive about things. He was invited to parties. He was likely to succeed, and grumpy jealous spotty pale blokes grumbled about him behind his back.

Michael was in the school theatre club and was big and strong and handsome and could act. There were more girls in drama club than blokes, so they did a production of Anouilh's *Antigone*: lots of juicy female roles. Michael played the old, heart-torn tyrant. He moved with a combination of bullish swagger and slight arthritic limp that left the audience astonished. Michael had conjured up the king.

His sport was long-distance running. The beefiness he inherited from his father was yet to develop; he maintained an easy luxurious swing to the way he moved. He combined beauty with a certain shy sweetness that did not threaten or repel, and his black eyes reminded people of a particularly friendly, lively spaniel. Indeed, he was very good with animals. He worked for the local vet part-time and had decided to become a veterinarian.

The nicest thing about Michael was that he was no snob.

Bottles was the unkind nickname given to a big-breasted girl who existed on the social margins. She was tall, big-boned, a little ungainly, with a certain daffy spinning to her eyes. Her classmates whispered about her with a fascinated prurience, because at sixteen, Bottles was living the life of grown woman. She looked 22, had adult boyfriends with cars, and spent weekends in clubs. Rumour was accepted as fact: Bottles did a strip show in the local pub.

Michael got to know Bottles on a school trip to Windsor Castle, an attempt to steep them in the mystique of royalty. They met over a joke.

As they got off the train at one of Windsor's stations, Bottles said to him, cheerily, 'My goodness, two train stations. Is that so the Queen can get away in case there's a revolution?'

It was 1976 and there was little to make any hungry

secondary-scholar feel wild, free and funny. Bottle's top was cut low, and her breasts were squashed together, showing pale skin and a hint of blue veins. She had been sent home recently for the unheard-of thing of piercing her nostril with an earring.

'I mean, do you suppose the Queen goes to the toilet in public? I'm being serious. There she is, waving to crowds and suddenly she gets caught short. Can she say, sorry everyone, I need a pit stop? Or does she just have to wait until she gets home?'

To a sixteen-year-old in the run-up to the Jubilee, this was scandalously original. Bottles began to walk in a clenched, constricted way and grunted in agony. 'One is so pleased to be hyah.'

Michael laughed, partly with disbelief that someone real could suddenly start saying such things. He laughed with relief because he found Bottles reassuring. Daftness is not only funny but very slightly pitiable.

Michael's laughter was constrained by fear, fear of being awkward or saying too much, and this constraint made it elegant. It was elegance that Bottles craved.

Both of them felt an irresistible tug of charm. Bottles suddenly put her arm through his.

'You,' Bottles announced, 'are a Louise.'

Michael's panic surfaced: how did she know? Had someone told her? If someone had told Bottles then maybe everybody knew.

She saw it and chuckled. 'Don't look so baffled,' she said, and stroked the top of his brown and flawless hand. 'Louise is a club. It's run by the most wonderful Frenchwoman and she's called Louise and so her club is too.' She lapsed into fake American. 'You wanna go?'

Michael beamed relief and friendship. 'Absolutely, without fail, please.' After all, he was the school's official American, and Americans are never supposed to be afraid.

She got the message. He liked her. 'Friday night OK with you?'

Michael offered, 'Or Saturday, Sunday, Monday, Tuesday . . .'

'Full social calendar, huh?'

'I'm a hot date, but I can squeeze you in.' Michael felt sophisticated, all of 22. 'I'm generally pretty busy except for weekdays and weekends.'

'Aw,' she said and gave his hand a quick squeeze. 'And you're the nicest man in the year.'

At sixteen there is something irresistible about being called a man, especially by someone who has had some experience of them. And with whom, for some reason, you feel both safe and giddy at the same time.

So that Friday they went to the Club Louise in Soho.

Michael loved it. It was full of other daffy people, starting with Louise herself. She sat in a basement cubbyhole, greeting teenage visitors from Bromley as if they were French aristocrats. She took Bottle's coat (long with a collar of black feathers that smelled of burnt sesame oil), and kissed her on both cheeks, and called her '*ma chérie*' with a skeletal detachment.

Bottles looked a cool 25 let alone sixteen. She ordered champagne. A woman called Tami bubbled up to them, nipping someone else's glass off a table en route. She held it up, empty, with a hungry grin. Tami wore black gloves with rings on the outside, something so chic it made Michael speechless with admiration.

Tami talked about American black music, how only American black music was worth listening to. Did he see Bowie at Wembley? Amazing, all done with just those brilliant white lights, everything black and white, and he just strolled out of this haze of light. 'I got so excited, I nearly mussed my perm.'

Michael loved *Station to Station*. Drunk, emboldened by moral support, he went up to the DJ's hidden booth and asked for his favourite track, 'TVC15'. Instead of curling his lip in contempt as Michael expected, the DJ said, 'Too right, mate.'

So up came 'TVC15', and Michael, out of sheer love, began to dance. This should have been terribly uncool. No one else was dancing.

But Michael was grinning like a monkey, and he had decided at the last minute to rent a tuxedo, onto which Bottles had pinned her earrings. Somehow that was just right. Suddenly, with an ungainly whoop, Bottles and most especially Tami joined him. That probably did it. An awful lot of people looking tough at tables were suddenly left behind as people started to dance.

Michael had trouble with conversation. He was always scared of running out of things to say. But dancing was inexhaustible, and he used dancing to communicate. He even did the terribly hippyish thing of linking arms, and got away with it. *Station to Station* kept coming back; people groaned and shouted when it was turned off, and Michael found himself in the centre of a circle of people who knew where the good time was.

The good time was him. Tami put all her rings on his fingers. They did a whip-round and bought another bottle of champagne, and Bottles, giggling, poured it over his head, like a ship being launched, knowing somehow that he wanted to stain those hired dressy clothes. At just the right moment she nipped him back to the table and stopped him drinking. She sat looking at him affectionately, introducing him to people. It was like having a mother who was truly cool.

The next day his real mother, bitter with disappointment and suspicion, said, 'Did you take any drugs?'

'No, Mom.'

'Who were you with?'

'A girl from school, Mom.'

'You were drinking. You're underage.'

His mother had a long pale face that had lost its prettiness quickly, lining in her thirties. Her hair was an unattractive orange pudding basin with its roots showing. Michael's Mum looked worn, downtrodden, and utterly wrapped up in her own unhappiness. She looked like someone who had been deserted. She also looked like someone who was enduring it.

'It's not a good way to begin life, Michael, drinking in clubs.'

Reality was returning like a headache.

'No, Mum.'

Her narrow face didn't trust him, and didn't trust itself. She didn't know what to think. And gave her head a shake.

'Your clothes are ruined. How can we turn them back into Moss Bros like that?'

'They're used to it, Mom. That's why people hire gear.'

'And they pay to have it cleaned and all. Do you have the money to pay for that or do you expect me to pay for it, Michael?'

Bottles gave him a call. 'Hiya! How's tricks?'

He didn't know what tricks were. 'Oh OK, but Mom's on my case about the clothes.'

Bottles chuckled. 'Fun costs, Michael. That's how you know it's been real fun and not TV.'

Michael thought of sports teams in California, and the coaches who all talked like General Patton. 'No pain, no gain,' he mimicked, calling them up.

'No pain, no game,' she corrected him. 'So, are you man enough for another night out at Club Louise?'

Perhaps he wasn't and that was the trouble. At the very least, he was scared that the magic wouldn't work a second time. At the most, Michael was scared that she would make a pass at him. He was confused, confounded by sex. Her big breasts had allure, but Michael also knew already that his future did not lie with women. He just had a lot of trouble finally admitting that to himself.

It made him awkward. 'Hi!' he kept saying brightly, every time he saw her, and nothing else. He could think of nothing else to say. He sounded like a chipmunk and felt five years old.

Michael wanted his more normal friends to see how wise she was, so he trapped her into a lunch with them. The girls, particularly, were fashionable and elegant and calm and confident and virginal and enclosed within a social circle. One of them grew up to be a newsreader; another was now a big cheese at the British Museum. They eyed Bottles, who plainly had a rich future as a floozy. The future newsreader widened her eyes and stared fixedly at Michael and that meant: 'What on earth are you doing with her and why have you brought her to our table?'

Ostentatiously, Bottles began to smoke in public in the school cafeteria. This was likely to get the whole table into trouble. The girls started to leave.

Bottles had no social circle, but promiscuously joked with anyone who would have her. Michael sat with her at these scattered tables surrounded by surly underachievers. His mouth ran away with him. He bragged to them about Club Louise. He knew it was a mistake, he could feel coolness slipping away, but he wanted everyone to know that they had gone to a club. So he repeated every last incident of their evening out, like it was some big deal, and Bottles ground out her cigarette with impatience.

Eventually Michael stopped trying to spend lunchtime with her. It was too painful. He started to nod at her in corridors as they passed, feigning mild friendship.

He knew Bottles thought it was what always happened to her, that there was something about her that put people off. She was fed up being too old for her age. Gradually, they lost touch.

Michael saw Bottles a year later. He'd convinced a bunch of people in his biology class to go to Club Louise.

Louise still greeted visitors as if to a literary salon, but inside the atmosphere was different. Tami didn't remember him. She went hard-faced and silent when greeted by this pale, stolid-looking nerd. 'Hmm. Hmm,' she said several times and pointedly moved on.

The music was terrible, like something recorded by amateurs in a bathtub. Michael asked for *Station to Station* and the DJ curled his lip. People sat glumly and defensively at tables, greeting only a very few people with effusive kissing on the cheeks that made plain to everyone else that they were not being kissed. People rolled their eyes as you passed, or said, 'Get out of the bleeding way. Honestly, these stuck-up queens.'

Bottles came in and at first Michael didn't recognize her. She'd cut her hair and wore thick make-up that made her look Egyptian. She was kissed into a table with gladsome cries of feigned elegance, and then they all fell into the same chill silence. A ferret-faced young man with dyed blond hair was giving a very hard time to some overly pretty old hippie who had cut his hair. In something like despair and panic the old hippie was trying to convince him of something. It was Malcolm and Johnny, and if that was the birth of punk, as far as Michael was concerned, you could keep it.

'Everybody's so bitchy,' despaired a member of the biology class. She played cello in the school orchestra.

'It used to be so nice. Really,' said Michael.

Like a basilisk, Bottles looked stonily through him.

The next time Michael saw her was in the 1990s on TV. She looked like Mo Mowlam, and wore pantsuits and sensible middle-length hair and was a spokesperson for an Aids charity. She was on the breakfast show, convincing people to come forward to have an Aids test. 'The main thing to remember is there's now some point to having the test. If we catch it early enough, we know the drugs can work.'

Sensible, modulated, contact-lensed and TV-ready. This was not at all the Bottles he remembered. Old for her age back then, she had grown up even more.

Michael was aware that he had grown down. Overwork, tight scheduling, embittered sex: all of it had made him hurried and crabby.

And what would have happened to him if he had kept on dancing? The answer, watching Bottles, was suddenly clear. He would have become a vet. He would have been a vet because he would have been less ambitious, less self-denying. He would have been more himself. If he had kept on dancing, he and Bottles might have stayed friends and he would have gone on with the amateur acting and the animals.

I should have told my polished little social circle to get lost. They dropped me soon enough. When I needed help.

That had never bubbled to the surface of Michael's conscious thought before, but it was true. The future newsreaders avoided him when he came back from California – they were not up to tending the wounded. Bottles had gone on to tend his dying friends.

Gosh, he missed her, now in this future he made for himself without any friends.

Bottles, honey, he thought. I need you. I'm sorry.

The air swirled, and Bottles bounded back into his life

wearing a tank top and clunky shoes and long hair. 'Babe!' she cried, 'Howya doin'?'

'I'm OK, Bottles,' said Michael, his voice warm. He was surprised by the flood of affection he felt for her.

They hugged and she pressed herself against him, and kissed him on both cheeks. Bottles said, 'It's good to see you. You know, it wasn't such a rocking good time without you.'

He'd forgotten how everything she said was quotes, in someone else's voice. He was touched by that now. Now she looked young and small and scared, but above all else, sweet.

Michael kissed her forehead. It was too much like child abuse otherwise. 'God they were dumb not to make more of you in our school.'

'Like I said, you were the nicest man in the year.'

'There wasn't much competition.'

'No,' she agreed lightly, and gave him a gentle little bat. She slipped out of his hug. 'But you haven't aged well. Too much science, love. I bet you went to university.' There was scorn in her voice.

'I did.' He had to chuckle.

'Ruined you for life. The trouble with being a swot is that you think you're dedicated to something else, when really, you're only dedicated to yourself.'

She turned back to him, appraising. 'You're . . . how old?'

He had to think. 'I'm thirty-eight.'

Bottles did not say he didn't look 38. 'So . . . that makes it sometime in 1998. Gosh, did the world survive that long?'

'It did, and so did you.'

She paused for a moment, considering. 'Hmmm.'

Impulsively, she flung herself onto the sofa, but kept her shoes hanging over the edge of the sofa arm. She looked like something from a Roxy Music album cover.

'I grew up happy, baby,' she announced. 'I'm fat and happy, and I never give Romford Comprehensive a moment's thought. The secret was to leave London and go somewhere where they make their own fun. Two days after school finished I ran off to Scotland with a real creep. On the way back, the train stopped in Newcastle. I jumped off it at the last minute, just grabbed my bags, said "Sod off" and stayed in Newcastle. I waited in bars, stuff like that.' Her voice went very small and quiet. 'I was on the game for a while.'

Suddenly, there was a spliff in her hand. She looked around the living room, the wall-to-wall carpet, Phil's paintings, his family's furniture, and the bay window. 'Posh,' she said, with little interest. 'Nothing much happens here, does it?' And then she said, 'I'm sorry, I didn't mean that. You've done well, Michael. You look so adult, like a kind of teddy bear.'

'That doesn't make sense.'

'You look like an adult teddy bear, a Papa Bear.'

'How did we screw up?' he asked.

'We didn't.'

'I mean, why didn't we stay friends?'

'Um. We were young and frightened and we fell in love in a kind of way and you weren't ready for it.'

'You know why we never did it?'

'Because I moved like a bison on a trampoline?' She had the habit of taking the piss out of herself. Her smile was crooked.

'It's true, you did, but I thought that was sexy. But I'm queer, and I wanted to tell you first, and I was . . . more scared than most of saying so.'

'I knew that!' she exclaimed.

'You did?' He smiled, embarrassed.

'Of course I knew that, Babe. That's why . . .' It was just the teeniest bit difficult to say. 'That's why I felt safe around you. Both of us ran away from people because we thought we were ugly.' Maybe Angels find it easier to say things than real people.

'You ignored me in Club Louise.'

She sighed and shook her head. 'You looked so naff. I mean you looked like one of nature's born Radio Three listeners. And punk was all style, and you can only keep up a style by being mean. So I was mean. Forgive me?'

He nodded. 'Yeah.'

'Can we have sex just once?'

He settled in next to her, and sucked the dope in, and waited

100

for it to buzz his brain. It never did, with him. Michael had marijuana impotency, too. But it produced a pleasant lazy atmosphere. She gave him a long lazy tobacco-and-peppermint kiss, and began to give his dick a rub.

'There's something else I have to tell you. I . . . I . . .' Michael sagged with disappointment at himself. 'Why can't I say it? I hardly ever get it up.'

'Hmm,' she said, cosily in his arms. 'That's OK. I never have orgasms.'

'What? You?'

She cradled him. 'Mmm hmm.'

'But you had all those men at school.'

'Maybe that's why, or maybe I was trying to prove to myself that there was nothing wrong. If there is anything wrong with not having orgasms.'

A pause. A beat. They both burst out laughing. 'It's fucking awful not having orgasms!' Michael yelped.

She nodded. 'I keep thinking I'm going to get there, I'm going to get there . . . and nothing fucking happens.'

'At least you can fake it. I just sit there dangling.'

'Hey, we're famous. The Dysfunction Twins.' She took another drag and said, 'We could have lived together and had the same boyfriends.'

'That sounds really good. We could have both disappointed them.'

'We could have cried on each other's shoulders and told the lot of them to go get screwed.' Bottles and Michael casually held each other like lovers, old lovers who are eighty.

'Men,' said Michael. 'They're no good to live with.'

Bottles adopted the tone of a school-ma'am. 'Never. Never live with a man.'

'They belch,' offered Michael.

'They fart on the tube.'

'They don't wash up.'

'Or they start to, make a big deal about how much they're helping, and then bugger off before it's finished.'

'They get mad if you don't call them, but they don't even notice when they haven't called you.'

'They want you to take care of them and then they go and fuck some other cunt.'

'Or arse.'

'Give me another kiss.'

They smooched. It was a theatrical kiss, a kiss in quotes, a spotlit kiss. It made her giggle.

'You've gone all butch,' she said.

'Me?' That was a new one.

'Yup. You used to be a little squit of a thing. Oh, very, very pretty, but I'd have been frightened of snapping you in two.'

So they smooched again. Her lips were fat, her breasts were fat, and Michael yearned to see her squirm out of her 1976 skin-tight jeans.

She peeled like an orange, and her body was in sections, restrained by straps. He sucked her shoulder. He tried to flip her breasts out of the bra, and then tried to undo it, and he got her tangled up, like a horse caught in reins. She started to giggle.

'You've never done this before. You have never got a woman out of her bra before!' she shouted and laughed.

He remembered how badly his copy made love. He tried to be better at it. He tried to delicately twitch her nipples. She giggled and kissed the top of his head. 'You're twiddling them like they're knobs on a stereo.'

So they just cuddled naked, deliberately kissing the neglected parts: elbows, ears, eyebrows.

He said, 'This is more fun than sleeping with a man.'

Bottles couldn't resist. 'I was about to say the same thing.'

'Oh cheers.'

'Men are always trying to fuck me without a condom.'

'Oh no no, it's just the opposite with me. They always have a condom because sleeping with me puts them at terrible risk. They couldn't sleep with me without a condom, they don't know where I've been. It's a good thing I liked being fucked, or they'd get nowhere.'

'I can't help you there,' said Bottles, sucking on a roach that would have required a microscope to see, let alone smoke. 'It seems to me that you urgently need to meet some nice men.' She offered him the roach, and after breathing out said, 'If you find one, let me know.'

This seemed to have introduced the topic of the episodes.

Michael began. 'Does . . . does it seem kind of strange to you that you're sixteen and I'm thirty-eight?'

She paused. 'Not really. But then the world doesn't really add up for me.'

'What do you know about yourself?'

She seemed to darken and go dull. 'That I'm . . .' She sucked on her teeth. 'That I'm some kind of construct. The real Maggie is thirty-eight, a single mum and lives in Islington. She's real and I'm not, but then I never really felt real.'

Michael explained the miracle to her. He explained why he needed her help.

She took it on the chin. She sat up and went business-like. 'I'm not the Aids expert. She is. I guess she'll help you. But. Don't call her Bottles. She hates the name. She's Margaret to strangers, Maggie to friends. She'll know something, dimly, about this. Like she's dreamed it, so she won't be entirely surprised to see you. She believes, a little bit, that women sometimes see things.'

Bottles leaned back, and looked up into his face, and it was firm. 'I meant what I said about swots.'

Why did everybody always have something perfectly justified to say about him?

'Go ahead,' he said, 'let me have it.' He wished he were dressed. His stomach was hairy and his dick shrivelled.

'You're so concerned about yourself that you're asking the wrong question.'

'So what question should I be asking?'

She told him.

'Oh God,' he said, and covered his eyes with shame. She was right and all. Right on methodological grounds. Right about the self-concern. He chuckled at himself.

'Can I go now?' she asked. 'The more I know about this, the weirder it gets and the sadder.'

'How come?'

103

'Because I'm dead. There hasn't been anyone called Bottles in years.'

'Can I see you again?' he asked.

'Yeah sure,' she said, in voice that meant no. 'Is it up to me?' There was no point pretending that it was.

'See you around,' said Michael, and she was gone.

Can I cure Angels who are sick?

That was the question to ask. If Michael could call up Angels and cure them, then he could make love to them after they were rid of the virus.

So, after making certain arrangements, Michael ended up in a clinic after hours. Margaret or Maggie was doing him a favour.

'It's not for me,' he had told her on the phone. 'It's a friend of mine. He won't come in for a test if I don't come with him and he doesn't get the answer right away. And . . . he's also paranoid about false results, so he wants to take the test two times in a row. Yes, I know, it's weird, but I'm really concerned.'

Margaret's voice sounded just the same as Bottles, as if it were the sixteen-year-old on the phone. Except that she didn't call him Babe and was content to stay with her all-purpose native London accent. Her voice was calm, and soft and business-like all at the same time.

'A lot of people are very frightened by the test, so it's good that you want to come in with him. Does he have any problems with confidentiality?'

'Um, in what way?'

'If he's paranoid about one thing he may be paranoid about other things. Like being seen by anyone.'

'Could we come in after hours?'

'It's an imposition,' she told him directly. 'But if it will make the difference between him coming in or not, then I'll do it. But it can only be this Wednesday night.'

Her clinic turned out to be attached to a hospital in the East End. The door was locked, but he rang and she herself opened it.

Margaret's hair was the colour of carrots, like his mother's used to be. Michael had the feeling that the hair and her long loose Chinese jacket were all carefully calculated to strike the right balance of flamboyance and reliability. She was like a civil servant with a past. I used to be quite interesting, but now I'm reliable. It was a balance inclined to create trust on both sides: the ill and the official health establishment. Her voice was motherly, concerned, and extremely cautious. Every word was carefully rehearsed; not so much chosen as identified over thousands of ticklish interviews as being the most appropriate thing to say.

Yup. Bottles was dead.

'Hello,' she said to Michael's companion, and held out her hand. 'My name's Margaret, I'm an old friend of Michael's.' She was searching his face with concern.

'So am I. My name's Mark.'

Mark was tall, broad-shouldered with wavy red hair streaked with grey. He had died five years before from Aids.

Michael had met Mark at Sussex University. Mark was in the Army, studying under some kind of Army grant, and he was big and muscular and freckled and slightly overripe. He wore cravats and played polo, and wore a green carnation in honour of Oscar Wilde.

Mark was one of Michael's more spectacular missed opportunities. They met in drama club and were doing an experimental piece that involved a lot of stretching, yoga and jumping about. It was easier than being talented. At one point they all had to lie on the floor on their tummies and put their heads on someone else's bum.

The entire time Michael's heavy head rested on Mark's bottom, he flexed his cheek muscles, up and down. Michael's head wiggled. Mark turned back and grinned naughtily. He had a general's face, lumpy and attractive rather than pretty, and he had a soldier's lumpy body. *Jolie-laide*, they might call it in France. Butch, Michael called it. He was unable to believe that someone so masculine and so military whom he fancied so very much could actually be gay. Instead, just to stop Mark's flexing, he bit the bum very hard.

'You must be hungry,' said Mark. He spoke rather like Noel Coward. 'Why don't you come back to my flat and have another bite to eat.'

Michael managed to pretend to himself that this was an invitation to supper.

So he showed up with a bottle of wine, and talked in a prolonged way about the director, a woman called Rosie. Mark began to look wistful. Rosie fancied Mark, and had asked Michael to find out if he was gay. Even this was not enough to trigger the conscious thought in Michael that the man he fancied might fancy him.

So Michael pumped Mark for information about his reaction to Rosie, which confused the issue more.

'I'm afraid I'm a bit inexperienced with women. I imagine you're not,' said Mark.

'Tuh. Not that much experienced. But I get along with them.'

'Well, perhaps you can show me how to as well.'

'I'd be really surprised if I had anything to teach you about women.'

When someone wants you, they admire you. You seem larger to them than you actually are, which is why it's difficult to believe they can or do love you, and not some image they've made up. It was hard for Michael to imagine that this strapping, athletic, outgoing, happy man admired him, respected him. It was simply unthinkable that he actually desired him.

So. Nothing happened.

There was a florid would-be Englishman at Sussex. He was in fact South African, and tried to live up to an image of England that had more to do with Bloomsbury than the new era of Margaret Thatcher. He kept talking about Virginia Woolf and Quentin Bell, and 'real universities' like Oxford. He ran the literary society and wore white suits and once, even a straw boater. Michael detested him.

About six months after his dinner, Michael saw Mark with this man together in Sainsbury's, plainly doing domestic shopping together, having a slightly acid conversation over the right choice of coffee.

Michael said hello, and Mark's chest swelled with pride as he introduced John, who said coolly, 'We know each other. Michael acts, doesn't he?' Mark seemed to display their married condition like another green carnation, and Michael ended the conversation, blinded by an inexplicable headache.

Mark and he stayed friends. The straw boater had married Mark in an attempt to marry old England. Mark realized this, as the bickering got worse. 'He's a bit of a fraud, actually,' Mark said lightly to Michael in the student bar. 'He's moved out. I'm doing some reassessing. I'm beginning to understand that, as much as I love it, the Army and I aren't meant for each other either.'

It would be illegal, in fact.

Mark became someone who added up. This made him less surprising. He dropped his science course, and took art history. He saved money to pay back the Army for their grants. He went on to run an art gallery. Somewhere in all those changes, he and Michael managed to become best friends, especially after Michael had met Philip.

Philip worshipped Mark. My ex-Army gallery owner who also plays rugby, Philip enthused, and took him to parties without Michael. Mark could more than hold his own at arty gatherings at which he doggedly wore blazers and cravats.

Mark never introduced his boyfriends. Mark's boyfriends evidently were not quite fit to be introduced. It was the first time that Michael noted a tendency in Mark towards secrecy. He kept aspects of his life in separate compartments.

Mark had developed a taste for leather and rough trade. He moved in with a rich banker, but they weren't lovers. They shared servants, and a games room, and gave parties in which people wore leather crotchless knickers. They called their joint townhouse the Cock Exchange. Michael never really felt comfortable with the grandees he met there, or the way in which the banker, especially, treated the people who worked for him.

Mark's face and manner remained disconcertingly fresh-faced. His eyebrows went prematurely shaggy, like an old general's, but there was something in his expression that reminded Michael of a child. He looked like a little boy who could play innocent.

Mark began to be away a lot on business or make excuses when invited to dinner, and to drive an old banger which he saw no point in replacing. He was ill and didn't want Michael to worry.

What do you say to someone who has died and who was one of the few people you could really talk to?

Perhaps you look at his face, suddenly returned to you, and consider saying all the things you never had a chance to say. You consider saying: you were a hero to me. You were so many things; it wasn't just the Army or the sport. There was your political work for the Labour Party, though everything about you signalled Tory. There was the way you knew the market value of every piece that came your way, including things you hated like the Pre-Raphaelites. There was the way you could explain to me how Picasso was a genius, so that I've seen Picasso differently ever since. There was the way you fixed your car, and the way you spent all Saturday afternoon playing rugby and two hours every Sunday morning tending your stocks and shares. There was the way you could give me advice on how to apply for research grants, advice that worked, or who at the Poly knew they had support in high places. You were astute and kind and sensible and strong.

All Michael said was, 'Hello old thing. Good to see you.'

They were in the car on the way to the clinic. Mark replied, cool and distant, 'Thank you.' Then he asked, askance, 'Why have you done this?'

Michael explained it to him, the miracle and what he thought it was for and why he needed Mark. It sounded so stark and self-interested that Michael apologized.

'Quite all right. I'm glad to be of use,' Mark replied. His

attention seemed be distracted. His eye kept catching on shop signs or *Evening Standard* headlines talking about the Labour government.

'Can we stop?' he asked. 'There's just a few things I'd like.'

Of course, of course, Michael said, and pulled over. Mark bought an orange and a newspaper. He left both in the white paper bag.

Introductions over with.

Once inside the clinic and sitting down, Margaret explained to Mark what the test was for and how it worked. 'We're going to take some blood and analyse it here. I'll be back in about forty-five minutes with the result. I understand you want two tests?'

'Ask Michael,' said Mark, detached.

Margaret's head jerked a bit too quickly towards Michael. There was something fathomless in Mark's response that she couldn't read.

'Two tests. Yes, please,' said Michael.

Sometimes shy or worried people rely on others to speak for them. Was this such a case? Margaret gave them the benefit of any doubt. 'No trouble. It will be a bit of a wait for you though. There's television and coffee. You could come back tomorrow . . .'

Mark cut her off. 'No,' he said. 'Thank you. I only have this evening.'

So he and Michael sat in the waiting area, a circle of comfortable chairs, and watched the seven o'clock news on Channel Four. On the clinic walls were A4, hand-lettered notices for social groups, aromatherapy, or stress management. Mark sat absolutely still, hypnotized by the telly. Sports results. Michael realized: he wants to find out how rugby union is going.

'Is this hard for you?' Michael asked.

'Up to a point,' Mark replied and fell silent. The silence persisted all through the sports news.

'We all miss you. Terribly. Liz, Tom, Martin, we still get together and have pub crawls along the river. The Mark Memorial Pub Crawl. We have one in summer, one in winter.'

'That's comforting.'

'Liz can't stop talking about you whenever we have one. I think she was a bit in love with you.'

'I proposed marriage.'

'Oh.'

'I thought she needed to be able to stay in the country.' Mark's smile was knife-thin and hard to read.

There had been other news since Mark's departure. 'Do you know about Rodger?' Rodger was the banker.

Mark's eyes were still fixed on football. 'No, but I imagine he died too. I imagine there's not much left of the old Exchange.'

The Angel of Death had passed over some doors as if lintels were marked. 'Harry's still with us, though.' Harry was Rodger's boyfriend who used to be tied up and left to the mercies of men who had since died. Harry was negative.

Laugh? Mark almost smiled.

The conversation was a knot. Michael suddenly thought honesty might cut it. 'Is dying very hard?' he asked.

'It's tough,' Mark said in an even voice. 'Unbearable, in fact. It's the worst thing you can know. So you seem to view it from far away. And then you don't know anything at all.'

'Is it true what everyone tells you? You float outside your body, and there's a tunnel of light?'

Mark seemed to chew over his response as if it were a plug of tobacco. On television, the news had moved on to Camilla Parker Bowles showing up in public with Charles. Mark turned to look at Michael, and there was something broken and rugged about his face, like one of those cliff faces that look human in profile. The face like a tumble of rocks seemed to ask: You really want to know?

'That happens, yes. But it's just an illusion. You are psychologically distancing yourself from what is happening. The tunnel of light is just the optic nerve closing down.'

Mark had looked healthy up until the very end. A few days before he died, his hair went snowy white, and he finally told friends the truth. This was his second bout of pneumonia, and it was by now what they had all suspected.

Michael had to go away to a conference in America. All he

could do was phone. 'I want you to know how much I've always respected you,' he said.

He didn't say: I loved you, once.

He didn't say: You see, Mark, I don't ask for things. I drift into things and let them hold me, instead of me taking a grip of them. Mark, something terrible happened to me that left me completely screwed up, which is why we were never lovers. And it makes me so angry that we never were, and now never will be. Would you have lived, if we had been lovers, Mark?

It was Phil not Michael who was with Mark when he died.

Now, in the waiting room, booming music announced the end of the news.

Mark said simply: 'The world moves on.'

He reached into his bag and pulled out the newspaper, and read it carefully, the paper crinkling like tin foil when he turned the pages.

Then he said, 'You miss everything.' Something terrible happened to his voice. It sounded like tape gone slurry from dirty tapeheads. 'You miss voices. You miss air. You try to breathe and there's no air. There's no taste, you're not hungry, you don't want to eat. You miss food. And colour. There's no colour. You miss having a life. You get so bored being yourself. A self just keeps asking: What do I think about next? What do I do next? And the answer always comes back: Nothing.'

They heard a door open. Margaret, Maggie came back. Michael could tell from her face: it was kept smooth and bland, but the smile was just a little fixed, and the eyes seemed to be saying no, not again, no not again, and they looked at Mark with sadness. Mark had tested positive. She would have done a T-cell count as well and would know: this is a dying man.

All she said was: 'All right, Mark, we're going to take the second sample now. Are you sure you want to go ahead?'

'I believe that is what Michael asked.'

Margaret glanced at Michael. 'Michael only wants to help you. Do you still want a second sample?'

'It's why I'm here,' replied Mark, detached.

You, commanded Michael to the Angel. You Mark are free from disease. You virus, commanded Michael, you the virus just seethe out of his blood.

I cast you out.

Maggie took Mark's arm as she led him to the cubicle, and her face was silently looking into his. Still everyone's mother, eh Bottles?

The telly battered on, booming about oven-ready chips. Jeez, thought Michael, all I want to do is sleep. What a leaden stupid unhelpful thought: life is strange.

Mark came back, and moved his chair away from Michael and the cushions made a squishy sound like a sigh. Mark reached into the plastic bag and pulled out an orange.

Mark's mouth lunged forward as he bit into the orange. Almost clear juice, with a bit of pulp, poured down his chin. Mark's eyes closed with pleasure.

Then he reached into a bag and pulled out a photograph. There hadn't been a photograph in the bag before.

It was an ordinary snap of a solid-looking middle-aged man with white hair.

'This is Robert,' Mark said. 'I never told you about him.' His thumb moved over the face. 'He was rather discreet. He was married, and a bit old-fashioned. RAF. When I got too ill, I told him I was fed up being his mistress.'

'Did he know you were HIV?'

There was a long pause. 'Yes.'

Michael looked at the face in the photo more closely. It was kindly, dignified, direct. That added up too.

Mark reached into the plastic bag and pulled out one of the very first Sony Walkmans, clunky and black, with the usual tangle of wires and earphones. Mark said nothing, but punched buttons.

From the distanced high singing, Michael knew. Mark's favourite opera: *Der Rosenkavalier*. Mark closed his eyes and ruminated on another section of orange.

Time passed. The cassette finished with a click.

Mark asked, 'Do I have to stay for the second result?'

Michael was surprised and slightly hurt that Mark didn't want to know. 'I'm afraid so. If you go, the samples will disappear.'

Mark rolled his eyes. 'Oh, God! That means she'll come out all worried and want to counsel me. And if the result is different then she'll want to take a third sample.' He put his head in his hands. 'I don't suppose it occurred to you that I've been through all this once before and that I never, ever wanted to go through it again?'

Mark's eyes glared up at him from under the bushy eyebrows. In life, Mark had never been this angry with Michael.

'It didn't really, no, I'm sorry.'

'If you want to have a fuckfest, you'll just have to take a few risks like everyone else, except that you never had the stomach for risk.'

Michael didn't know what to say. Mark turned the cassette over and went on listening to opera.

Finally, Margaret came back. Michael noticed that she had tiny feet. They gave her a delicate, slightly Chinese walk. Her face had gone splotchy. As she approached, she placed her hands either side of her mouth, as if to hold her face in place. 'Mark. I hardly know what to say.'

Mark stood up and began to wind the earphones around the Walkman. The opera kept playing.

Margaret reached out towards him and gripped his arm. 'Michael told me you are worried about inconsistent results. I'm afraid that the first test was positive and the second is negative. It's not usual, but it does happen. I'm so sorry. I'm afraid we'll need to take the test again.'

'That won't be necessary. That is all the result we need, thank you very much.' He jammed the singing Walkman into the bag.

'Mark, you can come in tomorrow, if you like.'

The tumble of rocks looked back at her. 'That won't happen. I am very, very sorry that Michael put you to all this trouble. I'm going to ask you not to worry me, or to try to rectify the situation. Thank you for your concern.' He turned and strode away on long legs.

114

Margaret followed. 'We might prove there is nothing wrong! There are treatments now, treatments that work!'

'Thank you!' bellowed Mark and let the door fall shut after him.

Michael stood up to go, sick at heart.

Maggie intercepted him. 'Michael, the first test showed almost no T-cells at all. He is already very sick. Michael, I don't know what your relationship is, excuse me, but should you have the test too?'

'No,' said Michael, suddenly bitter. 'I never slept with him.'

He died and I was in America. Michael's face crumpled and his eyes went bleary, and to escape he pushed the door open with his bum.

'Oh love,' said Margaret.

You think I'm a good person. You think I'm someone who's done all he can to help someone else.

'Give me a call! Tell him we can help him!'

That's the last Michael saw of her, in her Chinese shirt, reflecting in several directions as the door of her clinic swung shut. How is it that you care, Maggie? How is it than anyone cares?

Mark was two streets away, waiting by the car. He was staring up at the sky and listening to his Walkman. It still wheedled out *Rosenkavalier*. Shrill distant women's voices sang their farewells. Just for once, in London, there were stars.

'Can you send me back now?' Mark asked, without looking at Michael. He was quite calm, angry no longer, but his cheeks and mouth were covered with an even, glossy coating of tears.

'You could stay,' offered Michael.

Mark turned and looked at him with determined eyes. 'This is unbearable,' he said.

'Look Mark, I'm sorry for all of this; I shouldn't have done it this way. But if you stay, you could listen to music, you could go back to Robert, you could live.'

'It's unbearable, because once you're there,' Mark flung a hand up towards the sky, 'you don't really want to come back. You had no business bringing me back.'

'Just try, for a day or two?'

'I died Michael. I made them withhold treatment. Dying took hours, and I couldn't move or even see, but I could still think, and I had to think my way through dying. I had to work at it, it was an achievement. Can you please send me back now?'

'All right,' sighed Michael.

Mark made to put Robert's photograph into his pocket and then seemed to remember he could not take it with him. He put it back into the plastic Sainsbury's bag.

The great stone face turned once more to Michael. 'Don't do this to anyone else,' Mark said.

'Get ready then.'

'I am ready.'

'Goodbye, then.'

God, this was awful, it was like killing someone.

'Goodbye,' whispered Mark, his expression softening. His cheeks were pink and freckled and he reminded Michael of how he had looked at Sussex.

The singing of the Walkman stopped. Air closed over Mark like a lake and he was gone.

Michael was alone. Inside the bag, there was only the newspaper, and the orange, whole and uneaten.

The next day, Michael telephoned Margaret.

'Hello Margaret,' he began. 'This is Michael. I just wanted to say thanks for last night. Are you OK?'

'I'm sorry?' Margaret laughed indulgently, as if she were still Bottles. 'I'm a bit slow this morning. Michael who?'

'Michael Blasco, from school, I came round to the clinic.'

'Michael? Michael, hello!' Margaret was surprised and delighted. 'It's funny, I was thinking about you just the other day. How are you, long time no see!'

The backs of Michael's arms pricked up as if there were a cold wind. 'I'm fine. I, uh, I came round to the clinic Wednesday night.'

'Oh, dear.' Margaret laughed at herself. 'Did you? I've got a head like a sieve. I'm so sorry, I guess I just didn't recognize you. I mean, did you say "Hi, I'm Michael from school?"'

116

Michael considered. 'No. Not really. I popped in to get some information for a friend.'

Her voice modulated carefully downwards. 'Was it all right?'

'Yeah, yeah, he came in to the clinic and had the test. And it was negative. He's OK. I just wanted to say thank you for the work you do. It's good work.'

Michael ended the conversation quickly. He had learned one last thing.

If you were part of their story, you could be forgotten too. Oh, people could meet you both, shake your hands, they could tell you your friend was handsome and that they wanted to meet up again. And then they would forget. Not right away, but gently so everything healed shut. They'd forget everything, and if you were part of everything, then they'd forget you too.

Angels came, Angels were here, they could talk, and when they went, they were forgotten as quickly as dreams. And the stories they made were forgotten too.

Michael would be forever alone with his memories. Maybe we're surrounded by miracles, he thought. Maybe there're miracles every day, only we're programmed not to remember them. He opened up his notebook and read.

A physical copy
someone I know (later: also someone I don't know!)
in train, tube and 2 x in my flat, 1 x in office (location has no effect)
Can call up at will and banish (I may not know I've done it!)
other people appear to interact
His behaviour, my behaviour both sexual
the real person is straight (can be!)
copy says real person dreams what happens
Can't call up people without sexual element (sexual element can be love)
Can call up dead
Can control behaviour
They have free will until I override it
they can be male or female
they think they go somewhere (fiction continues elsewhere?)
they are a kind of fiction in flesh

they can change nothing
they are never really here
Then Michael wrote in the notebook, *Knowing does no good.*
And then he closed it.

Part II

What's so painful about love?

Henry came to stay with them. He had nowhere else to go, unless it was a burrow under the route of a planned bypass. He slept in the sitting room, on the sofa bed, and kept all his clothes rolled up in a backpack in the corner. The clothes were always neat and uncreased; Henry had a knack of packing clothes so tightly that they stayed pressed. The whole room smelled of him, a pleasant slightly earthy odour, like field mushrooms.

Michael assumed that Philip and Henry had sex by day on that sofa bed while he was at the lab. Throughout the night, Philip still cradled Michael in their big double bed, out of affection and habit. Michael was grateful to be held. He found he was scared.

So he made both of them breakfast and brought it out on a tray, and laid it out on the table in the bay window of the sitting room. Henry's arms were lean and pale and smooth as he pulled on his socks. His skin had a kind of silver sheen in the morning sun. He gave Michael a dozy morning grin under the thicket of his hair.

It was summer now, and dust danced in warm sunlight. Mild air drifted in through the open window; blackbirds made surprisingly beautiful sounds: Michael always expected them to caw like crows. He was lulled.

Michael needed wisdom; he needed advice and reassurance. He needed to talk. The song of birds, the clatter of cups and plates, Henry's smile all gave him courage. Phil came in, looking like someone who was late for work, and even that somehow reassured Michael.

'Something very strange has happened,' he announced, his hands occupied with cutlery. 'I suddenly find that I can make copies of people, people I want to have sex with. I just ask for them, and there they are. They can be male, female, alive or dead, but they can't be photographed and they can change nothing in the real world.'

Michael picked up the coffee-pot and it began to chatter as if it were cold and its teeth were clicking. He couldn't quite hold it or think what to do with it. 'I find the whole thing disturbing, to tell you the truth.'

Phil kept his head down. 'They do say it runs in families,' he murmured and spooned jam on his toast.

Henry very gently took the coffee-pot out of Michael's grasp. 'Some people might find that hard to believe. They would probably say you were making it up.'

'Oh, oh there is definitely something physically here. I can touch them. It's just after they've gone nothing they've done gets left behind.'

'That's why people might not believe you.' Henry had soft, brown, trusting eyes. But they could be firm and trusting at the same time.

'Well, I can fix that! I can show them to you. Who do you fancy?' Michael was feeling boisterous. He could feel his curly hair bounce and his voice boom. He tried to think of musicians who might be trendy among 26-year-olds and could only come up with the Labour Party theme 'D. Ream?' Michael suggested, surprised he remembered the singer's name. Henry appeared unmoved. 'Liam Gallagher? How about the Castro brothers from *Out Our Way*? Here, look.'

The air wavered and parted like curtains.

Out Our Way was an established soap opera about the East End. It had turned two bald, burly actors into unlikely sex symbols.

Suddenly two bald and burly actors stood looking dazed by sunlight in a hundred-year-old sitting room in WC1.

'Holy Jesus!' cried Phil, and pushed back his chair, which dragged on the carpet then gave a low crack and nearly pitched him backwards out of the window.

'Wha'?' said one of the actors, his brow knitting together.

Michael explained like a tour guide. 'The trouble with actors is that they usually show up in character. You get Valentino as the Sheikh, not Valentino.'

'What are these posh geezers doin' 'ere then?'

'The dialogue is always terrible,' said Michael, his face giving a series of nervous sideways jerks that were meant to convey that the whole thing was mischievous fun.

Henry had gone very still and watchful, like a cat crowded into a corner. He fixed the brothers with an adult eye and asked them, 'What do you know?'

'About what?'

'Why you are here.'

Michael, ebullient, intervened. 'It's for sex. Drop 'em, lads.'

The Castro brothers looked dazed and obedient, and they lowered their trousers. One of them was wearing no underwear under his jeans. Two perfectly average, plump sets of genitalia soaked up the sun.

Michael felt merry. He felt as if he were no longer alone. He reached across the table and pushed the tip of Phil's nose. 'You wanted to do a show called *Lust*. Now you really can.' Philip tossed his head as if an insect annoyed him. 'You want to have sex with someone, you can. We all can, all of us.' Michael suddenly felt familial; the gesture included Henry.

Henry blinked, hair in his eyes. 'We don't fancy them, Michael. You do. It's OK. We believe you.'

'You won't as soon as they go. You'll forget.' Michael began to feel afraid again, afraid to be alone. To encourage them to stay, he passed one of the Castros a cup of coffee.

'That's how it works. They're forgotten hours after they go.'

Henry said calmly, 'Everybody gets forgotten, Michael. It just happens faster to some of us.'

'Listen,' said one of the Castros, with studied politeness. 'We don't want to intrude or anything, you know?'

Michael protested. 'No, no, stay. They'll believe as long as you stay.'

Henry stood up and took the cup of coffee back from one of the Castros. He spoke to them as an equal. 'It's tough being temporary. Nothing you do matters.'

Philip looked up again in anguish at Henry. 'I can't deal with this,' Philip said. 'I . . . just . . . can't . . . deal with this too.' Henry put the coffee cup down on the table and took Philip's hand.

Shame-faced, the Castro brothers pulled up their trousers. Henry turned and looked at Michael with his round puppy-dog eyes and said, irresistibly, 'Michael, you've made your point.'

Michael closed his eyes and nodded. The Castro brothers faded like an afterthought.

Phil placed both his hands flat on the table as if to steady it and said, 'I don't know what it is we just saw.' His face was prim, closed, determined. 'I don't want to know. Henry and I have been hanging on because we could see you were in some kind of trouble, and I don't want to kick you while you're down, but honestly . . .'

Phil turned back to Henry, and he was pleading now. 'I just can't keep this up any longer.'

Henry lowered his eyes and said, 'OK.'

'We can stay at the Club,' Phil said, again to Henry. He turned to Michael. 'I'll do the washing-up.'

'No, that's OK,' said Michael. The person who made the meal always did the washing-up. It was the family rule.

Phil got insistent, a bit panicky. 'Have you heard me, Michael?'

Michael blinked. There was something he did not understand. 'I just said I'd do the washing-up.' He held out his hands to say: that's all I said, is there anything wrong?

Phil swayed as if under a burden, and he said to Henry, 'I'm sorry. You cope with this.' His hands rattling like the china, Phil began to clear the plates. The eggcups were his family silver, spindly on a single slender leg, and one of them toppled. Henry stood up and with Zen-like calm began to pack his shoulder bag. Philip gave up trying to get everything on the tray at once, and bustled away.

'We're going,' Henry said to Michael, his eyes sad.

Michael wasn't sure he'd heard correctly. Everything started to shake. 'Philip's left the cups,' he said. He took them into the kitchen; he needed to be in the kitchen with Philip.

Philip was sloshing water on plates, keeping his back towards him. Michael had to stretch round him to put the cups on the draining board.

'Phil? Listen, Phil, I need to talk to someone. I-I-I need just to talk.' Michael needed to have Phil around, even if it was mostly in principle, even if he mostly saw Phil when he came in late and surly.

Distracted, Phil fired a jet of water into a cup that shot back out, over his shirt.

'So. So. When will you be back?'

Very abruptly, Philip stopped. He put the cup down on the kitchen counter and pushed past Michael back into the sitting room.

'Will you talk to me?' Michael demanded.

Phil stopped, sagged, and turned back. He pinched his nose and closed his eyes. 'I won't be back, Michael. It hasn't worked, it isn't working, it won't work in the future.' Miserable, he began to weep. 'So I'm going. I mean, I'm leaving you.'

Michael started to babble.

'Buh buh buh buh, but doesn't the whole idea of it hit you? I mean you could use it in your work. I know you couldn't photograph them, but you could talk to them, fascinating people, old movie stars, whatever, and you could paint them, you could do new portraits of them.'

'What are you talking about?' Phil was gazing at Michael in something approaching horror.

'It could be a real opportunity for you, you know, the paintings will stay, at least we could try, right?' Michael stood, as if naked, looking hopeful. He saw it now. He needed to be more involved with Philip's work.

Phil's head was shaking as if in disbelief. 'You're crazy,' he said, and swung away. He went into the bedroom and pulled a suitcase out from under the bed.

'Phil? You can talk to them Phil. Philip, Philip, please Philip, don't go.'

Philip paused and left the suitcase open on the floor. He fled to the cupboard and, quivering, pulled on a jacket. 'I'll come back for my things when you're at work,' he said, moving back out into the corridor.

Michael pursued him. 'Philip, please listen. I told you because I can't believe it myself and I need someone to talk to about it. Philip, it's real, OK? It's real, it's weird and can be quite strange and that's why I need someone.'

Philip was at the door. His hand was on the doorknob and he looked directly at Michael. 'Sorry,' he said. 'Sorry, but I really can't help this.' His eyes had the utter ruthlessness of someone no longer in love.

'Philip, please don't go!'

Pity and disgust mingled in Phil's eyes and all he could do was shake his head goodbye. Henry joined him, slipping around Michael. They went into the echoing corridor beyond and Michael wailed after them.

'Philip! Phil-lip! Please! Come back!'

He heard the footsteps spiral down the staircase and the thump of the front door as it closed itself.

Michael kept talking to himself, quietly, under his breath. 'Phil. Please. Don't leave me alone. Phil-hil-lip. Pleeeeeeeeese.' His voice, constrained, wheedled like a rusty hinge. His legs folded under him and he dropped onto the floor of the hallway.

It was silent. The silence grew. The silence would continue. It was the silence of an apartment with only one person in it.

Maybe he'll come back. Maybe he'll get bored and come back.

Maybe he won't.

What do you want him for anyway? He was a pain in the ass.

I love him; I'll miss him.

You should have taken better care of him, then.

He should have taken better care of me.

Why did I tell him? Stupid, stupid, stupid, stupid. Who wants a miracle for a boyfriend? Things could have kept on just as they were; he was happy enough to have Henry on the side. Why did you do it? You only scared him off.

Who does he fancy? Ben Affleck, that's right, you should have shown him Ben Affleck, not those naff Castros from that naff soap, you should have said see, isn't this wild, fun, stylish, invite your gallery friends, you little social-climbing shit, you little Mr Trendy, you stupid untalented little fraud.

Don't blame him.

What do I blame, then?

Michael's knees hurt. He propped himself against the hall table and stood up. He walked back into the sitting room, still full of sunlight.

He looked at the carpet; it was the colour of sand, like a desert. The room would now have two phases: with Philip and after Philip. What was left? A few stains on the carpet from the early days when they still had parties here and wine was sloshed. There was the painting Philip did of Michael, looking stolid and holy. What else, indelibly, was due to Philip?

Almost nothing. Not the furniture, not the curtains, not the books on the shelves. Maybe that was part of the trouble.

A crawling loneliness spread out from Michael's stomach all the way to his fingers. He was alone. Alone because Philip had left, alone because he had been singled out.

He was a target for God's special attention. God had sent the miracle and the miracle had driven away the nearest thing Michael had to love. Who would have thought miracles felt so terrible? You could feel them break the universe. You could feel them break you.

Michael sat down on the sofa and it smelled of Henry. 'Why are you doing this to me?' he asked the sunlight. 'What did I do wrong? What am I supposed to learn?'

Learn that I'm impotent? Learn that I'm so scared of Aids that I won't kiss anyone? I knew that. Am I supposed to learn that sex is just an excuse to keep love away? Why would anyone avoid love? What's so painful about love?

What is so very painful about being ditched after thirteen years for a young man so beautiful that you'd have done the same thing yourself, so you can't even feel morally superior? Why would anyone mind that?

What's so painful about being bonded in your bones to someone who has to leave you to begin to breathe? What's so painful about opening up your entire life to someone, only to find that your life is rotten inside and both of you hate it?

And, once you learn that, what are you supposed to do with it?

The answer, it appeared, was nothing.

And, oh God, he had started his life with Phil so full of hope and trust and love. It had seemed as if his life had suddenly come right.

If you're gay and not very good at sex, people don't ring back. Nice people, handsome intelligent kind people who made you laugh don't ring back. You stop even asking for addresses, stop asking people back to the flat. You do it there, in the sauna, in the park. You do it with most of your clothes on and if you finish first, you get the hell out of there. And you tell yourself it's male sex instinct; you tell yourself it's gay culture. And you remember afresh all over again each time when they realize, pumping away at you, that your dick is not going to react.

Then, at 26, Michael had met Phil, and suddenly, none of that mattered.

'Show me,' Michael asked the air.

There was the sound of a key in the front door, and excited voices in the hall, and the clunking as the heavy fireproofed panels shut.

Phil's breathy voice said, 'But this is fantastic! This is it? This is our flat?'

'Yup,' someone said. A smooth pleasant voice with a what . . . Australian? . . . accent.

'My God,' chuckled Phil. His voice hadn't changed.

Philip stuck his head into the sitting room, and looked around goggle-eyed.

Was that really Phil? He looked almost skeletal, with a rockabilly haircut and jeans that swelled out at the thighs and closed at the ankles. He had huge brown eyes and bat ears and was still covered in spots. His hands darted up like startled sparrows.

This young Phil had a body language that was as delicious and as comic as Charlie Chaplin's.

'Gosh,' he said. 'I'll finally be able to have dinner parties.'

This Philip's face and body were different, the soul was different. This was a nice, young, innocent, frightened guy who had only just left home and who needed Michael for all these reasons. It was the younger Philip whom Michael loved and who was now no more.

Another Michael came in wearing a striped shirt that our Michael remembered. He was a fresh smooth square Michael, glowing pink with happiness.

Old Michael sat on the sofa bed that had not been in their version of the flat, and he was invisible to them. They thought that this was their first day. Michael had given them the grace of seeing nothing else.

Young Phil had to jump up to kiss young Mike, who was so much taller than him. 'Thank you thank you thank you.' Phil hugged him, and then leaned back to drink in Mike's face, the helpless stretched smile, the crumpled eyes brimming with love. They lunged at each other's lips and chewed them, making a smacking noise a bit like toffee.

An anguished flood of memory poured over old Michael. He had found this flat because he had found Phil. He had wanted Phil to have somewhere nice to live. Otherwise Michael would have stayed out in Harrow near the Poly. He remembered how they bought the sofa bed. They had bounced on it together in Heal's. They had wanted the staff to know they were lovers.

Young Mike shook Philip and chuckled. 'Oh, baby,' he said, words flowing thickly from a grateful heart.

'I love you,' said Phil, quietly.

Young Mike rested his head on top of Philip's.

'You said let's play house,' said Phil. 'But I had no idea you meant something full-size.'

'There's plenty of things around here that are full-sized,' said younger Michael. He sounded debonair. 'There's a full-sized fridge and a full-sized shower . . .' His body said that something else was full-sized too.

Oh you lucky guy, old Michael thought as the young Mike

enveloped his lover, and was gratefully received. The kiss this time was long and silent, and when they parted, there was unspoken agreement in their eyes.

'I'll show you the bedroom,' said Michael.

The apartment had not changed much in thirteen years. The Angels could not see the paintings on the wall that the young Phil had not yet painted. They hadn't seen the huge TV in the corner of the sitting room. They didn't see Michael's computer on the desk in the bedroom.

Their big four-poster bed had been there, though.

'My God!' exclaimed Phil and ran coltishly towards it. 'Wherever did you find that?'

Young Michael was beaming, flushed with pride and love and the pleasure of making someone happy. 'A barn in Lancashire,' he replied.

This may not have been their exact words at the time, but the spirit was right, the people were right. Young Philip flung himself onto the high mattress and kicked off his shoes, and young Michael went and pulled the bedroom curtains shut, and the wooden rings made a clicking sound that always meant they were about to make love. Then he rested his head, as if in prayer, on Phil's tummy.

The real Michael watched them make love. They were young, excited: young Michael almost got it up, Philip tried to allow him to penetrate him. Doubt crossed both their faces. Michael collapsed and groaned, and rested his head on Philip's shoulder. Philip kissed the top of his head.

'Don't worry, we'll get better at it,' Philip said. Michael leaned back to look at Philip. 'For some guys a hole is just a hole. You're not like that.' Somehow light danced in Philip's eyes. Young Michael breathed. Their eyes latched together, love and gratitude beaming out of them as steadily as headlamps.

They were too young to know who they were or what they wanted, so they were free to keep on trying.

Michael's heart ached all day as he haunted them, ached for what he'd lost and could not yet accept losing.

He watched them cooking lunch excitedly in their new kitchen. He watched them eat it without a table, plates resting on a towel on the living-room carpet. They ate it naked, passing the chewed food between them as they kissed. Entangled, they went into the bedroom again and failed again, and once again that made no difference.

They washed up and dusted and hoovered, delighted with their new domesticity. They read and reread the listings magazine and decided to see *Platoon*.

Day became early evening. They tried on different bum-freezer jackets. Philip decided to wear the brown trousers he later gave to Henry. They were new and crisp and sharp. Phil thought they were listening to Jane Siberry and went to turn it off, and then they both chattered off into the night, to hold hands (and indeed if memory served, something else) all through the film.

And suddenly old Michael was alone, in the dark. The weather had changed. In the real world, it was raining, heavy drumming rain that smelled of leaves.

Michael walked back into the bedroom, calling quietly. There was a sound like wind in the curtains around the bed.

'Hello, Phil,' he said to a shadow.

'Who the fuck are you?' It was the younger Phil. He scuttled back naked across the surface of the bed. '*Michael?*'

'Yes,' said Michael, sounding uncertain of that.

'You look so old.'

Michael sat shyly on the edge of the bed. 'I am old, baby. Thirteen years older.'

'You should start working out.'

Michael sighed. 'I do. Regularly. This is me looking fit.'

The Angel grew confused. 'This isn't a joke, is it?'

Michael shook his head, and tried not to get weepy. 'No, baby, it isn't.'

The Angel lost its innocence. 'What am I?'

'You're Phil. You're the Phil that was. My Phil.'

'I . . . I'm not understanding this,' warned young Phil, with a scared chuckle.

'We got older and different. So I called you back.'

There was a long pause. The darkness outside was as if all the lights of the world had gone out from neglect. The Angel looked about the room, processing sensations, how the world now looked. He looked at the tapestries that hung from the four-poster and seemed to see something new in them.

'I'm not the real Phil, am I?' he said, in a voice as low as the light.

Michael couldn't help but edge closer to him. He couldn't help but take him in his arms. It seemed such an imposition, a terrible thing to do to a young man in the first throes of love, finding the first anchorage of his own in the world.

'We broke up,' said Phil, his voice frail with disappointment.

Michael tried to cradle him, comfort him. 'We had more than twelve years, baby. That's pretty good going.'

'Why?' Phil pushed him away.

Michael retreated from him. 'You started to go places. You didn't need me there. I looked different. You didn't like what I did for a living, you were bored . . . and . . .' He sighed. 'Someone beautiful, something beautiful came along and took you. You tried to be good about it. Which only made it worse in the end.'

There was the sound of traffic, of tyres shushing over wet streets. Where had the day gone? He hadn't gone to work, or even rung them to say he was ill or whatever. This was worse than illness.

The young Phil looked askance at this strange man who had suddenly swollen out of the Michael he knew.

'You want to live with me,' the young Phil said, leaning backwards.

'I want you back,' said Michael, pleading against life itself.

'No,' said Phil.

'Why not?'

'Because you're not Michael.'

'I'm still Michael inside.'

Phil shook his head. 'Michael would never do this to me. And . . . I would never do to Michael what your Phil did. So things must be pretty poor where you are. You must have let things go pretty far.'

'Yes,' whispered Michael.

'Beyond repair?' Phil leaned forward, enquiring, like a friend listening in a coffee shop.

'And out the other side. I'm sorry. I'm sorry to do this to you. I want you to have hope. I want you to have joy.'

'I will, as soon as you put me back where I'm supposed to be. With my new boyfriend in my new flat.'

Michael nodded, once, yes.

'Will I know?'

My God, what if he did? What if he could sense it, back then?

'Can . . . can you feel attachment to the real Phil . . . in your time?'

Phil stared. 'Yes. Yes I can. They're watching the movie . . . and Phil, Phil's suddenly scared, he has a terrible sense that this can't last, that you will get old. I think he can almost see you on this bed.'

There is no time, where Angels come from.

'Send me back!' the Angel said, fear growing in his eyes.

Michael did. Air seemed to open, and to swallow him. There was a breath as it rushed in to fill the space Phil had occupied.

Michael looked up at the ceiling and saw the lights of passing cars move across it. This would be the first of many such nights.

There was another option.

The air puckered and blew, and Phil, the older Phil, was blown into the room wearing the clothes in which he left Michael.

Business-like, this Angel kicked off his boots and began to unbuckle his belt.

'Stop,' said Michael. 'Please? I want to talk.'

'Oh. I thought that this was what it was for. Another wank session together.' Phil sat on the bed and, bootless, lay back to stare at the ceiling.

'Live with me,' asked Michael. 'Stay with me.'

'Oh Jesus.'

'The real Phil has his new life, he has Henry, who is rather wonderful. I know you don't love me any more, but just do it out of kindness.'

This Philip was unmoved. 'Wouldn't friends get a bit confused to see me living in two places at once?'

'I could make sure that didn't happen.'

133

'Hmm. Whisk me out of existence whenever it got inconvenient. Charmed, I'm sure.'

'The real Phil would say do it. He'd probably say humour the poor bastard, it can't do any harm. Phil's still kind. He still doesn't want to hurt me.'

Phil crooked an elbow and lay his head on it. 'You're sure of that, are you?'

'Please,' pleaded Michael. He knew he was in a right old state, hair everywhere, face all red. Helplessness is so attractive.

With his other arm, Phil reluctantly took his shoulder and pulled Michael closer to him.

'Phil still loves you,' the Angel said, but his voice was business-like.

All of Michael's inner scaffolding sagged with the weight. But it didn't give.

Phil spoke in a voice that might as well have come from the grave, consoling, beyond reach. 'I still love you but for the wrong reasons. I moved in with you because I was terrified. I'd just left home, and you were my protector and for a while my provider. And I realized, if I stayed with you, I'd be terrified of life forever. I'd stay shallow and superficial because I would stay a teenager. Thank you for your offer. Thank you for making it an offer, when you could have made it a command. But I'm *Phil*.' The Angel seemed to stab himself in the heart with his hand. 'And Phil doesn't want to be here. I know what I'll become if I stay here. I'd still be a boy at sixty.'

There was an unspoken question lurking in the sound of the rain.

'And Michael, you would turn into stone.'

'*Il faut accepter*,' murmured Michael. It was something an elderly French woman once said to him on the Metro. She had caught Michael and Philip subtly mocking her dress and manner: the tartan skirt, the heavy sensible shoes. She told him how she filled her days since her husband's death and the departure of her sons, and how she had overcome her depression.

You have to accept. If you keep saying no, nothing moves on.

134

The curtains stirred as if the window were open. Philip was gone.

Michael stood up to make himself a cup of tea. He passed the dishes on the dresser and thought: the cups are mine, but most of the crockery is Philip's.

The downstairs buzzer growled. It was Henry.

'Michael? Can I come up?'

Was he supposed to say no? When he opened the door of the flat, Henry stood, dripping wet and looking sad for him. He carried an empty khaki bag. 'Hi. I hope it hasn't been too rough on you.'

Michael didn't answer. After a moment he stood aside to let Henry come in. 'Philip sent me back to get some of his clothes.' Henry shrugged. 'He's a bit of a coward.'

Michael closed up like a sea anemone. 'His things are in the closet there.' Michael walked away, back to his tea. Buggered if he was going to offer Henry anything.

Henry seemed to take forever. Cautious, calm little ruffling sounds came from the bedroom. Oh Jesus Christ, get on with it, can't you? It isn't the Crown Jewels you're packing up. Michael could see Henry, folding up the shirts, the jackets. He would tenderly adjust each sleeve.

That was my job once, except I never folded Philip's things tenderly. I rolled them up in a fury and dumped them in the laundry box and dried them in the dryer so the shirts came out as crisp as fallen leaves.

Michael could imagine Philip deciding which clothes he wanted. He would have kept changing his mind. He would want party gear, and jogging gear and formal wear. There would be a list, full of crossings out.

What on earth was Henry doing? Michael's smaller self began to imagine theft. He walked in on Henry to find jackets and shirts neatly laid out on the bed and on the floor a crossed-out list.

What, do you think you own this place? That's my bed, this is my bedroom. Michael's smaller self wanted to hurl the bag and all the clothes out of the window, or at least into the hallway.

Henry had the good grace to look embarrassed, and motioned

towards the list as if to say: Phil, we both know Phil. Michael remembered; this is Henry.

Michael said, 'I'm sorry you were saddled with doing this.'

'It's probably easier on both of you this way. I'll be done in a second.'

'Do you want some tea?'

'I'd love some. But can I finish here first? I'd like to talk.'

Cornered.

Michael sat waiting in the dining room like a schoolboy, ripping off the tip of his thumbnail. Finally, after five minutes, Henry came in and he poured the tea.

Michael couldn't think of any neutral way to start the conversation, so he asked, 'Where are you staying?'

'The Arts Club. There's a spare room.'

'Ah. That's why he wants all his trendy gear.'

'He's very upset.'

Michael sniffed. 'He can come back, if he's so upset.'

Henry said, with a trace of a smile, 'He may be coming back sooner than you think.' He reached into his woollen ethnic shoulder bag and pulled out a copy of a newspaper. Henry passed it to Michael and kept his eyes fixed on Michael's face.

At first Michael thought it was the *Financial Times*. The paper had yellowed. He was wondering why Henry had given him a newspaper and why he should be interested, when he saw a photograph of Henry. The light from the camera had penetrated his brown eyes so that they looked translucent and deep, like water through clear ice. His smile looked delighted, with good reason.

The headline read STUMPY UNLIKELY SEX SYMBOL.

Michael felt his eyes bug out. 'You're Stumpy!' exclaimed Michael. Stumpy was an anti-motorway protester who had caught the attention of the press about two years before and had become something of a celebrity.

Of course that's why he looked familiar. Though Henry did look a little different. Maybe he was just two years older.

Henry coughed, uncomfortably. 'Not exactly,' he said, looking at Michael with a sad wariness. 'I'm a copy.' He waited, and Michael began to understand. 'I was wondering if you could tell me anything about that.'

136

Michael processed, and Harry gave him time. Neither of them said anything, and then after a silence too long for comfort both of them began to talk at once.

Michael said, 'What do you mean, a copy?' and Henry said, with a relenting smile, 'Obviously you don't know anything about it.'

Then they had to pick up the pieces of the conversation. Michael said, 'Copy? Copy? You mean like an Angel?'

Henry had never heard the term Angel. He turned his head as if trying to hear better. 'No, no, I mean like the Castro brothers this morning.'

'Yeah, yeah, an Angel.'

Henry paused, pressing his two hands together gently. 'Yes, that's what I mean.'

Michael felt his heart thump. The next thought came to him sharp as a knife. Was there someone else who could do this? Michael did not want to be the only one who did this. He wanted someone else to talk to about it. 'Did someone else make you? Do you know who?'

This managed to throw Henry. 'Someone else?' He scratched his head and began to smile. 'I was assuming that it had to be you. In fact, Michael, I still am pretty certain it is you.'

'Why do you say that? I've hardly even heard of you.'

Henry's gaze at Michael was wistful, determined and sympathetic. 'Philip and I met at First Out. Suddenly I was just standing there next to him and asked if I could see his copies of the free papers.'

Henry's eyebrows raised as if offering up the story in evidence on a tray.

'That's how Phil and I met,' said Michael.

Henry nodded. 'He even said, "This has happened once before."'

It was as if Michael's heart were pricked with goosebumps all over. It's one thing to lose a property or a painting when a relationship breaks up. It is another to give away your memories. He went back and looked idly at the newspaper's date: 17 February 1998.

It could be that Henry wasn't telling the truth. Maybe he

was trying to shock Michael. Maybe he was playing a joke, or just wanted one up on Michael in some vague way because they were rivals in love. Michael looked at him, and Henry sat waiting patiently for him, calm and orderly and not at all fussed.

Whatever else Michael thought about Henry, he didn't think he was mean, or mad, or jealous for attention or any of the other things that would explain this if it were a charade. And if it were none of those things, then what on earth was going on?

Henry helped him out. Henry kept on talking. 'So Philip passed me the newspapers and I realized that I didn't really have any memories of anything else before then. I couldn't think how I got there. I knew it was a gay coffee shop, I had information, like I had been briefed. I knew I was supposed to talk to Philip and that I was going to fancy him. I said to myself, "Gosh, Stumpy would really like to know about this. This would really interest Stumpy; he's into mystical stuff."' Henry smiled and did a slight, self-deprecatory shrug that wasted not an ounce of energy. 'Then I realized that I was Stumpy. Sort of. When Philip said, "You're Stumpy," I said what I said to you. "I'm only a copy." But it was as if he didn't hear or couldn't remember. A few days later, there was something in the news about Stumpy being in Northampton and I knew I couldn't be in two places at once. So I knew I was in a bit of a strange situation. And this morning I began to understand what was going on.'

'But why would it be you?' Michael was suddenly sweating and his voice was raised.

Henry's voice was lowered. 'Philip said he'd always fancied Stumpy. He said he kept a kind of file? Of newspaper cuttings about him?' It was a question but Michael shook his head no, firmly. 'He said he did. But then he also said that he doubted you noticed.'

'So?' Michael was feeling unaccountably combative.

'Soooooo . . . I think you may have known about Philip liking Stumpy, but only just out of the corner of your eye.'

'So why would I be making up boyfriends for Philip?'

138

Henry smiled indulgently, as if Michael were sweetly old-fashioned. 'Because you love him and you want him to be happy.'

'At the expense of my own marriage.' Michael made a circular gesture of the hand that meant, come on, follow your own logic.

'Maybe you want to be happy too.'

It was like having a particularly annoying conversation with your mother, when she is all-knowing and wise and kindly.

'You think I did this to get rid of Philip.'

Henry's nod of agreement was almost imperceptible. 'People do things without knowing,' he said.

'Tuh!' Michael snorted and couldn't accept, but found that he couldn't fully deny.

'Innnnn any event,' said Henry, drawing the word out to buy a moment's time and staring at his hands. 'There is one way to resolve things. And if you were to do this thing, then you would get Philip back.'

'Oh yeah, and what would that be?' Michael felt his shoulders move like a bull lowering his head. He was on the verge of concluding that this was a scam and that Henry was about to demand money in exchange for Philip. Or the address of the lab.

'You could send me back,' whispered Henry. His eyes were honest and unreadable. 'If you send me away, then none of this would have happened. I imagine Philip would snap back into your sitting room like a rubber band.'

It took Michael a moment to change gears.

Henry gave the strangest, saddest smile. 'I just thought I would make sure you knew that was possible.'

He's volunteering, Michael thought. He's volunteering for non-existence. I can't think of another word for that other than goodness. Whether he's real or not.

And that's when he finally had to admit that what Henry was suggesting was likely to be true.

'Thank you,' Michael said.

Henry shrugged. 'You're the ones who are real. I don't count as much.'

Michael found himself saying, 'Yes you do.'

'I don't really exist. I'm not sure how fair it is on Philip for him to love someone who doesn't really exist.'

And Michael saw then in his eyes: he really loves Phil. And Phil must really love him.

'When this thing ends, Philip will never know I existed. It won't hurt him. I don't really exist. There won't be any memories for him to have, because I was never there. I couldn't even leave him a note.'

Henry held out his hands, smiling. He was, in fact, without hope. 'There's nothing I can change,' he said. 'Except you.' And for just a moment there was a fleck of light along the uppermost edge of his eye.

He sighed and sat up and looked almost merry. 'So. What are you going to do?'

'What, like destroy you?' Michael could only splutter and shake his head helplessly. He could of course do it. He could do it and get Philip back. He could return to the long lonely nights of not knowing where Philip was. Michael remembered uncomfortable evenings with Philip's arty friends. He could go back to silences over breakfast and to doing most of the household chores himself. Michael found that his heart sank.

'I think,' Michael said, 'I'm going to leave things as they are.'

'Do you have any idea why that might be?'

Michael shrugged. 'Maybe I don't really want Philip back.'

Henry reached across the table and took Michael's hand. The expression welling up in his eyes might as well be called love. 'Then. Maybe you did this to give him somewhere to go, so that you could move on as well.'

Michael felt rebellious. 'There are easier ways of getting rid of a boyfriend.'

Henry's smile was patient and unfooled. 'Are there? I can't think of one.'

The gleam came into Henry's eyes again. 'Is ... is there anything in your life you can't talk about?'

'Why, has Philip said something?'

Henry's smile was still sad for him as he shook his head. 'It would probably be something you couldn't tell Philip.'

Michael felt only slightly flustered. His eyelids flapped like butterfly wings. He thought he was calmly considering the proposition. He surveyed the history of his life and for the moment, he couldn't really think of anything like that.

'No. Nope. No, there's nothing.'

Henry looked a bit disappointed. 'OK,' he whispered, and smiled, and rubbed the top of Michael's hand. He quickly drank the rest of the tea. 'I think I'd better be getting back.'

'Sure. Sure, no problem,' said Michael, unaccountably veering all the way into an American accent, and he stood up jauntily, anxious for Henry to go.

'Thanks for the tea.' Henry stood up too and, with infuriating slowness, began calmly to arrange all his things in the woollen bag. Oh come on, you can just put things in and take them out later.

They moved into the hallway. 'If you ever want to talk just give me a call. Or you can just run up another copy if you like.' Henry smiled, but for once Michael was uncharmed.

Henry luxuriated his way into his long green coat with the torn pocket. He tossed the collar straight and then leaned over, legs straight, to pick up Phil's bag. 'I hope I see you,' he said. He meant it. Michael did not respond. Henry turned to go, but suddenly changed his mind. He even changed his mind gracefully. The coat swirled about him as he turned back around.

'Michael,' he said, suddenly firm. 'This is a miracle. It's something wonderful. Why don't you just use it to be happy?' Something in his eyes gripped and held. Michael remembered: this is a political leader. 'Why don't you just try joy?'

Why don't you just try joy?

The clinic had just been set up near Michael's work. It sold
Viagra and called itself the London Professionals Registry as if
it were American Express and you had to be invited to join. It
had a big polished black door, just like the Prime Minister's.
Inside there was an escritoire at which sat a woman in a tight
white uniform. Perhaps she was a nurse, or someone designed
to look like one. She talked in cool polite tones that perched
uncomfortably on the line between being polite and foreboding.
The wrong sort of person was not welcome here. The wrong
sort was someone who could not pay.

Michael was ushered into what once had been someone's *salle
de réception*. It could only have been called that: it was too gilded
to be fully British. It had sofas with blue velour upholstery, and
tables so fragile and flowery that they looked as if they were made
of porcelain. Lined up on the tables were *Tatler, Country Life* –
magazines found only in clinics. Michael had confirmed an
appointment for twelve, but was made to wait anyway. He had
time to consider the other professionals being registered.

A dignified old black gentleman with a cane sat with his wife
on the sofa. Michael presumed it was his wife. She wore a
brilliant blue dress and a hat, and she matched the sofas. Her
huge spectacles increased the firmness of her gaze. What are
you looking at? she seemed to say. You should have seen my
man when he was young. You've got a problem, too, or you
wouldn't be here.

Love.

An athletic young guy in his early twenties picked up a magazine from the table, went back to the sofa, stopped, put the first one back, and picked up another. He dropped down onto the sofa as if it were a piece of sporting equipment and crossed his legs. He flicked through the magazine at high speed, not reading. It was *FHM*, full of articles on how to deal with oversensitive women so they would give you sex.

What a thing to be twenty, big, strong, fleet and to end up in bed with just the kind of girl who tries to sound understanding and can't.

Michael waited 25 minutes. 'I'm sorry, I did make an appointment,' he said to the nurse in the corridor. 'Are you sure my papers went in?'

'I'll just check for you,' she replied, smiling. 'If you'd like to go back and take a seat.'

A few minutes later, a nurse came into the room and said, 'Mr Jones? Your prescription's ready.' The young guy bounded to his feet, and nipped out, as if skirting the defence in a game of basketball.

So he's already been seen. There is no queue. So they really are just keeping me waiting here. What on earth for? To make sure I have time to reconsider? To soak up the general ambience of money and importance? Or to soften me up? For what exactly, am I being softened?

Investment, he decided. They want to make sure I have already invested a lot of time in this. So it's difficult to say no.

Finally, his name was called.

A different nurse ushered him through another door, and down a perfectly domestic corridor into what had once been a maid's bedroom. It was tiny, without a window, and in it sat a bullfrog of a man. He sat behind another gilded table and did not bother to stand up.

'Take a seat.' He glanced at papers. 'Mr Blasco.' The voice was posh, the face overripe with too much old-fashioned drinking. He wore a shirt with blue stripes. His purple neck overflowed the top of his white collar. There was a signet ring on

143

his little finger and patches of worn skin on the backs of his hands. 'I'm Mr Fieldone. I'm a consultant with the Registry.'

Michael assumed that Consultant meant something fairly medical. Mr Fieldone spoke like a man who had, at most, fifteen minutes to spare, while reading Michael's papers, presumably for the first time, through half-moon spectacles.

'There are marvellous new treatments for sexual difficulties. But, by law, I'm afraid we first have to ensure that there isn't a previous medical condition that could cause problems. So I'm afraid there are some forms to go through.'

The questions started bland and increased in impertinence. Did Michael get morning erections? Would he describe them as full erections? Could he indicate the angle those erections achieved. Forty-five degrees? Eighty degrees? Perhaps Michael would just like to indicate the angle with his hand?

'Uh. I really don't know.' If only he had been brave. He wanted to say: I don't normally have my mathematical instruments to hand when I have an erection.

Did he ever experience erections while having sex? Did he have a regular partner? Do you have any other sexual partners? And how many of those do you have? Michael told him: about five per week. Mr Fieldone's eyes boggled slightly. He smelled of Imperial Leather soap, and his hair plastered low over his head looked like it needed a wash.

'Do you mind my asking if your partners are male or female?'

'Both. Well, mostly men.'

'Hmm,' he said, flicking back over the document. 'Yes. We see many people here, and we find that impotency often comes to homosexual men, particularly if they are a bit introverted or timid and can't fully commit to anyone.'

Michael felt something prickle in his cheeks.

Mr Fieldone continued, 'I would say that this looks like a psychological problem. I will be recommending you for a further physical exam, today if you like.' Michael agreed. Was he supposed to say no?

'It really is wonderful the breakthroughs of the last few years. There is a new drug called Sidenfil, which is quite effective. Now, the usual dosage is fifty milligrams, but such is the demand that we have only been able to procure – from *America* . . .' he said this leaning forward, to emphasize the trouble, distance and expense of such an importation, '. . . treatments in dosages of one hundred milligrams. We will of course, cut these in half, *professionally*, and give them to you in four test dosages. Your first fee will cover the cost of this trial prescription and today's interviews, tests and examinations and provision of results. If you decide that the treatment is for you, then a prescription of forty-two dosages will be available to you at a cost of £750. If you are in agreement with these terms, please sign here.'

'What? Wait, just a moment.' Michael's mind raced to divide and subdivide.

'Yes?' rumbled the deep imperious voice, all the cream of privilege rising to the surface. An eyebrow was raised.

'That's £350 for two tablets.'

'Including the work of three professionals.'

Ah, so you're the professionals being registered.

'That means you're selling me twenty-one tablets for £750.'

As if the case were closed, the salesman tapped all papers into a neat whole. 'I'm not selling you anything. By all means, take your time to consider, and we can file your questionnaire away?' His voice rose as a question.

This, thought Michael, is what it is. I knew what it was when I came here. They know I know what it is. The only question is: do I want to walk away from here with nothing, or do I want to walk out of here with Viagra?

'I'm only signing for £350. Right?'

'Only for the trial dosages, yes.' He was unwilling to say the price again. The form was pushed back at Michael to sign. Michael signed.

So he went to the doctor's office. The doctor wore a white coat, but otherwise looked like an ebullient stick insect. He was thrilled by something. Perhaps it was the money he was making.

'Hello! Good afternoon!' he cried as Michael came in. The doctor seemed to float, his spectacles reflecting the dazzling light. Life, evidently, was marvellous for a man who owned his own clinic.

The doctor explained, yet again, the necessity for a medical exam. There would need to be blood tests. 'You could have a Shunt. A Venus Shunt.' It had evidently been a rather celebratory lunch – his 's' sounds slurred as if on ice. 'An erection is made of blood and a Venus Shunt is a sort of short circuit. Lower your trousers please.'

A refreshingly cool jelly was applied thickly all over Michael's cock. It was rather like a prelude to something else.

'It helps conduct the sound,' explained the doctor. It did seem as if he was taking longer than necessary, applying the gel. His eyes gleamed. Perhaps he just enjoyed his work.

Being examined by the doctor was rather like being abducted by aliens. Something like a microphone that had won a *Design Week* award was run up and down Michael's penis. Tiny speakers connected to the computer produced a throbbing, shushing sound. This made the doctor giggle.

'Sounds like the music my son listens to,' he said. He was definitely drunk, and he was stroking Michael's cock in a friendly, offhand way. 'No. Nothing wrong there. Hear it?' Michael wasn't sure what he was supposed to be listening for. 'The blood is circulating beautifully!' He gave Michael's bare thigh an enthusiastic slap. 'Nothing wrong there.'

Michael discovered that once he had had a faint little hope. The little hope was that his impotence had a physical cause. Like a limb lost in a car accident, it could not then be blamed on him. Michael felt ashamed. 'The Consultant seemed reasonably sure it was psychological.'

'Oh *him*,' said the doctor. 'He's just a sales person.'

Michael knew exactly how to take this. 'Then what is he doing telling people that homosexuals tend to be impotent?'

'Oh Good heavens, did he say that? I am sorry, I'll have a word. You know how it is: everyone wants to partake of the mystique of medicine.'

He began to write something on Michael's papers, and then began to giggle. 'Poor old Far-Fars. Hmm hmm hmm. He never got over old Squeers.'

'I beg your pardon?' Michael asked.

The doctor waved his hand, the joke beyond explanation.

146

'Something that happened to him at school. Never got over it. Poor old Far-Fars.'

'You knew him at school?'

Michael suddenly saw: some old sozzled hack had been given a non-job by old school chums.

The doctor became suddenly serious. 'What we're going to do now, Mr Blasco, is give you a blood test. We don't do that here, that's done for us by another clinic, excellent, the Fairborough, just down the road. This will determine if you have diabetes and should also confirm you're not taking any other medicines that could cause problems.'

'You've already signed the prescription,' said Michael. 'What happens if it turns out I have diabetes?'

'Oh, we'll refund the cost of the test dosage.'

'But . . .' Michael had to chuckle. 'Should you really be signing a prescription before you know that it's safe?'

The professional leaned back. How can spectacles look as if they are grinning smugly? Oh come on, they seemed to say, we know what's going on here. This is a deal. You want it, we got it. 'We find most of our patients don't want to wait. They come back here and find the prescription is ready for them. If they fail the tests, then of course, we don't give them the drugs, and they only pay for the examination.' He paused airily and then asked, 'What's your line of work, Mr Blasco?'

Michael told him: a biologist.

'Ah,' the doctor said. 'A fellow professional.' He gained a conspiratorial air. 'Do you work for industry?'

'I'm an academic. We're funded by a research council.'

'Academic. And you're funded by government. Twice. That's clever of you.'

'A lot of private-sector research is funded in the same way.'

'Well. I'm glad that this current government is doing something for industry.' He was pissed and didn't care a bit if Michael might not be a Tory.

'Well,' said Michael. 'This current government lets you sell Viagra.' It was the first time during the entire process that anyone had called the drug by its brand name.

'And,' chuckled the doctor, 'keep its value inflated by keeping

147

it off the National Health. But then ask yourself, Mr Blasco, why should the taxpayer pay for that? When you are perfectly capable of paying for it yourself?'

It was all about money. Most people worked mostly for money. So why did it feel wrong that doctors should? Michael got his tablets. The nurses in the front office continued their conversation about the new tax-free savings accounts.

I suppose, Michael thought, I want other people to have a calling. Since I do not.

He got home and examined his prescription. The pills, of course, were not cut in half, professionally or otherwise.

Does Viagra work?

Michael tried it on Lawrence of Arabia and it did.

Michael had seen a television documentary years before about Lawrence and his sexual habits. He read the opening of *Seven Pillars of Wisdom* and wondered how there could be any controversy at all about it. The second page says clearly that he and the Arab warriors made love, supposedly because no clean women were to be had.

Michael found the passage about the Turkish commandant. Lawrence was quite clear there too. Violated and beaten, Lawrence discovered his taste for pain and humiliation. Michael focussed on an old photograph. Lawrence was wearing long white robes and had narrowed his eyes against the sunlight. He looked young, salty, tiny and beautiful.

Michael took his first Viagra and called Lawrence up direct from the Transjordan. Lawrence arrived and blinked. Michael had not expected Lawrence's eyes. They were as stilling as ice and the same colour and they fixed on Michael and were full of doubt. Lawrence was creased from too much sun, but otherwise, he had the face of a ruthlessly honest, difficult teenager. His long Arab robe was stained yellow. Michael smelled dust and eau de cologne.

Lawrence stood dazed for a moment. He stared at the huge blank staring eye of the television and then strode to the window and looked out over the street. The parked cars were lined up, the morning's light shower drying on their hoods. Lawrence was

149

slim and precisely placed, leaning sideways, his legs akimbo in the way a dancer's might be askew for effect. He held one forearm straight up, clenching the wrist with his other hand. Michael would have called him squiggly, which meant tiny and effeminate, if the gesture had not also given Lawrence the air of a warrior.

Michael coughed. 'Would you like to use the shower?'

Lawrence bowed once and said in a light voice, 'That would be pleasant. Thank you.'

'I'll get you a towel.'

Without any kind of ceremony, Lawrence began to disrobe. He calmly released and then folded his headdress over the arm of Michael's sofa bed. When Michael returned with a clean towel, Lawrence was nude, waiting patiently, holding his wrist again. His stomach was the flattest, hardest, most ribbed with muscle that Michael had ever seen. He could see the striations of the muscles through his skin.

Michael indicated the way to the bathroom and showed Lawrence how the shower worked.

'It has a pump?' Lawrence asked.

'Yeah, I guess so. There's a switch you have to turn on, only I leave it on all the time.'

'Water,' said Lawrence in a slightly wondering voice.

He made Michael feel graceless. Michael was never prepared for his creations to be more powerful than he was. And yet he should be prepared for it; they somehow were; as if they used him as a filter to strain their impurities. Thinking of the neighbours and what he hoped was to come he pulled the curtains shut. And finally, he picked up the blue and white paper that enfolded his Viagra and finally read its small blue print. The instructions said: take one hour before intercourse. Michael was going to have to engage Lawrence of Arabia in an hour's conversation.

Lawrence re-entered the room, moving without sound, without even disturbing the air. He was unashamed of his nakedness and was slightly erect, perhaps because his relative vulnerability excited him.

'So,' Lawrence asked, and began towelling himself vigorously as if to chafe away a layer of skin. He still smelled of sweat. 'What year is it?'

Michael told him.

'Is there a state of Israel?'

'Yes.' Michael felt awkward standing, but somehow unwilling to sit on the sofa.

'What has it done to the Arabs?'

'Moved them to one side. Integrated some of them into the state of Israel. Fought wars with the others.'

Lawrence rubbed; streaks of pink abrasion began to appear on his milk-white legs. 'Two great people destroyed. The last breath of British imperialism.'

Lawrence shook his head and sat down on Michael's living-room carpet with the abruptness of a wolf. He looked at Michael and Michael saw that yes, the blue-grey eyes were those of a wolf, in a boyish scholar's face, prematurely aged.

'Sit next to me,' Lawrence said, kindly. He looked utterly at home on the desert-coloured carpet.

Michael did, stiffly.

'I had a wonderful death. Don't you think? Still young on a motorcycle.'

Michael smiled at the pride. 'It is something of a prototype.'

'I hope that doesn't mean people imitate it!'

'No. But live fast, die young, James Dean, that kind of thing is around, but not really because of you.'

Lawrence's head dipped in frustration. 'My entire life was spent trying to avoid power.'

His skinny body, the slightly awkward way it moved – oh, God, it reminded Michael of Phil. The pubes were shaved like an Arab's. Like a young boy just come into puberty. How many people does this man contain?

'Why avoid power?'

The grey eyes looked up, undeniable. 'Because I could have destroyed the world. I had it in me.'

From nowhere there was a yellow, rolled-up cigarette, lit and smelling of hashish. 'And because wisdom does not lie in power. You must have the potential for power, but use the power for different things. I wanted to be wise. I failed of course. I wanted to be a poet and a warrior and an historian.' The face closed slightly with tension. 'Do people still read my book?'

Michael did not have the heart to tell him that he had read only parts of it and thought it was horribly overwritten. 'It's everywhere. Though, to tell you the truth, most people see the movie.'

Lawrence closed his eyes and went very still. 'They made a film,' he said, as if in dread.

'I've got it on video; do you want to see it?'

'No!' said fiercely. 'Thank you,' said gently. 'It was kind of you to offer. I can imagine that the movie is very romantic. For those of us who understand English, the verb to romance means to lie.'

Hospitality, Michael thought, Arab hospitality. He had difficulty fighting his way to his knees. 'Would you like some tea?'

'Tea would be lovely, thank you,' said Lawrence and rewarded him with the most beautiful of smiles under the most doubtful of eyes.

Lawrence made Michael feel lonely. Michael asked him, 'Come and talk to me while I make it?'

Lawrence slid to his feet, as if gravity worked in reverse for him. He padded behind Michael into the kitchen.

Michael asked, 'Is tea all right? Are you hungry?'

'I try to be independent of food,' said Lawrence smiling, grasping his wrist again.

Michael was cursing his ignorance. It wasn't that he had only skimmed *The Seven Pillars of Wisdom*. He realized he knew nothing of the history. There must be a thousand questions that an educated person could ask Lawrence of Arabia. Michael had only one.

'Is it true that you had many Arab lovers?'

'No,' replied Lawrence. 'I had very few.'

'Is it true that your book is dedicated . . .'

'Yes.' Lawrence cut him off with a single, perfectly timed downward nod of the head. 'We all have a love of our life.'

Michael lowered his eyes and lapsed into a podgy English miserablism. 'I wish I did.'

'Tuh,' said Lawrence, a kind of chuckle, dismissive but affectionate. He leaned against the archway into the kitchen. He looked like a teenage girl, a bold Italian gamine, leaning against the village fountain. 'You may just have met him,' he said lightly, his eyes hooded, his smile teasing. He was naked, but clothed in something other. It was Michael who was embarrassed.

Michael clattered the teapot and cups onto a tray, and carried it rattling into the sitting room. They sat down on the carpet again, and Lawrence imperceptibly took over the serving of the tea.

Lawrence passed Michael a cup. It went out like a heartfelt gesture. 'What the Arabs taught me is that eloquence, even when overwrought or extravagant as some of their verse appears to be in translation, has a shape, an architecture that carries its own meaning.' Lawrence placed the teapot and sugar bowl on the carpet in a pattern as formed as a cuneiform wordsign from Nineveh. 'This shapeliness is mirrored in their calligraphy, in which the writing becomes a dance. The strange effect of all this is that in practice, and I mean the practice of love, their sexual cues are verbal. Ours are visual, related usually to looks. Theirs are veiled physically, but naked verbally. They say things such as, "Love exists to grow a new part of the soul, as my love for you has done. So even in Paradise, there will be part of my soul called Lawrence."'

'Someone said that to you?' asked Michael in wonder. Doh. Lawrence's eyes were filmed over. His voice was slightly rougher when he said, 'You can sit closer to me, if that is your desire.'

Michael understood that this was an act of kindness, to understand and to do all of the work. Michael smiled at himself, to acknowledge that he was behind in the game. Feeling thick-arsed, Michael snailed himself in heaving stages six inches nearer to Lawrence.

'You have never suffered physically,' judged Lawrence.

Michael shook his head, no.

'I always made myself suffer physically, so that I would be enduring when I most needed to be. I would do without food or sleep or water. I would walk barefoot miles over rocks, so that I would disdain the physical.'

Michael was puzzling his way through the words. 'It's true. The worst I've had is a sprained ankle.'

'The heat and the dust and starvation all burn away illusion. The body is an illusion.'

Michael was beginning to fall in love.

Lawrence looked at him, fiercely. 'I have never,' he said, 'allowed myself to achieve a sexual climax.'

Michael was beginning to fall out of love. Lawrence of Arabia was barking mad.

Then Lawrence of Arabia pulled Michael to him. The arms were still hot from sunlight. The wolf eyes blazed with a demand. They were insisting. They were insisting on something that was only somewhat like sex.

'Be my desert,' Lawrence demanded. 'Be my sunlight. Burn me.'

Michael looked at his watch. 'I have to keep you talking for twenty more minutes.'

'Is this a spiritual exercise?' Lawrence asked, hungry to be told that yes, it was a deliberate act of withholding, a reining in.

'No. No, it's a medical one.' Michael's Viagra hour was not over. He checked for any of the side effects: flushed cheeks, a slight sense of palpitation in the hands and heart.

'Is the condition chronic?'

'Ah. Yes, actually, it is.'

'Then you do know pain,' said Lawrence, his voice sinking several octaves lower. 'Are you in pain now?' The thought seemed to entice Lawrence. He began to stroke Michael's temples.

'I am beginning to get a mild headache.' That was a side effect too. Gosh, Viagra was fun. Michael couldn't wait for the splintered blue plates in his vision, either, especially the ones with zigzag flashing edges.

'Then I bind myself to that vow also,' announced Lawrence, and sat back.

Then he announced, 'To be really alive, you have to be prepared to die.'

Michael thought: if Viagra can work against this, it can work against anything.

They spent the next twenty minutes discussing pottery shards. Lawrence loved his subject, Ancient Near Eastern

154

archaeology, and the excavation of Nineveh. 'It is a tonic against romance, to read the tablets. They are all contracts, the equivalent of shopping lists.' They finished the tea. Lawrence nodded and then turned and stretched himself out, face down on the carpet. He saw Michael's belt and asked to be struck with it. 'There is to be no indulgence,' he said. 'Use the end with the buckle. There should never be any shirking of the worst.'

Michael had never thought of sex as a trial of endurance. 'Um. Are you sure this is necessary?'

'It stops me becoming effeminate,' said Lawrence.

Oh no it doesn't, thought Michael.

The perfect buttocks wobbled. Without any fuss, no trumpets, or even any particular sensation, it was simply noticeable that Michael's penis was erect. His temples thumped with an increased flow of blood, and his thumbs felt curiously weak as they held the belt. Something was shivery and loose, not in his body, but in his mind.

Michael struck the buttocks, and they tensed. 'Is that enough?' he asked. Lawrence shook his head, no. 'Harder,' he said once. Michael struck again until the buttocks reddened and something like anger rose up in him.

Michael held down Lawrence's tiny arms and pushed him down flat and mounted him, definitively. Lawrence had an ugly anus, lumpy and twisted shut several times, rolling over itself. Michael forced himself through the resistance of the sphincter. Lawrence did not react. The cock pumped as if all by itself, and Lawrence looked grim as if enduring something dreadful. Michael kept pumping and pumping, and the idea came to him: perhaps science had freed him after all, given him back to himself.

But he didn't come.

Finally, he just stopped.

'You withheld,' said Lawrence. 'So did I.' He lay still as if broken. Michael slid back from him, and tried to coax him to roll over, to speak to him. Like a wounded child, Lawrence cast off Michael's hands.

'I have allowed you to violate the integrity of my body,' he said, and buried his face.

Michael felt like an unwanted guest at a wedding. He wanted to bring back the beauty of an hour before. 'Would you like some more tea?'

'I want some clean fresh air,' said Lawrence, angrily, to the carpet.

The hashish cigarette still smouldered on the fake wood tray. He's burnt my tray, Michael thought and then remembered. He can burn nothing; he's an Angel.

He's powerless. Michael looked at the unmoving body.

OK. He's from another age. All of this was inconceivably dirty and evil. Denial became all mixed up with the thing you desired. Denial made you able to ride in the desert with the Arabs. It made you tough. It meant that when you and they made love, you both understood each other's shame and guilt. They could respect and admire your shame and guilt as they admired your prowess. You are quintessential, Lawrence; you are genuinely warlike, as the English are. You are loyal and hard and self-sacrificing, and you regard militarism with its uniforms and flags and shouting and terrible music as irredeemably foolish.

You found yourself in Arabia, in particular circumstances. You found a kind of love, also in particular circumstances. It does not mean that you were not also noble.

Michael touched the small of the white back as if in benediction, and ordered Lawrence home, back to his desert and whoever it was had grown him as part of his soul.

I'm learning.

If you could sleep with anyone in the world, who would it be?

Sexually armed and dangerous, Michael now found there was no one with whom he wanted to have sex. This was, if nothing else, a serious failure of imagination.

There was a time when every afternoon's lecture presented Michael with students who seemed improbable miracles of health and beauty. Cosmopolitan London youths with V-shaped backs wore perfect white T-shirts. Their hips were slim, their crotches were full, their Scandinavian or Indic or West Indian complexions were unblemished, unlined, glowing. They had sat arrayed in front of him, legs wide, as if with the malicious intent of disturbing his calm.

Now Michael saw the imperfections that would distort their beauty with age, the gap teeth, the sunken eyes. For the first time ever, his students provided no sexual inspiration. In the mornings, the train seemed full of middle-aged men who needed exercise. Michael had to remind himself that some of them were, objectively, young and attractive. It was summer, the season of T-shirts and shorts and hairy knees. The beautiful naked legs had no effect on him.

Michael began to realize that he did not really like sex. He had only ever liked parts of sex, sudden jagged frozen moments. He would recycle them as images in memory or fantasy.

Often, the people in the fantasy did not matter. The core of the fantasy was the situation he himself was in.

These situations were not anything he would care to have written down. Just recently, one fantasy involved him being tied up in a Berlin dungeon. In another, he was pressed by a wall of waiting men in the urinals at Cairo train station. His potential partners in the fantasy might wear gelabiya or more Western dress. They could be Nile Delta plump or desert thin; young or old. Who they were did not matter.

In other fantasies, Michael imagined he was twelve years old in Carlsbad, waylaid on a beach and seduced into a weekend life in a male brothel. He imagined himself at twelve wearing the tight little trunks and dancing for men. He danced to T-Rex and put his finger on the cloth under which his sphincter lay. It made no difference if the customers were fat, black and middle-aged, or off-duty wrestlers still in costume, or fathers of childhood friends.

What made him come was the situation he was in and the different scenarios that could lead to. The dream was not of someone else, but of himself, changed.

Life had given him the wrong miracle.

Look, I said I kept fancying guys, but I don't. In fact, I think I don't really like most men. If anything, I am rather chaste. What I want is to be somewhere else, doing something I would never normally do. The fantasy actually is that I become someone different.

So that was what the miracle should have been. It should have changed me.

Michael looked at the escort ads in the gay press. The photographs were supposed to be genuine. They usually displayed the wares from the neck down: slim bodies with large cocks, muscular bodies with tiny ones. He could have any of them, just by asking. He didn't ask. Perhaps he was satiated.

Perhaps it was his computer course.

Seriously. The instructors had forgotten to set enough coursework to give final marks, so suddenly, week after week another report or essay or study was due. All weekend and most evenings, Michael read learned papers about Windows NT system design. Finals were coming as well, so he was having to memorize circuit diagrams. All of this was far from arousing.

Perhaps it was simply that he could have whomever he wanted.

When Michael and Philip used to go out together, the bars would seem to be full of delicious men served cold. When Michael went alone and sex was a serious possibility, the men all seemed to be ballet fans pretending to be motorcyclists, or over-coiffured skinny young queens, or bitter old ones, or flakes who believed in numerology, or fake rockabillies who talked only to each other, or men who lived with their mothers. Availability washed the bloom off the fruit.

Michael invited all of the team at the lab out to lunch. In the first flush of summer, they sat outside on a jetty on the river, crowded around two tiny silver tables. The day seemed to yawn and stretch in the warmth. Across the river were the Houses of Parliament, looking misty like an old aquatint.

'If you could sleep with anyone in the world, who would it be?' Michael asked his staff after three bottles of red wine.

No one answered at first. Who would you sleep with? is not a question anyone can answer easily. It's not only that the question is too personal. The answer changes, moment to moment. It could well be that at that moment you do not want to sleep with anyone at all.

Ebru smiled and said her boyfriend. 'Of course,' she added.

'Well . . . and who else?'

'No one else,' she insisted, smiling.

Michael turned to Shafiq and asked him.

'Oh!' said Shafiq, and looked pleased and embarrassed. 'Oh, I don't think I could answer that.'

'Don't say your wife,' said Ebru.

Emilio was humorously outraged. 'You said your boyfriend!'

'Yes, but that is the privilege of the one who is brave and goes first.'

'All right, I will tell you,' said Shafiq. His eyes sparkled with daring. They all waited. 'Sophia Loren. I like the mature women.'

Michael imagined sleek brown thighs in old-fashioned stockings, with a little wrinkle just above the knee. 'I can see that,' he said.

'They are more . . . you know. The young ones are beautiful, but . . .' Shafiq was shy and his smile overwhelmed his face.

I know, thought Michael. You can't imagine that the young ones are really interested in you.

Ebru kept up the attack. 'Emilio?'

'My girlfriend,' he murmured under a sheltering elbow.

'Oh dear, so unimaginative.' Ebru was teasing.

'We are all being that,' said Shafiq.

'There is good reason for that,' Ebru replied. 'We would all like to sleep with many people. But there are consequences in doing so. I would only do anything if there were no consequences.'

Michael could promise. 'There would be no consequences. Nothing would change. You couldn't get sick, you could not get pregnant.'

Ebru chuckled at her own naughtiness. 'And my boyfriend could not find out?'

'Absolutely.'

'Then . . . I would consider sleeping with George Clooney.'

'Oh dear,' said Emilio. 'And not Anthony Edwards?'

'He's bald. I couldn't. Now it's your turn, for you to say.'

'Anne Heche,' said Emilio, with an air of finality and a grin that was frankly smug.

'Oh, but you know that she is a lesbian?'

Emilio's smile went hazy and naughty. 'Hmm, maybe I like that.'

'Oh. We are learning many things about each other. It is good to be social so that we can all get acquainted better.' Ebru plucked each word like strings on a guitar. She turned to Michael. 'OK, boss. This was your idea, now it is your turn.'

Michael grinned and thought: I'm the only one here who can actually answer that question.

He drew it out. 'Well. First. Hmm. Who would I ask first?' Michael crossed his arms. 'I *think* it would be . . . Mother Theresa.'

Emilio yelped. 'Mother Theresa!'

Michael surfed it. 'Is she not beautiful?'

'Yeah, but to sleep with?'

Ebru was pleased. 'That is a very clever answer.'

160

Emilio couldn't accept it. 'It would be like sleeping with ET!'

'Hmm,' said Michael. 'I hadn't thought of that one.' He pretended to consider the proposition, rubbing his chin.

Ebru was proud of him. 'You see, Shafiq, Michael likes the mature women as well.'

'And then, after that,' Michael announced, and all conversation stopped: Michael was going to give them more than one? 'I think it would be . . . Johnny Weissmüller from the Tarzan movies.'

Ebru's eyes widened, miming shock, but she was smiling. She already knew.

'Right on,' said Emilio, which raised further questions about Emilio.

'And then it would be . . .' Michael took an olive from the dish, and chewed it, and they all waited him out. 'Taffy Duck from *Dumb Duck, Detective,* and after that . . . mmm . . . a girl from my high school.'

Ebru laughed some more and applauded. 'You win first place for originality. So as first-place winner, you now have to answer the next question, Michael. Who here in the staff of the project would you sleep with if it was no harm done?'

Michael smiled and shook his head. 'Oh no.'

Ebru drawled, amused, 'Oh, but you have to answer. It is the contest.'

'Oh no I don't.'

'I will tell you one other if you tell me.'

'OK, I will then.'

There was a quick exchange of nervous glances. No one, male or female, wants to know that the boss fancies them. 'Oh my goodness,' chuckled Shafiq and mimed getting up to leave. Michael should have studied drama. He looked at each of them in turn. 'I have to tell the truth . . . and say . . . that . . . I don't fancy any of you.'

There was a general groan of disappointment.

'And now Ebru.'

'No, no. I don't have to say anything.'

'You asked me the question and I answered it honestly. You wouldn't want me to lie, would you? So now it's your turn.'

Ebru laughed and picked at her fingernails, which did not look as if they had polish on them until you realized they were perfect and translucent. 'OK. Then it is Sean Connery.'

'Oh, everybody fancies Sean Connery. I fancy Sean Connery,' said Emilio. Which was probably just a shade too devil-may-care for it really to touch anything private. Michael studied Emilio: fresh-faced, a big nose, a shock of hair. Pretty, intelligent, lively . . . but no.

Icons, thought Michael. Everyone offers up icons. They're impersonal and safe and they never change and, for the most part, you even get people agreeing with you.

'I've got one,' said Hugh. The sciences can sometimes produce people who are colourless to the point of invisibility. Hugh had to say it again, amid the general clatter of disappointment at Ebru's answer.

'Hugh's turn, everyone,' said Michael, who knew enough to keep alert to anything that told him about his staff.

The table quietened down. Hugh was pale, with perfect jet-black hair and a neck so thin that it looked as if it could not support the weight of his spectacles. 'I saw a girl once, across the big courtyard at UCL. She was beautiful. She wasn't dressed like a student. She wore what I imagine very chic French women wear to work: a kind of brown jacket and almost a mini-skirt. She had beautiful legs and medium-length hair that was very tidy, and she was talking to one of the professors. No, actually,' he smiled to himself, and moved the spectacles up his nose, 'she was *listening* to him. Really listening to him. This bloke was a bit of a bad-tempered old hippie, but she was obviously asking him really good questions or something. He was taking it all so seriously. And suddenly she said something, and he laughed.' Hugh looked up and away, his smile growing. 'He laughed and laughed, and shook his head. And she said something else, and he laughed even more.'

'And so you have dreamed of her ever since?' Ebru had the good sense to make that a question.

'I asked the professor who she was,' Hugh corrected her gently. 'And he asked me why, and I said it was because I thought she was the most beautiful girl in the world.'

Ebru's face softened and she leaned forward. 'Oh, it is a beautiful story.'

Hugh whispered, 'Her name was Constanza Regina de Alencar Vrena. She was from Brazil, but she had an Italian father and she was a business major. So, I went to her class and introduced myself.'

Hugh mimed it. 'Constanza? Hello, my name is Hugh McPherson and you don't know me, but I would like to ask you out.'

Ebru's grin opened wide. 'You did that? You asked her out? Oh, but this is very romantic.'

Hugh's smile veered sideways and his eyes turned inward. 'She couldn't speak English. She couldn't understand what I said. She'd been telling jokes in Portuguese.'

'What did she do?'

'She smiled sweetly and walked away.' Something strange was happening in Hugh's face. It was becoming beautiful: the fresh skin, the black hair. Tenderness suffused it. He looked at Michael. 'That is what I would do. I would use it to make restitution. For all the opportunities that I missed.'

The men I slept with, did they make a difference?

In his youth, Michael had imagined that he would be a traveller, visiting India, China and the Andaman Islands. Thailand was as near to it as he ever got. Mark knew a Thai art dealer who stayed in Michael's flat, and who returned the favour.

Michael went to Thailand in 1985, and spent the entire trip in an agony of unfulfilled desire. The Thais were sleek and smooth and friendly, but he turned them all down. He and the rest of the world were terrified of Aids.

Bangkok was not. The Thai friend took him to see shows where naked boys danced: some were slim and effeminate; others looked like samurai. They sat on Michael's lap wearing nothing but dressing gowns and jockstraps. He bought them drinks, and under the cover of their dressing gowns, they flipped their erect genitals out of the jockstraps and used the heads of their penises to give Michael's bare arms butterfly kisses. He still turned them down. His Thai friend shook his head in disbelief. Michael saw some of the other Europeans at the bar: outrageous air stewards who were going upstairs with one boy after another, or ugly Europeans whose faces seemed puffed out with disgust or greed. This, Michael thought, would be a terrifically easy place to get ill.

He went to the far north, to the Mekong and the borders with Laos where tourism ended. The Communist municipalities blared propaganda from loudspeakers across the calm river.

Michael walked along its banks, and heard Blondie coming from a Buddhist temple, as if competing with the Communists. On tiptoe he peered in through a window and saw fifty Buddhist monks in training, all in their teens, bopping to 'Call Me'.

He walked on, until an uninviting soldier with a gun waved him back. When he passed the temple again, the same monks were all lounging on the river bank, sitting on upside-down, beached boats. They were young, bored and falling out of orange robes with unfulfilled desire. Their naked shoulders had the colour and gloss of polished wooden floors.

'*Parlez-vous français?*' one of them called.

Michael did his best. It is a heart-stopping thing suddenly to be surrounded by admiring young men.

'*Vous êtes riches?*' the young monk demanded.

They all laughed and giggled, and adjusted their dress.

No, he said, I am not rich, I am a scientist. This was a mistake. The boys veered away from any possibility of being kept by a rich Westerner. Suddenly they wanted Michael for his mind. They had only the dimmest idea of what a scientist did. Michael tried to explain: something about the brain. They all nodded in respect and looked a bit ashamed.

'*Je suis pêcheur,*' said the one who spoke, his smile dim with shame. He was a fisherman.

'*Vous parlez le français beaucoup plus mieux que moi.*'

The smile widened. '*Je suis vietnamois. Tous les vietnamois parlent le français. Je suis réfugié.*'

The boy explained shyly: his father had worked in the French embassy in Hanoi. He was not allowed to move more than a mile from the town.

The boys were interested in Michael and so demanded what in the West would be considered personal details. Was he married? No? Oh, that is sad, children work for you. Do you have a girlfriend? Michael lied and said many: he had many girlfriends. The boys all cooed and laughed.

One boy kept pressing questions on Michael: did he live in a big apartment? Did he have many clothes? Did he drive an ambulance? The boy was very pretty indeed and paler than the others, with a rounder face. Ethnic Chinese, Michael decided.

'Voo lee voo dang see?' the soft boy asked. 'Noo avong ung fate.'

Michael didn't understand. The fisherman explained. *'Une fête. Avec la musique. Il veut que vous allez danser avec nous.'*

The boys all demanded it in unison. They made it clear that it would be an enormous privilege to dance disco with a real Westerner. Michael could also see that some of them were telling jokes about his height and girth and hairiness. They would see Westerners as big, clumsy, slow and indelicate. He very nearly said no, out of humility.

But he loved dancing. In fact it would be easier to dance with the boys than to talk with them. *'Ce n'est pas une problème avec vos maîtres?'*

'Non. C'est educatif! Nous dansons avec un savant d'angleterre!'

So Michael bopped to Michael Jackson. It was the most enormous, innocent fun. Michel danced a reel and a jig, which made them roar with laughter. Each of the boys in turn did something silly to make him feel at home. Some of them made goofy demon faces; a big thick-bodied youth nipped onto his hands and walked on them; one of them moonwalked.

And then the little ethnic Chinese began a traditional Thai dance. There was no mistaking the hand gestures; the covering of the face, the alluring postures, the hands held out to ward off unwelcome advances. He was miming a female part. The boys chuckled but Michael saw them looking sideways to gauge his reaction.

The boy tripped up to Michael and, fully in character, made some kind of declaration or assertion. Suddenly sick in his belly, Michael knew that something was being offered, something he wanted. He pretended not to understand. Befuddled, he turned to his Vietnamese host.

'C'est une danse. Une mise-en-scène.' The Vietnamese started to laugh. He caught the eyes of his fellows, and slapped his hands together and turned away, grinning.

No harm came. The little Chinese seemed in no way offended or embarrassed, nor were any of the boys. They went on doing their party tricks, until an adult arrived.

The masters pretended to be horrified that the boys had imposed upon the gentleman, and insisted that they must not bother him any longer with foolish things. The boys protested that this was a scientist from London. So the *maître* honoured Michael with Nescafé. Michael was seated on a naugahyde sofa in a concrete office with a tin roof that served more as an oven than a shelter. He used a tissue like a windscreen wiper on his forehead as sweat drummed down. He tried to piece together a serious conversation with the master, whose French was for the most part incomprehensible. Was it not true that science was now confirming the teachings of the Buddha?

When it was polite, Michael stood up to say goodbye and asked if he might say goodbye to the boys. The master's smile explained: not possible; boys at prayer. Michael walked past the long, cool stone chamber and peered in on tiptoe. It was empty. Michael marvelled at the courage and beauty of the Chinese boy.

So, now, in his London flat, Michael made a restitution. He put on his old copy of *Thriller* and called all the monks up into his sitting room. The air moved like there was a bonfire. Suddenly, there was an orange swirl like flame and his room was full of young men in loose orange robes, bouncing as if made of coiled springs.

Let it go, he told them, for it had been something of a missed opportunity for them as well. The orange robes spun free.

They were beautiful: small and slim with perfect complexions, or large and beefy with spots on their cheeks. Michael bathed in them. He ran his hands over the smooth skin as they rippled past him, over him, under him. They felt like warm waves, until his fingers found sudden clusterings of hair. Some of them knocked away his hands; others were more biddable, caught up in the excitement of the dance. With a kind of baffled wonderment, they let Michael proceed. Others even knelt around him.

After they were gone, whirling away in rippling spirals of air, Michael listened to the silence. They would now be thirty years old, seasoned. Michael thought of the small Chinese.

Michael called him up, as he would be now.

The man looked almost the same; he was still slim, with an hourglass waist. His face was not more lined, but it did look plumper and wise. He wore black trousers and a translucent blue shirt and now spoke rudimentary English.

'You're not a monk any more,' said Michael, disappointed.

'No. Only monk for two years. We do Army, also we are monks.' He smiled and nodded, and the implication was delivered lightly: better monks than military. He ran a nursery in Chiang Mai. He showed Michael his card. 'Orchids, fruit. Big palm trees for the city. Work for all the husband of my friends' servants. I am very popular man. The ladies can have their husbands join them from the north. And they work in shade.'

He showed Michael photographs of his house. It was an old-fashioned teak house with a huge garden. 'You know Thai fruit? My garden have rambutan, and jack fruit.'

Michael suddenly remembered. 'Oh yes, rambutan. They're like clusters of lychees.'

'You like music. Music, boom,' he said. He made Michael understand the teak house acted like wooden speakers on the sound.

It was good to have someone spend the night. The nursery-man who had been a monk curled up next to and around Michael like a cat. His body was still hairless and hard, but he had become far more butch as he aged. He overwhelmed Michael physically, and when he slept, he purred. In the morning, the monk's black eyes shone with affection.

'You come to Chiang Mai, you give me call,' he said, and placed a card on the bedside table.

'You won't know me,' said Michael.

'Say a friend recommend my nursery. To buy rambutan for England. I will get to know you. I have no boyfriend now. I will like you.'

Michael remembered to write down the name and address before he disappeared. After he left, the card had vanished. But the naturalized Thai name and the address were real and belonged to a real person.

It was not until later, travelling on the tube, that Michael realized how this differed from every other encounter with an

Angel. The Thai had said: the real me will like you. Could Michael go to Chiang Mai to find someone he had never actually met? What could come of a love separated by seven thousand miles? Harm? That had been Michael's experience of love.

There were other restitutions to be made.

There was, for example, Al.

When Michael returned from California, Al was in Michael's year. Al was Asian, his name was actually Ali, but he had been adopted and had a Western last name: Wilcox. His eyes slanted down at the outside corners. They were dancing and dark, and seemed to reflect Michael's eyes back at him.

In the last year at school, Al's adopted parents divorced, and neither one of them wanted an Asian child. So he was left in an apartment by himself. His parents told him they didn't want to disrupt his studies. He knew well enough that he had been purchased at age four to help glue their relationship together and that he could no longer serve their purposes.

Understand this: he lived alone at seventeen. At seventeen, you are always looking for somewhere to do it: the backs of cars, alleys, behind the pillars at clubs, in darkened archways if the need is strong enough. Al had a huge bed in the middle of a studio apartment that he had all to himself. Understand this: he was beautiful and wanted to be a fashion designer and he had a white girlfriend with a harelip.

Al kept her photograph on a chest of drawers. She was called Tabitha. Michael liked Tabitha: he was young enough to confuse feeling sorry for someone with real sympathy. The part of his mind that always fooled himself said: see how nice Al is? He is wise enough to like Tabitha despite the lip. How I wish, Michael's befuddled brain whispered, that I could find someone as nice as Al.

They had history class together, and when Al wasn't looking, Michael's gaze would be fixed upon him. They had art class together, and everything Al drew was women in beautiful clothes: Audrey Hepburn in cocktail dresses; Asian ladies in big flouncy party frocks.

Al was lean and slim and, like Michael, was on the cross-country team. Once, after a long late run, they were alone in the shower room, and Al had swung back the door of his locker. He was naked and erect and he looked at Michael in a strangely solemn way.

Michael smiled tolerantly. The front part of his brain said: my friend's body has run away with him. It's hormones, it means nothing. Michael fooled himself into thinking Al needed reassurance, that it made no difference to him. Michael chuckled and gave the head of the penis an admonitory tap, as if to say: I don't mind, but put it away, mate.

By now Michael lived in terror of his sexuality. Michael had conjured out of his big athletic body a big forgiving athletic heterosexual. The heterosexual lived and breathed and took Michael's place whenever he was needed.

Al, shame-faced, turned his back to him and dressed, hunched and quiet.

But Michael could not be acting all the time. He must have been sending signals. He must have looked into Al's eyes at lunchtime, and smiled a big kind loving smile, all unawares. Once in the boys' toilets next to the showers Al walked past Michael's cubicle. The cubicles had no doors and were open to view so teachers could check for smoking or drugs. Al stopped and smiled, and Michael, caught as he was on the toilet, his dick jammed down between his legs, couldn't help but grin back. In that grin, he could feel all of his yearning flash out of him like a sword. There was complicity in that grin; I like being naked around you. He felt his legs unclench and open.

Some time later, Al invited Michael back to his studio. It was tiny, with big windows with net curtains pulled back. Anyone on the street could see them. That meant nothing to Al. He lolled like a tongue on his double bed, having changed into something comfortable: a T-shirt and very tight satiny blue running shorts.

Michael was trying to be good. This nice innocent boy, he told himself: Michael, keep your eyes to yourself. Al tapped the bed for Michael to sit next to him. Michael perched on its edge at a distance from him. He didn't want to take advantage.

Al heaved slightly on the bed, arching his back. 'My parents are worried about my living alone. They are frightened that I might meet a homosexual.'

170

'Where do parents get their ideas from? I mean, even if you did, it's no big deal, and if the guy wanted anything you could just say no, right?'

Al nodded, holding his chin up. 'I could, yeah.' He edged closer to Michael. 'Have you ever met anyone . . . like that?'

'Naw,' said Michael, going into big and butch mode. 'No, I never.'

And in big, blurting butch mode Michael had stood up, afraid, away from the bed.

Al had sat up too, and suddenly swung his feet onto the floor. A few more things were said, and then Al announced, his face closed and wary, 'Anyway, I got my homework to do.'

And outside the studio flat, Michael stopped. Next door was the newsagents where Michael glanced up nervously at *Gay Times*. He had to lean against the wall, and he nearly doubled over in rage. At first, he thought that he was outraged that a pass had been made at him. Then he thought he was enraged at the betrayal of Tabitha. Then he was mad at himself and mad at Al, and he did not know why. A blinding headache spread across the breadth of his forehead.

Michael could not remember what happened afterwards. He and Al seemed to stop talking. Something happened to Al during the last year at school. Michael saw it only from afar. Al didn't study for exams. His dark eyes were clouded and encircled with bags of even darker flesh. His tie was askew, his school uniform was untended. Al wore it with the bitter swagger of the unloved, the outcast. He dyed his hair a muddy, brassy blond.

Michael supposed it went something like this: my adopted parents do in fact care about me. They know I am stranded between two cultures. They don't want me to have to guess where my birth parents were from, and read about those cultures in books. They are worried that I will have no self-esteem. They are concerned that I am young and needing to be constantly reassured, partly because they deserted me. My parents would be horrified to know that I am haunting parks and toilets and taking older men back to my flat and spending all night in clubs. They don't want me getting into drugs and cock rings. It's just that my parents won't do a single thing to stop it.

Sometime before A-levels, Al simply stopped coming to school.

Michael still had fantasies that he had become Al's lover and ended up living with him. They would have moved to Sussex together and found a bedsit in Brighton and Michael would have gone to university and Al to art school. He could see the Cure posters on their wall and smell the curries they would have cooked together.

Michael kept an eye out for Al. He had no interest in clothes, but he read the fashion pages even so. Michael saw young British-Turkish designers become famous, he saw young Italian-British designers move to French couturiers. Al was not among them. From time to time he looked in the telephone directory for Al Wilcox, or rather Ali Wilcox. He looked at the photograph of any young Indian designer, in case Al had changed his name. Silence.

And something in that silence delayed him calling up an Angel now. He had felt that kind of silence before when calling up an Angel.

What was it that someone said? Fashion was moving in circles now because all the talented young designers had died?

If Michael had said yes to Al, if they had become lovers, would it have made any difference? Would Al be alive? It would have made a difference to Michael. He could have practised being in love, making a home, being human and close. Even if it had come to nothing, he would have begun to grow up at seventeen.

I have a feeling Al can make no difference now to anything.

Michael came home from a day back at the university sitting final exams and telling students to turn off their mobile phones. He sat in his darkened sitting room and thought about Al. He crunched a Viagra like candy, and waited for his hour.

He was a little bit scared, and that was good. Being scared, Michael had realized, means you're learning. I can edit this like a film, Michael thought. I can cut to the chase.

The air swung back like a locker door, and Al stood revealed, naked and solemn. His eyes were frightened and serious. This was nothing like a body running away with itself on automatic erection. This was a needy seventeen-year-old who had made a decision that required him to show who he was.

'Come here,' said Michael. 'Sit next to me.'

Al came to the sitting-room sofa, and curled up like a baby, caching his nakedness and resting his head on Michael's lap. 'I missed you,' Al said. 'I missed you for a long time.' Al lay still, and closed his eyes with what looked like relief. 'You didn't get fat. You didn't get boring. You stayed Michael.'

Michael found he was able to lean all the way down to kiss the top of Al's head. 'What happened to you?' he asked.

Al said. 'I missed the train.'

'What does that mean?'

'Oh. It means I died.'

Michael's heart groaned. Not another one. Michael's heart was fed to bursting with this stuff. It was like the war, his gay generation's war. Why didn't it stop?

'How old?' Michael whispered.

'Twenty-one. One of the very first in London.' Al, still curled up, raised a hand as if volunteering. 'They didn't even know what it was.'

Michael had broken out into a sweat and he made a shrugging motion as if he were in harness.

Al's eyes glittered up at him. 'Why did you turn me down, Michael? I wanted to be with you.'

Michael said, 'Because I think that if I make a pass at someone, I'll kill them.'

The words popped out, like a pip squeezed from an orange under stress, hard and bitter and glossy. Michael ran a hand over his brow. The words, he realized, were true. Michael chuckled. It was a strange kind of laugh that bent him over in the middle.

'Now it looks like I kill people if I *don't* make a pass at them.' He managed a sick sad smile.

Al was shaking his head. 'You didn't kill me.'

'Then why do I feel sick? Why does sex always make me scared?'

''Cause you're screwed up. We're both screwed up.' Al hung his head. 'I killed me, Michael. No one else did.'

Al reached up and played with Michael's long, curly hair. He leaned his forehead against Michael's as if in submission or final rest.

For the first time in his life, Michael's cock responded to emotion. Yes, it was also the Viagra, but the blood pushing into the opened veins of his penis was driven hard by a sense of farewell, of wishing someone did not have to go. It was the emotion you might have if your faithful lover was leaving for a month. Michael's heart yearned up through his penis.

Al could sense it. Something quickened in his eyes and he arched his back. He stretched his legs and opened up like a flower displaying its pistils. Michael's face slipped down the length of Al's trunk and kissed Al's penis and went further down to the neatly folded anus. The front of Michael's trousers had soaked through. His underwear was difficult to peel off. Al's legs went over his head, and Michael entered him and strained within him to reach further inside. All Michael saw was Al's eyes, and his delighted smile.

Michael lifted Al up, still joined to him, and carried him to the bedroom. He settled Al onto the edge of the mattress, and he kept standing and watching himself making love and that looked like a miracle in itself.

And the air whispered again. It seemed as if restitution had been pushed even further. It seemed suddenly that afternoon light was filtered through old-fashioned net curtains in a single window. Michael blinked at the illusion and it remained for a moment. They were back in a studio flat in Romford. He blinked again, and the room sighed with relief of tension, and collapsed back into its ordinary self, as both Michael and Al came together.

Al took his hand and rested it against his leg. 'It wouldn't have made any difference, Michael. It would have ended the same.' His dark pupils were holes that seemed to go on forever.

'I . . . I could let you stay here, Al.'

Al blinked.

'You stay here. You could live.'

His black eyes reflected little pin pricks of light, diamond-bright. There was no light in the room that was that bright. Al's mouth worked, as if he were about to say something.

Michael pressed home. 'Stay here and live with me.'

Al stroked Michael's forearm. He cleared his throat. 'Michael. There is a place without time. And we are there before we are born, and there after it. We are born with wonderful potential, and we live, and while we live, we fulfil it. Or not. In any case, when you die you are completed.'

The light in those dark depths was even brighter. 'I'm complete, Michael. That's my story now.'

'You're saying no.'

Al smiled sleepily. 'I can say yes or no to nothing. You can make me stay. For what it would be worth to you.'

Michael did not want to lose him just yet. He held him, and pressed his face against Al's brown firm chest. And felt love yearn out of him again.

Michael rolled the duvet over them both. Al spent most of the night curled like a baby. The sky greyed and for some reason the song of the garden's blackbirds was replaced by the cries of seagulls. Michael was both awake and asleep, his body unmoving as lead, and his mind dull. Michael thought to himself: all right then, go now.

In the morning Michael sat up in his big bed. Right, he thought, and stood out of bed alone. That is it. I am fed up with all this tragedy. Henry, he told the air. You were right. God dammit, I want to have some fun.

And, as if in answer, the curtains round the bed stirred.

That night, after work, Michael called up Bottles again.

Bottles showed up in her punk Egyptian phase this time, wearing a Tom of Finland T-shirt showing two men tweaking tits. She wore a leather glove with studs that was clenched around a bottle of champagne.

There was the elaborate ritual of Continental kissing. It had scared Michael once. Then he saw: we were poor suburban kids trying to be different, smarter, sharper, harder.

'You're looking so old,' she said. 'That's a compliment.'

'And you're looking so over the top. And that's a compliment too.'

She smiled in approval. You don't take any shit if you want to sit at the right table. 'I bought us a bottle,' she said with a swagger.

Michael led her into the dining room, where there were champagne glasses. 'Babe,' he said, expertly feigning a seventeen-year-old feigning sophistication. 'Tell me. Who should I screw next?'

'A woman,' she said and blew out smoke. 'A woman definitely. It's just so naff being trapped with one sex.'

'Well OK, but who? I've already slept with you. If you count as a woman, that is.' He opened the cabinet for glasses.

Her face started out mean and bitchy. 'If you ever sleep – get to sleep with me and I get to – oh bollocks!' She stamped her foot, and started to laugh at herself.

'The line you're looking for goes: if you do sleep with me and I ever hear of it, I shall be very, very annoyed.'

She nodded yes, yes, I screwed up.

'The implication is that my dick is so small you'd either be asleep or you wouldn't notice.'

'All right.'

Michael had another one at the ready. 'It's a wonderful old joke, I haven't heard it in *months*.'

Being bitchy was such a simple, innocent game really. Why had he been so scared of it? Bottles laughed and gripped his arm. 'All right then, but at least I bought us a bottle.' She was suddenly the gauche loud girl of years before. 'And, just to complete the image of sophistication, I bought us . . . a couple of straws.'

And that made Michael laugh.

They sat down at the kitchen table and Michael expertly turned the bottle around the cork and not the other way around so it didn't gush. This impressed Bottles beyond all reason. 'Tch. I usually get it down my front. Here you go.' In went the straws. They had accordion bendy bits, which Bottles adjusted to face each of them.

'Honestly, it's like we're at an American soda fountain or something.'

She nodded and laughed, yes, yes, that was the joke.

Something about Bottles changed who Michael was. Around her, he was able to tell jokes. 'Do you want to put ice cream in it? I mean, really come on like an urban sophisticate.'

Bottles mimed laughter silently. Silence was her way of controlling what she knew could be an ungodly squawk. Silence did indeed give her a certain lacquering of dignity. She wobbled her eyebrows, stuck the straw in, looked him dead in the eye, and began to blow into the champagne, frothing it up. Bottles doubled up with laughter, and let rip a horrible, piercing screech of a laugh. Michael looked at her, maintaining a stone face. That set her off again. Just as she was recovering, he leaned forward as if in sympathy, to pat her arm.

'Suck, dear. Blow is just an expression.'

Bottles had probably arrived stoned, which might account for the callisthenic effect the next laugh had on her; she looked like she was doing some kind of warm-up exercise. Conversation took a back seat to the recovery of composure.

Bottles wiped her face. 'Oh, man, if you had done that back in 1977, you'd have been in a band.'

'Now then. You will recall, we were discussing who I should fuck next.'

'Indeed. And I have just the gel for you.' She was imitating some kind of school-ma'am. 'That American singer you like so much. No, not Julie Andrews.'

It was Michael's turn to laugh.

'The other one.' Her voice returned to normal, perfectly serious. 'The good one.'

Why are men satisfied
with whores?

There were some pretty weird radio stations in Southern California in the 1970s. They were meant to lose money. Tax-loss radio, it was called. Tax-loss radio broadcast from trailers or the basements of disused churches. The DJs played whatever they liked: Black Flag next to Tony Bennett next to Miles Davis next to Magazine.

Next to Billie Holiday.

At fourteen, Michael didn't really know who Billie Holiday was, except that maybe she was something to do with Motown. Lost in the doldrums of knowing no one in California, being a teenager, being gay, Michael suddenly heard a voice that sounded like he felt.

Jazz was supper-club music for people who wore slightly transparent socks and liked it when Frank Sinatra sang 'hot damn'. It was in old movies. And in this old movie-music style was someone singing about a lynching. *The bulging eyes and the twisted mouth*, drawled a slow, sad, horrified voice.

There was something relentlessly modern about it, like someone singing Brecht or a song about a serial murder. It was perfect, just perfect. It was cool. Michael could see himself coming back from California with that kind of music and being cool.

He reckoned that the stores in the camp would be good on jazz, so he went there and asked by name for Billie Holiday.

They stocked a lot of her product. By luck alone, he landed on the fifties album, *Lady Sings the Blues*. He read the song titles, which for the last time, would mean nothing to him: 'God Bless the Child', 'Lady Sings the Blues', 'Strange Fruit', 'I Thought About You'. Walking back to the bus stop, he met someone who was almost a friend, a Marine's son on the baseball team. With him was the coolest guy of them all, the son of a black officer. His name was Hendricks, Rousseau Hendricks, and he claimed to be Jimi Hendrix's cousin.

By now Michael's taste in records was a reliable source of scoring social points for the children of Marines. Nobody, but nobody, bought Julie Andrews records except Michael. So when the white kid said, with a hooded smile, 'What have you got now?' Michael had a sudden surging stab of pride. I'll show you.

Out came the blue album. 'Oh, man,' said the white kid in real embarrassment. The record looked old.

But Rousseau Hendricks looked up, his eyes widening. 'You bought this?'

'Yeah, it's got all her best stuff on it.' At least, that's what the guy in the record department said.

'And that's the best there is,' said Rousseau. The white kid scowled. Michael had scored cool points plus. Michael knew then that his instinct had been right; Billie was what he needed.

Michael returned to Britain and scored cool points all through his brief period of glamour. He played Billie Holiday for Bottles in the long magic afternoons before parents came back from work. It was like listening to the Bible.

'Oh, that is the story of my life,' Bottles had declared. It wasn't then, but it was soon to become so, for a while.

Later, Michael read the biographies. Her voice had not always been sandpaper; she had not always sung in a heightened style. The recordings from the thirties were smooth, dapper, even merry.

It was that Billie he called up. She arrived direct from 1938, having left the Artie Shaw band.

Billie arrived unfussed, plump and pretty in a blue dress with white polka dots. She sat down on the sofa, lit a cigarette, looked at Michael and crumpled forward. She leaned back, smiling, narrow-eyed and took one long draught of her cigarette as if it were a cooling drink.

'Oh, baby,' Billie muttered to herself. 'Man.' She shook her head.

'What?' asked Michael nervously. 'What?'

Billie blasted smoke out of both nostrils. 'You don't even know what you want, do you?' Somewhere there were nerves; she suddenly reached up to tug on her hair. 'You going to offer the Lady a drink or not?'

'Sure. Um. Whiskey? Gin?' Michael tried to remember what he had in stock.

'A Grand Slam,' she said confidently.

'What's that?'

'Oh, man,' she groaned again. She strode into his tiny kitchen. 'Where do you keep the hooch around here?' She started to mix the drinks. It was Michael who was fussed. Michael fussed around the cabinet and the ice-cube tray.

'So. You don't know why you called me here.'

'I . . . uh . . . a friend suggested it.'

'Um,' she said, sounding completely unflattered. 'Maybe I ought to meet your friend instead.'

'I . . . I'm supposed to be exploring sex or something, and I guess I'm trying to do justice to women.'

'Justice to women. My, my. You reckon that's possible?' Billie unobtrusively took down another glass and started making him a drink too. 'Looky here. This is how you fix a Grand Slam.' She showed him, and passed him the glass. 'Here. You look like you need it.'

'Thank you.'

'You're welcome.' She said it because it was good form to do so, and comportment was important. 'So. What do I get out of this?'

'Well, some people think it's neat being alive.'

'I never did think that life was *neat* particularly. Death's part of the deal. Why should I be happy to be resurrected as a whore? Hmm? When I spent all my whole waking life trying to make myself a Lady?'

Michael coughed, with unease. 'Yeah. I . . . uh . . . I'm a bit English and to us a Lady is some old bat whose great great grandfather was good at railways or killing people and who lives in a stately home.'

Lady Day suppressed a prejudice of her own, visibly swallowed it. Who were more ofay than the English? Then something like sympathy swam into her eyes.

'A Lady is somebody with dignity. And nobody can take that dignity away.'

Sympathy swam up in Michael as well. 'Did you get there?'

'Yes,' she said in a determined voice. 'Yes, I did.'

And Michael wondered: how much of her future does this Angel know?

Lady Day was concerned about this present. 'So you see why I don't accept this situation. I was a whore at fourteen because my mama had just become one too, and it was the only way to put food on the table. I didn't want to be no whore, I was made to be a whore, and a stupid white judge put me into the workhouse at fourteen years old. She didn't jail the men who paid me that fifty cents. They knew I was fourteen. They didn't go to jail.'

Smoke poured out of her nostrils like scorn.

'Men like you. White men who would never have a black gal in their house.'

It was not often that an Angel expressed active, positive dislike. Michael wondered what to do. He could send her back, but that would be chicken-shit. So, Michael told himself, hear the truth, tell the truth.

'Not men like me. Those men were seventy years ago. And they weren't gay.'

'Gay?' She scowled and was bumped from behind by a chuckle. 'What, you a whore too?' Then she was bumped by the truth. 'Oh, I get you. You're a pansy.'

'Yup.'

'Aw hell, there was a pansy craze not so long ago. A lot of clubs had pansy comperes. A couple of guys in bands were like you and they were always pretty nice except Moose. He always used to get drunk and mean and call everyone else a sister. He hated women though he was one himself.'

Twang. Like a guitar string something snapped. Billie suddenly stretched out like a cat finding a warm place to sit. 'So. You been whoring around.'

Michael explained. 'It's like a gift. I can sleep with anyone I want to. Alive, dead. Except they're not real.'

Billie coughed a cigarette laugh. 'Man, you won the male jackpot.'

Truth. 'I'm impotent and it's ruined my life so far.'

'Ruined, how?'

'My boyfriend's left me, and I'm not concentrating on my work.'

'Sounds like life, baby.'

'No. Not when I can call dead people back to life.'

Billie thoughtfully plucked a bit of stray tobacco from the tip of her tongue. 'So. You got yourself a calling. Nobody said being called was any fun. I got myself a calling. It kept me alive a long, long time after all I wanted to be was dead.'

She managed a smile, held up her drink and toasted it, toasted her inhuman calling, toasted Michael's calling too.

'There was this time, I was singing against Baby White at the Apollo. And all the Apollo wanted was fast-time stuff, and folks who sang like it was opera, and they thought I was just imitating Louis. So I got up there, and I dragged anyway. Dragged behind the beat. I did *not* knock 'em dead at the Apollo. Not 'til ten years later, anyway.'

She growled.

'And then, there was this session with Teddy Wilson? Now, Teddy Wilson didn't even like me. John Hammond made him do it and they fast-timed "What a Little Moonlight Can Do". What nobody knew is what I could do and that the session clarinet was a guy called Benny Goodman. He was a wild cat, in those days. They fast-timed and Benny and I just said to hell with it, let's cook. And we did. And I heard it slot together. I heard the angels turning the bolts. And I knew. I knew then I was the best, and I knew it was going to take time. That bitch Ella had a better voice and she left people happier. But I was going to be the greater singer. And I knew it would cost, I knew those bolts were just another jail. God was always going to want me for something.'

Billie took a deep breath. 'And now he's gone and done it again.' She smiled, drank in liquor and smoke and then announced, 'I know what you got to learn.'

Michael felt slightly forlorn. 'I wish I did.'

'You,' she said, bracelets clacking slightly against the glass, 'need to learn how to have a good time.' Her eyes brimmed with something like mockery, but it was not unaffectionate. 'Let's see. This is London, right? I bet you don't even know where the hot spots are.' When she said hot, she meant hot. This woman knew how to swing.

'This is how it works,' she told him. 'You go to the swankiest place you can find where they play good jazz, because that is where jazz makes its money, honey. But you talk to the guys, and they get to know you, and pretty soon, you find yourself invited to where the action really is, where the guys go to jam afterwards. That's where you learn the music. That's where you learn the life.'

The only jazz place that Michael knew was Ronnie Scott's. He'd been there once in his twenties and his main impression had been that it cost a lot. There was a sudden blurring, and Billie's hair was suddenly conked and plastered close and she wore a clinging white satin dress, and round her shoulders a perfectly unfake fox fur.

'Where's the gardenia?' he asked.

'Gardenia?' Her face did a comic double take.

'For your hair. Um. They won't know you're Billie Holiday without it.'

'Gardenia, huh. OK.' And one appeared. 'Folks will just say she can't afford a hat.'

'It'll be your trademark.'

She adjusted everything, and turned, Lady-like, to be admired.

'They'll think you're a drag queen.'

Michael had to explain that drag meant something different these days. Lady was not exactly pleased to be told she could be mistaken for a man. 'So how come you got hair like Norma Shearer?'

'A lot of guys have hair like that now. In fact, it's kinda old-fashioned by now.'

'Tuh. It's never-was fashion where I come from.'

Michael wore his only jacket, a kind of brown-green with a zigzag tweed, and Billie just laughed at it. 'I hope the whole town doesn't dress like you.' She touched his mane lightly, and then tried to jab it down into some kind of order. 'Actually, you know, that hair's kinda pretty. So one thing here is going to be OK. The boys are prettier.'

They swooped down on Ronnie Scott's in a taxi. The foyer was charmingly naff. It looked like something from a 1960s James Bond movie, hanging red plush curtains, black leather sofas and hundreds of photos of jazz stars on the walls.

Just inside the entrance there was an ordinary business desk and an old white guy wearing clothes like Michael's. Sitting on the arm of the sofa just behind him were a gang of people who had the air of working there, sharing jokes. They looked like James Bond too, in jackets, turtlenecks and medallions.

'Mmm,' said Billie, approvingly. For her this was swank.

A tall gangling man was leaning over the desk, signing in. 'I'm a guest actually.' For some reason he was carrying a single trolley wheel.

Billie nodded at the wheel. 'You play that thing?'

'It came off. I'm the bass player.' He shuffled with humility, skinny but with broad shoulders, big flat fingers, and Farah slacks.

Billie teased him. 'Bass player. You'd make more money playing a wheel. No bass player ever makes any money.'

The guys on the sofa laughed. An older black guy, speckles of white in his hair, stood up and chuckled. 'Specially the way you play, Jack.' All Jack could do was shrug and smile and escape. Billie was already one of the gang.

Except for the little old white guy behind the desk. 'Standing room only. Cloakroom's over there,' he announced. Billie slaughtered him with a glance.

'Isn't anybody going to take a lady's coat?' Billie demanded, giving them lessons in manners. She shrugged it off to reveal her finery. 'Alphonse?'

She had decided to call Michael Alphonse. It amused her to show up on the arm of a certifiable nerd. Michael felt like an

Alphonse. He took her coat and he geeked his way towards the tiny cloakroom.

Billie looked egregiously resplendent. The old black guy strolled towards her. 'You don't have to try that hard here.'

'Try? You call this trying? You should *see* what happens when I try.'

She amused him. He ushered her up to the **Please wait to be seated** sign, consulted his book, and ushered them into the club.

There were ranks of narrow tables with little lights, and brass rails between levels and red tablecloths, and old fashioned straw lampshades that Michael wanted to call Tiffany. There were German tourists in long green gabardine coats and trimmed white goatees; skinny intense young men with black sweaters; a waiter with an Eraserhead haircut; women with hair as long and heavy as curtains with Dusty Springfield mascara.

Billie was fascinated. 'Everybody looks so sharp.' For her, this was all from the future.

They were sitting near the stage, and the lights spilled over onto her. Billie strode languidly to the table, milking the distance across the floor, making sure the satin caught the light.

They were going to have to share a table. Three rather large black men looked up, less than pleased.

Michael pulled a chair back for Billie, scraping it too loudly on the floor, for which Billie admonished him with her eyebrows, even though the sound made everyone turn towards her. She descended onto the chair as if it were a hereditary throne.

Alphonse was quite a fun character to play. Playing him gave Michael front. 'I'm Alphonse,' he announced to the guys. 'This is Billie. I'm just her foil for the evening. We don't sleep together or anything.'

The guys blinked as if swallowing something.

Billie opened her evening bag and flourished a cigarette. 'I don't suppose any of you gentlemen have a light?'

The gentlemen looked at each other uncertainly. 'Uh. I'm afraid the club has a no smoking policy.'

'A what?' Billie was outraged.

'At least down here in front,' said one of the guys in glasses, exchanging a glance with his bigger friend.

'It's bad for you.'

'What is this a sanatorium? If it ain't one kind of prohibition, it's another.'

They kept talking. Yes, they were musicians, yeah they knew some of the band this evening, uh, well, yes they're *pretty* good.

'So where do they play hot jazz in this town?'

Dave leaned back in his chair and folded his arms. 'Well, I don't think there is any. There's cool.'

'Cool, what's cool?'

'Uh, after be-bop? Charlie Parker?'

Billie was fearless. 'You'll have to educate me, I'm from 1938.'

Dave's smile was a little wayward: OK, he would play along. 'You haven't heard of Charlie Parker?'

She shook her head. 'Where's he from?'

'Kansas City.'

'Hmm. Good town. Basie's from Kansas City. I toured with him for a while. Basie swings. But then, he has my man Lester.'

Dave cocked a big, brown, doubtful eye at her. This Lady knew her stuff, but she must be kidding, or just out of her mind.

Dave had big broad shoulders, and thick thighs, and a touch of a potbelly under a fine red woollen sweater. Just as an aside, Michael quite fancied him.

'Well. Charlie and Dizzy came up with this new style called be-bop. And then there was this guy Miles, who was in on the birth of the cool, which takes us very speedily to the 1950s.'

'1950s. Shoot. Jazz in the fifties.' Billie made it sound like the next century.

The band came on. Jack the bass player thunked away happily. The singer was a well-known Ella mimic, who clearly enunciated her way through a set of very standard tunes to approving, undisturbed applause.

Billie groaned. 'Doesn't anybody in this town swing?'

'We do,' volunteered another one of the guys, in huge unflattering thick-rimmed spectacles, and only then remembered to check with the others with a sideways glance.

Dave took over again. 'We're going someplace later, if you'd like to come along.'

They ended up in a drinking club downstairs in Goodge Street. Billie did no entrance routine there. She folded up the stole like it was a sweater and crammed it behind the seat and asked, 'You fellas want a drink?' Michael paid.

The guy with the spectacles turned out to be called Alphonse too. So Michael and Alphonse exchanged sympathies for the name. 'Bill, John, Richard, anything. I said, Mum, why Alphonse? She said it was because it was her cousin's name.' Alphonse had a cold. He sniffed and pushed his spectacles further up his nose. He looked at Billie at the bar and leaned forward to Michael and asked, 'How for real is she?'

Michael said, 'Get her to sing, and you'll be surprised how real.'

Alphonse said to Billie, 'He says I've got to hear you sing.'

'Does he now?'

'Well, I think we all do,' said Dave, smiling. Wickedly, they suggested 'Lady Sings the Blues'.

'What's that, I don't sing the blues. No, I want to have some good times.'

'Well, you tell us what songs you know, and I'll see if we can play them.'

They settled on 'Miss Brown to You'.

Alphonse played piano and the piano was vacant. It was vacant mainly because there really wasn't room to sit behind it. So Alphonse played standing up, wedged against the slightly peeling red paint.

Billie started to sing in a thin rough voice with a timbre like a trumpet. Their faces fell, and kept on settling. Billie snapped her fingers, she swayed in place, she nodded appreciatively when Alphonse took over, and said 'Yes, yes, YES,' while he played. Billie did everything that was naff and old-fashioned but it was somehow indisputably the real thing.

Dave and a Brazilian called Jorge looked at each other and shook their heads, startled, amused and slightly beside themselves.

The band from Ronnie Scott's came in, to much shaking of

hands. Dave swivelled all his attention on to them. There was laughing about the night's set, scornful dismissal of a colleague who hadn't shown up, a reference to Dave's domestic situation . . . everything that could help make Michael feel spare.

Billie sizzled back to the table, ready to snap up more people. Alphonse sat next to Jack the bass player and started to sparkle, his eyes and glasses gleaming.

It was past Michael's bedtime. He was in a dive with Billie Holiday, and he kept nodding off. He saw the rest of the evening in a series of fast cuts. He glimpsed Billie back at the table, wreathed in smoke, barking with laughter. He saw Billie with eyes shut, swaying as Al and Dave played together. Billie and Dave danced. Dave, looking fat and awkward, tried to keep up with a woman who could genuinely do the Lindy Hop.

Michael looked up at Alphonse and said in a voice that sounded like dirty tapeheads, 'I'm not really up to having a good time.'

Alphonse laughed, and unsteadily gripped Michael's knee. 'You look shattered, mate.'

'Work in the morning,' Michael remembered. His watch said 2.00 AM. He stood up and murmured excuses.

Billie jumped up and smooched him on the cheek. He gave her the keys and explained how they worked and made sure she had the address. 'You take care now,' she said and sounded like she meant it. Michael stumbled out into the balmy night air and somehow staggered safely across Tottenham Court Road to the flat.

Very suddenly he was alone in his own bed, and wide awake. He thought of a potbelly under a red jumper. He was very sure that the skin on the stomach would be smooth and warm and the flesh loose and gentle to the touch.

Experimentally, he called up Dave.

Michael asked him, 'I don't suppose you would ever normally consider sleeping with me?'

Dave looked surprised and responded, 'Not to be rude, but normally no. I've got a wife. And a girlfriend. My time is taken.' The Angel began to look about the flat and wonder how he got there. Suddenly his hand went to the bridge of his nose. Knowledge had come to him. 'I'm . . .' he stopped.

The Angel sensed what he was, and therefore, what Billie was. 'That means that she . . . she really is . . .'

Michael nodded yes.

Dave bowed slightly to the miracle. Suddenly he chuckled, as if surprised by something. Smiling, he sat down next to Michael and reached up and pulled off the sweater. The real miracle was not that the Angels had physical presence. The real miracle was that no matter who they were, they wanted Michael.

Michael looked at the swollen belly covered in tight curls and remembered the clunking way Dave danced. It sometimes happens that when you see the body, desire burns away like a fog.

Michael remembered who he had spent the evening actually talking to. He remembered glasses and the coincidence of nick-names, and a hand on his knee. He called up Alphonse. Alphonse smiled sweetly and evidently did not need a miracle to make him say yes. There was no potbelly under his jumper. Michael did have a good time after all, within his limits.

Billie trawled her way back at breakfast time. Michael was downing repeated cups of coffee in an effort to jolt himself awake. Billie was listless, dragging her stole across the carpet. Michael told her, 'Go sit in the sitting room, it's more comfort-able. You want a cup of coffee?' Tame, somehow, she turned and went into the front room with its sofas and bay window, and she slumped, staring.

'Worse for wear, huh?' he said, trying to keep his own pecker up.

She shook her head. 'It's not that,' she said, and accepted the coffee. 'We all went back to Dave's place and they played me this stuff.'

She shook her head again, and sipped the coffee. 'Man I heard metronomes with more swing than that stuff. What did they call it?'

'Hip hop? Drum'n'bass?'

'Drum'n'bass. Man. I mean we had technology. We got mikes. We used it to make music more human. The mike meant you didn't have to shout at a song and deafen it. You could

189

seduce it, make it relax and start talking to you. I mean that stuff don't even have songs. It just goes tick tick tick as fast as it can. There ain't any time even for a tock.'

She rubbed her eyes.

'In the future,' Billie Holiday said, 'there will be no such thing as swing.'

Michael heard sadness in her voice, and sat next to her.

Her eyes didn't blink. 'It's all gone. My whole world. My music. There are no little clubs like I remember. The life isn't there, even the black folks've got their mortgage in the morning. They all think I'm just play-acting for a while. They don't know I'm stuck in it, up to my knees.'

Billie looked up at Michael. 'Guess what I'm saying is easy. They're all dead: Prez, Bean, Fletcher. We're just stuff in the history books that a few professors play.'

Michael put an arm around her. 'Everybody plays you, Billie. Anyone who likes music at all plays you.'

'Big deal. I'm talking about how a whole world can die.' She sighed and patted his leg. 'I get fragile sometimes. I get fragile and I slump back. Or I get high. You got anything other than hootch?'

Michael shook his head, no.

'Good boy. Keep it that way for mama. That stuff kills.' Billie sighed again. 'I would like to think that this had some kind of point. If I did sleep with you, what else would you learn?'

'I think I'd be like one of those standard tunes that you first have to teach to be still before you can teach it to swing.'

That's what she did. She kissed him as if he were a microphone, to amplify and quieten at the same time. He lazed in her grasp, kissed her beautiful breasts, let himself be played. Nothing much happened, except that it was happy and sad at the same time.

Even the way she made love was old-fashioned. No biting of nipples, no women on top. When Michael didn't get erect, she just shrugged.

'Between the booze and the scag, baby, half the men I've been with couldn't get it up. And in the end this is what they wanted, just this human touch.' Her fingernails traced some-

190

thing on his chest, like a child's drawing. 'I mean that is what this is all about, baby. People want love. I think I find it sometimes, but then it always seems to go away again. I get mean. Or worse, I turn into a doormat and eat my heart out for some worthless slicker.'

The hands suddenly seemed seized and she looked up. 'That's what I don't understand. Men and women, they're no different. They both want love. So why do you take it, this miracle of yours?'

'Take what?'

'Substitutes. The quick fix. Hell, opium is a better deal. I mean if I were you, I would go tell God to go monkey with somebody else's life. How is it that you men are so easily fooled?' Her eyes were outraged; she pulled back from him.

'What is it, Billie?'

Her head was doing quick little sideways shakes, rejecting something, fighting her way through it. 'That *look* on a trick's face when he's had a fourteen-year-old girl, and she's hated every second of it, but she's just kept smiling and smiling because she's scared and her mama needs the money. She been dry through the whole thing, and he sure as hell knows what that means. But he puts on his socks that his wife washes for him, and you know? He looks perky. He looks pleased. He looks like he's just had something real special and sweet from that young girl.'

Billie slumped back, shaking her head, now a slower gesture of stupefaction. 'Why are you fooled, baby? Why are men fooled by whores? We hate you sons of bitches.'

Michael was saddened. 'Do you want to go now?'

'Yes. Now.'

Billie stood up as if her joints were aching. Her eyes were desolate. Suddenly she was back in her polka-dot dress, as if it were a home or a bad habit. Her history, Michael saw, was always dragging her down, behind the beat.

'Anything I can do for you before you go?'

Her mouth did a disparaging downward turn that was also somehow amused. 'You keep talking about Angels. When I was a little girl, I always wanted to see an Angel.'

191

There was a swelling in Michael's heart that seemed to flower out into the world. There was a crackling sound in the air, as if roots were growing in speeded-up time. The air in the room blossomed. Petals of light unfurled.

In the centre of them stood Henry. The unfurling continued. Wings rose up behind Henry's back, silver and fleecy. Henry wore a 1930s dinner jacket, and on his arm, ready, was the silver fox fur.

'I'm just your foil for the evening,' said Henry.

Billie dipped slightly, calm smoothing her round high brow. She did her downward smile, pleased and gracious.

In December of 1938, Billie played downtown in a club called Café Society. Her new style transfixed the President's son and white society ladies who had married for money. In 1939, she recorded a draggy song with the Café Society Orchestra about a lynching. Columbia had refused to record it. In Britain the BBC banned it. Nevertheless, the first time the world heard 'Strange Fruit', it ground to a halt.

'My stole, please,' Lady Day asked the Angel.

Henry held it up for her and she slipped delicately backwards into it. Henry said, 'I'll take you to where the band is playing.'

The two of them walked arm in arm towards Michael's wall. He could see them walking well into the distance beyond the wall. Could he hear an orchestra? He saw Billie laugh and place her head briefly against her escort's shoulder. Girlish and lady-like, she did a little skip of joy, and told a joke that made the Angel laugh.

Do blondes have more fun?

So.

Michael finally went out and had some fun. There really was, on the face of it, nothing else to do.

He got his final marks for the first year of his degree in Computer Science and they were surprisingly bad: a 68 per cent overall. Despite his hours of programming, Michael had not performed well on the final.

I don't have the time to study, Michael realized. Suddenly he knew that he wouldn't start the second year in September. It was as simple as that, as simple as a flower opening. It didn't even feel as if he had made a decision. He felt relieved by the simplification of his life. He had other things to do.

Michael called up the entire New Zealand All Blacks rugby team. They looked so big and beautiful from a distance. Up close they were bulky and hairy and broken-toothed.

Michael pulled down one pair of black shorts to reveal a round, hard tummy and perfectly ordinary white genitalia. Michael knelt in front of them. The favour was returned. 'They're kinda sweet,' said the player, in mild surprise. 'It's not that bad.'

Michael called up a famous Maori player as broad as he was tall. The Maori's eyes glittered with something between rage and panic. He kept jumping; the miracle spooked him; desire was an affront. Michael assured him that all would be kept secret, that no one would ever know. In practice, the Maori was far more passionately accepting than his teammate had been.

To Michael's surprise, the warrior presented himself face down on the bed. Crowned with a Viagra headache, Michael prised open the boulder buttocks and pushed himself inside. It was like fucking a turtle; the brown back was sectioned with so many muscles it looked like a shell in patterns. The body was not used to being penetrated. The sphincter clenched and squeezed. This had an unfortunate effect of trapping blood in Michael's cock, making it bigger. The drag of inner wall across the head of the penis made Michael gasp. The Maori's face was contorted in pain, and suddenly, in one lunge, he extruded Michael's dick. Michael came while being pushed backwards.

The Maori left Michael with a quick post-coital word. 'Maori men don't sleep with each other. It messes us up. We sleep with white guys, and there is less contention. Thanks.' The Angel gave Michael a hearty athletic slap and rolled to his feet. His air of expectation left Michael no option but to fade him out.

It was a madness of the spirit to call up Harry Houdini. Michael had seen a nearly nude photograph of him in a review of a new biography. Houdini had loved his mother and loved being photographed wearing as few clothes as the law of his day allowed. The body in the photographs was without fat in a way that modern bodies never are. Despite the rounded muscles, Houdini looked malnourished, pale, and as hard as polished marble.

Michael called him and Houdini somersaulted into Michael's sitting room wearing baggy bloomers. He smelled of the past: sweat, hair oil and sauerkraut. Houdini pulled down his bloomers and begged, 'Photograph me! Photograph me!' The genitals were lost in a tangle of fur and looked unused. Michael coaxed him to the sofa. Michael touched his chiselled chest. No, no, it was all too awful, he could not contemplate it, though he writhed in Michael's grasp with the thrill of being exposed.

All Houdini wanted was to be stripped and bound and photographed. It was a bit cruel, but Michael explained to him, in halting German, that he could never be photographed. Then Michael sent him back to his mother.

Michael's greatest mistake was great indeed. He conjured up Alexander the Great on a wet Sunday afternoon.

It was just after a phone call from Philip. Philip hadn't found a place to live yet. Would Michael mind keeping his things a while longer? Michael now wanted nothing more than for every trace of Philip to be gone from his life. 'I've bought a whole new set of crocks,' Michael said. 'I need the space. I'll put yours in the basement, OK?'

'Yes, all right, thank you,' said Philip and his voice still chimed: take care of me, protect me. 'Could you pack them carefully? I mean it would be great if I could just come and collect them and they were all packed.'

'Come and pack them yourself,' said Michael. 'I won't break anything, Philip, but I do have other things to do!'

The call left him shaken and annoyed. No doubt they both wished their old lives could evaporate painlessly. It wasn't going to be like that. Michael found himself reaching for the whiskey bottle. He stopped himself. No, Michael, those are the old days.

Energized by anger, he did the craziest thing he could think of. Years before he had read, in floods of tears, *The Persian Boy*, Mary Renault's novel. As if tearing the reality of the London flat and his old life into tiny pieces of paper, Michael reached down in time, for Alexander the Great.

He could feel time, its depth and chill, as if he were reaching down the air vents of a seven-storey underground city. He could feel its dank breath on his face. The London air in his flat rumbled and rolled back like a giant stone in a tunnel passageway.

Something tiny and hard and alien thrust itself into his sitting room. Its eyes were wide and staring. It wore a crown of green and its skin was a battered, polished brown like an insect's shall. For just a moment, Michael thought he had called up a Martian by mistake.

Then he blinked and the thing came into focus as a human being. The crown was blonde hair, filthy and in spikes; the shell was leather armour. The saucer eyes still stared.

Alexander moved like a lizard, in swift halting gestures. Michael almost expected him to flicker a serpent tongue. He demanded something in a high, harsh voice that reminded Michael of dried and broken grass.

When Michael didn't answer, Alexander strode to the window and looked out. A car sighed past below. It was Alexander who honked like a horn in amazement, and his head jerked upwards, looking at the top of University Senate House, towering high. Alexander turned, glanced once at the ceiling, marched towards Michael, wrenched Michael's arm behind his back and pressed a sword against his throat.

Alexander barked at him again like a dog with its vocal cords cut. The stench from the mouth was appalling: rotten teeth, rotten meat and bad wine. Michael backed away, beginning to babble in terror. Alexander the Great sniffed him, or rather the smell of soap and deodorant.

Perhaps it was the scent that stopped him killing Michael. Nothing so flowery could be a threat. Alexander pushed him away, and strode out into the hallway. He saw the front door.

'I'll open it for you,' said Michael.

Alexander the Great knew nothing of doors or locks. He fumbled at the handle and its tiny knob for only a second or two, and before Michael could do anything else, he had jumped back and raised a horny, sandalled foot. Alexander kicked twice at the lock. The door could only open inwards, which meant Alexander had to shatter the lintel. He did it with the third kick, peeling back most of the frame around the door, and springing the hinge mounts free.

Alexander made a grave cry of triumph, and shouldered his way through the gap.

Michael was left panting. He thought of elderly neighbours being pushed out of the way by a drunk, mad, ancient Macedonian, and he whispered Alexander down to his own world. As if the doorway had blinked, the door and lock and hinges were back in place.

Well, thought Michael, at least it puts an inconvenient ex-boyfriend back into perspective.

And just this once, perhaps, a shot of whiskey was not uncalled-for.

Michael remembered his treasured issue of Q magazine, the

one with the nude photographs of Terence Trent D'Arby. As an antidote to Alexander, Michael called him up.

In the flesh, honey-coloured and slim, the Angel deferred and demurred. 'It's not really my thing but do what you like,' he said, amused. He smelled of lanolin. Michael rested his head on the soft belly and rolled his mouth back and forth around the apricot-like head of the Angel's penis, soothing semen out of him. That tasted of apricots too. Michael slept, with his cheek still resting on the Angel's stomach.

Michael had yet more mistakes in him. The next weekend, he called up the Bay City Rollers. OK, they were a thing from Michael's youth. They were even weedier in the flesh, and the clothes, all cut-off tartan and pixie collars, were more twee than Michael remembered. They smelled of stale crisps and had spots on their backs and Michael sent them packing before they had fully unpacked.

So he called up two Nuba wrestlers from Leni Riefenstahl's photographs. They were naked and enormous and frankly had no idea what it was Michael wanted to do with them. So he sat back and watched them wrestle naked in his sitting room. They slammed into each other like bulls, their rolls of muscled flesh rearing up and settling back in waves, and their elongated penises flying like flags of victory.

Michael conjured up a plumber who had ripped him off. Andy, he was called: broad-shouldered, athletic, with cute button eyes. He had a number-one cut and he had known Michael fancied him. Andy took advantage.

Andy tore up the bathroom floor and removed the toilet. Then he disappeared for four weeks. Michael had to hire a chemical john, like it was a camping holiday. Michael still fancied him when he came back, so he let him finish the job and paid him; only then did the new toilet back up and flood.

Such was the power of love that Michael hired Andy to instal the new fireplace, with its fake gas fire. It had a marble pedestal. Andy had to cut the rug, and got the measurement wrong, and cut away too much. Bare 1890s floorboards showed all around the polished stone. Michael traded the old pedestal for a larger one and paid the difference. Andy somehow managed to break the replacement in half. At this point, Michael finally sent him packing.

It was the most terrible abuse of power to make Andy's Angel lower his trousers and take it. It was as if the whole home-maintenance misadventure was finally worth it: we both get what we want. The Viagra worked a treat. A migraine blurred Michael's vision of his own cock plunging in and out of Andy's sculptured derriere. He even had the satisfaction of making Andy come when fucked.

'This isn't my usual sort of thing,' said Andy, confused.

Michael cooed in his ear, 'Maybe not. But you liked it. Do make sure the real Andy knows that.'

National Geographic had been one of Michael's few sources of thrills when he was younger. He remembered photographs of bountiful Amazonian Indians. They arrived squat and square with burnished hairless bodies. Michael finally got to see and touch what had been airbrushed out of the colour spreads. The Amazonians were amazingly loving and affectionate. They rolled over and over with him, giggling and teasing and kissing him, and pressing their foreheads against his so that they could stare into Michael's black eyes. They started to sing to him; rhythmic huffings and clickings and poppings that somehow expressed both energy and longing. When it was time for Michael to go to work they refused to release him. There was a long protracted ritual of goodbye. They clung to his wrists and made elaborate pleading noises. They encircled his midriff and pulled him back down among them, and gave him a breakfast of love. They made him late for the lab.

Michael called up Ernest Hemingway from a photograph of the old gent in his bathtub, proud of the erection that peeked over the top of the tin basin. Michael preened it and stroked it, and found that even after a few minutes' conversation, Ernest Hemingway was a black hole of boredom. Every single hearty thing he said – God knows, about bulls or fishing or shooting or his war wound or the nurses who tended him – struck Michael as phoney. Hemingway really seemed to think that shooting, fishing and boxing were what made you a man. When not having erections was his real problem.

Then there was the man Michael had glimpsed in the changing rooms of the Oasis public baths when he was ten years old. The man had been blond, pale, athletic and embarrassed, quickly lowering trunks and pulling on underwear. He showed up in his swimsuit, full of early-seventies misgivings. He kept jumping in Michael's embrace, nervous, uncertain, still not really believing that it was legal or decent.

There was the lead male actor of the old silent film *The Crowd*, angelically beautiful and distant. And in person, blind drunk.

There was the fruit-and-vegetable man who in 1977 first told Michael about the Clash. Then he had seemed an adult, all of nineteen years old. He had a head of permed hair that looked now like a joke wig, and huge beautiful front teeth. It was his face Michael remembered. The slim and rather indifferent body seemed to melt into the sheets. But he and Michael stayed up late drinking lager, playing the Pistols, the Clash, the Jam, the Vibrators, but they decided, finally. The Buzzcocks were best.

There was his barber, Italian and sweet, on whom Michael had had a crush all through childhood and who, to give the adult Michael a better blow job, pulled out all of his even white false teeth. His gleaming toothy smile had been why Michael fancied him.

There was even the porn star Brad Rodger, who looked impossibly beautiful in publicity photos. In person, he was tiny and slim with a dick that was large only in proportion to the rest of him. Worst of all, he was, not to be prejudicial, quite the stupidest person Michael had ever met.

'I really would like to do some serious roles.'

'You're kidding,' said Michael. 'You can't really think you'll get into serious acting doing the kind of thing you do.'

'I make up all my own dialogue, you know. I mean, I really improve those parts.' His voice did not rise and fall like a normal voice. Brad whined, like a caricature of the beautiful nasal stars wiped out by talkies. 'Like once, you know, they wanted me to say, like, oh give it me, give it me. I mean, what kind of line is that?'

Michael had to admit it didn't sound particularly original.

'So I changed it to fuck that ass baby. Fuck it hard. I mean, you know?'

Michael did his best with Brad Rodger, before the Viagra side effects began to grind away behind his eyes. He looked into Brad's pale blue blanknesses and decided it was too much like fucking a particularly pretty sheep.

There was the sweet Afghani who had asked him for instructions in the street, with unshaven stubble, and a slightly baffled air. Michael had held him in conversation. His name was Mustafa, and he was here studying engineering. His home was now rubble; his brother had been killed. 'My heart goes out to you, for being my friend,' he said. On his forehead was a callus where it habitually touched the prayer rug.

Michael called up Mustafa's Angel and found his only desire was to leave the innocence undisturbed. They sat eating chocolates and holding hands. And when it came to leave, Mustafa kissed him on the forehead. 'I love you,' he managed to say.

Michael was confused. 'Do you want to make love?'

Mustafa looked surprised, then coy, if not unpleased. 'Oh no. No, no,' he said, in a gentle voice a bit like a pigeon's. 'No. We . . . become romantic with each other.'

Michael saw in his eyes, a pleading: I want, but if I do, it cuts out the heart. Leave me the heart.

There had to be somewhere and somehow a way to combine the two, the heart and the body.

You discover two things if you can sleep with anyone. The first is that life is bountiful. It is more bountiful than an orchard at harvest time; more abundant than a pick-your-own field of strawberries that stretches beyond the horizon. The harvest of human genitalia attached to reasonably good-looking, reasonably behaved people is inexhaustible.

No matter how completist you are, you cannot collect the entire set. It grows too quickly: there are a half-billion penises in India alone. Like a kaleidoscope, ever blossoming, more and more genitalia, more and more beauty, unfold at high speed out of the old.

We walk around blind to prevent ourselves seeing this

bounty. Its vastness diminishes us; its availability makes not only ourselves but our love seem arbitrary accidents. If we did more than only glimpse it, it would drive us mad.

Secondly, in contradiction to this, you learn how rare attraction is. We don't sleep with most people, because we would not remotely enjoy sleeping with most people. They smell, they fart, they occupy our space, all the things people we love do and which make us leave them in the end. Only, we don't understand what these strangers mean. Their preoccupations are alien to us. We are unmoved by the thing that most moves them. Their genitalia look shrivelled, hairy, forbidding.

Only sometimes are there exceptions.

Michael thought again of monks, and remembered his time in California. He had often visited an old Spanish mission surrounded by fields and an ancient graveyard. It was the only thing in Oceanside that a Brit would recognize as history, and it was shaded and cool. In the old storerooms there were exhibits of early California life: dummy Indians grinding maize; a replica of a colonial bureaucrat's office.

The mission had been restored in the 1930s by monks. They smiled out of old photographs in the historical exhibition. Unlike most people in old photographs, they looked contemporary. You could see who they were. They were all in their thirties or forties, some plump, some slim. But they all looked secure, satisfied, and even merry. They looked happy slaving in hot sun while wearing thick woolly robes. They sang or joked in photographs posed to demonstrate the robust Christian life. It seemed unlikely even to Michael at sixteen that they could all be quite that good-looking by accident.

Michael invited them all home. It was a Thursday evening and he made a party of it. The Californian monks had come from Spain, from Costa Rica, from Ireland, and they sang romantic 1930s songs on the guitars that came with them. They made something like sangria with a different name and became boisterous. The Irishman sang an old love song in a high and wild voice that was only slightly off-key. They began to dance arm in arm around his apartment floor until the downstairs neighbours thumped on his door.

'It's a religious gathering,' Michael told his neighbours and invited them in. The neighbours were Polish and rather shy. Michael knew them only well enough to nod to in passing in the corridor. He learned their first names: Thadd and Marta Miazga. They spoke a strained and cautious English and were overwhelmed by the ten thumping, handsome monks who sounded like a jolly tower of Babel and who wore robes and sandals, and who welcomed them with cries and kisses and resumed their religious songs, as if around a campfire. At one point Mrs Miazga slipped out of the flat and returned with more wine. At 1.00 AM her husband shyly took the guitar and started to sing 'Good King Wenceslas' in a tired, happy voice. Michael suddenly saw that he was handsome too, and his wife. In fact everyone in the world suddenly seemed beautiful.

Finally, someone glanced at a watch. The Miazgas had hatched out of their shyness, into a pleased, flushed conviviality.

'It is so silly to be neighbours and not know,' said the wife, in a voice like someone drawing a bow across violin strings. Silly not to know that our neighbour is jolly and pleasant. They had become, at least potentially, friends.

All the monks gathered round them in the hallway, and shook hands and kissed Mrs Miazga good night. They all chorused good night, and then were gone.

Silence fell like a curtain. Michael sipped some wine, and considered and called back the Irishman.

The Irishman had a mop of straw-coloured hair, and a classic profile and milk-white skin. Michael felt woozy with sociability, wine and a broad and generalized love of the world. He popped his Viagra, and asked the Irishman to lie down next to him. The Irishman tumbled into his arms as naturally as dice, his legs crossing over Michael's. He rested his head on Michael's chest and started to talk.

His name was James. He had grown up in Clonmel in Eire. From the way he described it, the town was almost medieval: a big Spanish-looking church by a river; peasants, weekend markets, horsecarts in the streets, cattle fairs. Like other children he had swum in the river, toppled outhouses, stolen and smoked cigarettes, and attended mass. Then he had fallen in love with God. He wanted to be dedicated to God. Half asleep, he used the word 'married'.

Then his neck arched upwards, yearning, and Michael kissed him. The young monk kissed like a woman, almost chastely, shyly. He ducked away, like a nervous horse. Waiting for the Viagra to take effect, Michael asked him questions. Yes, he had been in love once. While still living in Clonmel, he had fallen in love with a married man.

'A great big fella with a handsome moustache. He'd go riding past in his plus fours on a bicycle, and he was the handsomest thing you'd ever seen. And he always grinned at me. And then he started stopping by to talk. And I realized there was this look in his eyes. And I thought no, it can't be, he's a married man. Either that or he doesn't realize. So we did nothing about it. And one night I was walking in the moonlight. It was a beautiful night, and I was just out for a stroll. And I heard his bicycle coming. Brother James, is that you? he asked. And I just said, Hello, Georgie my dear, because my heart was full. He took me off into the hedges. I still didn't know for sure what he was going to do until he took my hand.'

Scandal had been an ever-present danger. They had to pretend hardly to know each other. They would meet once a month, when George had a good excuse to be away from the farm. Once they were walking along the road hand in hand, when the last thing they expected in the world, or at least in Clonmel, came roaring up the road: a motor car. Its headlights blazed. They dived into a ditch, and the car roared on past.

James and George saw the car parked outside the local hotel and heard roars of laughter, and decided not to go in. Ah, it would be a great story to tell. Apparently the driver told it, roaring with laughter, buying drinks. These two fellows, he said, one of them a monk, and they both dived into a ditch! Maybe they thought it was the crack of doom.

The locals knew. Two men, one of them a monk, did not walk out together at night. The publican and his regulars neither knew nor really cared who the man was: likely a substantial citizen. But a monk was not exactly a man; if he went with other men then he was a monk who was doing the Devil's work.

'Would the monk be having blond hair?' asked the landlord, which earned a roar of steely laughter.

James was called into the Abbot's office, and the story of the motor car recounted as if it had happened to someone else. The Abbot said nothing too direct. A few of James's unexplained absences were noted, and he was asked, in the kindest, most helpful way, if perhaps he would not be interested in an exciting mission to California.

'So that was the end of George Kelly and me.' James seemed quite cheerful about it. 'At least I got out of Clonmel. And into all that sunshine.'

They kissed again, and the Viagra moved into the bed with them. James became suddenly demanding and masculine. In the street lights, Michael saw the outline of his lean stomach. Michael counted the years. If James were still alive, he would now be over ninety years old. James entered him.

I hope you found someone, James. I hope the sun and the sea and the health of California urged you to throw off your robes. I hope you moved to Santa Monica and met Christopher Isherwood, and set up a retreat in Big Sur. Or that you and one of your brother monks quietly and discreetly tied the knot. I hope you played guitar around campfires for many years to come, and that your God reciprocated your love.

Or maybe I'll wish even you another life in which George Kelly goes after you and comes whistling up to the mission over the brow of a California hill. I think I'll see that and wish it, and then I'll put you both there. Somewhere else.

'Good night,' said the monk, and kissed him again. 'I'd like to go home now, if I may.' He went with a sound of a whisper in the air,

It was two in the morning, and Michael was left alone.

The miracle was a wonder, but what good was it if it left you alone? What good did it do you if it meant you had no one in your life. What had Billie said? People want love?

'Henry?' he asked. 'Henry, are you there?'

Henry, naked, was suddenly at the foot of the bed, his wings folding shut.

'Henry,' Michael began shyly. 'Henry . . . could there be two of you?'

Henry rested his chin on his hands, tossed the tousle of his hair away from his face. 'There already are,' he replied. 'Me and the one asleep with Philip.'

'Well. If there are, could one of them live with me, too?'

It wasn't a handsome face, but it was a good face, and it widened in sympathy and a kind of amusement. 'You know the answer to that is yes. But is that what the miracle is about?'

'I don't know what it's about and I don't care.'

'Oh, you do care. Because you know that the universe can't keep twisting itself into new knots just to keep you happy.'

'That's why I want it to stop. I'm sick of people who fade out.'

Henry smiled. 'You're sick of Angels then. And what am I, Michael?'

Michael closed his eyes and sighed.

'Maybe it's time to try your wings,' said the Angel, and smiled.

Who's for real?

In the last days of his marriage to Phil, as promiscuity took hold, Michael often went to Russell Square.

Usually, he would be a bit drunk, having spent an evening with one of his own few friends. The controls would be switched off. Usually the controls warned Michael that what the Square contained was dangerous. Drunk, he didn't care.

In the early nineties, the untended shrubbery would be full of groups of men, some on their knees, others with shorts down. It was a curiously generous place, where strangers would give their all, or what they could.

A sweet and beautiful black man with liquid eyes would suddenly offer his rear. A German tourist would walk you safely home and say good night on the doorstep. An Israeli soldier, as big as Schwarzenegger, would shake with excitement in your grasp, and quickly go through every sexual motion, short of coming. There were people who wanted to pick someone up and take them home. There were people who only wanted to touch a dick with the tips of their fingers and then leave.

As the nineties progressed, the shrubbery was trimmed and the arrival of police cars grew more frequent. Circles of hardier souls would gather around a small public utility, rather like a gas meter or water pump that was camouflaged with a screen of green wooden slats. Inside those protective walls, it could be as crowded as a rush-hour tube train. Once Michael found himself wanking off an extremely well-endowed Australian, while his own penis was flailed with desperate vigour by a Japanese tourist who stayed completely zipped in. Whatever they wanted, they all kept Russell Square in a sealed compartment away from the rest of their lives.

Michael was here because he could not take people back to the flat. Michael's offer was clear. Hi, I have a boyfriend but we're not faithful, and I'm passive and here for safe sex.

Others seemed to say: I don't want love; love hurts. Or, I am HIV positive and I don't care who I make ill. Or, I am not HIV positive but I'm pissed and I no longer care . . . for now. Hiya, my name is Nick and I play the cello and live at home and I am very slightly crazy, enough to be on medication, and I am lonely and this makes me feel less alone.

Hello, I'm an American tourist and I come here once every five years and my wife back in the hotel thinks I am out for an evening stroll.

Hi, my name is Adam and I'm rich and sixteen and I have a car of my own.

Michael's idea of getting real was to go back to Russell Square. He popped a precautionary Viagra and went out.

He had forgotten that deep thrill of cruising at night. It produced a dragging sensation of mingled fear and excitement in his bowels. He could hear his own breath and found that his eyes flicked towards any movement in the darkness. Like desire itself, seeping out of your bones, men moved in shadows, behind trees.

A young guy, a skinny student in a baseball cap, walked past Michael stony-eyed. You could tell he was a student because the baseball cap looked fake. Students mostly wanted other students. Lurking by a tree was what looked like a very short, fat Italian waiter who stared straight through Michael. Even an old guy in the rolled-up sleeves of a striped dress shirt ignored him. He had metal-frame glasses and flyaway white hair.

Michael began to get worried. Usually, you had to find something you wanted quickly. If not you could spend hours circling in the dark, past the same men eyeing up the same you, in ever decreasing spirals of lust.

A tall man strolled towards him. He would be a bit younger

than Michael; white shirt, black trousers. A bouncer maybe, with a bit of a potbelly.

His eyes followed Michael as he passed, and they were blue, and his hair was a faded, natural blond. Michael couldn't help but turn his head. The man stopped, as if jingling change in his pocket. Michael felt a constriction around his heart and his breathing. The man started to walk towards him. Bingo.

'Do you live near here?' the guy muttered, the standard polite introduction. He had an Irish accent. Clonmel, Michael thought. In the yellow glare of street lights dappled through leaves, he saw a handsome, sensible face.

'I'd live anywhere you wanted me to live,' replied Michael, which was true for a moment.

As they walked home, Michael kept watching for disappointment in himself or the other, but it did not set in. The man was a few years younger than he was, and pleasantly talkative. He looked tired, in a worn, homely way. He smiled tiredly. His eyes crinkled and they were a very clear blue.

His name was Chris. Chris, Michael repeated in his head so he wouldn't have to ask again: Chris, Chris. Chris managed a pub, a quite nice one actually on this side of Euston Road. Tended to get the after-work crowd rather than the usual King's Cross lowlife.

'How much further is it?' Chris asked after they had walked only two blocks. They always got scared that it would be far or that they couldn't find their way back, or that they were being led to a sidestreet mugging.

Chris's eyes shone with relief inside the pleasant apartment. In the light his colouring seemed to heighten, his eyes went cornflower-blue, his hair golden, his cheeks pink.

'I've been working all evening and I'm a bit sweaty. Would you mind if I had a shower?'

Michael caught himself working magic. He thought at Chris as if he were an Angel: you've just showered. He felt something come up against the wall of reality.

So Michael said, 'Of course you can. In fact maybe I should too.' It was considerate, but taking a shower is a passion-killer. It is difficult to maintain a macho façade when you offer some-

208

one a towel in decorator colours. It is difficult to hold up the mask of fantasy as you peel off day-old clothes and used knickers that look like blotting paper. You are left naked, in a less than ideal body.

In the bedroom Chris turned away, and stepped out of his clothes cautiously, in that hunched and delicate way that makes people look embarrassed. He carefully hung his trousers over the back of the chair. He had a slight undercoating of fat all over his body, produced perhaps by nightly access to beer. Chris, who managed a pub, was not one of the great names or bodies of the century. Michael remembered discretion and hesitancy and withdrew.

He also remembered that this was not an Angel. You don't know who he is, Michael. He took his wallet and portfolio and hid them behind books on the shelves. Then he threw off his clothes and worked his way around Chris in the narrow bathroom. Michael showered quickly, giving his bum a quick scrub. He did not want to leave Chris unobserved in the flat. He shouted from behind the shower curtain, 'So um, did you close up early tonight?' He shut off the water and nipped out of the bath.

Chris was waiting for him, wanting to talk. 'No. This is my normal knocking-off time. As it were.' Chris grinned: it was his normal knocking-off joke as well, but it was enough to make Michael smile. Chris wore his white towel high around his midriff, to hide his tummy.

Michael blotted up water and hared after Chris and caught up with him in the bedroom.

'I'd say we're both getting a bit wet,' said Chris.

I hope he won't make jokes like this all night, thought Michael. He blinked back at him from behind his specs, feeling owlish. He had forgotten to take them off in the shower. Chris delicately removed them, and leaned forward and kissed him.

Chris still tasted of hops. He was a tall man and was at his best lying face down: his legs and buttocks were still slim, unlike his stomach. Michael had taken the Viagra before he went out, and it worked triumphantly, spiked perhaps by a tickle of fear and uncertainty that had long been missed.

Face down on the bed, Chris pulled his cheeks apart, and Michael suddenly wanted to feel himself inside there. Anxious lest the erection collapse, he pushed his way alongside, up to and then very suddenly inside Chris, real flesh to real flesh. Michael began to pump.

Without a condom. Michael had to repeat that. Michael, this is real and you are not wearing a condom, Michael stop. He wanted to go on and was suddenly aware that Chris would let him.

'This is silly,' Michael said. He half hoped Chris would say, never mind. Instead, Chris said, after a pause, 'Yeah, you're right.'

Michael pulled out. Condoms, condoms, where did he keep condoms now? It had been five months since he'd used one. As he pulled open drawers, he felt his erection subside. He raced back to the bathroom, catching his little toe on the side of the lintel. He hopped and hobbled towards his sponge bag and found both condoms and KY. Cursing under his breath, he winced back into the bedroom, trying to walk as if he hadn't nearly broken his toe.

Michael glanced nervously at his erection, which was now best described as a plumping of penis, like a fluffed-up pillow. It was soft but fatter than normal. He tore at the packet with his fingers and then with his teeth, and then he remembered where those fingers had been. Finally the condom was liberated and he checked it, and he slid it down his cock and it wasn't until it began to curl inward at the top that he realized he'd put it on inside out.

It would not roll up again. He had to pull it off as a whole, turn it inside out, and try to slip it back on like a pair of stockings. Chris lay dazed and luxurious with waiting passivity.

'Whew,' said Michael, his poor little willy wet and limp, as if sweaty from too much work.

Chris was covered with golden fur. It was very soft to the touch, and masked his anus which, considering the beauty of most sphincters, served only to increase its allure. 'Please,' said Chris, once, sincerely. He loved being fucked. Once Michael was inside him, Chris moved his buttocks quickly back and

210

forth, controlling the speed and depth of the thrust. Then he turned himself over onto his back, and raised his legs, his blue eyes yearning a simple request. Michael could do that, too, from the front. He could look into Chris's eyes. He could kiss him. He could arch his back and kiss Chris's nipples.

Michael could not come. Viagra had given him the means, but not the ends. Chris did not mind. It was half past midnight before Chris finally allowed himself to come, and Michael, out of a mingling of motives, pretended to come at the same time as well. He faked an orgasm. And then Chris curled up next to him, and placed his face against Michael's chest and talked.

The pub was Chris's whole world. The only time the job got a bit rough was after a match and people had to wait for a train. You had to get a bit tough with them then. The worst was when staff started filching drinks; it took away all your profit. It was such a thoughtless thing to do. At the end of the day, it was their jobs on the line as well. Finally you had to fire them; there was no alternative. That's why he preferred hiring women, older women, you know: they were just more reliable.

Chris wanted to be unburdened. He shared an ex-council flat with another guy. They weren't lovers or anything. The guy kept taking things from the fridge, which meant Chris got home late and found there was nothing to eat. Michael felt for him and kissed his forehead. Chris looked up, pleased and surprised, and they kissed again, tasting tongues. They paused a moment, and then Chris decided.

'I'd like to stay, but I prefer my own bed. Do you mind?'

They got dressed modestly again, backs turned towards each other. Michael still needed to pull on his socks when Chris said, 'Well, that's it then.' Then he said, 'Here's my card. You can ring me at work, if you like.' His expression was unusual for a man in his thirties. It was hopeful. He gave a shrug, as if to say, if you don't, you don't. 'Thanks,' he said, and something awkward like you have a beautiful cock.

Michael's big heavy door slammed grumpily shut, as if annoyed to be woken up in the middle of the night. The corridor outside had been newly carpeted. Michael couldn't hear the retreating footsteps. Michael pondered the meaning of that business card.

First time lucky, he thought.

The number of times Michael had brought men back: how often had any of them left an address? What a difference Viagra makes, eh? Chris liked being fucked and I could fuck him. That's a big difference. Chris had confused the Viagra for genuine sexual interest, perhaps even personal interest.

Chris was nice in a way that did not engage Michael. Michael suspected that he was boring. Chris would want cuddles and blockbuster videos on the telly in front of the sofa and would have even less to say about Michael's work than Philip.

But Chris had left a business card. A business card meant trust. It meant that he thought you could ring back and not be an embarrassment. He might even be slightly proud of you ringing back. The middle-aged women he so enjoyed working with might guess, and raise an eyebrow. 'He seemed rather nice,' they might say, wishing Chris well. A steadily maintained smile and a flick of the eyebrow could more or less reply: well yes, actually, he is rather nice. Guess my luck must have changed.

Has it, Chris?

Did Michael really want an affair with a bar manager on Euston Road? Michael could have a love affair with the young Rock Hudson, or Steve Reeves who played Hercules, or Henry James. Did Michael really want that everyday ordinariness: the quick hug, the bland well-meant concern. Hiya, how did it go today?

Do you like him, Michael?

Michael heard the very quiet sound of the battery-operated clock on the bedside table. He didn't know.

Viagra was like impotency. You didn't know where it stopped and you began. If Michael had really been able to fuck someone for hours, it would mean something. It would mean that the heart and body were both engaged. Chris had a right not to be misled. He had dilated like his arse; opened up and welcomed and taken a risk. Michael couldn't trust his body to tell him anything. All he could do was take a gamble, a flutter the English called it, a flutter of wings, of the pulse, of the heart.

He could call Chris's work now and leave a message. It would be there when he arrived in the morning.

Quick, Michael, before you lose the card and it drifts out of existence as surely as if it had come from an Angel.

'Hello, you've reached the Milliner's Arms, thirty-seven Euston Road. There's nobody here right now, but if you'd like to leave a message . . .' Chris's voice.

We'll get back to you.

Beep, beep, beep, beep.

'Hi. Um, this is a message for Chris, from Michael. Your card was *not* wasted. Can you call me at . . .'

They went to a movie together.

It was an American blockbuster, with a soundtrack of wailing Irish pipes. Halfway through it, the American heroine got real and danced a jig with down-home Irish, who were just so authentic, because they were poor and unselfconscious.

Chris was outraged. 'It's the bloody Americans being more Irish than the Irish again. Why do they always show us like that, like we're all fucking Leprechauns and can't go to the supermarket without dancing a jig.'

They went to a Pizza Express and Michael confirmed that Chris was a man without ambition. He talked about fridge freezers and plumbing. He talked about his Mum moving in with his sister. Michael's heart went out to him, because he knew that this was a man who wanted to set up a home with someone.

Chris probably saw that. 'I thought I might like to go to India, when I've saved up enough,' he said, a gesture towards the exotic. He still looked hopeful. Michael wanted to say something clever and a bit acid like, 'Travel narrows the mind.'

There was an awkwardness in the conversation where the laughs should have been. Unambitious people want comfort and fun: a bit of a laugh. Michael didn't do bits of laughs. Maybe I'm the boring one, he thought. He dredged deep to find something amusing to say.

He came up with his nest of stories about the Sacramento River delta: his hilarious boating holiday with his Dad. The story got interrupted because Chris wanted to know more about shopping malls and California dope. The story got going again, and Michael told him how they had boated off and forgot the dog on a country dock. Chris failed to see any humour. 'The poor thing,' he said.

'Wait a second. We came back, and saw a pooch running up and down the dock. And Dad said, Gosh, that looks just like Peaches the Pooch and I said Dad, that is Peaches the Pooch.'

'She was desperate, then, wasn't she?'

'Yeah, well, there was this sorta moment when we both realized what had happened. I stuck my head out of the cabin and called Peaches, thinking she'd be on deck, but it was the pooch on the dock that barked at me.'

Chris tutted and shook his head. 'Awww,' he said.

Michael persevered. He and Dad had dropped anchor out in the middle of the river. The next morning was the lowest tide of the year. They woke up to find themselves miles from land on a mud flat that reached the horizon. The boat was sinking in it. It leaned to one side and the kitchen cupboard sprang open, and all these tins spilled out and rolled all over the place like bowling balls.

'Anyway Peaches started running round and round the deck, and we couldn't figure out why. And suddenly I said, Dad, she needs to go for a walk!'

'Well, she was a poor little thing then, wasn't she? Why take her with you on a houseboat? Couldn't you have left her with friends?'

Michael relented. 'You know, most people find this story funny. I don't know many funny stories, and this is my effort to, like, be amusing.'

'Thank you,' said Chris perfectly seriously.

Michael took a deep breath. 'Yeah. You're welcome. Anyway, the dog can't take it any more and suddenly she just jumps off the deck and jumps into the marsh. And she disappears. She just completely sinks into the mud.'

Chris covered his mouth. 'Oh my God, what did you do?'

Michael was still waiting for laughs. 'I jumped in after her. And I sank too.'

Bubbles of marsh gas had tickled his feet and smelled like

farts. Michael reached into the ooze and pulled poor Peaches out. They both emerged stinking with no way to wash. Chris reacted as if Michael was describing a friend's death from cancer.

'Anyway, Dad said you're not coming onto my boat. I mean we smelled like a sewer. And so we climbed into the dinghy and just sat there.'

'Oh, it sounds disgusting,' said Chris.

'Actually, I still find it kind of funny.'

'Oh.'

'I was telling it as a joke.'

'Were you? I was thinking it didn't sound too funny at the time, being banished by your Dad.'

'I wasn't being banished. I mean, I couldn't go on board, that was all.'

'Sorry.'

So much for telling jokes.

'Actually, I was bloody angry,' said Michael.

And that made Chris laugh. 'I'd have fucking laid one on him.'

'Oh no you wouldn't. Not if you saw my Dad. My Dad was a really big guy. In fact, he was a Marine, which is why we lived where we lived near Camp Pendleton. No, he was a really big man.'

'He sounds fanciable, your father. Do you think you could introduce us?'

And Michael heard himself say, 'I did fancy him, actually.'

Yup. There you go. Chris's face froze.

Michael kept on like it was a funny story. It was some kind of revenge for the funny story. Part of Chris made him angry. 'Well, I didn't see him a lot; he never felt like my father and he was built like, whatever, and he was really handsome, and competent, and smart and I just fell in love . . . and one night . . . I made a pass at him.'

Chris went rather still. 'What did he do?'

Michael smiled. 'He went berserk. He rang my Mom.'

Chris saw the humour. He chuckled. 'That sounds awful. That sounds beyond awful.'

Michael didn't. 'It was a laugh riot.'

'I'm . . . I'm sorry, I shouldn't laugh, but it does sound like some kind of living end.'

'That and more. I'm impotent, Chris. Last night was a fake. It was a pill, it was Viagra.'

Chris looked suddenly dark. 'It still seemed pretty good.'

There was something else he needed to see.

'Do you want to see my father? Do you want to see how good-looking he really was?'

Chris began to look troubled, he sulked a bit; his hot date had turned out to be a flake. 'You have a photograph?'

'More than that. Turn and look at the men's room door, and in a second, he'll come through it, wearing nothing but those swimming trunks he wore all that summer boating holiday. Turn around, Chris. Look. Now.'

The doors swung open, and out came a man wearing surfer shorts. The shorts were blue with a half-inch band of white around every edge. He was tall and square at the same time, with shoulders like volleyballs, and a bare chest that seemed to support breasts, and a collarbone that was parallel to the floor, stretching his trunk wide. He had a face a bit like a more thickset, Latin Gregory Peck, decent, almost wise. The eyes were absolutely black, darker even than Michael's. The crew cut was savage, unflattering. The thighs and calves were a particular feature; this was a big man who could sprint.

Marine Staff Sergeant Louis Blasco. Eventually made Master Sergeant, the last two years Michael knew him.

Staff Sergeant Blasco paused, looked confused, as if he'd lost his way. Drugs, you would think. A man wearing nothing but swimming trunks stumbles out of a toilet and looks confused. Conversation in the restaurant settled in a hush like the surf on Oceanside Beach.

OK, Dad. Michael toyed with the idea of making his father drop his shorts. To avenge himself. So that big uncircumcised American head could show itself. So Michael could see it again.

Michael said, 'He's dead now, actually.'

He made his father march quickly out of the restaurant.

*

216

Back home, Michael called up Henry. His Angel sat at the foot of the bed.

'Henry, it didn't work.'

'What happened?'

'The same thing that always happens. I sent him away. I've spent all my life sending people away. I told him something I've never told anyone else.'

'Ah,' said Henry and sat back.

'It just came bubbling out of me. I was mad at him, and I just suddenly heard myself say it.'

'What did you say to him, Michael?'

Michael felt a rush, as if he were in aeroplane, and it was taking off. 'I told him something about my father.'

'Something you've never told anyone else?' Henry took hold of Michael's hand and coaxed him by rubbing it.

Michael just nodded. He let go of his breath. He'd been holding it without realizing.

'Maybe the time's finally come. Why don't you tell me?' the Angel asked.

So, finally, Michael did.

What's eating Michael Blasco?

At twelve years old, Michael believed in love. He believed that love was the natural state. If you were out of love, then through a kind of natural gravity you would roll back into it. Michael believed that some day he would roll home.

Home was probably Romford, though Mum still sounded like she was from Sheffield. Michael was a mystery to his mother. His underwear was going crisp and no one had ever told Mum about wet dreams. She accused him of masturbation, and knocked on the door of the toilet when he read comics, demanding 'What are you doing in there?' Michael's puberty had been more traumatic for her than for him.

Michael's visits to California became an escape to another world of beaches and palm trees. Coming back every two years was like visiting another self. This self was called Mikey or when he got older, Mike. Mike had his own room, which was full of things, neat things his Dad had bought him, boy things. They were just where he left them: well almost. His Dad had maybe moved the boy things forward to kind of emphasize them – the baseball glove, the Swiss Army knife, the bicycle-repair tools.

Michael would come back at twelve or fourteen, to find all of Mikey's old things there. He could sit up late at night and read his old *X Men* comics. Sometimes there was a sense of homecoming. Hiya, how ya doing, his California self would say, perking up after two years without being used. Sometimes

Michael would settle into Mike as if he were a sofa. Other times he was a bit frosty with his old self. At sixteen, his lip curled. *X Men?* You're still into *X Men*, oh God, they're terrible.

Michael would play his old records. His first love had been Mark Bolan and T-Rex and then, glistering with make-up, dear old Bowie.

This could cause some tension with his father. Dad thought rock music was socially destructive. He had few records himself. Staff Sergeant Blasco owned *The Sound of Music* and *My Fair Lady*. In a strange convoluted way, this was to do with his Latin background. The Blasco family had been in California for 100 years and were thoroughly Americanized. That meant the Catholic League of Decency, and that meant Family Entertainment. At ten, at twelve, Michael heard and learned to love *Camelot* and *Mary Poppins*.

While other twelve-year-old kids were buying Grand Funk Railroad, Michael was seeking out the Original Cast Recording of *Cinderella*.

Michael played *Cinderella* year in, year out, at twelve, at fourteen, even at sixteen. Maybe it was the link with England. Or maybe it was identification. In 1957, Julie Andrews had been twenty-two, the same age as Elvis Presley. Polished, operatic, old-fashioned she may have been, but everything she did crackled with a youthful energy that made Michael bounce. It was a feminine energy, something he could identify with. And this Cinderella was like him, stuck powerless and dreaming in a family that didn't quite work.

There was one song, about sitting in your own little corner and dreaming of adventure, and that was what Michael was doing. There was magic, and Michael always loved magic. Cinderella insisted on it: impossible things happened every day.

And there was the soppy song about love, which Michael was ashamed of loving back. It was a song of disbelief, that the one we love is so beautiful.

Every year his father would greet him at the airport with a great bear hug. 'Hey, Mikey, how's it going?'

'Fine, thanks Dad.'

Michael would be pressed up against the T-shirted pectorals and surrounded by the melon-like arms. Michael would look up to see something like his own face, as he wanted to be.

His father had a thick neck: it went straight down from his ears. His square jaw never seemed to need shaving. Mirror shades, laconically rotating chewing gum and a brutal crew cut all added up to the desired image. This was one tough hombre.

Michael would be both agog and dismayed, buffeted by alternative breakers of admiration and self-denigration. How could he ever hope to match his father?

Dad looked like someone who starred in police thrillers. He wore grey T-shirts with AFL logos. The tops of his father's bare feet were always coated in sand from surfing, jogging or volleyball. Michael's Dad played basketball with the Latino kids on the beach; he jogged from the camp to the power station beyond Carlsbad and back; he played touch football nearly incessantly. Every part of his body from his cheekbones to his feet was bronzed, lean, rounded, veined and gritty. He looked like Michael's more popular older brother.

When Michael was ten his Dad was Senior Drill at boot camp in San Diego. Staff Sergeant Blasco spent his days barking orders at intimidated new recruits. Michael sometimes watched from the back of the drill hall. 'Tiger! Tiger! Kill, kill!' the recruits would bellow in unison.

'We break 'em down to build 'em up,' his father said once, on the drive back home. Michael's first two experimental weeks in America were spent in the top floor of a duplex near San Diego airport. 'You see, Mikey, if there ever is a war then those guys won't have time to think. We don't want them to think. We want them to do. So we have to rehearse everything so much that they just do it automatically. That's why we do all that animal stuff. I don't want you to be embarrassed by it. All that animal imagery is real important to the psychology.'

Michael sat looking at the billboards on the roadside, feeling pale and weedy.

His father wanted high spirits. 'So what animal are you, Mikey?'

'I don't know. Probably a chicken.'

'Oh, man. We gotta do something about that.'

Sometimes Staff Sergeant Blasco was more like a Mom. He'd say Mike was looking kinda pale. Was he getting out? He was looking thin; maybe he'd like to stop and get something to eat? He'd slap Michael's back to get an idea of its fleshiness. Didn't Mike's Mom feed him anything?

'We gotta get you out on that beach. What sport you doing these days, Mikey?'

Michael dreaded that question. Just the question alone made him feel cold and shivery and skinny. 'Um . . . snooker? That's something like billiards.' California sunlight made Michael squint.

'Uh-huh,' his father would say, without commitment. 'Snooker sounds cool. Listen, I know you have a lot of studying to do in England, but now that you're here, maybe you'd like to join in with some of the stuff that's going on in San Diego. I know you don't play basketball or any of that stuff, but there's a sailing club, tennis. All kinds of stuff. Some of the NCOs have set up a kind of sports club for the kids in the camp. Maybe you should check it out.'

When Michael came back at twelve, his Dad had just been promoted from Staff Sergeant to Gunney. He worked in Camp Pendleton and so they lived in camp accommodation, a regulation bungalow with a regulation yard.

Dad would have the guys in to watch the game, or he would host a staff barbecue, or there would be a sailing club annual accounts meeting. Marines with wives from Manila or Topeka would mingle in a tiny condo without a single book to talk a mix of baseball statistics, camp politics, shopping tips and the latest model cars.

Sometimes they talked movies. An old guy, somebody's granddad, asked Michael, 'Have you seen that movie *Poseidon Adventure* yet?'

'I thought it could have been better,' said Michael. 'I thought the ship turning upside down would be magic, but it wasn't.'

'Huh, huh, I love that accent of yours, Michael. Hey Louis, your kid talks better than you do!'

221

'Don't I know it!' Louis shouted through the open back door. He was grilling hot dogs on the barbecue.

Michael was still trying to talk movies. 'I really like *Planet of the Apes* movies.'

'Yeah, my grandson loves those too.'

'He gets it all from his mother. She's English!' Louis called back, dumping chicken wings onto a plate and family history at the same time. His calf muscles looked like drumsticks, brown and sinewy.

The old man asked, 'You live in England most of the time, Michael?'

'Yes sir.' That 'sir' was American.

'So you think you'll probably be coming over here to live?' The old man's eyes narrowed and his mouth went thin from expectation.

This was a trope. The little kid from England was now supposed to say oh yes, I want to live in America more than anything because there are beaches here and job opportunities and liberty and the Constitution and you can go to football games.

Michael was English enough to resist being bullied into unwarranted enthusiasm. 'I might come here, I haven't really thought about it.'

Michael had recently found himself corralled into the camp's 4th of July pageant. He had to stand up on a stage in a hall and recite: 'Hello, my name's Michael. I'm from England and I want to know more about the Declaration of Independence.' At least the kid from Chile got to ask about Daniel Boone.

The old man took Michael seriously. 'The schools here are real good if you're thinking of going to university. Good colleges around here too.'

Michael's father shouted from the kitchen, 'Mike's the only guy in the family with any brains. What was that exam you took, Mikey? The elevensomething? Well, anyway, it's like he's a straight-A student.'

'Is that so?' the old man intoned. He didn't have that much time for grades.

Something in Michael wanted to twist the knife. 'Actually, I can't live in California. I'm allergic to sunlight.'

'Allergic to sunlight.' The old man cast a look back over his shoulder in case this was new to Michael's father. 'What are the symptoms, Mike?'

'I go this strange shade of brown all over.' It was a joke. It was a joke about Britain, you know, we never see the sun, so we don't know about tanning. Unfortunately Michael had committed a breach of etiquette. You never tell a conservative American a joke without first signalling and confirming that what will follow is a caprice meant only to amuse.

The grandfather leaned forward, serious and concerned. 'I mean strange how?'

'Dead weird. I mean, where the sun doesn't hit, like under my shorts, it stays white, and you can see the line where the brown stops.'

The old guy blinked in confusion. 'But does it interfere with your activities? Sports, going to the beach, community work?'

'Oh it doesn't hurt or anything.'

'Well. How does it differ from a tan?'

'Tan?' Michael said, rounding his vowels to Terry-Thomas proportions, 'Whot's a tan?'

A shivering nervous laugh, and the old man's steepled hands moved towards the thin little smile. 'Oh. Ha-ha, I getcha.' There was a long uncomfortable pause and he fought his way to his feet. 'I'm going to go and see about those wieners.'

Michael felt pity then; the poor old guy had only been trying to be nice. He felt sorry for himself too: now he would have to talk baseball statistics.

He could at least talk to American adults. American kids seemed to Michael to be unbelievably obnoxious. It was like someone had granted them Asshole Licences that weren't revoked until they were twenty-five. Well, at least the sons of Marines commanded to play team sports. They shouted a lot and could be quite funny, unlike their cautious, thin-lipped, watchful parents. But the humour was loud, often cruel, and consisted of set phrases that Michael simply didn't understand.

'Big man he got money in his hand. Hey big man, whoo-hoo!'

They roared with laughter.

'Hey, he's got a man-tan, man!'

Michael could even begin to join in. He listened to the radio, he watched TV, he tried to understand. A local DJ had an ID that rumbled 'The Big Man'. But most of it remained mysterious. Maybe it all came from going to Oceanside High School together, stuff they made up. In any case he was irredeemably out of it. And as Michael played baseball, basketball, volleyball, tennis, etc, only when he came to California, i.e. every two years, he was hardly going to win respect on the field.

One of the kids asked in disbelief, 'Are you really Sergeant Blasco's son?' The kid was big, blond, lean and spotty. Despite expensive dental work his face looked like someone had bashed it in with a spade. Aggressively, he drove the hardball into his own mitt, breaking in a new glove.

Michael had to concur. 'Yes. Hard to believe, huh?' He squinted into the sun, sitting on the bench, dreading his turn at bat.

'You got it. It must be something to do with how they raise 'em in England.'

As the summer wore on, it got worse. The accent was an easy target. Americans couldn't hear the difference between posh and Romford-Sheffield and didn't want to.

'I say, old man, just how did you get to be such a discord?'

'Ooh rather.'

'Spastic, I believe the term is.'

'Hey, Spaz, can you get your poop in the pan, yet?'

At twelve Michael had no defence against this. He was small and pale. Without even trying to, he lost his native accent in a protective camouflage of likes, you knows, sos and I means. It worked; Americans regard their accent as a symptom of strength and virtue. They assumed Michael had wised up. Then Michael went home.

At fourteen, it was different yet again. Michael's father had moved into an Oceanside condo that looked like something from Cape Cod. It was made of wood and was painted white and blue. It had security gates and was on the clifftops right over the beach.

His father was proud of being so adult. 'I could have stayed at the camp, but you see guys who do that and they don't get into the property market til it's too late. Do you like it, Mikey?'

Instead of playing on a team, Michael ran cross country with his father. Michael would meet him every day after work at the camp. This filled his father's heart with pride and companionship. Michael heard his father on the phone. 'Sorry, sir, but unless it's urgent, I always run with my boy at five PM. Yes, sir, from England. He's just here for the summer. Well, he beats his old man now, sir.'

They used the showers at the camp. Marines with the bodies of young bulls would stroll idly past, stark naked. They would murmur politely, 'Good afternoon, Sarge.' It was as if beautiful horses had learned how to talk.

'Afternoon, Clancy. This is my son, Mike.'

'Hey, guy, how's it going?'

'Real good,' said Mike, monkeying about with his accent. Acting the butch little American helped control Michael's eyes. They kept veering downwards, like World War One aircraft. The bobbing heads of the circumcised cocks were framed with girdles of muscle found elsewhere only on classical statuary. Michael felt something like awe, a yearning for both attainment and possession. He still could not quite focus on it as lust.

Michael and his father would run out of the camp, down the hill to the harbour and from there to Oceanside Beach. As they ran his father talked, between breaths: in, out, in, talk, in, out, in, talk. He ran barefoot, making scrunching noises in the wet sand that formed the commas and punctuation of his speech.

'Forty-three past ... I think ... we'll do it ... one hour twenty ... easy.'

'Yeah.'

'Y'getting good, Mike.'

'Thanks.'

'You thought of going serious?'

'Sometimes.'

'Could get you a coach.'

'Maybe.'

'There's a military academy in Carlsbad.'

'I know.'

'They get real good SAT scores . . . good school.'

'Uh huh.'

'You could go there . . . do this every day.'

Michael turned and there was this big tough guy like Clint Eastwood only for real, and he was beaming, face shiny and oiled with sweat. The gloss on his face reflected sand, sunlight, blue sky, sea, just like his huge mirror shades. He was beaming at Michael.

'So how 'bout it?'

It's hard to keep your voice soft, to make it communicate that you're deeply touched, when you are breathing to fuel a run, and your voice rattles each time your feet thump down onto the sand.

'I'll uh . . . think about it, OK, Dad?'

That was all Louis wanted. His chest seemed to expand and he looked out on the beach as if he had suddenly inherited it.

'We could getcha running real good.'

They would shower together, and all of his father's body was gleaming with sweat – the broad back with two bands of muscle either side of the spine, the dimpled shoulder blades, and the arms as curvaceous as a woman's body. That was Michael's favourite moment. His father would dive into the showers as if they were waterfalls in the desert. He would rub his face and hands and torso. His father loved the water cold.

Afterwards, he and Michael would go to Café 101, which served old-fashioned greasy spoon food: huge hamburgers, peach pie, meatloaf and breakfast all day. That would be their supper: no frozen peas, no boiled spinach, no wet new potatoes.

The whole condo smelled of men. It smelled of his father's fellow officers who piled in after a game of football on the beach, and then stayed to watch the fight away from their wives. The bags of potato chips and empty beer cans would be there the next morning.

It smelled of his father. Dad left his laundry until the basket was full. He lost track of what sheets were washed and which ones were not. Each night after their ritual good nights – Good

night, Mike, see ya in the morning, guy. OK Dad, see ya –
Michael would settle into a bed that smelled of his father. It
smelled of aftershave, thin acrid sweat, talcum powder and
liniment for his sprain. The sheets steamed pheromones, for his
father had been spending his nights alone too.

One night Michael deliberately touched his father's hand. It
was after all their male things – after their run, after the showers,
after their meatloaf and gravy, and milkshakes and cherry pie
à la mode. It was after the chores were done – the moving,
oiling, tool cleaning and boiler checks. They were putting up
new racks in the garage. Michael passed a drill bit in such a
way that he could stroke the palm and fingers of his father's
hand. His father's hand was surprisingly soft and smooth. It
was like it was made out of tiny satin pillows that someone had
warmed by sitting on them.

That night Michael masturbated for the first time. His friend
Ali had told him about it. You keep stroking until it shoots out
stuff. For some reason, it had never occurred to him to try. Just
this once, he promised himself. He felt male, full and swaggering
with maleness, he had spent the day being male. He had no
real idea what would happen.

He just kept stoking himself. It didn't go very hard, but then
he didn't really know how hard it should get. What he was not
remotely expecting was orgasm. It was as if he were on some
kind of donkey cart with no brakes, steering wheel or anything
to drive or control it. He watched helplessly as it rolled down
a hill. There was a terrible sense of acceleration, of going faster
and faster, higher and higher, and as if in crash, a sudden loss
of all control, and a tumbling fall.

Michael lay stunned and messy and embarrassed. He would
have to wash. He didn't know there would be so much of the
stuff, or that it seemed to crawl everywhere as if it had a life
of its own. I'll get the sheets dirty, and Dad'll know, Michael
thought.

He pushed his pj bottoms down with his elbows and kicked
them off. He didn't want to touch anything with his hands. The
doorknob became an obstacle: it would not turn between his
two elbows. He gave up and used his hands, but they were too

227

slick with semen to turn it. Would he have to call his Dad? He decided to sacrifice a sock. He stuck his hand into it like a glove puppet and managed to open the door. Padding out quickly to the bathroom, he kept his pj top hanging low. He washed his hands for ten minutes, and then the sink and the taps several times. Then he snapped his pj bottoms back on.

He felt abused. Orgasm had come as a thumping physical shock that left him a bit weak in the stomach and knees. It was as though something that was not himself had temporarily taken over his body. It made him feel a bit soiled, a bit guilty. He told himself: I only did it to see what it was like, and I won't have to do it again now.

Michael wanted to talk to his Dad. He could tell his Dad about it and his Dad could tell him what to expect from sex. His Dad would be good about it, no shock or outrage.

Michael stood outside his father's open bedroom door. His father left the door open in case Michael needed him. If Michael stood in the doorway, his father would say: 'Mike? Is there something wrong?' Michael stood and waited. He could hear his father breathe, a delicate hissing sound that reminded Michael of baby rabbits. He could smell his father's breath too; sometimes it was stale, mostly after he'd overdone the exercise and hadn't drunk enough water. The sense of his father's physical presence was overwhelming.

Michael wanted to sleep next to his father. He wanted to curl up beside him, and smell the big bear-like smell and be cuddled. He wanted to have long conversations about life, and about the future, and what it was to be an adult. He even wanted to smell his father's breath.

He waited, but there was no invitation, and he wasn't brave enough to invade. He could talk about it in the morning if he still needed to.

So Michael crept back into bed, still breathing in the scent of his father, and pulled the pillow round and hugged it from the side, as if it were his father's torso, and a great heaviness, a stillness settled over him, like liquid lead was oozing out of every pore. He had a dream about melting, as if he were wax.

*

When Michael returned at sixteen, it was altogether different.

First off Michael flew on his own from LA International to San Diego. He had to find his own way across the huge airport to a domestic departure lounge. He had to carry his own bags onto the runway, and leave them on the cart beside the tiny aeroplane while the guy tagged them for him. Doing all of it unaided made Michael feel he had glimpsed what it was like to be an adult. It also meant that his father thought he was old enough to handle all that.

This time, Michael and his father were the same height. 'Hey, Mike, you've grown up, guy!' They hugged in a guy kind of way and patted each other on the back. His father had the same battery of teeth, the same shaved head. Ultraviolet radiation may have creased the face a little bit more, but that only wreathed the smile more. Michael pulled back to look at him and was stunned again.

Everything about his father pulled at his heart. If Michael had seen his father for the first time in a restaurant, he wouldn't be able to take his eyes off him. If he had wanted a guy for a friend, somebody who could teach him about all the things he knew he needed to find out, somebody who could give him anti-dork lessons without making him feel like one, it would be his father. If he wanted a companion, someone to share a house with, it would be his Dad. He wanted to spend his life with him.

And this time, at sixteen, Michael recognized the undertow, that pulling, for what it was.

'So how's the cross country going, Mike?'

'They need me. They want me.' Michael slipped into this new self as if it were a body stocking.

'Good man!' His father slapped his knee.

'So, like I'm in real serious training now.'

'Sounds good to me.' His father was being laid back, changing gears like he was playing ping pong.

'So like, I really need someone to run with and stuff.'

'Well, I was kinda planning on doing what we were doing the last time you were here.' His father was looking out the window, at the distant billboards, as if they were passing women. 'If that's OK with you.'

229

'Do a beach run every day.'

'If that'll do the trick. I don't know.' Finally Joe Cool looked back around at his son. 'It depends on what you want to do. We may be looking at getting you some professional coaching.'

Michael was brisk. 'I'd rather run with you, Dad.'

'Well maybe. But you gotta consider how far you want to take this thing and how well you want to do it.'

'Maybe we could do both. I was ... uh ... kinda thinking ...' Michael seemed to be hurling towards some kind of decision; the sensation was not unlike the acceleration towards orgasm. He suddenly sharply knew what he wanted. He could see it, there was no doubt. A couple of hundred still images flickered in his brain: them in the apartment together, at the beach together, chores together, breakfasts together.

'I'm thinking I might go to school here, you know, college, and um, work on my running, you know, maybe be on the team while I study.'

This had never been discussed with his mother. Michael had just invented it. He was betraying his mother to talk in this way, to make this offer without her knowledge.

Michael pressed on, like a car careening zigzag across a roadway. 'I was thinking it could be UC San Diego. Um. I don't think it would be fair to make Mom pay and all.'

'No, no, no,' his father said and seemed to have to stand up in the front seat, like he was having to break hard, in an emergency. Michael was perfectly aware that he was offering his father the thing he most wanted in the world.

'So. I was kinda thinking I could, like, you know, live with you.'

His father was not looking at billboards any more. His father was looking straight ahead. 'You'd have to make sure UCSD was good in your subject.'

'Yeah.'

'Maybe we could drop into the school now. It's on our way.'

Michael nodded slowly, surely, as if this were something considered and serious. That would be good.

The Chiclets chewing gum stopped clicking. His father's jaw clenched, and then he swallowed. 'I would like that a whole

230

bunch,' he said, and then he turned and looked at Michael, and nodded, and smiled a strained, tight smile. His eyes were impossible to read behind the mirror shades. All Michael saw in them was his own reflection.

They stopped at UCSD and wasted an hour. Michael's flight had got in at 3.30 PM, and it was late to show up on a huge campus and expect to find somebody to answer their questions. It took them fifteen minutes to find out where they were supposed to park, and another twenty to find the registrar's office. A woman behind the counter spent another ten minutes showing them on a map where the Sciences Administration Building was. The office would close at five.

This was not his father's world. Dad looked like a truck driver, ill at ease and dusty. The woman behind the counter was stylish, black, and thin like the Duchess of Windsor. Her hair was pulled back and her earrings folded into themselves in stylish swirls. 'And you sir, are you enrolling in a class too?' she asked.

'No, that's my son,' said the Marine. He had a high-school diploma. He was proud, pleased to be taken for twenty, and insulted all at the same time.

'Uh huh, OK,' she said, processing information at high speed as the clock hands spun. She passed Michael booklets and forms.

In the car roaring back to the camp his father asked, 'What does your mother say about this?'

Michael felt the first uncomfortable lurch. 'I haven't really said anything about it. In fact it's all been kind of a spur-of-the moment thing. In fact, I just decided right now at the airport, when I saw you again. I just knew it was what I wanted to do.'

'Uh huh.' His father nodded, and the face gripped itself. Out from under the mirror shades, some water started to creep. 'Well, you know you gotta talk to your Mom about it.' His voice was rough and slurred.

Michael felt the second uncomfortable lurch. He didn't want it to mean this much to his Dad; his Dad was supposed to be unapproachable, like a fortress.

His father coughed to clear his throat. He started to talk

231

exactly as if he were running, short of breath, gasping. 'And, we'll need to get you a driver's licence. And you know, find out about a qual . . . oh, shit.'

His father flicked the black stick and the car made a bink, bink, bink noise and it eased over to the side, his father carefully looking behind. It went onto the paved shoulder and stopped. His father jerked on the handbrake, and rested his head against the steering wheel.

'Sorry, son, sorry.' His father's voice sounded like it was glued with drying saliva.

'Dad? Dad?' Michael was worried.

'I'm sorry I fucked up your life. I'm sorry I left your Mom, she's a great lady, and she sure as hell deserved better than me. I did the best I could. But I messed up.' He sighed and gathered breath and turned. 'And look at you. You're big and smart, you grew up so well, and it's nothing to do with me. But I'm going to make sure that you're not disappointed in me.'

'Disappointed? In you?' Michael was incredulous.

'Ah, what the hell.' His father suddenly sounded normal. He took off the mirror shades. The action made him look older and more fragile, like the skin around his eyes was crêpe paper and could tear. He wiped it with the heels of his hands. 'What say we go get ourselves a burger at the 101?'

'Right on!' said Michael. And they slapped hands.

The brute fact was that Michael had fallen in love with his father. It was a romantic and sexual attachment. Michael wanted to marry him.

There is only one word for love and it blurs many dividing lines. There was nothing in his father's manner that could signal to someone who was in the first full flood of love that he did not want the same thing. His father's face softened and went tender as they planned when Michael would move in with him. He evidently, despite everything he said, wanted Michael to be with him as quickly as possible. He offered to move closer to USCD, to buy a house instead of a condo, asked Michael if he wanted a separate place with a face haunted and shadowy and sad. His father's face opened up like a sunflower when Michael said, no, no, the whole point was to live together.

'You'll need a car. We could let you have this one. What do I need a car for? Or would you rather have the Jeep? Your choice.'

Dad got excited planning joint trips. 'I never took you to Aspen. I can't believe that. I took all those bimbos, and I never took you! Yosemite, Alaska. There's the John Muir Trail.' As long as the length of the trail would be with Louis Blasco, Michael wouldn't mind.

'That'll be fabulous!' said Michael.

His father laughed. 'We'll take a tent, get in the Jeep and just take off!' His father's hand soared like an aeroplane. 'Or, there's the Sacramento Delta. Man, it's the size of the Mississippi and nobody goes there. Get us a houseboat? Just the two of us?' His father's eyes shone with love.

Michael could understand it now. Now he knew that his father had needed tenderness. You can train your mind to kill if a silhouette of a soldier flips up out of the corner of your eye. You can become adept at breaking the spirit of kids who are only a few years older than your broken-spirited son. You can do that, and it will only make the need for tenderness worse.

You drive home alone from Camp Pendleton every Thanksgiving and Christmas to be with a big established Latin family who all went to university except you. You have no one of your own to love except your son, who is gone for two years at a time. You don't have a grey suit; you don't talk like your lawyer brother. When you are out of uniform people think you are an illegal immigrant, which is why certain white women fuck you. You drive home through Oceanside, California, which is full of floozies. There are sixteen-year-old drug-addicted whores who hang out in the back of gas stations just off the I-5. There are clubs with neon signs that look like they're from the 1950s, with cartoons of women dressed in swimsuits with tails and cat ears, all in pink. You can buy some women, or seduce others because you are Latin, smoother than most and built like a tank. And that's what they want you for. Either that or the 50, or 90 or 100 bucks.

And you are strong and you are physical and you are sensual and you are loving, and what you see is what you get – a woman

233

with liquor on her breath. You want a nice girl. But you don't want a Catholic-ridden, uneducated, old-fashioned Mexican girl, and you don't want a slut of an Anglo, and you won't get the kind of girls your brothers marry. Their wives came from good homes, spoke Spanish with an American accent, cooked chicken in chocolate sauce, and went on to higher degrees.

The English girl from Sheffield had seemed a perfect way out. She had red hair, and a kind, long, fragile face that was ordinary and kinda classy at the same time. She was all agog with Louis for all the wrong reasons. He was a way out for her too.

God, the things Michael's mother gave away without realizing. She really didn't understand that a Marine Sergeant would not have a lot of money. The upholstering of American life is very difficult for a Brit to read. An American can have a house in some exotic-sounding California town and it can have a swimming pool, but that does not mean he is rich. His brother may be a lawyer, but that does not mean, as it assuredly does in Britain, that he is likely to be from the top social drawer.

His mother's sexuality had betrayed her spirited but fearful self. She married for love, but she didn't really want to live as someone with a Spanish surname five thousand miles away. If she had been braver and less tough, if she had moved to Southern California with her handsome husband, she might have been happy.

Instead, she insisted her husband stay in England. It was not her way to clean house and pretend to be all glamorous. She relaxed into being a housewife and began to look dowdy. There was no way he was going to quit the Marines, and in any event, what was he supposed to do in England? He had no hold on English culture, English life, English power. So he went back and she did not.

In a curious way, a woman with a child does not need love as badly as a man who has no wife and not much social standing. A man like that might need love more. Maybe a man from a big, loving Latin family would inherit a great and unused capacity for love.

And suddenly there is his son, his English son, a bit stuck-up, a bit weedy, kind of a bookworm, but you know? That kind of makes his old man proud of him. It makes his old man think: I can help make somebody who turns out that different from me. And I can tell my own mother, hey Mom, I didn't let you down. I didn't become no lawyer like my brother, and I got divorced, but I did one good thing in my life. I made my Michael. And you know Mom, my Michael wants to live with me. This guy could go to Oxford, he could talk with the children of aristocrats, hey, he doesn't even like Southern California. But my son wants to live with me.

All that summer, Michael and Louis made their plans.

Michael would pass his GCSEs in June the next year, and then spend six months studying to take the SAT test. Then Michael would apply for a dual passport. He began to sign his full name: Michael Louis Oliveira Blasco.

Using his Latin name made Michael feel wobbly inside, as if he had changed his name to join his father, as if indeed they had in some way merged identities. It felt as if he were going public, as if he were promising someone never to love anyone else. He would repeat that new name to himself over and over in a whisper.

Thoughts of his father drove out thoughts of anyone else. The beaches of California are not short of handsome men wearing little clothing. They had no power to turn Michael Louis Oliveira Blasco's head or heart. The magic of naming echoed what had happened in biological fact. Michael's ego had melted down and merged with someone else's. He had married his father.

Mi macho, cómo te amo.

There was nothing else in Michael's life for over a month. Love made him numb. He and his Dad came back from a movie and a slightly beery dinner. It was eleven at night – eight in the morning in England. Michael rang home and finally told his mother of his decision, and then took everything one step further.

His father had drunk a bit too much. He couldn't handle

drink that well. He was a bit woozy and his black eyes swam with love. Michael wanted to kiss him. Instead, he took his hand and said, 'Dad. I've decided. I'm not going to go back to England.'

His father's eyes dimmed. 'What do you mean?'

'I'm going to stay here. At the end of this summer? I'll finish high school in Oceanside.'

'Oh man.' His father let Michael's hand drop. He covered his head with both hands. 'Man, oh man.' He swayed as if under a burden. 'You can't treat your mother like that, Mike. You're too old to give in to emotion like that. You got to do the right thing.' The words were laboured, like he was remembering lines from a John Wayne script. 'You got to go back home to your mother and we'll do this thing the right way.'

His face looked blue-white and blotchy.

'It's what I want to do.'

Isn't that what you want?

His father sniffed and moved away from him, took a swig from the bottle and as if he had heard Michael's unspoken question, shook his head, no.

Michael went to bed a bit drunk, and slept well enough until about 5 AM, when he suddenly was awake, wide awake, with the truth as clear as if it were squatting on his chest.

I love my own father like I should be loving someone my own age.

Michael, Michael, what do you think you're doing? There is no one else in the world doing this, there isn't even any name for what you are doing. You are out there, man, you are way, way out there.

What are you doing to your mother? She's the one who's actually been there all your life, she's the one who's done all the paying. Now, just when you're growing up and she's getting old, you want to take off and leave her.

And you want . . . there really was almost no way to say it. You want your father. You want to settle in with your Dad and you want . . .

Though he's a Catholic he was born semi-circumcised so the head of his dick always shows and it's always clean and before

I sleep and when I wake up I think of the head of that cock in my mouth. It's all I want.

You have to stop it, Michael. This is crazy. Go on home at the end of summer and get over it. That's all he wants. Go home and let the whole idea of living with him in America dissolve.

What are you going to tell him? Are you going to say, Dad I'm a faggot and I'm in love with you and I want to live with you like a pair of hairdressers? No, you're not going say that, so what the fuck are you going to say?

You're going to say, Dad, I've changed my mind, I don't want to live with a dumb Marine. I'll say I've decided that English universities are better.

He'll pretend that's OK, OK with him, and he'll cough to clear his throat instead of crying, and he'll put on those mirror shades so I can't see his eyes, and when he drives he'll thump the steering wheel hard for no reason.

Real great, Michael. Superb. Either way, you're going to hurt him. Aw shit, what have you done?

It was a long time to stay in bed, staring at the ceiling. Michael was not strong. He slipped back into reverie. He imagined that Louis was not his father at all, and that they had gone backpacking in the wilds, washing in lakes, and holding each other at night. He imagined them making love, imagining trailing his face down his father's body. He masturbated, imagining making love to him, and mopped up with the tissues he now kept by the bed. He fooled himself with imaginings. He went to sleep and woke up, lulled and soothed, with the feeling that it would all be OK somehow.

Michael walked out to the kitchen later, in his Y-fronts with a morning hard-on.

'Man, you look like I feel,' said Dad, a remark open to interpretation. He reached for the coffee-pot. 'You're like me, you can't wake up without caffeine.'

Flawless, unchanging California sunshine came through the windows. It would be another beautiful day, with Oceanside ten degrees cooler than anywhere else.

Michael couldn't even remember why he had been so concerned.

His Dad went to work, and Michael lay on the bed and masturbated again, dreaming of him. The dream this time was more direct: they were still father and son, but no one knew anything. They lived together as partners, they slept in the same bed and Michael swung his bag of books into the car every morning and drove off to UC San Diego. It took people years to realize what was going on. They were shocked at first, Mom, Michael's uncles, but when they saw it was love, they got used to it. They grew to understand. It was the image of sleeping all night, his face cushioned on his father's breast, that made Michael come.

Then he got up and looked at the curriculum covered by the SAT test, and made a list of American textbooks and thought of joining summer school. And after that there would be nothing to do except loll on the beach all day dreaming of his father. And he would go to the camp, and see his father in the nude, and run with his father and dream with his father of the life they both wanted to build together.

Driven mad by the imperatives of love, Michael became sure his father wanted the same thing.

As they started the run, Dad slapped Michael's butt. He looked at Michael in the shower and said, 'Man, what do you call that thing? Is that a dick? It looks like it belongs on a horse, man!' His father walked on the pier with an arm on Michael's shoulder. He hugged him as they watched television on the sofa.

The liquid looks of love, the hugs, the sudden rufflings of his hair, the kisses sometimes even on the mouth, thrilled Michael, and warmed his heart, and made him dream, and convinced him that they were, in everything but consummation, lovers.

Michael did not imagine, even in his daydreams, that they would proceed immediately to sex. Sex would emerge almost as an afterthought, almost as a by-product of complete intimacy. They would share meals, share showers, share food, share beds, and at some quiet moment, foreheads touching, they would proceed to make love.

Michael dreamed of the moment that his father would finally say something. He imagined it in some detail. His father would begin quietly, shy. It would be no easy thing for a Marine to admit that he – and he would look down, smiling – that he loved Michael. He knew such a thing was a bit unusual but he had seen something in Michael's eyes, something that at first he wanted not to see.

Michael was romancing.

He began to be sure, from his father's eyes. He was sure from the totally comfortable way that he would sometimes break into terrible campfire songs that he loved him too. His father was too shy to say so. His father had always been so masculine; so conventional. It would be hard for anyone to accept, let alone a conservative man whose utterly traditional American values were underpinned with an equally unforgiving Catholicism.

The thought came: you have to help him, Michael. You can't leave him in doubt. It'll be easier for you, Michael: you're from the younger generation. And then it will be in the open. And then it will happen.

Michael began to rehearse how he would do it. He would sit and start a serious, adult conversation. Dad, he would say, let's be honest about this . . . what's happening. Let's just say it. Dad, you and I well . . . we are . . .

Every time, imagination faltered. Every time the words, the magically correct words, would not formulate themselves. The right words were like the Loch Ness monster, expected, believed in, but swimming in the depths.

Michael convinced himself that it was his duty to make the situation clear.

And all the while love grew stronger. Michael would deliberately make his bed with his father's old sheets. Night after night, he would breathe him in. Michael would take his father's underwear, his swimsuits, anything personal and touched by him. He would take the swimsuit to bed with him and press it up against his face. Or he would wear his father's underpants, to feel his genitals cradled where his father's had been cradled. He would wear them secretly all through the day, as he drove to UCSD library to see what a university science course really expected you to know. It was as if he could feel himself cupped by his father, held.

By the end of those two months, everything about his father, from his name to his eyes, to his hands and feet, to the spreckles of his urine on the toilet seat, to his dirty knives and forks, to his hairs in the hair brush, to old photographs of him when he was Michael's age, to his letterman's jacket, to his tight jeans, to his loose shorts, to his white running socks, to the warmth he left behind him on the sofa, to his footprints in the sand and the imprint of sand on the bum of his wet swimming shorts, to the sand that fell from his feet when he dried them on the landing of the condo – everything about him made Michael feel loose and shivery, could moisten the tip of his penis.

It became, simply, an overwhelming, instinctual imperative. Michael needed his father to penetrate him, to leave his seed.

Every time his father laughed, every time he lightly touched Michael, every time he wrestled with him out of sheer high spirits and physical boisterousness, intertwining arms and necks and legs, Michael became more convinced.

His father wanted it too.

Why couldn't either of them say anything?

You're old, Dad; you come from a religious background. You're a big bad Marine, Dad. All of that makes it hard for you. I'll make it easy.

The words fail because they just say it, and that makes it sound weird and strange and it's not. It's just love. So why use words?

All I need to do is come to you, Dad. All I need to do is lie next to you and kiss you, and we will be together.

Michael, why are you such a coward? Michael, you know it's up to you. You can't just lie here night after night, dreaming of him, hearing him in the next room, seeing him day in day out, seeing him naked, seeing the way he looks at you. Michael you must, Michael you have to. Just do it, Michael. Just be honest.

So finally, a week before he was due to go back home, on 7 September 1976 at 2.00 AM, having lain awake for four hours, Michael finally said to himself, That's it. I can't stand this. This has to end. It has to end now. He kicked off the covers.

Do it, Michael.

He stood up.

I'm actually doing this.

He felt the cold, cup-shaped American doorknob.

I'm going to touch you there. I'll know what it's like.

Michael listened as the door clicked open.

I'll finally, finally know what a cock is like in my mouth. I'll finally know what your cock is like. I don't want it from anyone other than you.

Can you hear me, Dad; can you hear my feet on the carpet? Have you lain awake all night, thinking of me? Are you sitting up with a start, thinking, is that Mike? You'll say, naw, he's just going to the john. He doesn't even know what's going on. Mike's innocent.

Well, I'm not innocent, Dad. I know what I'm doing. I'm doing it for both of us. We don't need to be afraid. We don't need to tell anyone what we've done. We can live together, father and son. You'll know when I touch you. You'll know when we kiss. I've just got to do this. I'll bust wide open if I don't.

The door hangs open. I can smell you. I can hear you breathe. I stand over you. How do I do this? You look so sealed in the sheet, all wrapped around, how do I peel it? Do I just land next to you? Will my weight hurt you? I'm not so little now, as I used to be. Do I just lie down on the edge of the bed and kiss you?

Dad, help me, I don't know what to do.

Maybe you'll just keep on sleeping. Maybe you'll never know. Maybe I'll just touch you, hold you and you won't notice. You'll think it was just a dream, something not real, something that happened another time, another place.

No harm done.

So Michael sits down on the floor and feels the rough fur of the carpet on his bare ass, and he reaches in under the sheet, and goes up the cool soft thigh and feels the tip of his father's big-headed penis and takes it firmly in his grasp.

Everything is still for a minute. Then Michael moves his hand around it, over it, to feel its sleeping shape. At last, I'm touching you; I'm holding it. It feels just like I always imagined, big and small, swollen and soft. Sweet. It feels sweet. It feels like it is meant for expressing love.

Suddenly, his father's eyes snap open and glare into his.

There is no confusion, no awakening befuddlement. His father's eyes are hawk-like, angry, watchful, and they stare into Michael's face. It is as if they are made of ice, at sea, and glow faintly in the dark.

'Jesus Christ, what the fuck are you doing?'

And his father scuttles back from him.

Sergeant Blasco crowds himself against the back of the bed. 'What are you doing, Michael?'

He lunges sideways, fumbles with the neck of the lamp, and switches it on. Michael sees the eyes again, and thinks, oh fuck, oh no. Something seems to be sucking his stomach out through his ass.

Michael knows instantly, with horrible, shrivelling certainty, what the situation is. He was wrong, he had been wrong about it all. But his mouth, and another part of his brain, carry on, try to make the situation change, by a miracle, by sympathetic magic.

'I was trying to make it easy for you.' Michael feels skinny, like a concentration-camp victim, naked with ribs showing through, and he is nervously biting both the tip of his index finger and thumb.

'Trying to make what easy for me, Michael?' His father has pulled up a sheet over his loins. He jerks it higher, to cover his tits.

Michael starts to blub, he can't say it because to say it, and see the reaction would be the final end of the dream.

'You were stroking my dick, Michael!'

His father has gone relentless, professional. He is trained to seek out problems and hound them. 'Make what easy for me, Michael?'

Michael blubs it out now, as a confession, an admission of error with no hope of making anything right. 'To make love.'

His father thinks he hasn't heard right. 'To make love? Is that what you said? Is that what you said to me, Michael?'

Michael nods, knowing his whole face has gone as bleary as semen, all tears and spit.

'Jesus Christ.' His father digs his fingers into his hair, and his hair stays upright. 'What, you wanted to fuck me?'

It wasn't like that; it didn't feel like that. It was love. 'No,' Michael whines in an utterly bereft voice.

'Suck my dick, or what?'

Michael can only make a noise. All Michael can do is haul in enough air and force it through the glue to say, 'I love you.'

His father strides forward on the bed, towering over Michael, big enough to snap him in half, his bare shoulders still beautiful. 'You're a faggot. You're a fucking little faggot and you touched me. You touched me.'

His father is now striking at Michael's chest with just the tips of his fingers like a goose attacking with its beak. 'You *touched* me, you fucking little fruit. Your own father!'

And his father pushes him to the floor. Michael hits his head on the edge of the open doorway. His legs lift up and his smooth bottom and smoochy little anus are visible, and this drives his father crazy, as if his son were doing this deliberately to lure him.

'Get out of here, get out of my room, you fucking faggot! You fucking fairy!'

His father starts to kick him, in the butt, on the back of his legs.

Michael can't talk. 'Dad. Stop,' he tries to say, but it comes out as a bubble of something. He rolls over onto all fours and tries to crawl.

That sticks his bare hairless ass in the air, like a porno photo of a dame in a fuck magazine.

'Just get the fuck away from me.' His father doesn't exactly kick him, more like pushes him with his foot. Michael falls forward and friction-burns his elbow on the rug.

'Go on, get out!'

Michael scurries forward on all fours. He manages to run mostly on his feet, except for the odd, steadying fist on the carpet. He scuttles into his room and closes the door. He waits, fearfully.

Michael begins fully to understand what has happened. The dream has collapsed. He won't be studying at UCSD. He will never live in any house in San Diego or Carlsbad, at least with Dad. There won't be a garden. There won't be skiing in Aspen or a walk along the John Muir Trail. He won't become an American citizen. He will never be Michael Louis Oliveira Blasco. He'll go back to England. Will he ever see his father again? Maybe yes, after many years, after all this wears away.

Michael tries to think of something sensible to do. He does realize that his nakedness infuriates his father. He starts to dress. In the condo hallway, there is blood on the white carpet. That will stain, he thinks dully. He pulls on underwear, jeans, T-shirt, gets a towel from the bathroom and drenches it under the tap.

He kneels and starts scrubbing the carpet. At first the stain reminds him of the skids on his own elbows. But as he scrubs, the stain spreads, and the thought comes, it will never come out, never, never. And then it looks just like what has happened, a terrible bloodied wound that will mean the carpet is never the same.

'Never, never, never,' he says and he scrubs and then he breaks down. His hands go too weak to hold the towel. They rise up helplessly and waver like the necks of swans in a mating dance, and he sobs and chokes.

And his father walks out of the bedroom. His father has dressed now, and he looks at Michael with hatred and disgust.

'Don't look at me like that!' Michael wails.

His father has come to do something else. He walks into Michael's room. Michael trails after him.

'What is this?' His father holds up a book of *Alice in Wonderland*, and throws it down.

'What's this? Batman. A guy in leotards. What have you brought in my house? Huh? You fucking fruit! Were you looking at me? Were you looking at me in the showers? Huh. Huh? Were you looking at my men? Did you come every day into the changing room just to watch the men?'

It's going to start again, his father's hand jabbing into him.

'I did it to be with you.'

244

His father stops. There is almost sympathy in his face. Now the anger has somewhere to go. His gaze lights on the records.

'What is this? Huh? Fuckin' *Cinderella*. You're the fucking Cinderella. Fucking *Cinderella*.' And Dad works the album back and forth, cardboard crinkling until the album snaps.

'Dad, don't,' says Michael, but what he means is don't be this angry, don't break us.

'What's this? And this? All this faggot stuff.' He starts flinging books and records to the ground.

'Dad, stop.' Dad has hold of a book and he is tearing its binding down the middle and he's throwing the pages at Michael. He suddenly wipes all the books off the shelf, and he throws the stereo at the wall and it cracks with the sound of plastic breaking. He shoves the TV to the floor. Miraculously, only some knobs are broken off.

'You get all this stuff out of my house! I don't care where. It just goes!'

His father storms out of the room.

Michael goes quiet. Well, Michael. This is what it is. He didn't love you that way and now he doesn't love you at all.

He knows what you are, that's why. He never would have loved you, the second he found out that you're gay. It never would have been any kind of love as soon as he knew who you were.

How ... could ... you ... be ... so ... dumb?

Michael starts to slap himself. He slaps himself really hard, to wake himself up.

'You stupid fucking little idiot!' Michael growls at himself, and cuffs his ears and temples, and keeps his fist rolled and punches himself in the face.

There was only a week to go. If he'd left it a week, he would have got onto the aeroplane, gotten over whatever held him. He could have come back at eighteen without Dad ever knowing.

Michael stands in the middle of the room and looks at the bare light bulb, and feels the heaviness again. His fingers feel like fishing weights. They feel like they could pull the line all the way out of his reel. It's late, he has no energy, no tears. He might as well finish clearing up.

245

Michael picks up the broken record. You can buy another. He puts the books back on the shelf, moving as if in a slow-motion study. The book torn in half is a veterinary textbook, one he was reading for UCSD. He might as well leave it torn, leave it here. He won't have any use for it now – he won't be studying at UCSD. The stereo is fucked, but what does that matter? He only uses it when he's here, and he may never come back again. He turns the TV on and it's a late-night Italian Western, claustrophobic voices in studios mismatching lips. He goes back to scrubbing the hall carpet, listlessly, mechanically, continually and to some effect.

Michael begins to be aware of a shower running. There is a noise coming from it, as if there is something terribly wrong with the plumbing. He thinks he'd better see what's wrong. Then he thinks, If I go to the shower and he's naked he'll think I've come for him again. The towel has turned pink. Michael needs to rinse it. He goes to the kitchen instead, rinses the towel and comes back and recognizes the sound. It's someone crying.

'Dad. Dad, is something wrong? Dad?'

The door creaks when it opens like in a horror movie. The shower is running and something dark is on the floor behind the frosted glass, and there is a shredding sound.

'Dad, Dad are you OK? Dad, just say something.'

Michael opens the door and his father is slumped on the floor of the shower and he's fully dressed with water running and he has been eating towels. Big, plush, California towels. The threads of them lie wound all over his black slacks. They coat his mouth and make him look a bit like the Cookie Monster. His accusing eyes look up at him.

'Dad, get up.'

His father grunts and tries to and can't quite get his legs to unfold, and Michael becomes seriously worried, but he can't think of any way of helping that does not involve touching his father. His father's dark eyes warn him: do not touch me. Michael backs away hands raised as if to shield himself, mime helplessness, display his innocence.

Outside the bathroom door, Michael starts to pace. He paces the hallway, and tries to collect his thoughts and can't. They scatter away from him like pearls from a broken necklace rolling away down an escalator. He can't think of anything to do.

He decides to pack. He will have to leave. In the bedroom he takes his shirts out of the closet. He can't remember how to fold shirts so they stay flat. He remembers how his father and he worked together doing the laundry, just that morning, washing, sorting, ironing. 'Hey Mike, I never did this as well by myself. When you move in, we'll have the cleanest laundry ever.'

I guess we won't now, Dad.

I really should go to bed. Michael has just about convinced himself that that is all he can do, since he can't find his socks or his favourite pair of running shoes.

Then abruptly, determined, business-like, his father enters the bedroom. He's changed into dry clothes, a form-fitting T-shirt and slacks. He's still barefoot. He's breathing heavily, through his nose. His lips are pressed shut.

'What time is it in England? What's the number?'

'What do you mean?'

'Whot do you mean?' His father is doing a hate-filled imitation of an English accent. 'I'm going to ring your mother and let her know what a terrific job she did raising you.'

'You're going to tell Mom?'

'No. You are.'

'Me?' Michael sounds like a scared little boy.

'Don't you think she has a right to know? Are you ashamed, Michael? Are you ashamed of what you did?'

'Yes,' says Michael, miserably. 'Please don't tell Mom.'

'You should never do anything you're ashamed of, Michael. It's five hours to New York, say eight to London.' His father counts forwards from 3.00 AM. 'It'll be eleven in the morning, right Michael?'

His father backs away into the hallway, and walks towards the phone in the kitchen. Michael follows, wretchedly.

'Please Dad, please don't. Don't do this, Daddy, please.'

His father gets out his tiny, khaki-coloured pocket diary and starts looking up the number.

'Dad please, look, I'll go to a psych, I'll do anything, but please don't tell Mom.'

'You sure as heck will be going to a psychiatrist.' Dad listens to the dial tone.

Michael remembers shoes. He kept outgrowing shoes, and his Mom on her teacher's salary had to find money for shoes. They always bought the specials or nearly out-of-dates in super-markets. Her boss told her to smarten up how she dressed when she was teaching but she never buys clothes for herself.

'Everything you do has consequences,' his father says. 'It's time to grow up.' His voice changed. 'Hello Mavis, this is Louis. No, he's not fine. If you wanna know, he's just done something pretty godawful. Michael. Tell your mother what you did.'

Michael is sobbing helplessly now, and is shaking his head, no, no. He can't even imagine saying the words.

'You start growing up now, Michael.' His father holds out the phone like a club.

'No.' Michael is wheedling, like he's wet himself in public.

'Michael.' His father is starting to get angry.

Michael howls, and covers his face, and bolts from the room. The gesture is perfectly sincere, but Michael is also aware of very slightly overplaying it. He is offering up the shame and guilt and self-disgust his father wants him to feel. He runs out the front door, and down the steps.

'Michael! Michael!' his father shouts after him.

Michael has forgotten the key and the security gate is locked.

'Michael!'

He hears the apartment door slam, and feet on the steps. The gate and fence are metal poles with something like spikes on the top, with crossbars only at the top and bottom. Michael jumps and hoists himself up. His shirt catches and tears. He stumbles and kicks and topples forwards, hands reaching out to take the blow. Grit is driven into them and his knee thumps hollowly on the sidewalk. He stands up and his knee is weak under him. He has to hobble along the sidewalk. It runs parallel to the fence, and on the other side of the fence his father strolls alongside him, on his way back to the condo staircase.

'I'll keep it simple, Michael. I'll just tell her what's happened. I won't make any trouble. You'll have to face her sooner or later, boy. And yourself.'

And his father climbs up the staircase to the waiting phone.

Michael hobbles on towards the beach. He can hear the sea, shushing like a mother to quiet his fears. 'Oh man, oh man.' Michael says to himself, over and over.

At 3:15 AM there are birds singing somewhere and there is a steely hint of dawn. He stomps flat-footed down the steps from the cliffs onto the beach. There is no one, just security lights blazing in shrubbery, street lights, the odd light bulb over the driveway into holiday apartments.

What Michael wants to do is flee. He wants to slip back into the apartment when his father is at work and pack up his things, maybe take some food, and not go back to either home. He can't stand the thought of being back in either home. He just wants to disappear.

He flings himself down onto a hollow in the sand, in the dark, hoping that no one can see him.

The breakers keep pummelling. They keep coming back, one after another. You imagine a little kid in them, and he keeps getting knocked over, and the kid wonders why they don't stop. They pull out for a little while, and the little kid thinks oh good, it's gone, I can swim now, and then the wave hits him again.

There is no way this is going to get better. Everything, everything is going to change. He saw his mother's long face. What is she going to make of this? What is he going to tell her? She knows I wanted to live with Dad. Now she'll know why. She probably knows that now, right now. And she'll know that Dad will want her to pick up the pieces again. It would be hard enough for her to find out I'm gay, but that I was crazy enough to make a pass at my own father. That I would be that dumb, that sicko.

Of all the guys in the world, why your father?

Because he's beautiful. Michael saw his father's face, his body, and the colour of his skin. He remembered the smell of him, the smell of his mouth, the feel of his lips. The love, the sexual love flooded back. In the end losing his father hurt the most, or rather, losing the dream of him. That's why I did it; that's why I dreamed myself into a hole. I could have shut up, not told him, lived my little dream. For how long, Michael? He

249

would have started to ask you about girlfriends. He might have noticed my eyes straying. Sooner or later something like tonight would have happened.

Michael faced inevitability. This was always going to happen, he realized. From the moment I started making my plans, this was waiting for me.

So it really wouldn't have been any good if I'd been smarter. Dad never would have loved me.

Michael started to weep again, for that lost dream; it had been his life over the last two months, and he had no other life to mourn. He'd already left his old one.

Michael must have fallen asleep in the end. Suddenly there was sunlight. Seagulls made exhilarating noises, one after another like the bells of many churches. There was a paved road along this stretch of beach and all along it old ladies were walking their dogs, or businessmen were jogging in grey tracksuits. For a moment it was beautiful, and then Michael remembered. He looked at his watch. It was 6:10. What if Dad came looking for him?

Michael stood up and started to hobble further down the beach towards Carlsbad. Between Carlsbad and Oceanside there was a marsh, a wildlife reserve with a lagoon and birds. The main road raced through the middle of it on a causeway. So did the railway on a separate series of bridges. If Michael slipped under the railway, he could hide from the road, amid the reeds. Then maybe about ten o'clock he could go and have breakfast at Café 101. He could pack some stuff and take off.

Well maybe. How was he going to take off? By bus? How much money did he have? What was he going to do? Say: Hey, Dad, I'm running away from home, can I borrow the car? It began to feel like another dream. He had developed distaste for dreams.

He felt exposed, naked in the wide expanse of beach and brilliant sunshine. He turned off the beach and limped as fast as he could up onto the railway. He scanned the road, slipping on gravel, for any sign of a blue Ford. He hobbled along the tracks, visible all the while from the road.

Finally he saw the pathway under the railroad. He skidded

down the bank, and ducking low, scampered under the bridge.

The lagoon was lined with the backs of expensive homes and the railway. There was no road anywhere near it. Michael squatted on the banks and looked at the insect patterns imprinted on the creamy mud. He waited.

He remembered his Dad used to bring him here, to look at the birds, and spend an hour or two fishing. It was always hot and still. What do you think of your son now, Dad? Michael asked the memory of his fishing father. The sun pounded like unrelenting boredom.

Hungry, Mikey? You've still got the price of a Huevos Rancheros in your pocket. In a week you won't.

Just how much of a baby are you, Michael? This is what a five-year-old does. He decides to run away and gets halfway down the block before realizing that he can't cope.

Michael slapped his own face again. He had to slap something, he was so mad, so bereaved, so ashamed. He couldn't stand it. He couldn't stand being inside his own skin. He seethed under his skin, like oil in a joint being roasted in the oven. You're not hitting hard enough, Michael. He really slammed himself on the cheek. It went numb. He picked up a stone and drove it as hard as he could into the centre of his face. His nose started to bleed. Drops of blood dotted his trousers.

Stupid fucking fairy, what the stupid fucking hell good does that do? He broke down again, and started to cry. It was late and getting hot and he was sick from hunger, bleeding, and lack of sleep. Ten AM. Maybe it was safe to get going.

A train roared overhead, hooting and rocking the track from side to side like a crib. Michael toyed with the idea of waiting for the next train and walking under it. That might even look like an accident.

The thought of Huevos Rancheros made him decide he wanted to be around. And that made him laugh and snuffle at the same time. All I've got to look forward to is a 101 breakfast.

He strode alongside the tracks, perfectly safely into Oceanside. He climbed up another bank onto a side street and walked among all the whispering ranch-style homes, with their lawns and succulent ground cover being automatically watered.

Michael was watered too. He washed the blood off his face.

He turned up the street to the café and went in the back door from the parking lot, and the first person he saw in a booth was Dad. Michael thought about turning and running and realized that he didn't have the strength.

'Hiya Mikey,' said his father, in a voice that seemed to come from far away across a valley. 'Have a seat.'

And you thought you were being so smart: he knew you'd come here all the time. Michael sat down. The booths had tan upholstery and individual jukeboxes at each of the tables. They didn't work.

'You been in a fight? Who did that to you?' His father's voice really was different, it was higher and more gravelly at the same time. His sunglasses were different, old-fashioned, dark green, not mirrored at all.

Michael considered making up a story about how homeless people had chased him and beaten him up. But he didn't have the heart for it.

'Me,' he said. His own voice was far away too and now he understood why: neither of them wanted anyone to hear.

'You. You did that to yourself?' His father's mouth opened and shut helplessly. Michael couldn't see his eyes.

Then his father reached across and touched the bridge of Michael's nose, and made him turn his head. His father's implacable face remained mostly unmoved but the voice shifted down an octave. 'You've broken your nose, Michael.'

In that gesture, Michael knew it hadn't gone away. The tips of his father's fingers were soft and cool. This guy was his ideal man – big, masculine, kind. Michael still wanted to marry this guy. He wanted to take him in his arms, and kiss him, and live with him. Whatever this was, it would not go away.

'What'll you have to eat?' his father said, business-like.

'I'm not hungry.'

'Yes you are, Michael.'

Michael's head hung in shame. What could he do to make up for it? Starving himself wouldn't do any good, if a broken nose couldn't. He asked for a Huevos Rancheros.

His father paused at this and seemed to ruminate. It seemed

to Michael he was thinking: I thought we'd be doing this a lot. He pretended to study the menu.

'I . . . uh didn't tell your mother everything. I just outlined some of the basics. I couldn't say it, Mikey. I just couldn't say it about you.' He kept looking at the menu the whole time.

Michael felt relief, and felt cowardly for being relieved. 'I will tell her. After a little while.'

'I bet,' said his father, darkly.

Another voice spoke. 'Hi, what'll it be for you folks?' The waitress was too old and thin to fit the stereotype but her smile was huge and professional.

'Huevos Rancheros. Two big cups of coffee. Maybe a Danish.'

The waitress had picked up on something. Her smile went rigid and her eyes skidded sideways towards Michael. There was a bruise across his face now, he could feel it, and his clothes were torn. She looked back at Michael's father with suspicion. We look like it, thought Michael, for the first time we look like an older faggot and a poor kid he's picked up and is bribing with a meal. His ears burned.

For the first time ever his father asked, 'You wouldn't be able to serve a beer this hour of the morning would you?'

Two days later, Michael was on the aeroplane. His mother greeted him wearily at the airport, circles under her eyes. She was wearing a beige mac in summer; it was drizzling a bit. She took him in her arms and gave him a hug that was meant to say: you're still my son, whatever happens.

'Welcome home, Michael.'

What the hug actually said was: Michael, you will never go home.

Home will always be with the man you love, and nothing else will ever be the same again. The externals of his old life, everything he had thought he would escape, closed over him.

As for his father, well, early to mid-forties is a bad time in the military. If you start slipping, your career almost certainly will end. They give you courses in making the transition. It's still too big a shock for many people, to go from an ordered environment where people respect each other and work together for common aims, to a world in which loneliness and justified suspicion is the basis on which everyone must live their lives.

Dad got taken in by an investment scheme on the Salton Sea. How, they reasoned, can you ever lose on property? Look at what happened in Palm Springs. The folks who bought there early doubled, even trebled their investment. Now, this is Palm Springs with water, a lake even. A salt lake.

Michael's legacy from his Dad was an empty plot of land, on a named street without a single house on it.

His father never could handle booze. He just couldn't metabolize the stuff quickly. Nor, at forty-eight, could he get a job anywhere. He tried to stay in shape, hung around with floozies more and more, sold the condo in Oceanside for something right in the heart of where all the whores hung out. He drank and whored, which on the coast of California almost certainly means he also did drugs. He started to get fat.

He shacked up with a tough little Mexican lady. This most American of men was continually asked for his passport or identity papers. When he passed out on the street people started talking about illegal immigrants. Finally he moved back to LA, and tried to set up in his brother's law firm. He wore a suit and tried to find something to do: accounts, sales, even typing. He had a fight with his brother, and that's when he and Michael's mother lost touch. Michael's uncle said he'd heard that Louis was working as a gardener now, in Beverly Hills. 'A sad case. Not something we like to talk about, really.'

When Michael was in his twenties, his mother got a letter. Michael's father had died. The family were terribly sorry, they'd only found out themselves weeks before. They'd collected his ashes from the cremation agency and scattered them on the vast training grounds of Camp Pendleton.

'They may be sorry, but why couldn't they have told us when the service was?' Michael's mother looked baffled. Michael did not say: they didn't want us, Mom. They don't want me. They know what happened, and you don't.

Michael had a fantasy that lodged in his brain. He would return to it, even when he lived with Phil in their first full hormonal rush of love. He returned to it even now, when he loved nobody.

His father hadn't died. They made a mistake, and mis-indentified someone else's body. And one night, Michael is at an international biology congress, in LA, and for some reason it's raining, but there is a bar next door to his hotel. Michael doesn't know it's a gay bar, he has no idea. He just goes in to escape the unruffled anonymity of the hotel.

And he's leaning against the bar, and something about all these men together, big and butch or pretty and merry, starts alarm bells ringing. He's just beginning to realize what kind of bar it is, when a warm tender voice behind him says, 'Hello, Michael.'

He turns and his father is there, alive. He's still a big man, white-haired and a bit portly now. His skin is sallow, rather than brown, but he's stylish, all in black, and his eyes sparkle with love and regret. He's braver now, more willing to accept the truth. Michael books him into the room next to his in the hotel and what happens next varies, slightly, according to the scenario.

So what do you want, Michael?

Henry waited until long after Michael had finished speaking. Then he crawled up the bed in blue jeans and brown shirt and snuggled up to him.

'You know, Michael, I saw a TV programme once. There's a syndrome. Brothers and sisters who have never seen each other before, or fathers and daughters who meet for the first time as adults. They often fall in love. It's how we're designed. Either we go for someone who's totally different from us genetically. Or we fall in love with someone close to us genetically, because it's worked before. So it's not that you were perverse or bizarre or sick or just plain dumb. It's what people do.'

Michael was not to be mollified. 'So why doesn't everyone fall in love with their father?'

Henry sighed, and kissed him on the forehead. It was as if they had been lovers for decades, comfortable and relaxed and kind. 'The programme said that what makes the difference is living with them when you're young. You have to know them in childhood. There's a kind of barrier kicks in then. In China they sometimes choose a bride for a baby boy . . . she's a baby girl . . . and they grow up together and almost always they hate the thought of getting married. They feel it's incest.'

Michael lay still. 'So what do I do about it?'

'What you're doing now. You talk about it. You put it behind you.'

Michael laid his head on Henry's chest. 'Anything else?'

256

'You could fall in love with someone.' Henry was smiling at him.

'I tried that. It didn't work.'

Michael's face must have looked forlorn, because Henry suddenly looked forlorn too. 'I know. It hurts.'

It was late again, they had been talking all night, and Michael need to sleep. He looked at Henry's face and a phrase came to him. 'Guardian,' he said. 'Angel.'

'That's right,' said Henry. He bundled Michael closer to him. 'If I stay the night, will you try to sleep?'

'Hmmm mmmm,' promised Michael, and felt himself settle as if sinking into Henry's chest. It must have been all he needed, because in the morning, when he woke, Henry was gone.

Michael went to work the next day feeling bright and happy and alert.

Which was good, because there was a lot to do. The deadline for the next grant application was looming, but there was also the paper he had promised for the congress in America, and several offprints that he really should read. He had even fallen behind simply signing off invoicing and accounts.

He and Ebru charged at the in-tray. She sorted all the piles of paper into different sections, and they went through it, letter by letter, invoice by invoice. He couldn't help hearing a certain note of exasperation in her voice. But there was relief as well.

By the end of the day, all her invoices had been signed. Orders had been approved for stationery, feed, even capital expenditure in the form of a new statistical software package. Ebru was happy and joking again. She even stayed late to get it all in the post.

Michael stayed late too. He got through all of his e-mail. Even after he got rid of the spam there were still forty-six real messages to be answered. He went through his paper in-tray and threw out all the sales pitches for conferences and courses. He bundled up all his journals into his bag to be read. He scanned the employment notices from the university in case there was a post coming up. Ebru stuck her head in through the door.

'My, that is a beautiful desk,' she said. 'It is so nice to see the top of it. You should let people see the top of it more often.'

'It certainly looks good,' Michael agreed.

'So nice and tidy,' she said, and made a kind of pinching gesture with her fingers that Michael did not understand.

On the Thursday night, Michael got a phone call.

'Uh, hullo?' said a voice Michael didn't recognize.

'Yes, hello,' replied Michael cautiously.

'Oh, that *is* Michael. Hello.' Long pause. 'Sorry, this is Philip, Michael. How are you?'

Philip sounded hesitant, well-behaved and cautious.

'I'm OK, thanks.'

'Look, Michael, I'm sorry to bother you. Are you going to be around this weekend?'

'In general, yes, why?'

Exasperation stirred. Do get on with it, Phil. Michael was disoriented. This was not like talking to Philip at all. It was as if he were talking to a particularly diffident stranger who needed to use his loo.

'Well, we've finally found a place and if it wasn't inconvenient for you, I was wondering if I might finally relieve you of all the things I've left cluttering up your flat.'

Philip sounded like his father, pure Surrey.

There were a hundred questions. Is it a nice flat? Where is it? How on earth did you afford it? Neither of you has any money.

But you don't ask a stranger things like that even if you once were married to him.

They agreed Saturday. 'See you, then,' they said as blandly as possible.

Philip showed up in a white rented van with the real Henry. They were having a row. Neither one of them was used to vans or vehicles and they had no idea where or how to park it.

Phil had gone fluttery and shaken. 'Oh, for God's sake, just leave it parked on the pavement outside the door. We're loading furniture.'

Henry looked worn. 'It's illegal to park on the pavement. We'll get a ticket.'

'So we'll have to pay the fine. I'm not lugging chests round the block!'

258

Michael was embarrassed and very slightly pleased. He leaned into the window. 'Hello, hi. If you leave your emergency lights flashing, the police are generally pretty good.'

'Hello, Michael,' said Philip, looking relieved.

It was surprisingly good to see him. Michael's heart warmed instantly, and he chuckled. 'How are you, Phil?' It was remarkably like seeing family, a cousin perhaps.

'Oh. Fine. Usually.'

'Hi, Henry,' said Michael. He had to remind himself. This Henry is not exactly the same one I talk to. He's a different copy.

'Hiya,' said this copy of Henry and they shook hands. There was a sense of loss with this Henry. Michael wanted to ask him: do you know that we talk?

'Come on in, have some tea, and just relax for a bit.'

As Michael unlocked the door of the flat, Philip stood like a bunny rabbit holding two paws up against his chest. He was scared of what he would feel once he saw the old place. Michael felt the undertow of the old patterns; Michael wanted to protect Philip and shelter him, as if he were a child. The old door clunked and groaned in bad temper. 'You won't find much difference.'

Philip shivered a little unhappy smile.

The flat hadn't changed. It couldn't change. Philip looked around at the hall chest still in place and the mirror hanging over it. 'It's all just the same.'

Thirteen years seemed to whisper around them like the sound of wind.

Philip was remarkably well-behaved.

There was a lovely little impressionist portrait Philip had bought at a student show. 'I know I bought that picture, but it was always meant for the bedroom, and it just won't be the same without it.'

Michael could see: Philip wanted the flat to stay the same. 'It's up to you, Phil. It's your picture. I won't mind if you take it. You're an artist, you should have some pictures.'

'Well. I suppose . . . I'll leave you your portrait, OK?'

Michael grinned. This was all a bit painful. 'A Philip Tolbarte

259

original. That'll be worth something, some day. Thanks.'

Michael had been good too. He had wrapped all of Philip's family silver in soft blue protective cloth. Philip's big desk had been dismantled into parts for lugging downstairs. All his *Trance Dance 97* compilations were crated up in old wooden wine boxes. Finally, all his pictures had been carefully tied into blocks, sheets of packing paper between them.

The fridge, the cooker, the washing machine were all part Philip's, but he wanted Michael to have them. There wouldn't be room where they were going, he said. Michael began to hurt for him: Phil was poor. Michael wrote out a cheque for half the value of the things new.

Philip hesitated. 'They're old, they're not worth that much.'

'Take the cheque,' said Michael, playing father. Philip reluctantly took it.

'Take the chairs, too.'

Philip shook his head no. 'That's all right.'

'Phil. Take something. You're setting up house. You'll need them.'

Henry said quietly, 'He's right, Phil.'

The logistics of loading chairs, desk, paintings and chests full of porcelain gave them all something else to think about. They spent half an hour outside in the street, trying to find ways to tie everything up so it wouldn't shift or fall. Henry hated vans, but he nipped like a monkey around the furniture, tying and securing. Henry was practical.

'Well,' said Phil. 'I think that's everything.'

'If I find anything else, I'll bring it round.'

'Oh, I nearly forgot.' Philip took out an old Tesco receipt and wrote his new address on it. It was out near South Quay on the Docklands Light Railway. Michael had never even heard of South Quay.

They shook hands outside on the street. Philip's eyes focused into Michael's wistfully. 'Thanks,' he said in a whisper.

Michael watched the van go and waved as if they were weekend guests taking leave.

'Well. That really is that,' he said aloud to himself.

Upstairs in the flat, there was a pale patch on the study wall where a picture had been. Some of the drawers were empty. Now that Philip's desk was gone, there was space in the small room for a bed again. Those were the only signs of Philip's final departure.

How could the flat be even more silent this time?

Easy. It's less full. Philip really, really has gone.

Michael sat on the sofa and sipped a sherry, like his mother always did.

So come on, Michael, he said to himself, with his mother's voice. Do you want him back, or not? And if you don't, why on earth are you sitting around feeling sorry for yourself? You've got to decide, love. You don't want someone real, you don't want someone made up. Well, love, there's nothing in between.

So what do you want, Michael?

Love. Again, that's what I want. Love.

You are a person?

Michael had all the discomfort of being a teacher's child. When he was nine, he and his mother even went to the same primary school.

Every morning there would be a harassed routine of cornflakes and bathrooms and shoelaces. His Mum couldn't afford a car, so they took the bus and walked into the playground together.

Michael was in some danger of being bullied when he was smaller. Once, a gang of older boys surrounded him and started pushing him. Michael looked up and saw his mother turn and walk back into the school, clasping her hands in front of her. Michael understood and was even grateful: he would have to cope with this himself. So he pushed back.

Michael's good grades were regarded with suspicion. His minor misbehaviours were abruptly punished to avoid any accusation of favouritism. One teacher, Mrs Podryska, who didn't like his mother, was not about to do Michael any favours. 'And did you do this homework yourself, Michael?' she asked in a loud, clear voice in front of the rest of the class. Michael still remembered Mrs Podryska's pleased little smile.

Saturdays were spent on domestic chores. His mother would hum to herself all morning, polishing furniture and asking Michael to give her a hand with the vacuuming. After that she would take Michael with her to the supermarket to help carry the bags. Then Michael would have his homework to do, and she would sit through it with him. 'Come on now, Michael, you know how to divide numbers. And no, you don't use your calculator, you use your head.' Blanched with exhaustion, she might watch the television, or talk to her sister or her mum on the telephone.

On Sunday, after breakfast, they would go and visit Granny Hobart. Gran lived in a self-contained flat for old people in Royston where Michael could watch the TV quietly and again help with the washing-up. Sometimes, for a treat, they would go to the cinema together, at 3.00 PM. Again they would take the bus, and it would be full of giggling gangs of independent kids who had escaped their mums.

The quiet time for both of them was Sunday morning. On Sunday morning they had a big breakfast together: bacon and eggs and toast and jam. They would go through the Sunday papers, scrunching toast.

That was how, at nine years old, Michael first saw a photograph of Pablo Picasso.

By tradition, Michael saw the colour supplement first. He turned a page, and there was a picture of an old man in tight briefs. The old man had planted his fists high on either side of his chest, which was puffed out as if he were a muscleman. He stood on a beach and in the background people wore funny masks, all bright colours. The old man's head looked like a bullet, the eyes were dark and staring, merry and challenging at the same time, as if he would head-butt you for a joke.

Michael, even at nine, was forced to acknowledge that something happened when he looked at that photograph. He skimmed the rest of the magazine but kept turning back to it surreptitiously. Michael knew it was somehow wrong that it was a man, and somehow even worse that it was an old man: but he wanted to keep the picture.

His Mum stood up abruptly from the table. 'You won't forget to wash up now, will you love.' Michael's breath went icy. Mum usually took the supplement into the toilet with her.

'I'm still reading this, Mum,' he said.

She wasn't bothered. 'I'll take the Arts instead.' When she

was out of the room, Michael quietly tore the page out of the magazine. He didn't want his mother to know it even existed.

For the next few weeks, while his mother did the laundry, or rang up about the broken Hoover, or shouted at him to get ready for school, Michael hid in his room and looked at his secret photograph. It was embarrassing, something you couldn't talk about. Michael wanted to dance on that beach, be part of the parade with umbrellas and people in masks. He wanted to be enveloped and hugged in those brown arms. He wanted to see what was inside the briefs.

Michael was not the only one. Many people lusted after Pablo Picasso, even at a time of life when most men are age-spotted ghosts of their former sexual selves. How can a photograph convey that? It was as if it were something that wafted around Picasso, a miasma of power that seeped even onto film. Michael at nine would look at the photograph, and duck away coyly. Coyly, he would look again.

At nine, his father's absence was like a grey mist everywhere. Michael eyed men in the street: is my father like him? A big breezy Romford guy would stroll past wearing a football scarf and Michael would think: I'd like to have him for a father.

Michael wanted to sit on Picasso's lap, and snuggle up against that old chest and be held in those arms, and feel those bare legs under him.

Sitting on his bed before school looking at the photograph, Michael realized: this is how men look at photos of women. This is how girls look at pictures of Bobby Sherman or the Monkees. I feel about men the way I'm supposed to feel about women. I'm the wrong way round. I'm queer.

This was a shocking thing to realize at nine in 1969. You could be called Big Girl's Blouse or Poof. Everyone knew what poofs were and they were horrible, and everybody laughed at them all the time. And he was one of them. He was a poof. That scared him. He was what he was not supposed to be, and Michael was otherwise a good little boy. He put the photograph away and then somehow, without meaning to, lost it.

Michael forgot about Picasso. The next year he went to

California and he found his dream beach and his dream father. A-levels and university left him little time for art.

It was Mark, the rugby-playing art dealer, who finally kick-started Michael's interest in Picasso. 'I once popped in to a little exhibition of his work in the Camargue,' Mark told him. 'It was seeing them all together, actually, that did it for me. There was one whole wall of them, painting after painting in the most beautiful colours, and you began to realize the fantastic productivity of the man.'

Late in life, Michael read the biographies, and those demanding, sullen eyes began to work their way into him. The young Picasso was not handsome. Unlike the unambitious, famous people are often not more beautiful in youth. The young Picasso had a fat face, flat greasy hair and a double chin. His expression was disgruntled, and he was bundled in scarves against the cold. He looked older than he would in his forties.

In his forties, Picasso posed as a boxer. His short arms and legs were rounded enough to imitate muscles. He wore baggy briefs that revealed his thighs and chest. The cloth was jammed up into his crotch, as if to show off his dick. Which was surprising as objectively speaking, he had hardly any dick at all. His body at forty, when most men are grizzling all over with greying fur, was as smooth as a girl's. His expression was serious, and his eyes obviously black.

Thirty years later, Michael sat and sipped his mother's sherry. From nowhere, like a bubble rising up from the floor of the sea came a single word.

Picasso.

Before he had time to ask, the air of his flat welled up in ripples like muddy water.

In Michael's sitting room was the most sexually powerful man of his time.

Picasso was tiny, with a round, demanding face, blunt nose and black eyes that seemed to pop out of his head. He was already balding, which in his case simply confirmed his masculine state. A thick woollen jacket was thrown over both shoulders, and the sleeves were left empty. The effect was curiously feminine.

Picasso ignored Michael. He sauntered in a semi-circle around the sitting room, his face curdling with bored disapproval. He sucked on a cigarette, then blew out the smoke.

'*Personne ne vit là,*' he said.

Michael dragged out his schoolboy French, kicking and screaming. '*Moi, j'habite ici.*'

Picasso turned a shameless gaze towards him. '*Vous? Vous êtes une personne?*'

You? You are a person?

Michael had the power of creation, however, and was growing used to it. '*Oui. Je vous ai créé.*'

Picasso looked genuinely bored. '*Moi,*' he said and let the word rest a moment. '*Je me suis créé.*'

Picasso was still scanning the room. His eyes flickered at Philip's portrait of Michael, as if it gave him an attack of the vapours.

'*Mon Dieu,*' Picasso murmured. '*Ça a l'air d'avoir être frit dans de l'huile d'olive.*' It looks like it's been fried in olive oil. Like an athletic teenager Picasso spun around and flung himself sprawling onto the sofa. '*Du vin, s'il vous plaît*', he said, as if to a waiter.

All right, thought Michael. I'm up to this. I'm more than up to this. From nowhere, by magic, he called up a small table with an ashtray, and a glass and a bottle of wine from 60 years ago.

The Angel's mouth made a quick downward turn. Michael had succeeded in giving Pablo Picasso a moment's pause.

Michael told Picasso, 'Please use the ashtray.' Michael pressed his advantage. 'You are a copy of a masterpiece,' he told the Angel. 'I am the student who has copied you.'

Picasso had already recovered. He sniffed and poured himself a glass of wine. He had a private little smile, and his eyes said, be wary, student, I am more than a match for you.

Michael got the preliminaries out of the way. 'Are you willing to make love with a man?'

Picasso flicked ash into the tray. 'I would do so if I wanted to destroy him. Though I am not a destroyer. Unlike you, I am a creator, not a copier. Ultimately, I have no time for destruction.'

'Except perhaps for making sure than no exhibitor would show Gilot's work after she left you?'

Picasso kept smiling undisturbed. 'Is that what she said? Has it occurred to you that she was exhibited only because of me? And perhaps her work is not all that good?'

They were negotiating. 'Might it interest you to find out how I am able to raise the dead?'

Picasso sipped his wine. 'It interests me to be alive again. And relatively young.'

He lowered his gaze at Michael, like a bull lowering his head to charge. He took a contemplative sup from his cigarette, his eyes appraising Michael. Then he ground out the cigarette, stood, walked across the room and grabbed hold of Michael's face. He pushed Michael's lips out of shape, into a parody of a Boucher mouth, and he shook Michael's jaws.

'I fuck you. You never touch me as a woman, ever.'

Picasso relinquished Michael's mouth, but kept a hand hovering as if to slap him.

'That's all the same to me,' said Michael.

The hand was lowered and it unbuttoned the front of Picasso's trousers, and Picasso indicated what he wanted Michael to do. The tiny brown penis was erect, straight up and hard against his belly, as it was almost every time Michael saw it. Michael knelt and swallowed. Picasso kept drinking his wine. The penis was spicy; it reminded Michael of nutmeg, in its colour and scent.

Picasso grew tired of standing. 'It's late, we go to bed now,' said Picasso, patting Michael affectionately on the top of his head.

Picasso claimed Michael's side of the bed and snatched up the newspapers, and began to read, lips moving, eyes burning through them.

'*Je ne peux pas lire l'anglais facilement. Traduisez,*' he demanded, pushing the papers at Michael.

So Michael found himself reading laboriously through British politics in bad French.

'So there was a socialist revolution in *Britain*?'

'Of a kind. They unelected it thirty-five years later.'

'Tuh. That is why English medicine for warts does not work. They have never had a real revolution. I hate England. The stupidest things about my work are all written in English. My friends translate them for me. I'm tired.'

Without asking, Picasso nipped sideways and turned off the light. Quick as blinking, it was dark, and Picasso had somehow enveloped Michael in his tiny arms, thick short legs. Picasso twisted Michael's head around and kissed him with a passion that bewildered Michael. This was a man who basically preferred women. His breath was heavy and scented with cloves and he sucked in Michael's spittle. Before Michael could quite adjust to being so swept up, he was hoisted onto all fours and found himself, with no preliminaries – cream or tentative, gentle penetration – being fucked.

The penis was the right size. It was so small and comfortable that Michael tightened his arse around it, to hold it, caress it. Suddenly impatient, Picasso unfurled and reared up, balancing on the balls of his feet, and began to thrust himself in and out of Michael's body with a speed Michael had never encountered before or even imagined. Picasso was otherwise silent. He came quite quickly and then collapsed. Michael, bewildered, had by accident come at the same time, into his own hand. Picasso rolled off him and looked at Michael and said, 'If you were a woman I could have really fucked you.'

Then he kissed Michael on his nose. 'You make a funny creator, my friend.'

And, just as instantly, he was asleep.

Picasso snored, loudly and incessantly, as if he had an appetite for it, as if he claimed space by doing it, as if he snored to proclaim his genius.

He grew suddenly affectionate in his sleep, and clamped Michael from behind, and snored like a camel directly into Michael's ear. Michael fought his way free. Picasso snorted and then chuckled. In his sleep he began to laugh, continuously, uproariously.

'Are you awake?' Michael asked, feeling battered.

Picasso grunted and rolled onto Michael again. His dick was hard, and Michael was surprised at his own compliance. His arse wasn't sore, and he made no protest. The penis entered him again, and this time it was gentle. It lapped inside him like waves. Michael was to discover that the only way to stop Picasso snoring was to let himself be screwed. And then together, like a boat untethered, they could drift away together.

Michael woke up and it was still dark, and Picasso was still inside him, and around him. Picasso had been inside him all night.

'Hmm,' said Picasso and began to rock inside him. He nuzzled and then chewed Michael's ear. 'You are life,' he said. 'You give me life. I will give you life in return.'

And this time the fucking, though slow, was hard and slamming. Picasso's flat belly thumped into Michael's backside. The penis went all the way out and all the way back in with one thrust. Michael began to make noises he had never made before: he couldn't stop himself. He groaned and grunted and sighed like a bad actress in a porno movie. Picasso seized hold of his long hair and pulled back hard on it, like reins. Michael came before Picasso did, whinnying like a horse.

Picasso finished, slapped Michael's buttocks, and hopped out of bed. 'You are dirty, wash,' he said.

He commandeered Michael's kitchen to make coffee. Michael padded dazed and flushed from the bathroom. Picasso was wearing a pair of Michael's best long grey knickers, but he used one of his ties to make a kind of pirate sash around his waist. He was so short he had to lunge forward on tiptoe to reach things on top of the counter.

'We will move,' Picasso announced.

'I'm sorry?' burbled Michael.

'This apartment faces east, good, but it is low down and has trees in front that block the light. And it is too small. I cannot paint here. We will move.'

Michael felt a jumble of feelings. No other Angel, no other man had ever made the decision so quickly and simply to live with him. No other man had demanded that Michael sell his flat after the first date.

Michael said, 'I like the trees. This flat is worth money because it faces a garden.'

'Humph,' grunted Picasso, unimpressed.

'It's not that easy.'

'I will make it easy.' Picasso turned and his expression surprised Michael. Picasso was smiling, affectionately, gently and sweetly. Life is ours, the smile said. We can do with it what we want. It was a smile that promised: no harm can come. Michael found that he would do anything to make that smile continue.

Picasso passed him a tiny cup of what looked like tar. 'You cannot make coffee. I can tell.' He led Michael out to the sitting room, in front of the bay window. It was only just beginning to get light and everything was grey, as if wrapped in cushioning plastic. They sat at the table in the bay window.

'My friend,' Picasso said. 'You give me life, and I am grateful. You are like a mother to me. You are like a physician who asks only kindness in payment. It is easy to be kind, that is why I don't trust it. But I will be kind to you. You are a sweet man. So understand. I will give you kindness and love, but I will want to screw women, so I will bring them back. Don't try to stop me; that would make me mad. If you are a jealous man, that will be a pain in your heart, not mine, so learn not to be jealous. All right?' Picasso's own eyes were kind, and stroked Michael's knee.

'All right,' agreed Michael.

'All right,' said Picasso, grinning and slapping his knee. 'So now we look for a new place to live. How do we do that?'

'I don't know,' Michael admitted. 'When I first came here to live, I rented, and then they sold it to me for a low price. So I don't know how to find houses, or get another mortgage.'

Picasso tutted. 'You are a child. Are you poor in spirit to stay here without thinking? For how long have you lived here?'

'Thirteen years.'

'You need a new life?'

Michael found that the answer was, 'Yes.'

It was a trifle. 'We move,' said Picasso. He stood up abruptly, walked away, and came back with heaps of newspapers that looked like an unmade bed. He pushed these at Michael, and growled, 'My baby boy. My baby boy needs to grow up.'

It could get awfully tiring living with somebody who went straight to the truth without passing Go.

'Here. They have ads for houses? You read the ads, I will go get us bread to dunk in the coffee.'

Michael began to look. Everything seemed to start at £200,000. Picasso came back from the shops with croissants. He flung the grease-spotted bag on the table, dunked a croissant in Michael's cup and demanded, his mouth full, 'You have found somewhere?'

'It's not that easy.'

'And that one there?'

'I've already looked.'

Picasso seized the newspaper and read out loud in criminal English: 'Two-bedroom apartment three floor roof garden? Garden. Camden Town. One hundred eighty thousand. Sounds OK!' he declared and pushed the billows of newspaper back down onto the table.

'Sounds good,' repeated Michael, mystified, and picked up the newspaper again to look again at the page of ads to make sure it was actually there, and try to understand how he could have missed it.

'We have to make an offer quickly, if it is a bargain, yes?'

'I think so. But I have to go to work today.'

'No you don't. No one has to do anything. They choose to do it. You choose not to work today, so that we can buy this apartment.'

'I'm sorry, I can't do that.'

'Hmm.' Picasso looked suddenly worried and concerned, and he swallowed. 'My friend,' he said and took Michael's knee again. 'Look at me. Look at me in the eyes. I am hungry to paint. If I think you are stopping me painting, I will go evil. Do you believe me?'

Michael rang in sick.

Picasso sang while he washed up, and Michael looked at his pay slips and his bank balance and tried to find ads for apartments similar to his own to see how much it might be worth. He only earned £35,000 a year, partly from the lab project and partly from teaching. The bank would be nervous about the temporary nature of the project, but even so, he should be able to get a mortgage for about £99,000. If you called the study a bedroom, this was a two-bedroom flat. One of those in a mansion block around the corner was selling for £350,000.

He could do it. He could do it and make money.

Michael looked at the sunlight streaming in through the bay window, on the old sand-coloured carpet, the old sofa, and the old wallpaper. There was a butterfly fluttering inside him that made him smile. It was time to go. It was time to find somewhere new.

Picasso had them down into Goodge Street tube station by 8.15 AM. He breathed in the stench of the trains and strutted up and down the platform, taking possession. He looked at the posters and beamed.

'I was right,' he said. 'This is my world. I made it.'

He pointed to a poster for *Fear and Loathing in Las Vegas*. A computer-distorted Johnny Depp grimaced out of a field of white, amid Gerald Scarfe-like splashes of black. 'That is a photograph, yes? What did that to a photograph?'

'It's a computer graphic. *Ordinateur*. Oh shit.' Michael took a deep breath and tried to explain computers in French. He knew none of the words. He got across the idea that it was a machine that could add and subtract, and could turn anything into numbers, even images. So by changing the numbers, you changed the images.

'You can make anything.' Picasso looked impressed.

'They made dinosaurs.'

'Tuh. They did that in *King Kong*.'

'These looked real. They can make people look real.'

Picasso's jaw thrust outwards. 'You have one of these *ordinateurs*?'

'I use them at work. I also have one at home.'

'You have one at home? Do many people have these things at home?'

'Yes.'

Picasso laughed aloud and did a little dance. 'I am in the future. You have brought me into the future, my friend.' His eyes were sparkling.

272

The apartment looked unprepossessing. It was on a corner over a shoe shop, with a battered multi-locked door on a side street facing a recently closed ex-supermarket. Picasso rang the buzzer and then shouted up, 'Hallo. Hallo. We want to buy your apartment!'

A woman looked out from the top of the wall. Evidently, she was sipping coffee on the roof. 'I'm sorry, but you will have to talk to the estate agent first, if you want to see the property.' She had what might pass for an American accent. She did not look at all offended. If anything, she was rather amused.

'Estate agent, *qu'est-ce que c'est?*' Picasso demanded of Michael.

'Hold on, I'll be down,' the woman said.

Michael tutted. 'It is not possible to arrive at people's apartments at this hour of the morning.' They heard footsteps. The door was opened by a tall woman, grey-haired in a blue-patterned kimono. She explained. 'Estate agents *sont agents immobiliers.*'

'Uh, estate agents!' huffed Picasso. 'They are only after your money. It is us who want to buy your apartment.'

The woman chuckled. 'Well, OK, come in.'

She spoke French and was Canadian and her name was Mirielle. Mirielle led them up a staircase that was crammed with bicycles. On the landing there was a toilet in a kind of booth that had been jammed against a sloping roof. It looked like a set from an early German Expressionist movie like the *Cabinet of Dr Caligari*.

Past more banisters and they were in one huge room. One wall was lined with kitchen sink and encrusted cooker. Two other sides were crowded with bookcases, desks and sofas. All along one wall arched windows faced east, dancing with light. Picasso was overjoyed. He turned and rubbed the top of his head in a circle against Michael's chest.

Mirielle led them through a door out onto a flat rooftop, lined with big red pots holding giant ferns, bamboo and evergreens. 'This is the garden. We would sell the plants with the flat. Do you like gardens?'

'He does,' said Picasso and pointed to Michael.

The banisters led up a staircase that smelled of sawdust, to two bedrooms. One was long and dark with a sloping roof, and the other was a garret with another huge window. It was full of canvases lined up like cards in an index file. Picasso rifled through them. His cheeks rose up like buns. There were Goths with facial tattoos, cross cut on the same canvas with the backs of turtles. Magicians in top hats were under the sea, but the seabed was an aerial map of New York. 'You are one of my children,' Picasso said.

'Oh really,' chuckled Mirielle. 'And what is your name?'

'Pablo Picasso,' he announced. Um, thought Michael, that might be a mistake.

'Funny,' said Mirielle, without missing a beat. 'That's my name too.'

'We will buy your flat,' Picasso said, airily as if it were nothing.

'For my asking price?'

'Is anyone else asking?'

'Now,' said Mirielle, 'we need the estate agent.'

'And a glass of wine, to celebrate. My friend has a bottle,' said Picasso and winked at Michael, and Michael for once was quick on the uptake. Out came another bottle of 60-year-old wine. Mirielle looked at its old-fashioned label, with its plain black print. *Mis en bouteille 1932*. It was too perfect, so she laughed, and brought out glasses.

'I will work here,' Picasso announced to Michael. 'I am your new life.'

There was just one problem: who would buy Michael's flat?

Michael remembered his Polish neighbours downstairs. The husband had been made redundant and they needed to sell their larger flat with its Council Tax and ground rent. They had a buyer for their place: but they had been gazumped on the flat they wanted to buy. They had nowhere to move to.

Mr Miazga was alone in the apartment, still dressed as if for his work: a neat grey shirt of some interesting fabric, black slacks and black jacket. Yes, yes, it would be ideal.

'My wife, you see, works at the School of Eastern European Studies, which is just near here, so she can walk to work. That is why we are here in England.' He had a neat, quiet way of

274

walking and talking, as if he were continually picking lint from his suit. His eyes never quite met yours.

Picasso began to slump and look about the walls, and huff. Shy quiet people made him impatient.

The Miazgas were shy but talented. The wife was doing a thesis on the pre-Christian Balkans. Mr Miazga had until recently worked in an architects' office as a programmer.

'That means he writes programs . . . uh . . .' Michael searched for the word in French.

'. . . *logiciels*,' Mr Miazga said, with his unfaltering, mild smile.

'Computers.' Picasso sat up. 'You work on those things?'

'Well,' said Mr Miazga, 'I write the instructions that make them work.' He glanced sideways at Michael: how is it that this man has only just heard about computers?

Picasso kept pushing. 'You know how they work. You write down the numbers.'

'That is one way of putting it, yes.'

'Do you have one? You could show me how it works?'

Mr Miazga did not want to teach this bumptious man anything, but he was trapped by his own good manners. He avoided answering. 'The architects ask me to use the computer to show our clients how the buildings will look.' He used the present tense as if he still had a job.

Michael offered compromise. 'Why don't you just show us something you've worked on?'

Mr Miazga showed them a virtual shopping mall that was to be built along the A40. He guided them down the covered walkway, past the Pizza Shack and Ameriburger franchise and into the bowling alley. There was the sound of a strike and the clatter of falling pins.

The father of Cubism saw: this was the real way to display all sides of an object. He leaned forward and irresistibly took control of the mouse. He scowled, his eyes widened; the whites of his black eyes were illuminated like a glass of milk with a light bulb in it.

Mr Miazga explained, 'This way, the client feels work has begun on his project. While the surveyors are still specifying the materials and checking our estimates, we have something to show.'

Picasso only sniffed. He moved forwards and backwards through the design. He tried to scamper across the ceiling upside down. He could not. He chuckled. He drove the mouse straight into a wall and through it and he laughed. 'You are God,' he said. 'You can change the rules.'

'It can show what the blueprints will look like,' corrected Mr Miazga, who detested all overstatement and vulgarity. His black suit and designer shirt would have looked better with a huge gold brooch.

Picasso ignored him. 'The artist is the one who makes the space. The audience uses it. It is much more like life. But . . .' He slapped his thigh and stood up. 'The power of the artist has not changed. It is his world the audience enters. Thank you, Mr Miazga. Please, would you be able to show me more about how this works?'

'Certainly, if you wish,' said Mr Miazga. He was beginning to rise.

'You could do it today?' Picasso asked.

Mr Miazga faltered. He batted his eyelids like an embarrassed girl. 'I . . . I plainly have nothing else to do.'

Picasso sat down in his chair. 'Excellent, excellent. You and your wife must come upstairs and have dinner with us tonight. Is that not so, Michael?'

'Indeed,' Michael began.

'There will be a lot to celebrate.'

Mr Miazga could not help but smile. It would indeed be a relief to be able to sell their big flat and move on. He nodded in agreement.

'Michael, you have things to do with banks and lawyers, yes?'

Michael was beginning to get a bit peeved at being directed all the time. Picasso looked around at him and suddenly he had a face like a bloodhound: doleful eyes and drooping jaws. 'Don't you have a lot to do? I'm sorry, is it possible that I can help you in any way? I don't speak English. I am weak in such situations.' He was apologetic and undeniable.

'No, it's for me to do.' It was just that Michael wished he were doing the driving. It was his money that was buying the flat.

'I will cook!' Picasso announced, his eyes dancing again.

Picasso did not cook. He concentrated on a complicated sauce involving cream and tomatoes and basil and berries and apple liqueur and butter and a teaspoon of grated onion. Michael did the shopping. Michael cooked everything else: the boiled potatoes, the salad. The Miazgas rang on the telephone first, to tell them they were on their way: one floor up.

'Remember,' Michael told him. 'You cannot be called Pablo Picasso. Everybody in the world knows who Pablo Picasso is.' Picasso looked like he was picking his teeth after a good meal. 'You'll need to be called another name. I suggest Ruiz.' Michael paused. 'It will be easy to remember.'

'It is my father's name.' Picasso curled his lip.

'That's why it will be easy to remember,' said Michael, backing away to the door. And, he thought, it's your real name.

The Miazgas came, scrubbed and pressed. Their ageing beauties had been pinned back into place. Mrs Miazga was big and blonde and just the slightest bit blowsy. The academic Laura Ashley dress was so flimsy and pink that it might as well have been Zsa Zsa Gabor chiffon, and strands of her blonde hair kept rising and falling. Mr Miazga looked braced against a further onslaught from Picasso. He had spent the afternoon with this man, and now faced a whole evening of him.

Picasso bounded up to them and kissed Madame Miazga on both cheeks. His arms enfolded Mr Miazga, and wrenched him down to his height. Picasso kissed him full on the lips.

'This man is a genius!' Picasso declared of Mr Miazga. Mr Miazga was in the process of recovering from the kiss. 'He has taught me so much.'

Mr Miazga pulled himself up to his full height, as if to imply that a kiss on the lips would normally follow a proper introduction. He had not come to live in England to be battered by such behaviour. 'May I present my wife, Marta.'

Marta cooed and offered a tiny, polite hand. Mr Miazga continued, 'Marta this is Mr . . . Mr . . .'

'Luis,' said Picasso. Whose father's name was that? His eyes were on Michael and the whites looked tobacco-stained with knowing. 'Luis Ruiz. It rhymes. It is easy to remember, yes?'

'I am sure I will have no difficulty remembering your name at all,' said Marta Miazga, who had always been more outgoing than her husband. 'My husband is called Thaddeus, or Thad for short, and so the English call him Tad the Pole.'

Michael found himself chuckling along with her. Though Picasso could not possibly have understood the joke, he laughed too. Mr Miazga sucked in air thinly between his teeth.

Over dinner Picasso talked. Michael started to uncork the wine, and Picasso said no, no, no and took the bottle from him. Picasso kept talking as he showed the best way to uncork and pour it. He told Michael where the oven glove was. 'Yes, yes, I put it on the lower shelf where I can reach it, we keep it there from now on.'

Picasso talked about computer graphics. 'They defy gravity. Things are pasted on them, things are stretched, everything blurs into a dream. It is as if you take the human mind and plug it into the electricity grid. The results have ceased to be entirely human. If not used by artists the results are distinctly unpleasant and alienating. These graphics reveal a desire for perfection. Perfection is for people who want to work and who are scared that they will run out of ideas.'

Mr Miazga coughed.

Picasso talked about Monet's water lilies. He enjoyed them in a scanty kind of way, but like all impressionism, its fate was to be used on greetings cards. Its innovations were all technical. Its artistic message was too often merely pretty.

Marta mentioned the curious art that was now winning awards. A dead sheep in formaldehyde. Picasso laughed, and stomped his foot. 'That is either very good or very bad. It is reaction against computers. Did he enjoy winning his award?'

'I think so, yes,' replied Marta. Her sentences seemed to wear glass slippers – they tinkled and you were afraid they would break.

'Ah, then the art will be very bad.' Picasso munched his lamb heartily. They all waited.

'Why would that be?' Mr Miazga enquired.

Picasso swallowed. 'There are people who Are and there are people who only Have. The people who Have must be good at getting, and they are polite. The people who Are . . .' His hand trailed away.

'Don't need awards,' said Michael.

Picasso nodded once, firmly. 'The awards are there to make the people who Have feel like the people who Are.'

Mr Miazga enquired, 'And those who Are, what are they good at?'

'Whatever they like,' said Picasso with a shrug. 'Defeating others,' he added, shamelessly.

At the end of the evening, the Poles seemed suddenly to remember it was Michael's flat. They thanked him in English for the meal, for the move. Michael said how that the timing was lucky for all of them. 'The apartment will be ideal for us,' enthused Marta.

'You know we have been saying,' said Mrs Miazga with a confirming glance at her husband as she took Michael's hand in friendship, 'we have been friends for so long that we don't even remember when we first came to this apartment.'

About three weeks ago, thought Michael. The Miazgas couldn't remember the Angel monks and the singing at 2:00 AM.

Michael eased them down his hallway. Marta thanked him for Picasso. 'It was wonderful meeting your friend! It was just like meeting . . .' She sought for someone to measure the impact. 'Matisse.'

Picasso's smile temporarily lost its balance. The dapper Mr Miazga shook Michael's hand. Marta waved to Pablo. '*Enchanté*,' Picasso said.

The door swung shut. Picasso held out both arms, and sighed and spun around. 'I can eat, I can drink, I can read, I can learn, I can work!' he said, and did a little dance. He pulled Michael to him, and looked up, his small round face suddenly like a child's, stretched tight. 'And all I have to do is love you,' he said.

'Is that difficult for you?'

'I am a woman's man,' said Picasso proudly.

'One . . . one man I brought back, who had been dead. He told me never to do it to anyone else.'

'He turned down life?' Picasso was incredulous. 'He was a fool.'

'Mark was no fool. I love your painting because of him.'

'Now I know he was a fool,' said Picasso. He stood back, to regard Michael as if he were a painting. 'You are not such a price to pay for life. You have beautiful hair and beautiful eyes. You look like a man, you are big and you are strong, and so don't cause comment on the street, and you are smart and soft, soft for me and I like that.'

Michael advanced; Picasso didn't like being pressed up against him, it revealed too ruthlessly how short he was. Michael dipped down, bending neck and spine, and they kissed. Their tongues seemed to glue to each other. They parted with a smack, and Picasso said what Michael was thinking: 'Delicious.' He reached up and rubbed Michael's neck. 'You want me to fuck you,' he whispered.

'Yes,' Michael said from a place so deep inside him the words felt as if they came from his stomach.

Picasso was so short that his arms encircled Michael's ass. 'I take you,' Picasso said, and picked him up from the floor and hugged him into the bedroom. The tips of Michael's toes dragged across the carpet. Picasso let him fall onto the bed and pulled down Michael's trousers so hard they tore.

'I fuck you face to face,' said Picasso.

'Face to face,' said Michael, and knew that he was in a kind of love. Throughout the act, he looked into Picasso's eyes.

The move was upon them before Michael was ready.

Picasso took charge. The van was to arrive on Thursday. Wednesday evening, they started to pack. Big tea crates arrived: Picasso kept popping out of them like a jack in the box. He thought this was very funny. Michael was not in the mood.

In fact, Michael was cross. He had wanted to clear things out before he moved; at the same time he also wanted to save everything. There were Phil's old toiletries, bath foams and aftershaves that Michael had bought for him. Michael sniffed the tops and smelled Phil. He started to chuck them, but at the first clinking of glass in a bin, Picasso, wearing nothing but shorts and sandals, flapped into his bedroom.

'What you throw away?' he demanded. 'This is good, no?' He splashed himself with aftershave: 'Oh, I smell like Monet's lily pond now,' he joked.

'You smell like Phil,' murmured Michael.

There were all the old receipts, gas bills addressed to Phil, old photos of trips to Paris. There were books Phil had given him with cards inside showing two cats entwined. There were old socks. There were magazines saved because they recorded the top 100 albums of all time according to *New Musical Express* in 1990: *Pet Sounds* at number 1 apparently. There were invitations to Phil's early exhibitions; old clothes: cowboy shirts, torn PVC, Lycra bicycling shorts. Phil's unwanted wardrobe was a history of ill-advised eighties and nineties fashion.

Cups and saucers: things Michael had given Phil that Phil now did not want; beautiful heirloom silver spoons that Phil had given to Michael that he had not wanted. His old life was stripped bare. His old life naked looked like an empty room. He was leaving the carpet and the rosewood fireplace.

Michael started to cry. Picasso was overcome by kindness. 'Oh, my love,' he said, which in French is something you can say more easily between men. 'Hold, hold.' He chuckled sympathetically, and held Michael's shoulders. 'It is always hard to move. You know, when I was young, we moved here, we moved there. In Spain when you move, everyone speaks a different language. This is just to Camden Town. Eh? Eh?' Picasso held up Michael's chin, and made him look into his eyes. It worked. Michael smiled, embarrassed by his own weakness and by love.

'I help you!' Picasso exclaimed and flung out his arms, to greet the changes.

So Michael's old life was packed away into tea chests, except for the four-poster bed from Lancashire. That had been sold to the Poles. Michael slept in that bed for one last night. Picasso did not snore, placated by the reassurance of sex. He slept umbilically attached to Michael, planted deep inside him.

In the morning, Picasso jumped about the flat as if the floor were a skillet. Michael heard him from the warmth of the duvet

clattering away amid the kitchen things. As if Michael were a
nervous invalid, Picasso arrived with breakfast on a tray: croissants and coffee. 'Here, a last breakfast for the condemned
man,' he said, gesturing at the tray. Michael took a tiny sip of
coffee to savour it. Picasso gulped down half a cup and one
torn strand of croissant before jumping up again. He would
have nothing else to eat until supper that night.

Picasso darted up and down the stairs like a muscular squir-
rel. The moving men thought he was a porter who was paid to
help with the move. Picasso wore overalls from 1916. The legs
had a sewn-on lower half of a different colour. He pointed,
clicked his fingers, grinned and somehow acted so completely
like a mover that the movers began to follow his instructions.
Picasso made sure the sofa bed was loaded last, facing out from
the back of the lorry. He indicated that he and Michael would
travel to Camden Town sitting on it.

One of the moving men said, 'Tell him he mustn't, please,
it's the insurance.'

Michael shook his head. 'It won't do any good telling him
anything.'

The mover was old and reliable, and he looked at Picasso as
if accepting some fundamental fact of life. 'It's your funeral. I
hope not,' he said.

Michael and Picasso stayed in the back of the lorry. It jerked
and thumped and squealed its way up Tottenham Court Road
to Camden Town. Picasso sat on the sofa, looking out the open
back. Somehow he had spirited a bottle of champagne from his
other world, the eternal past from which Angels seemed to
come. The ink on the label was as thick as a rubber skid mark
and the font plain, listing the name of a village. Picasso began
to sing an old, strange yelping song. Michael was to learn later
it was *cante hondo,* the only music Picasso really loved. He
waved a bottle and irresistibly forced Michael to sing along.
Canta la rana, y no tiene pelo ni lana! he announced. The frog
sings, though she has neither fur nor wool.

The van took fifteen minutes to coax itself backwards into
their narrow side street. Picasso manhandled packing cases with
the gusto of a bullfighter. He nipped so quickly up and down

stairs that he reminded Michael of a silent flickering film, a two-reel comedy short.

Picasso was untidy and disordered; everything he did was a kind of unintended blurt. Their new flat rapidly filled with papers, boxes, chairs, CD racks, suits on hangers, lamps and cutlery. They were piled high in unsorted and unnecessarily exciting piles that threatened to spill paint or crystalware onto the floor. Picasso flung himself onto the toilet, fully clothed, in order to sit down, and announced with a sigh, 'We are done!'

Michael looked around forlornly. A heap of previously sorted lab reports slithered onto the floor as if depressed and exhausted.

Picasso gulped water from the tap. 'We go!' he announced. 'We help your friends.' He took the keys and locked up, and Michael found himself heading back to the apartment that was no longer his.

The Miazgas had economized. They were carrying their own furniture up the stairs. Picasso hoisted the Poles' piano on his own back, and twisted it sideways up the circular staircase. He carried Marta's valuable china in an orange washing-up bowl. The plates and glasses clashed and tinkled as he bounded up the stairs. Picasso pogoed down them again on two feet, like a child splashing in mud puddles. He gave Mr Miazga orders and Madame Miazga compliments. He let Marta mop his brow and he mimed having a fever, panting with the heat she generated.

Somehow or other, once in the flat, it was Michael and Mr Miazga who did all the less spectacular lifting. Picasso stood back with Marta and conferred and suggested the best places for the furniture to go in their new and cramped surroundings. For this Picasso had absolutely no talent. He suggested their enormous rubber tree stay in the hallway, where it would have no light and block access. With minimum ceremony, he dumped most of Mr Miazga's suits on the kitchen table.

Michael was by now exhausted and dazed. An avalanche of other people's things poured into what still felt like his home. He kept thinking he would offer people a drink: the tonic water was in Camden Town, the ice was melted. He wanted to comb his hair, but his comb of course would no longer be in its accustomed place on the mantelpiece. Except that it was, poor forlorn, forgotten comb, faithfully waiting his return. See, Michael thought, I haven't forgotten you. If he felt that about a comb, what did he feel about a man? A whole habit of life?

Michael combed and recombed his hair and watched Picasso. Picasso had flung himself down on the sandy carpet as if it were a bed. He lounged up a hand to accept a cup of tea that Marta had managed to assemble from the scattering of her kitchen.

Picasso was vain; he seemed to think the smell of his sweat was manly, virile. He did not bathe every day.

The smell of Picasso permeated the flat. It was not an unpleasant smell, certainly not to Michael. It was a sexual smell. It was as if the very air were stuffed with Picasso's penis. All three of them, wife, lover and anxious husband, could not think of anything other than those powerful genitals.

Mr Miazga was pale and thin-lipped, and sat on edge, hands clasping his knees, his delicate down-turned face looking as if someone had farted. Mrs Miazga's movements were anxious, faltering. She was disoriented. Her fine blonde hair came increasingly undone. It seemed to be falling out, drifting to the floor.

Michael took stock. Well, he told himself, you could have had a very clean pub manager instead. Instead you chose Pablo Picasso. It will be exciting, Michael. It will not be easy. And it may not last forever.

Michael could see the moment when Picasso wanted to get back to painting. In one single rolling motion he was up from the carpet and pounding the palm of his hand with his fist. He looked around the flat as if all of it, the original ownership, the sale, the move, had been his own work. He nodded as if to acknowledge the good job he had done. He said, direct to Michael, 'Come, we go to our home.'

Then Picasso took Michael's hand. It was evidently unpremeditated, thoughtless, sincere.

Michael found himself grateful and slightly weak at the knees. So, evidently did Mr Miazga. He settled back in his chair from relief, and his chest expanded, and his eyes zipped left towards his wife, and then widened, once. See? he seemed to say. I told you. They are lovers. You get all excited over a man who is homosexual.

After they left, outside on the landing Picasso promised, 'I will have the wife.' His voice was airy, amused, and he spoke out of the corners of his mouth as if Madame Miazga were a cigar.

The new flat in Camden was dark and in disorder. Street lights outlined the crags and valleys of jumble. Michael was given no time for regrets. Picasso herded him to their unmade bed, driven by a lust that Michael knew that he himself had not inspired. Picasso wanted Marta.

Picasso dozed and then woke up with a snort. He flung off the single summer sheet, and padded into the sitting room, leaving Michael in the bed. Lights blazed around the edges of the bedroom door, and there was a sound of assembling, plugging in, mild swearing. Michael finally admitted that he was awake and would not sleep. He stumped downstairs into the sitting room and saw Picasso at 2.00 AM, sitting in front of the computer playing *Myst*. His bare buttocks hung over the edge of the chair as round as peaches.

'Hmm,' said Picasso. 'This is not three-dimensional . . . you just move closer to the drawing.' On his right, there was a pad and scrawled sketches of the Myst world populated with drunken people and smiling goats. Their smiles were drawn as a series of single unbroken spirals describing cheeks. Michael glanced down over Picasso's body. Picasso worked erect.

'Coming back to bed?' murmured Michael.

'I don't know,' grunted Picasso.

In the morning, the bed was cold and when Michael went downstairs Picasso still sat in front of the computer with a cup of cold coffee and strewn stale bread. Had he been up all night?

'You eat too much,' Picasso announced, in a bad mood. 'You will get fat. You will become a drunken boor.' He sighed, as if it were inevitable. 'Do not expect me to cook you breakfast,' he said. He slip-slopped his way out to the roof garden, carrying his coffee, escaping Michael. It was summer, warm, with beautiful light over the ferns. Michael joined him and Picasso said,

'You missed work yesterday and the day before. If you were more dedicated, you would do a better job.'

Picasso wanted him out of the flat. Michael showered, and deliberately took his time over coffee and yoghurt and bananas, and pointedly washed up – not a Picasso habit – and left at his usual time feeling bloated around the eyes and saddle-sore.

No one at work mentioned that Michael had missed two days. He began to explain that he had had to move flats suddenly. No one asked him any questions about it. Ebru and Emilio were quiet, brisk and business-like, as if Michael were a customer they would attend to in a moment. He filed slides and looked at data, and by the end of the day realized that he had spent it alone.

When he got back home, he found Picasso at the computer, now wearing Michael's best Japanese bathrobe. The game was noisier and the images moved. A tiny alien leapt and jumped and avoided being fried by robots.

Picasso kept playing. 'She is softened and ripe and if you are a man at all you will have her,' he said. Then he looked up. His eyes were angry and hungry. 'Do it because I tell you. I will like fucking you better if I think you are a real man.'

Upstairs, Mrs Miazga was in Michael's bed. She was huge, pink and dishevelled, her hair in Pre-Raphaelite waves. The room smelled of her hair, and of her body, opened and reopened during the course of the day.

'Visit me,' she said in a warm and friendly voice, and held out her arms. She looked dazed and dazzled, her blue eyes warmed like a southern sea. She smiled in complicity. I know you are lovers, we will be his lovers together, love me too.

Well, thought Michael. He could just surf it. Let himself be carried by the wave of adventure.

He went into their new bedroom, stuffed with boxes, some of them full of shoes and vinyl records, and found his sponge bag. He crunched his Viagra into a bitter, tongue-curling paste, to make it work faster. Then he cleaned his teeth to rinse away the bitterness.

The taste of Mrs Miazga's mouth was edged with hormones and a scent he did not quite like. But her huge soft, smooth body was a wonderful maternal harbour. Michael weighed into her, waves rippling around him. There was an excitement about being where Picasso had been, in the folds of flesh still moist from him. Perhaps it was the Viagra kicking in early. Whatever it was, it joined forces with Michael's reluctance to have sex with a woman. Conjoined, they had an unexpected effect. Michael rode Mrs Miazga for forty-five minutes. He did not come, but she did, three times. 'My God, you are super lover,' she said in fractured English. Her fingers strutted pleased up the side of his arm. 'I can tell, you have had many women through your hands.'

Picasso was standing in the doorway. He chuckled approvingly. Much of the time his eyes were kind, as now. 'My big friend loves life,' he said proudly. He mimicked the gesture of Madame's fingers, and strode forward. 'Now I show you,' he said. With no manners, Picasso pulled Michael away from her. He grinned down at the woman. 'I am back,' Picasso said, his teeth bared, and she looked up at him adoringly conquered.

Michael was relieved to be relieved. He went downstairs, clothes draped over his arms, showered and sat in the sitting room. He poured himself a whisky and ate crisps. For the next two hours, the man he loved was in the next room fucking someone else. Michael turned on the television, low. He was just as alone as when he had been living with Phil. OK, you learn. Having a lover, husband, whatever, does not stop you being alone.

Michael had power. He could get rid of Picasso whenever he liked. He could walk in there now and banish him, leaving Marta stranded and shocked.

Except that that had not been the deal. Picasso had given him what he asked for in exchange for life. And why did Picasso want life so very much?

On the sofa, on a sketchpad, there was a drawing of Michael. It was one continuous line of charcoal, a single gulp of information, stylish and twitching as a cat's tail. It was a drawing of a man who was windswept as if at sea, eyes narrowed in the face of some invisible force. The tiny Chinese eyes each consisted of a single charcoal line, but you could tell they were about to weep from wind blown directly onto the cornea. The

287

mouth was downturned, enduring and elated, somehow just about to smile, as one smiles in a storm, from exhilaration. It was a drawing of a man caught up in a miracle. It was a new Picasso.

And it would disappear the moment Michael sent Picasso away.

Madame Miazga darted into the bathroom, a towel wrapped around her. The water suddenly hissed and she began to sing as she showered.

Picasso emerged in Michael's boxer shorts, strutting like a welterweight champion. He slapped his belly and announced, 'We go drinking!'

Madame threw on her light and translucent dress. She smiled warmly at both of them, and giggled with delight. Only a certain hardness in the contrast between her blue eyes and the mascara around them gave a clue that this was a woman who had mastered academic politics. She put a longer finger that was exactly at 90 degrees to the floor against her freshly glossed lips. Sssh, it meant, this is our secret. Her eyes went soft, forgiving, pleading, in memory of her husband. She loved Mr Miazga, but perhaps found him too fastidious.

They separated in the street, waving good night. In a local Camden pub, Picasso played cards and smoked and joined in a game of darts with fat bearded men in black t-shirts and earrings of whom Michael was very slightly afraid. Picasso's cigarette balanced on his lips all night, and he nodded brusquely when his turn came. When others played he sipped beer, looking serious and constructively occupied.

They left at eleven o'clock and for some reason Picasso was angry with Michael.

'Those people were trash,' he said. 'They have no conversation. Why did we go there?'

Michael was dismayed at the unfairness of it. 'Because you wanted to!'

'Are you alive or dead? Don't you know where the interesting quarters are? Or do you live inside your computer? I will have to find the interesting people. I can see that I will have to do everything. I even have to find women for you. I even have to cook! What do you do well, eh? Anything?'

Without waiting for an answer, Picasso flicked open the double lock on their door and raced up the steps ahead of Michael. Michael listened to the rapid fire of Picasso's feet. He felt leaden. He did not want to go in. It was not his house or his bed. Come on, Michael, he told himself, you have nowhere else to go. But his legs simply would not move.

Michael had thought he was happy and that Picasso liked him. Michael thought: he can snatch away happiness like a scarf. The reversal felt complete. It felt as if all love were gone and the relationship over. Like a ship in warp drive, space seemed to travel around him, and Michael arrived at the opposite pole of the universe. He imagined moving out, selling the flat, sending Picasso back. He considered going direct to a hotel to spend the night. He wanted the affair to end. Michael's eyes ached with loss.

'Henry?' he asked the night air. 'Henry, I need you.'

There was a tap on his shoulder and he turned around, and there was Henry, hair in his eyes, waiting.

'Henry, I'm in love and it's all going wrong.'

Henry looked sad while smiling. 'He's impossible.'

'Yes.'

'He says things that are so unfair you can't believe he said them. They're outrageous.'

Michael found himself pausing, and waiting. The set-up was too neat. Henry had something to say. 'That's about it.'

'Everyone's impossible to live with, Michael. Even saints. I lived with a saint for years. Most of the time he was wonderful, but sometimes all he seemed to care about was his research.' A smile kept playing about Henry's face.

Picasso was something like a saint and nothing like one.

'There's nothing for it, mate. You just hammer each other into each other's shape. And either it gets comfortable or it doesn't.'

Michael half-chuckled. 'You're not much comfort, you know that?'

Henry reached up, and there, in the street in Camden Town, started combing Michael's hair with his fingers. He looked up and down Michael in tenderness. 'You look great.'

'I feel awful.'

'You look . . . adult.' Henry's eyes sparkled. It was love. Love of a particularly airy, open, fleshless kind.

And Michael felt a kind of hesitation.

Henry gave Michael a little push towards the door. 'Go on. Have it out with him. See who wins.'

Michael hesitated. He would rather stay there, with Henry.

'I'm an Angel, I won't always be here. You mustn't get dependent on me.' Henry started to walk away, determined. 'Go on. It's down to you.'

There was nothing for it. Michael went in.

Upstairs, Picasso had changed into boxer shorts, and was reclining on Michael's sofa bed. 'Miguel Blasco,' he said, with real affection. 'I like you really. Come here.'

Michael yelped. 'You just told me I wasn't good for anything!'

Picasso chuckled at himself as if he had done something silly and amusing, like trying to roast potatoes in the fridge. 'I did not like that pub.' He patted the sofa. 'Sit next to me.'

Picasso Mindfuck, really! Michael's eyes felt heavy, like two hard-boiled eggs. He hated feeling the surrender and gratitude that welled up in him. He wanted to stay angry. He shouldn't allow himself to be jerked this way and that like a puppet.

Picasso stood up. 'Don't be mad over something so small. Mmm?' Picasso encircled Michael with his arms and stood on tiptoe to kiss Michael's shoulder. 'See? I am so small to be mad over.'

Picasso had given Michael a choice: he could go on being angry and have a major row, which would almost certainly fail to change how Picasso behaved. Or, he could weaken as he wished to do, be carried off by Picasso's return to kindness.

Picasso seemed to sense him relenting. 'My maker of Angels.'

I'm in love and I'm helpless, thought Michael. I am shooting whitewater rapids of love. All I can do is hang on and try to avoid the rocks.

Picasso leaned around and kissed him, and the river bore Michael away.

The apartment never recovered from the move. As fast as Michael tried to put it in order, Picasso created another row of jam jars full of brushes in the bathroom, or a pile of printed help files on the floor. There were heaps of opened boxes from amazon.com. Half-read books were left open and face down on the floor. Sandals, socks and paint-stained newspapers stayed where they fell. It had never struck Michael until then that he himself was basically a tidy person.

'Leave it, it will continue to protect the floor,' said Picasso, bemused by Michael's protests.

'It's a horrible mess,' said Michael, going firm.

'That is a matter of aesthetics,' Picasso replied. 'I will not be bullied by you over aesthetics.'

Something shuddered in Michael and went still.

Paintings began to appear, stuck to the walls with Blu Tack: gouache on crumpled paper: a parrot in blue and green and red; a vaguely African-looking pattern in black and ochre with white dots in swirls, a tunnel of blue and white light. A sculpture in Blu Tack was stuck to the coffee table, a kind of amused Isis with hips and breasts, and a shocked open mouth. Michael asked who it was supposed to be. Picasso had to repeat several times before Michael penetrated his accent: it was a Blu Tack Geri Halliwell.

Picasso developed a bewildering affection for the Spice Girls: he played the CD over and over.

'Why don't you stop?' Michel asked him.

'I will when I understand it,' said Picasso. In self-defence, Michael bought him a compilation of Asian dance, *Anohka*, and Madonna's album *Ray of Light*. He bought him Philip Glass and Arvo Pärt. 'They are no good, they try to be intelligent,' Picasso said, dismissing everything else except S Club 7 and Steps.

Picasso loved CDs. In the world music section of HMV he found compilations of Europop and Brazilian brega. He played CDs incessantly. 'They do the same to music, make it perfect but inhuman.'

Picasso loved Pot Noodles and disposable cameras; he was entranced by Play Station and tried to get Michael to buy one and a samurai game called *Soul Blade*. 'Tush. You buy rubbish that does not move. I want *Ade's Oddyssey*. I want *Sonic Hedgehog*!' He kept buying glossy magazines – *Q, Maxim, Elle, Vanity*

Fair, Empire. He would tear them to pieces and Blu Tack together mosaics out of fragments of shiny, laminated print. Discarded corpses of shredded journals began to litter the flat. He made himself little bracelets of Blu Tack, he stuck shards of magazine colour to his T-shirt with Blu Tack. In the corners of the room or running along the picture rail were little families of creatures not entirely unlike mice made out of Blu Tack.

'You practically breathe Blu Tack,' said Michael. He was being driven, slowly and without cessation, out of his box. The first of his blinding headaches arrived, after a glass of wine on a Friday evening.

Three weeks later, Picasso called him to the screen. 'The first,' he said.

It took a moment for Michael to understand what he was looking at.

It was pieces of his room. When Michael moved, flesh-coloured fragments moved in shards. The videoconferencing camera on top of the computer was feeding what it saw live to the hard disk, and those images, refracted and broken, were made part of a series of mirrors. The series of mirrors formed a face, in the same way that feathers form wings.

It was a portrait of Michael, in fractured, virtual mirrors.

The head could be turned, rotated and sometimes, as if at random, the entire face would blossom outwards, the mirrors separating and reassembling into a portrait from a greater distance.

'It's your face when I fuck you,' said Picasso.

Each time the portrait reassembled, its eyes would gleam brighter and a smile would assemble in sword shapes.

'The audience can choose all angles, but each time they choose, the program will force the image of you closer and closer to joy. You look like that. When I fuck you, you have a joyful face. You look like a young man!'

The face assembled and reassembled every time something moved in the real world.

'Then you come.' Picasso mimed something explosive with his hands, fingers outstretched. 'You will break up into pieces of light. And you are reincarnated.'

No one had ever done anything like that about or for Michael before. 'Do you . . .' Michael wondered how to proceed. 'Do you love me?'

Picasso shrugged. 'I ponder you. You have this miracle, and you don't use it because I satisfy you. There is an economy about that which I like.'

The face on the screen grew brighter and brighter and more joyful, unavoidably, pre-programmed. That was what Picasso wished for him.

Picasso said, 'You have nothing. No money, no morals, no interests, no conversation, no friends to speak of. But you Are.'

'What am I?'

'There is no word for what you are. You just Are. Ah, watch now!'

And the mirrored face dissolved.

Michael's heart swelled like a satsuma growing wings, and rose up as if wanting to be born, jamming in his throat with love.

When Michael came home at night, the whole apartment would smell of eggwhite, turpentine and glue. Suddenly the walls were papered with new Picassos, their colours like tropical glazed pottery: greens, reds, blues and yellows. The whole flat seemed to trampoline off itself with joy, bouncing back and forth between its own exhilarating surfaces, the spaces between gaping with amazement. The only possible response walking into the room was: who the fuck has done this?

When Mr Miazga came to give Picasso his lessons, he was stunned, his mouth going slack and sad. It's not fair, his eyes seemed to say, that my rival should be such a man.

Mr Miazga looked forlornly at Michael. Help me, he seemed to say.

Michael found his return glance said: you help me first.

At eleven o'clock one night about three months after his arrival, Picasso barrelled into the flat with ten boisterous, excited people whom Michael had never met, except for Phil's friend, Jimmy Banter.

Jimmy's eyes boggled. 'My God it's M'n'M! You did land on

your feet with this one, didn't you? So what's the story? Is he gay?'

'No, but he sleeps with me.'

'I wonder why,' said Jimmy. 'I mean, if he isn't gay. I mean, you were a man the last time I checked. Dear old Philip's not doing too well.'

'I'm sorry to hear that.'

'No, you're not.'

'What's wrong?'

'Lost his way, I would say. Says he's suffering from a crisis of direction.'

'Maybe he's finding a direction,' said Michael.

'He's painting portraits,' said Jimmy, miming horror.

The guests studiously avoided saying anything about the work on the wall. They stood back, and raised eyebrows, and waited for someone else to say something first. Michael offered them drinks, and learned that some of them were dealers.

Among the influx was the art critic of the *Evening News*. The critic's accent was ludicrously posh, a deliberate effort to be noticed and to give affront to an egalitarian world. He fearlessly gave affront to Picasso. 'Are you unable to experience any anxiety of influence?' the critic demanded. 'You do know of course from whose work you are stealing?'

'No,' said Picasso, looking smug. 'Tell me.'

'Hockney,' said the critic, as if barely able to bring himself to say the name aloud. 'In his dreadful Picasso period.'

Michael passed the critic his gin and tonic. The critic turned on him succinctly. 'You are the maid, are you?'

'This is my flat,' said Michael.

'I see,' said the critic. Even his smile was designed to annoy. 'And how long do you think *he* will be living with *you*?' The 'y' sounded like he was about to throw up, the 'ou' hooted like an owl. Michael's riposte was succinct. He took back the gin and tonic and began to drink it himself.

Picasso pronounced the critic. 'Noel Coward,' Picasso said, pointing. 'During his precipitous decline.' It was a miracle Picasso could pronounce the word: prayssheepetooose. It was effective enough. One of the many things Picasso knew is that it is more valuable to make enemies than friends. You can always make up with an enemy, but friends hang around as dead weight.

It was instructive watching Picasso at work. He strode around the flat arm in arm with an apparent favourite, expansively describing the work. The critic laughed at him. 'He is like a very bad wine, one is amazed he has the effrontery even to wear a label.'

The dealer didn't care; he was in this for the money, not to defend the sacred flame of art. The dealer began to roll a joint expertly, one-handed, while Picasso talked. Picasso stood in a combative pose, telling a story about a bullfight. Picasso could strut even when he wasn't moving. Only once did his eyes flicker sideways to another dealer from New York. This dealer was much older and better-dressed than the joint-roller. Though Picasso ignored him, the man's stone face looked neither annoyed nor forlorn.

Michael had spent years cruising gay bars and he knew: Picasso was making a pass at the older man by playing up to the younger. Did the New York dealer know that? Come on, Michael, this is the air these guys breathe, of course he knew. The younger guy probably knew. What they all actually knew or rather had decided, was that this Luis Ruiz, wherever he was from, was a player. Right at the end of the evening, the New Yorker quietly passed Picasso his card.

'Boy,' said Jimmy Banter to Michael as he left, 'am I going to make Philip jealous.'

'Why would you want to do that, Jimmy? Just tell him I still love him, will you?'

Jimmy had the grace to look chastened. He gripped Michael's arm. 'Just my little joke,' he said, and left. Camp will always let you down.

When they had all gone, Picasso was slow and well fed, like a bullfrog. He put a hand behind Michael's neck and said 'I like being with you. You are useful.'

Tender words. 'I keep you alive,' said Michael.

'You will find when I am being good and you have not made me angry that I am good to you.'

The thought arrived whole and clear and quiet. This is love, and this is adventure. But this is not good for me.

Michael had assumed that love was always in one's interest. If love was a stone that rolled you naturally home, it must be a good thing. The idea that love could smash as well as build a home or roll you further and further from your self had never occurred to him.

Michael's entire flat became a workshop: a pottery wheel appeared in the bathroom, with sacks of clay. When he was not painting or computing, Picasso was sawing wood from pallets he had found at Camden market. He would scoop up scraps of fabric, a baby's shoe, or the skull of some small rodent picked clean. Everything entered the maw of his art and was taken back to the flat to be used.

Adoring women arrived. They no longer wore X-Files T-shirts and Camden nose rings. They were smart, bright young gallery assistants from Notting Hill or Bond Street. They wore slim black slacks, graceful shoes and medium-length, artfully tinted hair which they tossed from time to time to indicate fascination.

'Hello, Michael,' the gallery assistants would beam at him when he arrived from work, as if genuinely pleased to see that their fascinating new artist lived with another man. 'I'd better be going,' they would offer, standing up after a decent interval.

Picasso kissed their fingers, between the knuckle and first joint. 'Oh, but you will come back, I hope.'

Amanda, Diana, Jill, Cecilia; apparently they did come back, judging from the state of the bed linen. Michael gave in and began to sleep on the sofa bed in the living room. His headaches started coming regularly. When do you get headaches, Michael?

When you're angry.

Michael came back from going to see *In the Company of Men* alone, to find Picasso painting another portrait of him: this time as a weeping clown. Was Michael flattered? He was certainly enveloped, and perhaps being digested.

'People call idiots the Clowns of God.' Picasso touched Michael's nose with the tip of the brush handle. 'Clown,' he pronounced him. 'You are in an unequal contest with God. This is foolish, but inescapable. I learn new things from you, Michael.

I did not know that the privilege of saints was to fight with God. Most of us don't even touch Him.'

Picasso painted either in great easy sweeps, or impatient jabs and lunges that left the canvas or the previous layer of paint showing through in streaks. This was an impatient painting. Picasso had scrawled tears in the jagged, staring diamond eyes.

The next night Michael came home at 6.30 to find Mrs Miazga beside herself in what was now Picasso's bed. She was red again, but now it was from irritation. Perhaps she had found evidence of others. She looked miffed when Michael stumbled in to fetch shorts and a T-shirt to wear in the house, unconsciously imitating Picasso. They both stared, wishing the other gone, wishing themselves gone, wishing him gone.

'I'm sorry,' said Michael, coldly. 'I didn't know you were here.' She drew the sheet up higher. She shrugged, but could only just bring herself to say, 'It's your house.'

Michael found a private corner in the sitting room in which to undress so he could shower. His towel, he remembered, and his bag of toiletries were still in the bedroom. Damn. He marched back into the bedroom, his trousers wrapped around his midriff.

'Where is he?' he asked, rifling amid Picasso's trash for his own few things.

'I don't know,' she said, after a pause. 'He left suddenly. I thought you were him coming back.'

Michael blew out air from tension.

'I know,' she said, and swung her feet out from the bed. She fumbled for a cigarette. She sighed. 'If you let me shower first, I could be gone.' She looked forlorn.

'OK,' he said.

He sat in the front room, and looked at the paintings, the new ceramics, the boxes of wood stuffed with found objects. How on earth, he wondered, do I end this?

He doesn't allow other people to end things; leaving must be up to him. It would be hard to have him go, because it was a fascinating story to live beside: to see an artist climb. Especially one who climbs quickly, rather than slowly, painfully, humiliatingly as Phil had done.

It would hurt, to tear Picasso out of his life. At first. But to live with someone you love who does not love you is indeed to eat your own heart. You have to live through clichés to realize how powerful and apt an expression they often are. Michael was eating his own heart out. He would have no heart left.

Michael was good at avoiding decisions, at letting life decide. Life decided. 'Enough,' Michael said aloud. He had had enough. He looked at the paintings on the wall and had two goals: to get Picasso to go, and to save his art.

So the next day, Michael took another long lunch break, and visited Mr Miazga in the flat that had once been his own. Mr Miazga was working alone at his computer, with the resigned grimness of someone unemployed at fifty.

'My wife is not here,' Mr Miazga sighed. 'Is she perhaps at your house?'

Michael tried to think of what would be polite, and realized that nothing would be. 'I don't know. It's possible. I try not to go there.'

'I hate that man.'

Michael sighed too. 'Sometimes I do.'

'You? You love him.'

'The two are not mutually exclusive.' Michael looked at the Zip-drive disk in his hand. 'Thaddeus,' he began. 'I have a lot of respect for you, and so I am going to ask something that I would not ask from just anyone.'

Mr Miazga kept keying in a program. 'OK. Ask.'

'I want you to redo all his work.'

Mr Miazga sniffed. 'He should make backups.'

'He does. I do. But that won't work.' Michael had rehearsed this next part. 'It would be difficult to explain how I know this, but believe me it is true. Every trace of his work will disappear when he dies.'

'A fault in how he programs?'

'Stranger than that. I can promise you that all his paintings and ceramics will disappear as well. That would be a loss. But, consider if his new work in computer art would disappear as well.'

Mr Miazga shrugged. 'I am not a critic.'

'No, thank heavens. You are a creative technologist. So, ask yourself this question. Is he not finding out what can really be done artistically with this stuff?'

Mr Miazga went quiet. 'What are you asking?'

'I'm asking you to rekey in any code he makes. I'm asking you to redo every gif. I'm asking you to rescan every graphic. That way the work will survive.'

'Why?' Mr Miazga turned to him, his bafflement shot through with something genuinely enquiring.

In his shoulder bag Michael had volume two of the John Richardson biography. The books are laced with every existing photograph of Picasso, often in his workshop. Michael opened it at the chapters dealing with the early 1920s. Silently, he kept turning each of the pages.

Michael could see the exact moment when Mr Miazga understood. He jumped as if someone had stabbed him with a pin. 'It's him,' he said and turned to Michael wide-eyed.

'The rules are simple. Whenever he goes back to wherever it is he comes from, everything he has done in this world will vanish.'

Mr Miazga rifled through the pages. 'It . . . really is him.'

He looked at Michael with something like horror. Then he crossed himself. 'Is this some kind of miracle?'

'I don't really know. We could talk about it all afternoon and still not understand it. Can you believe me, Thad?'

Mr Miazga went back to the photographs. He gave a nervous laugh. 'It is remarkable.' His eyes said: is it God or the Devil who has done this?

'If you do this I will tell him what you are doing. If it's a choice between his work surviving or Marta, I imagine your wife will be safe.'

Mr Miazga chortled, ducked and smoothed down his impeccable hair. 'A man might prefer to have his wife back for other reasons.'

'I . . . imagine she still loves you. I imagine she will be grateful that you are still there to pick up the pieces . . . And . . .'

OK, here comes the second impossible thing.

'Can I promise you something, Thad? When he goes, she will

have no memory of him. Neither will you. It will be as if he never existed.'

It was all beginning to be a bit too much for Mr Miazga. He expelled air and pulled his hair back even flatter.

'I imagine that you are aware of the value of his work. And that, whatever the personal situation, you can see that there is value in making sure the work survives?' It was a question, left for him to answer.

Mr Miazga covered his face with his hands, and appeared to wash his face with them as though they were flannels.

'OK, I will do it,' he said, snatching his hands away. Then he seemed to crumple. 'Oh, I am a weak man.'

'You are in control of your emotions, Thad. Whatever the situation with your wife, you are still able to see clearly. And you are a normal man who wants his marriage to survive.'

Mr Miazga looked round at him slowly, his face more creased than usual, in folds. 'And you do well, too. You get him back.'

'I don't have him, Thad. And I'm doing this so that I can send him away.'

Mr Miazga looked at him for a few moments and said, 'For you I will do this. Not for him.'

Michael returned to work elated. He boomed hello at Shafiq and Tony, and bounced so effectively at Ebru that she had no time to say anything about his absences. He kissed her on the cheek, talked to her about her trip to Turkey, and asked her to run a report on their data using different variables.

Then he slammed into his in tray and got a fair way through it. He saw from the papers that it was too late to agree to speak at the American conference. Well, OK, you can't do everything. He tore up the correspondence, threw it in the wastebin and e-mailed an apology. At 6.00 PM, he tapped all the remaining, older papers into a neat pile and put them in a folder. He was the last to leave.

Michael wandered in a circuit around Archbishop's Park. It was the day before the clocks went back and it was nearly dark. There was no one else there, though it was still warm and the trees had all their leaves. Michael's feet began to drag, as if he had forgotten to drink any water during the whole of the day.

Michael avoided going home. He finally took the tube and ended up in the Camden bar. The red-faced, bearded men ignored him. He watched other laconic, unfearful souls play darts.

It wasn't enough to have love. You needed to have power. The two were so much alike. Love and power only exist between people. Both come from inner liveliness. Perhaps they were the same thing, since to fail at one seemed in some way to be bound up with failure in the other.

Michael finished a pint of Becks and finally went back to his flat.

'This flat, it is mine,' Michael said. 'I bought it.'

'Hmph,' said Picasso from his computer. He turned and glowered a warning.

'You're welcome to stay. If you still need to. You can sleep in my bed or on my sofa. But please stop bringing women back.'

Picasso smiled. 'You are jealous.'

Michael smiled. 'Not at all. It is inconvenient to come back and find my bed occupied.'

Picasso seemed to swell and darken like clouds. 'Do not threaten me.'

'How have I threatened you? I have asked you to keep strangers out of my bed.'

Picasso said, 'You will make me angry.'

'Why? Because I ask for good behaviour?'

'Yes. It is bourgeois.'

'Oh please. It would be bourgeois to sit by helplessly while you turn me out of my own house. If you want to make a mess and fill a flat with whores, go find one of your own.'

Picasso finished keying in with a musical flourish. 'I will do so.' He turned and challenged Michael, his jaw thrust out.

'Good,' said Michael.

That night Picasso noisily made up a bed downstairs. For the first time in months, Michael slept in his own bed alone. He felt the separation, like scar tissue from his sternum down to the top of his penis. It's over, he realized. It really is over. There was sadness like a story ending, and another sensation that was like fear.

Trepidation we'll call it. Unease. Michael knew that it was a necessary unease. It was the unease you feel when you lose a tooth, or change jobs. It was the unease of learning.

I love you, Michael accepted, and it will have to end. He wept one long slow hot unwilling tear, and that was all.

In the morning Michael went downstairs and Picasso was making coffee. He looked smaller. He turned and smiled and said good morning and pushed an empty cup in Michael's direction.

'You have set me free, haven't you?' Picasso said.

'Yes.'

'You will let me live.'

Michael nodded. Picasso chuckled and gave his head a funny shake. 'You have become tired of me, but you don't threaten me. That is good,' he said. 'It is economical.' He made a fist to emphasize the last word.

Michael allowed himself to be drawn. 'Economical how?'

'Toh!' said Picasso and spread his hands out over the self-evident, empty table. 'One should never give everything. It is wasteful. It tries too hard.'

His eyes said: I am going to live. I am going to live without conditions.

Two weeks later Picasso stood at night on the doorstep. He had a new leather jacket slung over one shoulder and a shaved bristly head and a stud earring. He had started to sell pictures; his agent had found him a flat. He was in an expansive mood.

'I am going to live!' he said, rocking on his heels.

'Indeed,' said Michael, smiling with him.

Picasso took his hand. 'And the work. It will live too?'

'For as long as you do. When you go . . . the paintings, the sculptures will disappear.'

'Like the flowers,' said Picasso, and his face was impossible to read. It was regretful but happy.

'Except for your computer pieces. Uh . . . I have not told you this. Mr Miazga. I made a deal with him.'

For some reason, Picasso threw his head back and laughed aloud.

'He is keying in all your work again. So it will remain. It will stay.'

Picasso was still laughing. 'Poor Miazga. Regard! There is a man who gives everything!'

'The deal is that you stop screwing his wife.' It was terrible, but Michael was grinning too, without knowing why, and he suddenly spurted out a laugh.

'He can have her!' declared Picasso, with a wave of his hand, dismissing her, it, everything. He did his little dance in place. His eyes looked at Michael, brimming with affection.

'You,' Picasso said with one finger, 'Are.' Two fingers together made a sign like a blessing. He gave Michael a hug and whispered in his ear, 'But I really hated screwing you.' The words broke apart like rocks with laughter.

'Liar,' said Michael. 'You were in me all night.'

Picasso stepped back. 'True,' he proclaimed. He spun around and held up a hand to wave goodbye. 'True!' he bellowed as he walked away without looking back.

And Michael for some reason felt a wild unaccountable joy. It was as if there were a giant tiger lily flower all red, spangled with yellow, and it was just beyond the sky, filling it, invisible. I am going to live, Michael repeated. He watched Picasso's retreating back with love and gratitude and relief.

What am I looking for?

Michael finally cleared his in tray and saw in it a reminder: *Deadline for grant proposals*. He lightly thought: why have they sent me this? The answer seemed to thump him in the heart.

Because you didn't do the application.

No, I must have. Didn't I? Michael couldn't remember *not* doing it, but then you don't remember not doing something. He was sure he had done it. Well, or rather, it felt as if he had.

But his only memory of application forms was, he realized, from last year, for the six-month initial grant. He opened up My Documents, he did a Find, and there was no file called *application* or *council form* or any other likely name on either the server or his hard disk. He must have sent it out, he couldn't have been so stupid. He sorted all his e-mails by address and looked at everything he had sent to the Council. Only one had an attachment, and that was simply the first progress report.

Michael went out and asked Ebru if she still kept a record of all outgoing and incoming white mail.

'Mmmm hmmm,' she said, and handed him the register.

'Good girl,' he said wistfully, looking at her brisk, pinched face. And she was a good girl, better than he was, to record each outgoing item of post. It wasn't as if she were a secretary; she was a postgraduate researcher.

Michael went though the list line by line for all of August and September: there was nothing, no conventional mail what-soever to the Biological Research Funding Council.

'Do we have a record of courier dispatches?'

Her eyes said of course we have. 'Yes; that what you were looking for, Michael?'

Ebru's gaze was upsettingly direct and unfriendly. She was plainly fed up with him. There was nothing in her manner to encourage him to tell her what had happened.

Michael lied. 'I sent back some faulty software, I need to know when.'

'If you'll tell me where you sent it, I could find it for you.'

'Well, I know roughly when and I know it was sent by ordinary post, so it'll be easier if I just scan for it.'

Her grey eyes rested on his, and then she shrugged, and then she passed the dispatch courier receipts in silence.

There were only three dispatches in August and none of them was for the Research Council.

Michael slowly closed the register and found that his limbs did not want to move.

There would have been no funding after September. They should have enough to finish the light learning experiment, but that wasn't the point. The point was to use the current study as a benchmark to see how other learning activities produced different results. They'd talked about it, the team expected it. Michael could not believe he had done it, that he had fucked up that badly, that he was so stupid, so incompetent. His flesh seemed to crawl nervously all over his bones. Part of him was trying to take action, or perhaps, escape himself.

He rang the Research Council. The conversation left his heart shrivelled with shame. The neurology contact was a man called Geoffrey Malterton; he was, as ever, pleased to hear from Michael. Geoffrey sounded ebullient and efficient – nothing out of place in his life, then. 'Whoa, you're weeks too late, months too late. It's all been snatched up, I'm afraid. I'm sorry, but you know how fierce the competition is for grants. What, is your project still unfinished?'

'No, no, not at all, it's just that we've had some new ideas.' Michael tried to sound bright and alert.

'Well, then you can always apply next year. The answer is no for this year's money, I'm afraid.'

Michael asked Emilio for the project accounts. He avoided asking Ebru. As soon as he saw the spreadsheet, their situation was so obvious that he wondered why the staff weren't talking about it. Simply there had been no income except interest since April 1. It was now late October.

Did they have enough to continue? Michael had supposed he would be able during the year to raise more money from other sources. They had roughly one month of money left. He recalculated their budget, remembering extras like stationery and an unpaid water bill, and had a moment's panic. Then he remembered: interest was compounded quarterly and that would be paid in at the end of November. He had to track their steadily decreasing principal and try to calculate the interest. It was all back-of-an-envelope stuff, but the interest made the difference. They would be OK. OK meant that there was enough money to give all the staff their contractually required one month's notice.

It could all be made to seem deliberate. They had enough basic data for this particular project. Michael could just ignore the idea they had of following it up. They should make sure that all the data were entered and correct and then run the reports. There would even be time and money if they needed one final trial, one more order of chicks, to fill any gaps in data or design.

There was always a problem with staff near the end of research projects. You tell them the project will end just when their work must be at its most meticulous. Yes, they had known all along it would come to an end, but yes, they have living expenses, so they have to look for the next contract or post. They often leave before finishing, especially when the end of the project is unexpected and they have not been able to plan.

He went to the cold store. They had done a good job while he was going crazy. The slides were all in order and labelled. The salami wafers had all been stained and stored. With something numb and slow, part way between dread and relief, he saw: the project had been well done.

Michael went into the soft, dark, red-lit room. There were the chicks, his chicks, peeping out of need and hunger. They were warm and feathery in his hands, as light as dust, kicking and struggling for life. They would be the last batch to be killed.

And suddenly Michael saw them afresh; they were like his Angels, all his beautiful Angels alive and hungry and here for such a short time. He was surprised by a sudden welling up of tears. He loved them. He was going to lose them. He loved them and he didn't want to kill them. He stood transfixed by confusion, torn by irreconcilable emotions, for the chicks, for his research, for his old life with its mild addictions to science, order, and shots of whisky and of semen. He had no desire or idea of what to desire. Simply, he was unmanned, meaning he had lost a self. He could not answer the question, what do I do next? He stood in the dark, cradling a little chick, weeping for it, making peeping noises himself.

Please God, make it stop. Please God, just take it away! I'll be good. Just tell me what to do, and I'll do it.

The world is not to be seduced by words. The world stayed the same, waiting for him to act.

Michael remembered the first day they had moved into the arches. Ebru, Emilio, Hugh inspected their well-resourced lab, running around the cold room and the darkroom and the emergency generator like kids. Ebru had kept deferring to him: Michael, where do you want this? She had called him Hoja, which meant teacher or master in Turkish. She would never call him that again.

Michael took a deep breath. A parental voice from somewhere said, Do it, Mikey. Get it over with.

Shafiq was in his box. Ebru and Emilio were together in the front office. Hugh was hunched over the camera. Michael asked to see them in his office in fifteen minutes. He spent those fifteen minutes rehearsing what he was going to say, with his fingers spread out across the top of his desk as if they were roots drawing strength from it.

Their body language alone was enough to wrench his gut. Ebru slouched in, her arms crossed in front of her, her mouth pushed to one side with sour suspicion. Shafiq stood like Prince Charles, erect, his hands clasping each other behind his back as if to stop him hitting someone. His plump face was turned upwards as if absorbing a blow. Emilio looked bored, irritated, impatient. I spent so much time building them up into a kind of family, Michael thought. I've destroyed it.

'There's no good way to say this, so I'll be brief. We've collected enough data which thanks to all your efforts is in super shape, really, it's all recorded, the data entered, everything in cold store . . . well done . . . really.'

They were as frozen as the samples. They knew what was coming.

'Which means that the project is entering the home stretch. We still have some slides to photograph, which I see Hugh has well in hand. What we need to do now is just make sure we have enough data, all in order, and then try to turn it into some kind of information. Which I reckon we can do before the end of the calendar year.'

Ebru flicked hair out of her eyes.

'Um. That means the project will end and that I'll be giving you formal notice today. You've been a terrific team, and I wanted you to have the news as soon as I did.'

'You forgot to apply for the grant, didn't you, Michael?' Ebru said it.

'No. I uh took advice from the Research Council. They said it was probably best if we tried to wind the project up as a second grant was highly unlikely.' Michael wiped his mouth.

Was she going to call him a liar as well as incompetent? Ebru hovered for a moment like a hawk over a motorway bank. Then she shrugged and went silent. She couldn't be bothered.

'Any questions?'

There was a beat. Ebru shook her head and murmured, 'No.'

'Well, if you have any, just ask. Ebru, you and I will need to go over all the contracts and make the nuh-non-renewals official. Hugh, there is the photography to continue. Emilio, you and I will need to get going on the data processing.'

Silence.

'I uh, was wondering if people wouldn't like to get together today for a lunch. My treat?'

Never had words of his sounded so much like a creek running dry.

'I would like to say thank you.'

The team glanced at each other. Ebru said it. 'Maybe later, Michael. When the project ends, the last day or something.'

'OK,' said Michael. His hands did something awkward in mid-air. 'OK, thanks, gang.'

They started to file out.

'Oh. One other thing. Um. We really have a lot of data. And I was wondering if we really need, need any more. Which would mean . . . I want us to set this last batch of chicks free.'

That was enough to make Ebru stop and turn around. 'Oh that is a good idea,' she said, without any tonal variation in her voice.

'Well, they're such beautiful little things, and we've got a lot of data and it just seems such a shame . . .'

Oh God, oh no. He could feel his face. It was crumpling at the corners of his mouth, and his cheek was twitching up towards his eyes. He was starting to cry, and he had no real idea why.

It is a very strange sensation to break down in public and for that public to stare back at you stonily, completely unmoved by anything like sympathy. Cry, you bastard, their eyes seemed to say. Cry for your little project.

'We could just let them go, in the park?' He was begging.

Ebru said, 'That is illegal.'

'It'll be an illegal little party.' Michael bounced in his seat, trying to communicate that it would be naughty and fun.

'It's stupid, they'll die, it isn't even kind,' said Ebru and turned and walked out. Shafiq shuffled away. Hugh said, 'I'll get going on the photographs.' Emilio said, smiling but with a direct gaze, 'Whatever you're on, Michael. Stop taking it.'

They processed the chicks without even telling Michael they were doing it. They did it very quickly, and neatly. Michael went into the photography room. Hugh was photographing as before, but Ebru was staining samples.

'Those are fresh,' said Michael.

'We have to do it while they're young, Michael. Otherwise

309

they will be too mature to compare with the other samples.'

'I asked you not to do that.'

'When?' Ebru turned and her gaze challenged him, challenged his right to give any orders at all. 'When did you ask me not to, Michael? We discussed your idea about setting them free and decided it was wrong. And we decided that it was stupid to waste them, and so we follow proper procedure.' Her hand made an involuntary little wave, sweeping him away. 'We will do everything in order, Michael. You don't have to do a thing.'

'I'm very unhappy you did that.'

Ebru held out her hands in something like helplessness. I am helpless to help you, Michael. I am helpless to say anything other than that your unhappiness makes no difference.

Michael had nothing else to do, so he typed all the official notices of non-renewal. He went over the accounts and planned the new expenditure. That is the kind of thing a good little boy does when admonished. There is no coming back from being justly admonished by your staff, and then being defied by them.

He worked alone in his office, deliberately until late. No one popped in to say good night, see you tomorrow. At 8.30 PM he did a round of the lab, turning out a few lights. In the reception box, the night guard was pleased to see him. He was a Londoner, ex-Cockney, a vanishing breed. 'Hello, sir,' he said, perking up. 'I haven't seen you this late in ages. How are you, sir?' He sounded genuinely pleased to see Michael.

'I decided to give up all that staying late.'

'Oh, very wise, sir, very wise. My wife says the same about me at my age. But the money's good, and between you and me, it gets me out from under her feet.'

It was terrible to be treated with friendliness and respect.

The leaves had begun to fall in Archbishop's Park, and they had blown across the street, crunching underfoot. Walking back to Waterloo seemed to take forever; he shuffled with dream-like slowness. He'd fucked it. He had well and truly fucked it. He stood stricken on the platform at Waterloo, wanting to hide.

310

He walked back to his old flat near Goodge Street on automatic pilot. He got all the way to looking up at his old window, and seeing his ceiling illuminated through it and a moving shadow, he thought oh good, Phil's home.

Then he realized no, he's not. No one is at home. Home is over, home is gone. My animal brain just walked me back here.

His animal heart stood outside the building yearning upwards at the light on the old ceiling. I want my job back, my beautiful project. I want my partner, my flat, my peace of mind. I want my old life back.

Too late, Michael, you're not going to get it.

The idea of walking back to Goodge Street tube, and going all the way to Camden, made him close his eyes with fatigue. He wondered if he could just ask the Miazgas to let him back in, for ten minutes' snooze. He just wanted to clear his head. But he would have to explain to them, and worry them, and involve them again in his life.

So he turned, dazed as if on painkillers, and dragged his way back to Goodge Street station. Everything around him – the Eisenhower Security Center, the cenotaph in front of it – was like reassuring old friends seen after a divorce. There was the Reject Shop . . . no, it wasn't. It was now something called Cargo. Change swept over everything like a tide; turn your back and it's as over as the First World War.

Michael tried to find the flower. The flower was whatever he had touched when Luis had left him. The joy in the world, in himself. I have seen it. It was real. It can come when things go wrong.

It's strongest when you have been brave and strong – not when you've fucked up, messed everyone over, lost it. Not when you've thrown your life out of the window.

There was now a porn shop on Tottenham Court Road.

Well there would be; they had been moving north out of Soho for some time, as real estate got too valuable even for the sex industry, and only cappuccino, it seemed, could turn a penny, or rather, enough pennies. GAZE the WORD the shop called itself. There were ribbons of coloured plastic across the door. There always were, in porn shops. Like ketchup bottles always looking the same.

'Well hello, Professor,' said a voice.

Someone was standing in the doorway. Michael blinked; it took him a moment to recognize who it was.

The guard from Goodge Street station. He was wearing a fancy T-shirt, the kind you're not supposed to tuck in, and the same blue security trousers that made his legs and butt look somehow bolshy.

'Have a look round, don't be shy,' the Guard said. He looked chunkier. Perhaps he had been working out, but his mouth still habitually sneered. He held apart the plastic strips as if opening a dressing gown.

'Come on. I'm sure I've got something for you.' He emphasized 'you', as if he knew and understood Michael.

Michael had no direction, no reason to do anything else, so he went inside. It was bright like Christmas, full of colour.

'I expect you're surprised to see me here,' said the Guard. 'I suppose you could say I found my metier.' He grinned cheekily. 'Here, have a look at these.'

He handed Michael video boxes covered with coloured computer printout. The images were of naked men.

'I get these from round the world,' he said. He dipped down behind the counter, and pulled out a folder. He opened it up, to show clear wallets full of more laser-printed images.

Rancho Rauncho, one of them boasted. *Starring Spike Harden and Mustapha Most.*

'American,' he said proudly. 'Uncensored. You won't find this sort of stuff for sale anywhere else in the West End. Not at these prices. Beautiful stuff.'

Michael noticed: he's wearing a wedding ring.

'Look at this. Now this is the guvnor . . . Max Schnarr. He goes all round the world: Russia, Eastern Europe, Quebec, all sorts of strange places. Picks up all the best-looking men himself, and they're so besotted with him that they let him make a film. He's in 'em himself. This one's from Venezuela.'

Michael stared, bored beyond description, bored into some netherworld where nothing you said made any difference.

'Hold on.' The Guard leaned forward. 'I've got some really special stuff, if this kind of thing is too tame. Red, yellow, brown.' He leaned back, and waited.

'What do your mates next door think of this?' Michael asked. Goodge Street station was three doors down.

'That lot? I just tell 'em what I'm making these days. It beats working for London Underground, I can tell you.'

'You're not gay,' said Michael.

'Doesn't mean to say I don't like pleasing men.' The Guard gave a wobble of his eyebrows, and something queasy washed off him. It was attraction, but attraction as if it were music played backwards. It was revulsion so strong that it mimicked attraction.

'Listen, you're not in this line of work, I'll tell you how I do it?' His blanched skin and blue blank eyes shone. He wanted the Professor to understand that he was not some stupid oik. 'You can buy this stuff with copyright off the Internet. You just pay a one-off fee. It's expensive, but it comes with all rights, and you download it at three AM when the lines are clear. And it's lovely quality, MPEG 2 compression. You can transfer it to DVD or video. The punters could do the same, but it would take them forty-five minutes to download, and they're bound to lose the line halfway through. I got in a leased line, that costs, I can tell you, but I got a thriving mail-order business. In fact, I had that before I opened the shop. I want to become the main source for gay porn in the entire UK.'

Michael started to look through the files.

'I tell you some of this stuff is really strong. I mean, under-the-counter even in America. You've seen nothing like it, mate.' The Underground Guard leaned forward. 'Come on, tell me what you're into.' Michael could feel his breath on his cheek: he could smell it. Mint on mint; there was a Polo circling his mouth even now. It clicked every time he spoke. 'I've got it for you, or I can get it. Come on, you can tell me.'

Latin Manhattan. Ghost with the Most. A Lad In with His Wonderful Lamp.

Michael remembered Phil in his porn phase. 'They cost fifty thousand dollars to make and return two hundred and fifty. Do it six times and you're a dollar millionaire.'

The Guard was pleased. 'You know how it works then. I mean, I'm looking for an Angel.'

Michael looked up. 'What?'

'Angel. You know. Theatrical investor. To put up the money. I'm trying to make a video of my own. Because I mean you're absolutely right, the money gets made in production. It's not like that for any other part of the film industry. For regular films it's distribution, but with this stuff it's all under-the-counter, which is too expensive and slow, or on the Net, which frankly is too cheap. You're giving the stuff away on the Net, which is why it's available on one-off. I'd love to turn it around and sell distribution back to the States. Hey. The British are coming, eh?'

'That could be the title,' said Michael.

The Underground Guard was getting excited. He chuckled. 'You're dead right.'

'My project just closed down,' said Michael. 'I have no money to invest.'

'Ah well, one day my ship will come in,' said the Guard. 'In the meantime, think about what you're into and let me know. Like I say, if I don't have it, I know where to find it.'

'Don't . . .' Michael stopped at the door. 'Don't the police bother you?'

'Naw. They'd rather people got into this stuff than pick up some disease. But only because the drugs are so expensive on the National Health. Sooner or later, I'll end up in jail. Goes with the territory.'

His blunt pale face established beyond doubt; he'd do well in prison.

Michael thanked the Guard and left.

The logical part of Michael's brain got him home, regretfully, coldly.

Michael sat in his flat in the dark, listening to traffic and the shouts of kids from the clubs.

Michael tasted emptiness. There were times when he wanted Luis back. But that would prove Luis's point in a way. He would even take Philip back. He would take anything, Michael. It is getting hard to see any progress in all this.

314

He thought of the Guard's stubby pale body, its little potbelly, the undoubtedly uncircumcised cock, and the thought produced a weary sort of sexual response.

OK. Come on then.

The air wavered and parted its lips, and the Guard stepped into Michael's sitting room.

Why does God suffer the Devil?

'Nice place,' the Guard said, casing it.

Then he said, 'Shit.' Then he had to sit down. He'd understood faster than most what he was.

'You're not real,' Michael said, still bored, still exhausted. 'You're a copy. I make copies of people I think I want to have sex with. It's a miracle. If you can figure it out, tell me.'

'Do you mind if I smoke?' the Angel asked.

Michael waved, go ahead. It makes no difference. Once you go, my lungs will clean up again.

The movements of the Angel's pale, pudgy hand were jagged, as if pins were prodding him. With one hand, he flipped out a fag and then a match. His left hand tapped out a nervous rhythm on his thigh. The Guard had broken out in a sweat, and his eyes grew narrower and brighter as he looked about him. His eye fastened onto the wall covered with jumping Picassos. 'Did one of us paint those?' he asked, jabbing a finger at them. 'One of us copies.'

'You're quick,' said Michael.

'Have to be. Everyone in my family's a thief.' The Angel tapped the end of the cigarette on the matchbox before finally lighting up. He drew in gratefully, then blew out. 'You eaten anything?' he asked.

Michael had to think. 'No,' he said quietly. 'I meant to get a takeaway, but I forgot.'

'It's all right, I got plenty of dosh, I'll go get it for you.' The Angel bolted up from the sofa as if it were electrified.

'That wouldn't be honest,' said Michael.

'Why not, I bet I make more than you do.'

'Once you go back to whatever it is you come from, the money you gave the man will disappear. It would be like stealing. I'll give you my money.' Michael heaved his wallet out of his trousers.

'Disappear?' The Angel did a little shuffle in place.

'Mmm hmmm,' said Michael, and held out a tenner.

He took the money, then he said, 'I'll need the keys.'

Laboriously Michael passed those and then he said, 'You don't come back with them, I'll wipe you out of existence and they'll be back here in my pocket.'

'Not if I give them to the man. Then they'll stay there, won't they?'

A long pause.

'You don't really know what would happen with either the keys or the money.' The Angel rocked back and forth slightly on his heels.

That's right, Michael didn't. Another experiment he could make, if he had the heart for another experiment. If he hated killing chickens, why would he want to wipe out the Guard to discover if he got his keys back? And what would happen if his keys stayed lost?

'Knock and I'll open the door,' said Michael. 'Sorry, but you did say you were a thief.'

'I never. I said my family was. I tried all my life not to be, and I'm not, see?'

Michael nodded.

'Though . . . it does kind of leave you crook inside. Bent, in all kinds of directions.' The Angel smoothed down his hair, like drivers do after they've done something stupid like veer out of their lanes. Michael walked down the stairs with him, to let him out. The air felt like glue he had to fight his way through.

The Guard stopped to breathe out smoke. 'Funny, innit? I already know, nothing I say or do can make a difference to anything.'

'It's a shortcut to a lot of things, being an Angel,' said Michael.

The Guard said, 'Angel, huh. That's what you call us.'

'What would you call yourself?'

'Oh, a right little devil. What do you want to eat?'

'There's a little takeaway place, it looks like a minicab office. It does steak sandwiches. Turn left and left again. You'll find it, just follow the smell. Get something for yourself, too, if you want.'

'Right. I'll be back then.' There was an awkward smile and Michael rocked himself wearily to his feet. They thumped down the hollow wooden steps together, each of them sounding as real as the other.

Michael let the Guard out, and gave him a wave as he walked across the street. Michael discovered he had no energy to climb the stairs. He sat down on them instead, and waited. He thought of the Guard, the pale glow of his sweatiness, his pudginess, the crispness of the gelled hair, the rounded jelly of his arse in the tight trousers. It was as if repugnance were a sock that could be turned inside out. Michael thought of the wedding ring on the Angel's finger. He thought about that business of being bent in all directions. We'll do it if he wants to, Michael thought. That was the extent of the attraction.

Michael wished again that he were in love. If he were in love with someone, it would be sit-down meals and not takeaways. He would have someone he could talk to about the grant and the project and how he was to live through it. There was wisdom in love. Without love, wisdom stayed unformulated simply because there was no one who cared enough to talk.

There was a thumping on the door. Michael groaned to his feet, fumbled with the lock, and the Guard burst into the stairwell wafting a kind of freshness, interwoven with a delicious smell of steak.

'Brrrrrr, it's parky out there,' the Guard said, and bounded up the stairs. He strode ahead of Michael into the kitchen area. Cold vapour steamed off him. 'I should have borrowed one of your jackets. Right. I'll just put this away to keep warm.' He peered at the cooker and deciphered its ancient markings. 'Where are the plates?'

'Top shelf over the cooker.'

318

'Might as well warm the plates as well.' The Angel cast him a sideways glance. 'So. Can I spend the night here?'

'Yes, if you'd like.'

'Thanks,' said the Angel. 'Where are the place mats?'

'Um.' Michael couldn't remember. He had to remember where the place mats were and when he went to get them, he walked as if he had lead boots on.

'Knives . . . forks . . . salt.'

A lovely little setting for two was laid out on the table. Michael was aware of something like a mismatch between the man and his behaviour.

The Guard sniffed. 'You got anyone to clean this place?'

'No,' admitted Michael. 'I probably should. My last boyfriend wasn't exactly tidy.'

'Not exactly, no,' said the Angel. 'The whole place is covered in china clay. Did he do all those paintings then?'

'Yup,' sighed Michael. 'He's only been gone a couple of days.'

The Angel's back went very still. 'Where'd he go to?'

'His agent found him a place. He has his first exhibition next week.'

'Ah . . . so you do let some of us live, then?' The Guard said it as he stood up with candles for the candlestick.

Michael wasn't sure why he didn't like the Guard saying that, knowing that. He didn't have time to work out why he didn't like it.

'There we go,' said the Angel, holding out his hands to the professionally set table. He's worked as a waiter, Michael realized. 'You got any serviettes?' the Angel asked.

Later, Michael waited for him under the duvet of the bed. The Guard was one of those people who brush and spray. They try to wash their private parts without making a sound of water splashing, and they powder themselves. Michael knew the result well: the Guard would taste of alcohol base and smell like the ground floor of Selfridges.

The Guard walked back upstairs from the john wearing Michael's robe and holding in his tummy. He still had on his socks. He would have been handsome if he didn't leer and his body language had been less jerky and angular.

319

The Guard dumped himself next to Michael. He did indeed smell like a floral tribute. But the body was alabaster – smooth, plump and cool to the touch.

The Guard asked, 'What do you like doing?'

'It's more important to know what you like doing,' said Michael. 'You're married.'

'Yeah, well, I do other things too.'

'What, are you bi?'

'Yeah, sort of. I'm not a thief, but when I was younger . . . well I got sent down. My brothers needed some help on a job and I got caught. I wasn't so big then, in fact as it happens I was a bit small for my age. Anyway, while I was in the nick I sort of found out that if you let the other guys do things, then they weren't so . . . I don't know, aggressive. They were still right little bastards . . .' He managed a kind of sneering chuckle. 'But they were placated.' He propped his head on his elbows. 'And you. What do you get up to, eh, with this little miracle of yours?'

'Too much.'

The Guard liked that. He settled down with a chuckle. 'Ho I bet. Come on, tell me, what you been up to? Who have you had?'

'Um. The New Zealand All Blacks. That high diver who's a Brit but his family's Italian. A very nice black musician . . . loads.'

'What, and they just come and perform for you?'

'Yeah. I think the real miracle isn't that they're here, it's that they want to sleep with me.'

'It's not surprising. You're a very good-looking man.' The Guard gave him an encouraging nudge.

The words sounded false. Michael suspected that he was being flattered. 'So who would you ask for?'

'Ooh. Someone like you.' The Guard grinned. One tooth was outlined in silver.

Michael knew he was being flattered. 'What would you like to *do*?' he asked, again, insisting.

The Angel ventured, as if onto thin ice. 'Well . . . would it be all right if we just . . . cuddled?'

320

'Yeah sure fine,' said Michael who was hardly up for it anyway.

On the night after you discover that you have destroyed your job, it is reassuring to be held. It was pleasant, even necessary, for Michael to feel a warm, smooth, soft body enveloping him from behind, as if it were there to shield him, as if it were offering him love or stability or both. There was a simple, catlike sensuality about feeling the other body stir, of taking its hand, of hearing someone murmur sleepily, 'You'll let me stay, won't you. Please?'

Michael awoke in the morning to hear a sizzling sound. He thumped downstairs to find the Angel at the stove, frying bacon and eggs. 'I couldn't find the coffee,' the Guard said.

The kitchen looked brighter as if the sun were out. The floor, Michael saw, had been cleaned. The Angel picked up his gaze as if it were a tip.

'I washed the floor for you,' he said. 'This place is filthy. There's shadows on your sheets. Probably skidmarks and all, only I didn't want to look too close. I still can't find the coffee as it happens.'

The Guard gave Michael a full cooked breakfast. Michael offered to do the washing-up, but the Guard said, 'Hadn't you better be getting on? Look, why don't you let me stay here and clean up a bit?'

Michael couldn't help but smile. 'You really want to stay as long as you can, don't you?'

The Guard grinned inexpertly – smiling was not his strongest suit. 'I like to make myself useful.'

'OK, stay and clean up,' said Michael. He found that the thought of going to work and facing the team all over again made the Angel seem a refuge of domesticity.

'I should have asked your name,' Michael said.

'Nick. Just plain Nick. Nick Dodder.' Then he said, 'Here, your tie needs straightening.'

At work that day, Michael tried to be committed. He started out well, planning expenditure until the end of the project. Then he had a bit of a blow. Emilio handed in his notice. 'I had an offer already, you see, for when . . . uh, this project finished.' He pronounced it finish-shed.

'When will you go?'

Emilio flinched and didn't answer. He probably wanted to go as soon as possible. Emilio was the project's IT man. Any real problems with the network, or any fresh programming to be done and they would miss him.

Michael sighed. 'OK. Well. Your contract holds us both to a minimum of a month's notice, and I'm going to need you to work out your notice. Basically, we need to audit what we've got in terms of reports, generate any new report forms, and train up Hugh and Ebru to use them.'

Emilio looked discomfited. 'If . . . if I finish all that before the month is up, could I go? It is three years' work, Michael, guaranteed.'

'I'll think about it,' said Michael. He meant no. 'Thanks for letting me know.'

The day darkened, Michael slowed down. The truth was that he had destroyed his project. This truth did not go away like an unwelcome guest. The truth stayed, like a dysfunctional family, like your inescapable self. Michael hid his face.

And when Michael got back home, the flat smelled of roast beef. The entire ground floor was in order. The books were on shelves. Places had been found for all of Luis's canvases, bags of clay, splattered wood, old newspapers, plastic ice cream containers, rope and bits of tyre.

Nick was pleased with his work. 'A lot of it's upstairs if you want to go through it. Personally, I'd just chuck the lot. Have you insured this place?'

'Yes, why?'

Nick took Michael's shoulder bag to hang up. 'Because if your friend has even started to sell his stuff, each one of those paintings is worth at least three hundred pounds. And there's forty of them. That'll be worth twelve k. You like roast potatoes?'

At dinner Nick was full of schemes. 'You should do this place up and sell it. Those are Regency banisters. You could do up the whole place as Regency. It's just opposite the tube, it's got a roof garden, only one point of access on the street, no neighbours. If you put in a second lockable door at the head of the staircase, this place would be worth three hundred, four hundred thousand. Hell, two bedrooms, Camden Town, I tell you, a year from now it would be worth half a million. If you needed help doing it up, I'm pretty handy, as it happens.'

'It might be a good idea.'

'It's a brilliant idea. It'll be work, mind you.'

'I'll think about it.' It was what he had said to Emilio. There was something Michael didn't like.

'Come on, get up off your arse, this place will never get back in order if you don't get into some habits. Why don't you let me wash, and you put away? You know where things go?'

So rather neatly, as a team, they got the dishes washed. Nick soaped them lavishly, rinsed them in water so hot it steamed, and shook them.

'This thing of yours, this miracle,' he said, scrubbing between the teeth of Michael's forks. 'You say you can call up anybody? I mean, we could call up James Dean? He was gay. He'd be happy to do anything. From the sound of things, he did.' Nick chuckled darkly. He rinsed a glass. 'People would pay to see him do it as well.'

'What, do you mean make a film?'

'We could do, yeah.' As if it were Michael's idea.

Michael had an answer. He shook his head. 'The instant he went back, the film would show nothing. And that I do know for certain.'

Nick seemed absorbed in polishing a wine glass. He held it up to the light. 'So you mean they can't be photographed?'

'The image only stays as long as they are here. Every trace of them goes. Think of it as a fast death. Like I said, being an Angel's a shortcut. It's what happens to all of us. After we're gone, the children sell the house, the new owners tear out the garden to make a driveway, and throw away our old photographs. It just happens quicker to Angels.'

Nick tried to look philosophical. He succeeded in looking like a contestant on a quiz show. 'Yeah,' he said, his brows touching. He put a plate in the rack. 'So. If they hang around, these Angels, their photographs stick around as well?'

Michael imagined them, hundreds of Angels hanging around

Camden Town so people could see them wanking in films. 'That,' said Michael, 'would be like a run in reality.'

'Reality's already running, mate,' said Nick, with eyes like cash registers.

And after dinner Michael found himself caught in a fleshy hug. 'Hmmm,' said the Guard, kissing him as if he were still washing plates. There was something awkward in the way he did it; his arms pushed Michael away as much as they held him. Nick leaned back and looked at Michael, in what could have been affection, if it hadn't looked appraising.

'I'm into a lot of things,' the Angel promised, rubbing his crotch against Michael's. You couldn't fault him for being over-subtle.

There was one side of Michael's sensuality which had not been explored of late. He crunched a bitter pill, and Nick offered up his buttocks. Michael was surprised. The things that were unattractive on the front of Nick – his pale plumpness – were beautiful from the back. His buttocks were white, flawless mounds. Though his body gave evidence that it had been penetrated many times before, Michael was aware from the clenching of Nick's jaw that it was not comfortable for him. But that was not what Nick said.

'Shall I stop?' asked Michael, pulling back.

'Naw, naw, it's great, go on.'

Pumping from Viagra, headachy and breathing thinly because the drug had swelled up the inside of his nose, Michael came, squirting from a penis that was artificially clogged with swollen veins. His cock felt like a cake decorator squeezing out icing from a tiny hole. The orgasm kept coming, as it were, until his balls ached and he felt drained, and he actually wanted it to end. Someone Michael didn't even like had just given him the most thorough orgasm of his life.

So Michael woke up once more with Nick in the flat. This time, Nick was putting away his clothes. 'You,' said Nick, 'need to do your laundry.'

Yeah maybe, but it's my laundry, thought Michael.

'You have a washing machine?'

Michael knew what was coming. 'No.'

'Well, I can go to Coin Operated while you're at work if you like.'

'What is it with you? I can do my own laundry.'

'Do it yourself, if it suits you.'

Michael hated the whole business of going to the laundry. 'I'll give you some money.'

'Wouldn't want to rob the coin-op, would we?' Nick grinned.

That night Michael found all his socks individually stored in transparent plastic bags, and sorted by colour, blue, black, brown, white.

'Why did you do that?' Michael demanded, feeling trespassed upon.

Nick was cooking again. 'Stops you losing them, mate. Otherwise they get separated and nobody needs a drawerful of half pairs of socks. Trick of me Mum's. You can say thank you if you like.'

Michael felt helpless. There was absolutely no way to say that it wasn't useful. You could even see which colour each pair was.

'Just . . . just ask me next time you're going to change something.'

Nick bowed. 'To hear is to obey, oh Master of the Lamp. Incidentally, I'll be polite about the contents of your fridge, but let's just say that some of it had prices on in shillings and pence. It's all still in the bin, and if you want to go through it, please feel free.' He canoodled his way forward and gave Michael a kiss. He was actually wearing an apron. It was like watching a character in *EastEnders* who the writers have decided would go suddenly gay.

At dinner he helped himself only after first serving Michael. 'You don't use it for anything do you? This miracle of yours.'

'I get my socks put in plastic bags.'

'Well there's a thrill. Look, why don't you let me make a few suggestions.'

'You did.'

'Well, let's make some more, see who we can get in here. It's such a waste not to use it. What? You go and ask any other bloke in the kingdom, gay or straight, what they'd do if they could have anybody they wanted and they'd tell what they'd do soon enough, I can tell you.'

'And that would be what they say. Not what they'd do.'

'Look. Let's go to bed after dinner, and see what takes your fancy. If there's something you really want, I'll just hive myself off. Give me the power to come back by myself and I can come and go as convenient.'

Michael lied. 'I can't do that.'

'Have you tried?'

Michael lied. 'Yeah, a couple of times.'

Nick seemed to find it funny. He chuckled. 'Like hell you did.'

There was some kind of issue about power. Michael now knew that.

In bed, Nick insinuated himself next to Michael. 'Now, let's see. Who shall we have then, eh?' He mentioned a boyish, not-so-young film star beloved of young girls. Nick nuzzled up against Michael. Michael didn't fancy the little squit.

'I'd like to piss on him,' said Nick, with a sudden surge of aggression that made Michael go still.

'I wouldn't want to do anything to him at all.'

'He is a bit wimpish. Maybe you'd like something a bit more butch.' He mentioned a boxing champion, low of brow, high of aggression, who was currently in prison for pummelling a waiter in a restaurant. 'That could be a bit more of a challenge. I hear he's hung like a horse. Talk about biting off more than you can chew, eh?'

'Oh, all right,' sighed Michael.

The brute arrived in an Italian suit, with a neck that was wider than his head.

'Imagine that on top of you. You wouldn't need the Viagra with him, he wouldn't care if you were hard or not.' Nick's merry little eyes said: you didn't know I knew about the Viagra, did you? He nudged him. 'Look at the size of it. That would cure your haemorrhoids.'

Michael felt something move in the air that was also a tickle inside his head. He felt it move and clench and try to hold.

'Go on,' said Nick, to the boxer. 'Drop 'em.'

326

Michael extended himself into the air. He felt himself grapple with something. Michael pushed it back down, and saw a tremor in the muscles around Nick's mouth. Nick had tried to make the boxer lower his trousers.

'I call the shots,' said Michael.

Nick chuckled.

Nick had tried to take control of the miracle.

With a single swipe, Michael pushed the boxer back to where he had come from. He felt his eyes blaze.

Nick looked surprised. 'All right, you didn't like him.'

Michael was angry but could find no words.

That was not Nick's problem. 'I was just trying to find something you might like. Or do you only want me?' His eyes, made of blue ice, simply could not do melting warmth.

'I may not want you at all,' warned Michael.

'Aw baby.' Was he being sarcastic or affectionate? Michael couldn't tell; both explanations fitted his behaviour, his tone of voice. He stroked Michael's arm. 'Let's just go to sleep.' Nick turned off the light and swung his best feature towards Michael. Michael felt his penis creep out of its shell. In the dark, Nick's body was as warm and as comforting as a lover's.

Nick was loyal. Nick never left him. Nick never gave up thinking of things to do for him.

'I thought I'd finally tackle the old studio today,' Nick said at breakfast. He meant the place where Picasso used to work. It was still crowded with stuff the artist had thought he might use: bicycle wheels, a single fur-lined glove, masses of magazines stained with paint, sheets and towels crusty with dried colour.

'Don't do that. Let me call Luis and see what he wants from it first.' Michael looked at the flat, with the newly polished wooden floors and clean kitchen counter tops. He thought of Luis and knew: Luis would demand he keep it for him.

'No. On second thoughts, just chuck it for me.'

Nick passed him a packed lunch. Michael ate it alone at his desk: chicken sandwiches, an apple, sticks of celery. He got back from work and Nick said, 'You got the Internet, right? Do you think I could use it?' The throw rugs were out on the roof garden, drying.

'What for? No downloading whole videos.'

'No, no, just a few images. You're a mean bugger, ain't ya?'

'Yes, I am. How many images?'

'Look, I'll be careful, all right.'

Each night, dinner was direct from cookbooks: *boeuf en croûte*; curries with raisins and homemade chapatti. Every day a different part of the flat would have been scrubbed and polished.

Michael would come home to be presented with Internet images of twelve-year-olds in loincloths; students in a wrestling school in India, pubescent under folds of cloth. 'Doesn't that look sweet? Go on, admit it, they're lovely.'

Nick moved the computer into the bedroom. He downloaded images of a man who had cut off his penis and was now hammering nails through his testicles. The man had posted it himself, with an e-mail address for responses. Nick giggled. 'More like an e-nail. I mean that one would let you do anything to him, anything at all.' Nick's eyes burned with a tiny pin-prick light and his high greasy forehead gleamed like an icefloe.

Michael would be reading a book in bed and Nick would call, 'Here, you got to see this.' Michael looked up wearily. 'Look at this fat old whore. She loves being made fat. Look, she's got a progress chart here, she's fattening herself up like a goose. She says she wants someone to keep her in a dungeon, and force-feed her and then cook her and eat her!' This struck Nick as being wildly funny. 'I mean she actually wants to be cooked!'

Michael looked at the woman's face. She was smiling, bright and intelligent. She looked like someone who might work for him. He felt sick. 'I want that stuff off my hard disk. I want you to go and empty the cache and make sure it stays empty.'

Nick laughed at him. 'Oh-ho-ho man, you don't know the half of it. You really don't.'

'And I don't need to. That stuff is illegal and it's criminal.'

'No, it's not, they do it to themselves.'

'They do it to themselves because . . . because their imaginations have been corrupted.'

'Oh-ho man, listen to you. You sound like someone's maiden auntie.'

'People just do not naturally cut off their cocks. They do it because it has a social meaning. That's why they want people to send them e-mail. That means there has to be a social system for it to have meaning in the first place. And people like you are creating it.'

Nick was still roaring. 'Ah-ha-all right. I'll get the stuff off your bleeding hard disk. I'll bring it in on video instead!' This struck him as particularly funny.

And sure enough, Michael came home the next day to find a video from Russia playing on his television. A soldier was being lifted up and lowered onto a waiting cock. He winced from pain. He glanced directly at the camera, hoping for it to stop. Then he threw his head back in pain. The two men who bounced him up and down glanced nervously at each other. Was this right?

Michael punched off the power. 'What would have happened if I'd brought a colleague home with me?'

'You'd have changed channels.' Nick giggled.

'I would have turned you off.'

'That's what I meant.' Nick's laughter subsided. 'You really wouldn't have the right to do that, you know.'

Nick stood up to face Michael. He was smiling with some kind of catlike satisfaction. His voice started out silky, but roughened as he spoke. 'Whatever I am, Michael, I am a living, thinking, feeling being. You have no more right to switch me off or send me back than a mother has a right to throttle her own child. You got that? You think about it, Michael. While you're being so high and bloody moral about everything.'

Michael had no answer.

'I'm not one of your bleeding little chickens. You called me up. Now you're responsible for me. What am I supposed to do, eh? Run around and pick up your shit-stained underwear and wash it just so you'll let me stay alive? Am I supposed to go back to my trade? Which incidentally I was doing very well at. Don't you think people might notice, Michael, if two Nick Dodders showed up in the same business in the same town? I'm here because of you, mate, and you're stuck with me.'

329

Michael was caught completely off guard. 'You could get a job.'

'Oh cheers, thanks, charming. Without any papers, without anything to prove who I am, except someone else who lives with his wife in Vauxhall. Yeah, a job, right. So we're agreed then, are we?'

Michael was lost. 'Agreed about what?'

'I get to stay here until I find a job and can support myself?'

'I need to think about that.'

'Well you better think about it, Michael, because I don't have anywhere else to go.' Nick's voice rose, extremely effectively, to a bellowing roar of outrage. 'And I am fed up with you threatening to kill me every time I do something you don't like! Got that?'

Michael found he was shaking.

'Sorry to shout,' said Nick, deflating.

I'm stuck with him, my God, he's right, I'm stuck with him.

And after dinner, Nick slid next to him under the sheets and said, 'I'm sorry, Mike. I lost my temper, all right? It's just this whole thing gets on my nerves. I'm an active guy, no pun intended, and this hanging around the house just isn't good for me. Look. I've got an idea. See us both out of a hole, all right?'

'What is it?' Michael said, knowing he wasn't going to like it.

'There's no point me applying for ordinary jobs, I got no skills, and even if I could prove who I was, all it would do is show I got my education in the slammer. So, I've got to work for myself, right? Now I got an idea for a bit of what's called basket-weave marketing.'

'It's porn, right?' said Michael.

'It's better than that, mate. Picture this. You're a retired Bengali millionaire, right? You're fat, you're old, you're rich, and you're staying in a posh hotel. You go on line, and you see a lovely bit of video, and it's got this beautiful blond hunk, hung like a horse. Well you're as black as the ace of spades and you got a kink for blonds. And it says, no money upfront. You can have this beautiful blond hunk. Just pay us when he shows up. Well, you're a bit suspicious, but you done something similar before, so you have a go. And five minutes later, shall we say, miraculously, there is an Angel on your doorstep. With a big blond dick and orders to shoot. And he doesn't do nothing until we receive your securely encrypted credit card number.' Nick's eyes were glazed; he seemed to be staring into some kind of paradise. 'Huh. You can even download the video as a souvenir.'

Michael wanted this not to work. 'There would be no video, it would disappear when they did.'

Nick cuddled up to him. 'Well. Part of the idea is that our Angels wouldn't disappear. No offence, but the way you treat us is a bit exploitative. Tuh. You send us packing as soon as you've used us. Now. We'd keep our Angels. And that would be good for business. Cos, you see, you never really take off as a business if you stay a takeaway. You got to have premises. People like to eat out sometimes; sometimes it's a bit inconvenient with the in-laws staying. People like to see a real address in the real world; they won't pay the bill otherwise. So we'd keep 'em all in a hotel, all our Angels. Maybe lots of hotels, once we got going, all around the world. And that would be the pitch: see the video, have the hunks. Eat in, eat out.'

Michael was caught off guard. 'That would cost a fortune.'

Nick lolled his head on Michael's chest. 'Not as much as you think. You see, normally you got to pay a living wage. I mean, your staff have to eat, right? Wrong.' Nick groaned to himself with genuine pleasure. 'We wouldn't even have to feed them. Angels don't need to eat. Did you know that?'

Michael looked blank.

'You haven't been watching. I've been going without food. I don't even feel hungry. I don't even need to wash. Haven't you noticed I stopped doing that? But I still smell of roses. I don't need to buy clothes. I just call up one of my old suits. Naw. We just keep 'em, hundreds of them, as long as we want them. In basements until we get going.'

Michael didn't have to think. He just said, 'It sounds like hell.'

'Well, not once we get enough dosh to fix the places up.'

Michael was certain of one thing. 'I'm not going to do this.'

Nick fell coldly back onto the bed. 'Well. What are we going to do then?' He looked back at Michael. Perhaps he saw something gather in Michael's eyes. His own went soft and begging.

'Please don't kill me, Michael. All right, I'm inconvenient. I didn't ask to be born. You brought me here in case I was a good fuck. And I was. I don't like being fucked, Michael. But I let myself be fucked, because the alternative was not being here at all. And that is why I say, what are we going to do about this? Hmm? You have to be part of the solution, Michael. You got to take some responsibility.'

Michael was cold all over, and sweaty. He ran a hand over his forehead. This was always coming, he realized. Sooner or later I would call something like this up.

I either kill him or I let him live.

I've never stood for anything in my life; I never marched in protest, I never turned down a job because it was immoral. I guess I thought I was a good person because I paid my bills and hadn't actually killed anyone. And that so far is the meaning of my life. No harm done.

'I don't like . . .' Nick bit his lip and looked pained. He shrugged his eyebrows as if to say, it's best to use the honest word: '. . . blackmailing people. But this could get really nasty. I can be nasty sometimes, I just can't help it, there's too much gone on in the past. Look, I was on the game for a while, all right? I got kicked out of the house, and my house was a house of professional thieves. I was too much even for them. There's nothing I haven't done. I don't trust myself staying here with you. I advise you to get rid of me. Strongly. So, that's why I'm asking now . . . what alternatives do we have?'

That was exactly what Michael was thinking. I could give you money, but that would mean I would always be giving you money. I could get rid of you, and tell myself you were never real. But unfortunately, you are right. You are a thinking, feeling being and I do not have the right to destroy you. And I could let you do what you want to do, which . . . which I think is some kind of betrayal of what all of this is about.

Nick pressed his advantage. 'You could give me money to

make a film. That might do it. Do you have a spare fifty k? Or, I suppose, I could go and talk to my opposite number. By which I mean, Nick. I suppose I call him Nick.'

The Guard gave a little wave with his fingertips and mimed a cute embarrassed hello. 'Do you think he'd be pleased to see me, Michael? It might take some explaining. But it would also prove that I wasn't lying about the man in Camden Town who can call up Angels. And at the end of it I think he might be just as interested as me in the commercial possibilities. Only, the real Nick Dodder wouldn't be in your thrall, would he? And that Nick isn't one bit nicer than this one.'

Michael thought: I'm being threatened. He still held Nick in his arms.

'Or we maybe could go ahead with my takeaway idea. You provide the cheap, raw materials and I do the rest. If you were smart, Michael, that's what you'd do. Because if you did that you would be rich.'

It was as if the crumpled bed were a plain. They were looking down on it in the dark, in a Camden bedroom, and they could see an entire world. It was a world in which mankind finally had what it wanted: an inexhaustible supply of whores who were, at last, actually subhuman. Torture, bondage, snuff, all of it. And no harm done.

Nick chuckled. 'We could mix and match. You know, build the perfect man. A bit of Brad there, a bit of a buck porn star where it counts. Pretty little boys with holes just above their cocks, so you could fuck them frontwise. People could pay to sleep with Elvis Presley or President Kennedy. Or Marilyn just after she snuffed it. We could offer hot or cold running Marilyn.'

Trying it on, it's called. You step just a little over the line, to see what you can get away with.

'It'd be a public service. We could get the serial killers in. Lovely little things they could do to our Angels, and in the end, no harm done. It would save real lives, that would, Michael. The Dennis Nilsens of this world could cut young men in half and leave the drains unblocked.' Nick chuckled.

You try it on and if nothing stops you, you go on until you

destroy the world. Or rather sell it until nothing worth having exists.

'No? Naw?' Nick's cuddle became a little shake. 'Naw. You got everything you want don't you, Michael? You've got no ambition, you know that? No ambition except . . . you just want to be left alone. Hmmm? OK, then here's something else we could do that would leave you alone.'

The King James Version of the Bible calls them the little foxes. It's a mistranslation. It really should read the little fruitbats. The little fruitbats land so lightly, and nibble at the edges, leaving toothmark scrapes on the skin of the pears. You can't believe anything so small could become such a threat so quickly.

Love starts small too, a pleasant smile over drinks that grows into a lifetime of care. This was the opposite of love and it starts out with a quick fuck.

Nick kissed Michael on the cheeks.

'You'd never see me again, I promise.' He smiled. 'All you have to do is . . . give me the power to make Angels.'

Michael was quick. 'I can't do that.'

'Hmm? You can give me different clothes. Have you tried to give someone else the power? You haven't, have you? So you don't know.'

Michael understood something and went cold. 'You've already tried to call them up by yourself.'

Nick chuckled. 'Of course I have. You don't think I'd just sit around all day by myself, surely? Go on, give it a go. See if you can.'

'I'm sure that I can't.'

'You mean you're sure you won't. You don't think you're being just the slightest bit territorial here, Michael? It's like: "I have the power, nobody else is going to get it." '

'It's not mine to give.'

'Bullshit. Whose is it then? God's? I wasn't aware that you scientists had proof that God exists. You don't know what this is for, Michael, or where it comes from.' He imitated Michael, sounding nerdish and American. 'It's not mine to give.'

'Well. It's plainly not yours to take. Is it?' At last Michael had said something undeniable.

Nick sighed. 'No. It's not. Look, we're both tired, let's just sleep on it. Maybe we can find a way for you to help me make my film. That's all I want, Michael. Just find a way to make a bit of dosh. All right? Good night.'

After all, making dosh was what was really valued. Making dosh was good. Nick kissed him on the cheek, turned around, and was soon asleep.

He left Michael turning and twisting, staring into the darkness. I'm a prisoner, he realized. He's got me. This little horrible turd has got me stitched up. He thinks.

Michael sat up, and looked at Nick in the dark. He listened to Nick breathe.

He is alive, Michael thought, but it's a different kind of life. It's a life I can control, and because it comes from me, perhaps I can see what is always there more clearly. Like the extraordinary circumstance of breathing, just of breathing by itself.

Oxygen invades the blood, carried by blood cells which feed the mitochondria the element they need to spark fuel into energy, to maintain the slow-burning fire that is life.

The brain doesn't even need to think about it. It is delegated. The brain puts together sound and images. It harvests the world, and gives it shape, sounds, smells.

And then it can think about it all, creating ever-growing forests of abstraction. Invisible codes: names, equations, rules for handling the world. And desire. Desire, perhaps the biggest miracle of all. Desire the imperative, without source or logic or cause. Desire, simply there in the bones, the brains. Desire that sets the priorities for the self and all its processes. I need this; what do I do to get it? Now I need that, and move to get that too.

Nick looked so harmless, asleep. His face in the light from the window looked young and without blemish. His breath smelt of innocence.

Is this what a parent feels? To see in someone else so clearly just how extraordinary the puzzle is? Breath, blood, food, sweat, bones, teeth, eyes – how they all fit together, a million miracles, more miracles than you can count. All boiled down to one particular miracle, the one that you fed at your breast, the one whose face looks like its father's, the one you named.

Parents love like God. They say my son is a murderer, but I don't stop loving him. My daughter is on drugs and calls me bitch and whore, but I don't leave her. Desire makes life and life makes responsibility, which sounds so dull and wearying. But it's the goal of lust; it is what lust strives to produce: responsibility.

OK, my little vicious Angel. All you can see is greed, and you are far too old for me to change that; and you're driven by all the men who fucked you when you didn't want it, because . . . because you didn't know you were a miracle.

I could get inside your head and try to cure it forcefully. Who would I turn you into, Nick? I could make you into oh, someone who wants to do good in the world. You could go and work for an Aids charity. And all I would have to do is completely reconstruct your personality. And do I know how to do that? Can I give you a happy childhood in say, Slough, with weekends in the country? And if I could, would that be enough to make you kind and good? I would need to invent parents who believed there was more than money and conflict and status. So whose parents would I give you? I'd need to give you their loving genes as well, since I don't know enough about the mix of inheritance and upbringing. And that would mean you would have a different face.

In other words, I could replace you with an entirely different person. And how would that be one jot different from killing you?

I don't know enough, my Angel, to stir that little head of yours around as if it were soup.

I have to remember, however clever you are, that you are a poor, powerless creature. You want to make hell, but you can't do it without me. So you won't do it. You will, however, do whatever else it is in your nature to do.

Michael knew then what he was to do. He felt calm. He even liked himself. He gave the sleeping Nick a kiss on the cheek, and covered Nick's bare cold arm with his own.

In the morning, Michael was up first. It was he who cooked breakfast. Nick stumbled out, scowling with sleepiness, surprise and turned tables.

'My turn to cook, this time,' said Michael.

'What are you so bloody cheerful about?' Nick slumped into the chair.

'Life,' said Michael. He presented a plate of bacon and eggs to him. 'And, I've decided what I'm going to do about you.'

'Oh yeah,' sniffed Nick, smelling of sleep and trying to sound unconcerned. 'And what would that be?'

'Absolutely nothing.' Michael smiled.

'Oh yeah.'

'Yeah. There's nobody responsible for you mate, but you. So go ahead. You want to stay in this world? Be my guest. Like everything else, human or Angel, you'll have to decide what to do next. How you're going to live, where, how. Go ahead. Decide. That's life.'

Nick's jaws worked. 'You'll never get rid of me that way.'

'Who says I need to?'

Nick coughed. 'Suppose I smash the place up.'

Michael chuckled. 'Does it look like I care about this place?'

Nick was waking up. 'Suppose I go to the real Nick Dodder?'

'Go ahead. I don't suppose the real Nick Dodder gives a flying fuck about anybody, does he? What's he going to do, give you half his income? Say move in with my wife? Listen mate, Nick Dodder is a shit. He gets a certain perverse satisfaction pandering porn. He wants to hurt as many people, human or Angel, as he can. He's a real nasty piece of work, who cheats on his wife, and who, if the world let him, would poison it. But you. You are no longer Nick Dodder. You have an opportunity, mate. You can become different. You could become a nice person if you put your mind to it. But in the end, it's all up to you. Even if I were your Dad, or Lord God Almighty, it would still be up to you and not me.'

So Michael put on his suit, and pulled on his shoes, and Nick ate slowly, sullenly, ignoring him. So Michael said again: 'Up to you, Nick. Oh. And don't presume. I am no saint, Nick. Do anything to hurt me, and how do you know I won't lose patience and send you back?'

Nick blinked at him.

'You don't,' said Michael.

337

Michael went to work and sat down in his office to look at reports.

He heard a peeping sound.

He nipped out of his office to the warm and darkened, red-lit chamber. It was full of chicks. He had a single moment of profound confusion. Michael stood in the circle of his own self, which is timeless. For a moment he thought that these were the last batch of chicks without quite understanding why he felt so shocked. Then he remembered: we killed them.

Michael gathered himself in, and feeling delicate walked into Ebru's office rocking like a table with uneven legs. 'Ebru. Why did we order more chicks?'

She looked up. 'I . . . ah. Sorry, Michael. I don't understand you.'

'When did we order more chicks?'

She looked at Emilio.

Michael could feel sweat on his upper lip. 'If we need them for more data, you should have asked me. We need to control expenditure.'

Ebru went very still. Her eyes widened and she looked worried, and she said extremely carefully, 'Michael. What are you talking about?'

'The darkroom is full of chicks, how did they get there?'

'Michael. I cleaned the darkroom out yesterday. There is nothing there now.'

'It's full of chicks. Come and see.'

Ebru rolled her eyes, but they stayed wide. She looked like someone whose boss has finally gone mad, and is beginning to wonder if she herself has not helped drive him over the edge.

The eyes got wider as she heard the sound, the sound of need driving new life: chicks peeping.

Ebru followed Michael through the double sets of doors, which stopped all light entering. The room was thick with the smells of straw and faeces. Ebru took her head into her hands, and saw in the red light. In their warmed cages were 24 chicks.

'This, this was empty, Michael. I did not do this. Maybe . . . No. No, I don't think anyone would do this without consulting.'

And Michael understood: I did this. I've restored them. He

picked up one of the chicks and felt it shivering. I need, the shivering pleaded. I need food and warmth. I need to be held. I need my mother. I need to live.

I restored them because I love them. And that means the miracle is not for lust. It's for love as well.

Lust, love, driving life.

You were dead, Michael thought at the chick. We killed you. And so, I brought you back. He lifted the chick to his lips and kissed it. 'Angel,' he pronounced it. He looked at it in the red light. Murder undone. Restitution.

He came up with an explanation that would appear logical. 'We . . . probably ordered these some time ago, and they just arrived.'

'But who hatched them? Who put them in the cages? Who brought the cages back, Michael?'

Michael shrugged. 'Hmmm. Who knows? Somebody who was doing their job. But Ebru, I don't want these chicks killed, all right?'

'Absolutely not, Michael, certainly, certainly. No.' Ebru was fierce; something had gone wrong and she was mortified.

'Nobody is to blame, OK Ebru?'

'What will we do with them?'

'Feed them. We still have some feed left over, don't we?'

'Yes. I was going to throw it all out.' Ebru made a desperate gesture, with her hands in her hair.

'Don't worry, Ebru. It's fine. It's all fine.' Michael still cradled the little chick to his bosom.

Ebru stood still. Her cheeks were outlined in the red light, but he could not see her facial expression. After a moment she said, 'You love them, don't you Michael?'

He sighed. 'Yes. Yes I do.'

She chuckled, nervously. 'That is not a scientific attitude.'

'Oh, I don't know. It just depends on the kind of science you're talking about.' He thought of life, of how it extended to wherever Angels came from. And if you could make Angels out of chicks, what did that mean for humans?

She stepped forward and lightly touched his arm. 'When the project is over, we will talk, OK?'

339

He nodded.

'There is a mystery here, Michael.'

'Yes,' he said. 'There certainly is.' Ebru left, and alone in the dark, he began to think.

Dominion over the animals. Over the fish, over the fowl, over the cattle. We never knew what that meant.

Responsibility. We are responsible for them. They are our children too.

Michael sat on the floor of the darkroom, and held up the chicken to look at it.

'What shall I call you, eh?' he asked it. The beak was stretched wide open, hungry for everything. 'I could call you Ali, or Bottles. I could call you Johnny or Mark. Maybe I could even call you Nick.'

Michael stood up, and gently tipped the chick back onto straw. 'Learn,' he told it. And he went and turned on the lights. Light flooded the room. Experiment ruined. No reason to kill them a second time. He left the lights burning, to make the point.

Michael finished his day's work well. He was determined that the lives and deaths of the previous batches would not be wasted. They would be wasted if the evidence were not in order, or the results without meaning. He melted through the reports. He saw what the stains meant. The stains went into incredibly convoluted patterns.

Patterns, he saw, that were already there.

We are born with our potential.

Even chicks, their brains extend beyond this world back, forward, wherever it is we come from. Silent as settling snow, experience falls on prepared ground.

At the close of that day, the world made sense for Michael. He went into the offices and said good night to them, Ebru, Emilio, and they said good night back, as if pleased to have him return.

He walked back to Waterloo station, his feet crossing in front of each other again, but not from exhaustion, but from a kind of joy.

When Michael got home there was a mass of pink flesh

mewling on the carpet. It looked a bit like an unshelled crayfish only it was the size of an Alsatian.

Nick leaned against the wall all sweaty, and pale and ill. 'I nearly did it,' Nick said. 'Not quite what the porn market demands right now. But I'll get better.'

Michael paused. 'That was meant to be a copy of me, wasn't it?'

'Yeah.' Nick's laugh was a shiver. 'Serve you bloody right mate, let you know what it's like.'

Gently, Michael waved it out of existence.

Nick's eyes. They were metallic, like the heads of drills that were somehow pointed inwards. 'I'll keep going. I'll keep going till I do it.'

Michael sighed. 'Not while I'm here, you won't.'

There was something in the air and in Michael's head at the same time. Something like a tentacle, or an arm . . . a member shall we say, and it rose up and tried to touch Michael or rather Michael's power. Michael grabbed hold of it, felt it twist and turn in the air, and he wrestled it to the ground, and pushed it back and down. Nick even, involuntarily, made a swallowing sound.

Nick was covered in sweat. 'I'll go cook dinner,' he said. He stumbled into the kitchen. He cut up an onion. He started to sing 'Zippity do dah!' He left the knife on the counter top. The onions sizzled. Michael sat down and took off his shoes. He had a corn on his right toe and it was twitching. 'I'll give you a hand,' he said, out of habit. He went to the kitchen counter. 'Can I do anything?' he asked. Nick turned and drove the knife into Michael's heart.

Michael didn't feel anything, except a kind of inconvenience in the chest. Breathing had become choked and unnecessarily difficult. The knife was lodged deeply, and blood was pouring down his shirt into his trousers. It'll be hell to clean up, Michael thought.

'So,' said Nick. 'I guess you won't be here then.'

There was very little time left, no time to be afraid. Everything closed around Michael in a rush. The floor felt like a bed, cushioned and soft, and there was a reassuring sound like rain

341

on a roof, a sizzle like onions, the hiss of white noise on a stereo.

Michael floated as if in a warm bath somewhere up towards a corner of the kitchen. Nick and Michael, their little drama, seemed further and further away. He saw Nick lean over Michael. He saw the fat glisten on the wooden spoon. He saw the eyes go still and dry. Nick knelt next to Michael, almost as if he were going to help. The emotions Michael felt were the same. Poor boy, he felt for them both.

Dying was delicious, like lying in late, like being on the beach at twelve years old, when you wanted nothing more than to be. It was as if all work had ceased, and everything been done to perfection.

Death was like deciding, just this once, not to take out the garbage or not to do the ironing. It was like all the times when need is not strong enough to make you move. Death was like fulfilment: desire was no more.

There really was no longer any need to look at anything. So Michael ceased to see.

Vision was blotted out by direction. Michael felt a tug and looked inward. All he could see was a tunnel of light.

Yes, it was the optic nerve closing down. That was evident to Michael as soon as he saw it. It looked like a scan for glaucoma, when light is flashed deeper and deeper into the eye, shifting from yellow to red as it penetrates.

You had to understand, as Michael did, what the optic nerve was. It was a flow of time. Light triggers electrochemical pulses, which flow along the nerve in the current of time, deep into the head. It is broken apart like a sentence into a thousand grammatical parts. These are sent to a thousand different parts of the brain.

Now I am the light, Michael realized.

And he travelled, in time in one direction only, up the nerve, into the self.

Michael was read, like grammar.

Every cell in his brain that had ever been fired was fired at once. And he felt the whole lifted up, like a giant tangle of Christmas tree lights, lifted up as one final shape.

And it moved outside of time, to where time was not, and nothing more could happen. It preceded Michael, entered eternity, and froze. Its final frozen shape, spangled with light, seemed to be like a giant illuminated flower, in reds and yellows, sparkling with dew.

And Michael dying, still barely in time, was able to survey it. He was without location, without volume. He was a centre of gravity contemplating his life, able to think of something new one last time. Able to call for salvation, able to regret, able to feel joy.

In that eternal life there was Michael flinging snow in the High Sierras, there he was toting his bag to school, there he was in the Rialto cinema, Oceanside watching *The Sting*. There was Michael on a small funfair ride with his Dad at La Jolla. He had forgotten that.

There was little Michael taking a bath in a washing-up bowl, and his mother blowing bubbles at him. There was Michael, in his bedroom at night memorizing lists of endocrines. There he was pumping weights, there he was in Thailand, there he was bicycling in France with Mark sipping *calva* outside a *bar tabac*. There he was, making love to a 24-year-old from Brooklyn whom he had forgotten. There he was, staring down a microscope into the stained patterns of a chicken's brain. There he was on the platform at Waterloo station, cursing himself, cursing life.

And there were the dreams. They were real to the self. There were dinners of dogs' heads in his mother's kitchen. There were missed trains that turned into scarves trapped in car doorways. Michael's mind, saying to itself while consciousness slept: wake up Michael, you're forgetting something. Wake up Michael, you're walking the wrong way. Michael, look at me, I am here.

Michael saw something under the petals of light.

It snagged them, held them, twisted them, shook them.

It was dark, like a shadow, and it still lived, and it heaved and it dragged.

Michael saw all the parts of his brain that had never been fired.

343

They had been there before he was born. They were waiting for his birth, to become real. He had lived a life and never used them.

They were the wastes. They howled, these wastes. They were enraged. They shook the flower of light, wanting to be born as light.

The wastes were desire. And desire did not want to die.

There in that desert, Michael was not.

There was Michael not loving Mark.

There was Michael not travelling to India or China. There he was not, not riding a Jeep over the mountain terraces of Yemen. There he was not, failing to hold his own children. There he was not, bringing meals to his sick, dying brothers. There he was not, omitting to call his Mum. There he was not, never an actor on a stage. There was Michael without the brothers and sisters he never had. There was Michael not with his father for the last ten years of his life. There they were not hiking the length of the John Muir Trail. There was the Michael who had not known his father as a little boy. There was the Michael who had never known true love.

And above all, there was Michael, who had not slept with his father.

Dad, Dad, Dad, Dad, Dad . . .

Hello Mikey, a voice seemed to say. *Hello my beautiful boy.*

Dad, Dad-dy . . .

I picked you up when you were born, all wet, and I held you up to the light and I said Please Jesus, let this one live, let him be all he can be.

Michael wanted to be held and to hold in return. It was too late for that.

And I left you.

We carry our dead around with us as patterns we have learned. Love injects them into us. Semen is only the faintest physical mirroring of it. The patterns are as alive as we are.

The voice of Michael's living father told him, *You don't want to die, Mikey. Nothing happens after you die.*

The shadow wastes howled forever mourning. That howling would sear like sand blown in wind. It would burn like fire.

And it would never cease. Desire was immortal and continued after death. And that was hell.

Heaven was what had been achieved.

You can't make up for things. You can't make anything right. Nothing can happen.

This, thought Michael, is the wrong time for me to die.

He saw his desire formless and aching and true to itself. He saw it trying to twist the flower even in death.

Desire tried to twist the nothingness. Like gravity it tried to wrench being from nothing. Desire reached out in rage and thrashed and seized and shook.

It was as if the shadow cast the light and not the other way around. The darkness was the spider that spun the cobweb on which the dewdrops hung.

Michael had always had a talent.

He could absorb people into his bones out of love, and could make his bones and mind move like they did.

If he were thwarted enough, he could wrench the molecules of the air and make them move and leap and think.

Michael knew, then. He had made the Angels himself of headaches and grief and rage.

Desire made Michael want to live. Right, thought Michael, and desire blossomed in him like a dark flower blooming out of his heart.

Right, he said, prising open reality, forcing it like an arsehole to accept him, the wrong way through the valve.

Right, and Michael tore reality.

He saw.

Nick was propping open one of Michael's eyelids. Nick contemplated this stare, quizzically, as if it were a painting of his own that he was judging. Poor Angel, thought Michael.

Michael saw again what he had seen the night before: the potential in the translucent skin. Again, it was the waste that Michael saw. It's what a parent sees and aches for and forgives. And punishes.

Out of love, Michael called up his living father.

His avenging father wore mirror shades and his Marine uniform and stood six foot four. He put a hand on Nick's shoulder. Nick spun around and gaped in terror. Michael's father hauled him to his feet and held him and bore him off.

Michael sent Nick back up the nerve into eternity to Nick's own unilluminated self. The air closed shut over them all.

Did we learn anything?

Michael woke up in crisp white sheets. He smelled them first, and then opened his eyes, and saw pale blue walls. Ebru was sitting on a small hard chair, legs crossed, reading a magazine.

Michael wanted to ask her the time. He couldn't talk. Something harsh and foreign was stuck into his nose and down his gullet and it was long and slithering, and he thought it was some kind of worm. He cried aloud and tried to hoist it out of him.

Ebru's head snapped up. *Inshallah*, she murmured and launched herself beside him, grabbing his wrists. 'No, Michael, no. It's OK, Michael.'

'Awwww!' was all he could say. His throat was unbelievably parched. He could feel these things reaching all the way down into his belly. My God, what were they?

'Sssh. Rest, Michael. You have been sick. You are in hospital. Sssh.'

He calmed down, panting. He ached in all his joints, and his feet felt huge and his knuckles looked swollen – swollen and gnarled at the same time.

'Do not try to talk, Michael. OK? OK Michael, you just nod your head, OK. I am going now just to get the doctor. Leave those things, OK.' She ran out of the room and her sneakers on the linoleum made noises like mice.

Michael looked around. Hills and valleys of sheets rippled over him. There was a drip feed into one of his arms. The skin

347

on his hands had gone scaly, and his wrists and forearms were the same width. There was tape, like a very thick moustache, on his upper lip.

He tried to think, but it was as though his brain was elsewhere, huge and fiery and unwilling to cram itself back into his tiny skull. It waited, half-unsure that it wanted to be there.

Nick tried to kill me. That's why I'm here. In sudden alarm, his hands skittered down the hospital cloak, to his chest. There were no bolts and stitches, no swollen tissue. The knife wounds were gone.

The door thumped. Ebru stood in the doorway holding it open as if remembering her manners, her eyes round with something like fear. A male nurse bustled in around her. He was small, neat, pale, friendly, cold. He reminded Michael of Nick.

'All right, Mr Blasco, let's have a look at you.'

'What day is it?' Michael sounded like Donald Duck.

The nurse chuckled. 'I wouldn't try to talk if I were you.'

Ebru still clung to the lintel of the door. 'It's Thursday, Michael.'

He'd been out of it for several days.

The nurse leaned over and propped open one of Michael's eyes and shone a light into it. 'Do you feel dizzy or weak?'

Michael nodded his head.

'I'm not surprised.'

Neither am I. I came back from the dead.

'You're not that bad, considering. If you're awake, we can probably get rid of the tubes. Hold still, this is going to give you a free shave.' The male nurse grinned as if he'd said something funny.

As it was torn off his upper lip, the tape sounded as if the nurse were ripping up Michael's best shirts. It did hurt, uprooting stubble.

'Are you ready? These are coming out now.'

With a certain degree of professional skill, the nurse began to haul at the tubes as if pulling a barge. It didn't hurt, exactly. It was just horrible having something slither up through the hiatus valve, then up his gorge. Michael began to retch. The tubes heaved their way through his nasal membranes, burning with stomach acid and smelling of vomit. Michael coughed and expelled the tubes at the nurse, with fluids.

The male nurse smiled and sneered at the same time. 'Right,' he said, wrapping up the tubes and placing them in a bag. 'We can feed you properly now. Which is more than you were doing for yourself.'

He began to haul off surgical gloves, like a trick anxious to get home whipping off a condom. 'You've been a silly boy, haven't you? You'd have left us, if your colleague here hadn't come to find out where you were. So, they're going to send you to some counselling. Find out what that's all about. Otherwise, you'll be fit as a fiddle in no time.'

'You sound,' croaked Michael, 'as if you think I don't deserve to be.'

The male nurse didn't respond. He polished off the task of throwing out the gloves as well. He sealed the bag in silence. 'Dr O'Connor will be here soon,' he said to Ebru. Then he was gone.

Ebru stared at him for a few moments. 'Michael,' she said, shaking her head. 'Michael, what happened?'

Michael wasn't sure. 'What do they say is wrong?'

'They say you must have had nothing to eat for weeks.' Her hands twisted. 'They think it is an eating disorder.'

Aw. Michael understood. Nick had done all the cooking. All those takeaways, curries and stews; they were all undone. All those neatly packed lunches. They now no longer existed. Angels cannot really even care for people.

'I'll show you what happened,' said Michael.

And he called Nick back.

The air did a belly dance and unveiled, and Nick came back.

'Oh shit,' he said. And then. 'Ooooh *shit!*'

Ebru gave a faint little cry.

Michael told her. 'Keep well back from him, he is dangerous.'

Nick froze, looking watchful.

'I'm going to let you live, Nick.'

Ebru was at some kind of end. 'Michael, what is this?'

Michael kept talking to Nick. 'I'm doing this for my sake,

because I do not kill. Also, I wanted my colleague here to know that I am not crazy.'

'I've learned my lesson,' said Nick.

'Oh no you haven't. It will take a lot longer than that for you to think your way through it.'

Ebru was still hiding her heart under her hand. 'Michael, where did he come from?'

Nick answered her. 'From eternity, love. I'm an Angel. Michael makes what he calls Angels. He thinks he's God.'

'No I don't.'

The blue eyes were fixed upon him. 'You're God to me. Shall I tell you what's going to happen to you, Michael? You're going to have the same life that God had.' Nick gave a narrow amused little smile. 'And God has had a terrible life.' He sniffed. 'He keeps trying to do good.'

'I'm going to put you where you can do no harm. You know how they seal radioactive material away? They drop it into salt caverns a mile deep and the salt migrates and closes, so nothing can get out. I'm going to put you into one of those caverns, Nick. And I'll give you companions. You can make a kind of porn with them, if that's all you think they're good for. They can be your little demons.'

Nick was sourly resigned. 'I always said. Prison went with the territory.'

'Then maybe prison is what you want.'

'Watcha.' Nick made his fingers into a pistol.

You could have been such a handsome devil, Nick. You could have been one of those bitchy stand-up comedians who trade on their whiff of cordite, and who mellow with success. A chat show host? Or a racing car driver, something flash with sporting gear and sponsorship but nothing actually athletic. Anything that required aggression and the common touch. What you will need to become now, is a philosopher.

'Be yourself,' said Michael, and cast him down.

The air folded around Nick like a pair of closing buttocks.

The room was still, except for the sweat trickling down Ebru's forehead.

'Michael. What was that?'

350

Michael sat up. He was very weak, but he had been fed and rehydrated. He felt light as if his bones were hollow. Michael felt like a bird.

'I'll explain,' he promised. 'Excuse me while I dress. There is something I need to do.'

'You will stay here, Michael,' said Ebru, folding her arms. A trolley with food came. A cheerful black lady came. 'I am your nutritionist,' she announced. 'This may not look good, but it is delicious.' It was a kind of pabulum with mashed bananas. Eating it gave Michael stomach cramps, but soothed his throat.

It was night by the time the doctor had examined him, and the discharge papers were filled in. 'Thank you, Ebru, thank you for helping me. Do you think you could come with me to the lab?'

Ebru took him by the arm and walked him to Goodge Street tube station. Michael was too weak to talk over the noise of the train. It lurched and made him feel queasy.

He thought instead of what he was going to do. He saw himself setting the chicks free in the park. They were nervous at first, clustering around his feet, their down blown in different directions by the wind. Then suddenly they spread out around him, showing against the dark grass as if fluorescent.

As Ebru led him from Lambeth North, Michael told her every-thing that had happened since the first day of the project.

'I would not even begin to believe,' said Ebru. 'If I had not seen with my own eyes.' She pointed outward from her cheek-bones as if warding off the evil eye.

'There will come a time, Ebru, when you won't remember this. All you'll remember is that I was ill. But you'll think more kindly of me.'

'I always thought kindly of you, Michael.'

Shafiq was at the security desk. Ebru called to him. He looked up in alarm. 'Shafiq, it is only us,' she said. Reassurance seemed to slim Shafiq down; he grew sleeker. He stood up grinning. 'Michael. You are all right! They said you were . . .' He looked at Ebru, for reassurance. 'Not well.'

'I'm OK, Shafiq. I . . . I would like us to let the birds loose.'

Shafiq and Ebru glanced at each other.

Michael insisted. 'They can't die, Ebru. They don't need to eat.'

'So, they stay cold and miserable all winter long,' she said. 'These are the ones we killed.'

Ebru said, 'No, they're not. See for yourself.'

She helped him down the corridor, which was longer than he remembered, to the darkroom door. She swung it open. The light, as he had left it, was on. They would have seen light for a week. Ebru picked one of them up and gave it to him. Already, the creature was bigger, older, than any of their chicks had been. It looked up at Michael with reptilian eyes.

'They are already different,' Ebru said.

Michael smiled at himself. 'So, I could have set free a race of immortal superhens in Archbishop's Park.' He saw them chasing children. He saw vermin control gassing them to no effect.

Shafiq tried to help. 'We thought we might sell them to a chicken farmer.'

'Yuck,' said Michael. He thought of someone eating Angels.

There was only one thing to do, really, faced with it.

'Goodbye, then,' he said to his children, and he sent them to rejoin their immortal selves. The air throughout the darkroom roiled as if full of evaporating gas fumes. The chicks were gone.

Shafiq gasped and looked round-eyed at Michael. Michael didn't have to look at him to know that. He kept his eyes averted.

'It's just something temporary, Shafiq. It's just something temporary that I can do.'

And it will be a good sign when it stops, for that will mean the wastes have stopped howling.

Michael sighed and slapped his thigh, as if closing a boot, and he asked Ebru, 'Well, did we prove anything?'

Ebru paused for a moment, as if asked to cross a chasm on a rope bridge.

Michael asked again: 'Our experiment. Did we learn anything by killing all those chickens?'

Ebru considered. 'We prove they learn. But we also prove that what they had to learn was in their brains to begin with.'

'Is that something worth knowing?'

'Yes,' Ebru said, and then again more fiercely, 'Yes, it is.'

'Was it worth killing them?'

Ebru sighed. 'You need to find your own answer for that, Michael.'

Michael rubbed his eyes. Was there a chair? He needed to sit down. 'I know what the chicken's answer would be.'

Ebru shook her head. 'But you don't, Michael. You can't know. That is the whole difficulty.'

She took him by one arm, and spurred by her example, Shafiq took the other. They led him hobbling back to the soon-to-be-emptied office where he could sit down.

Michael slumped into his chair. 'We're real,' he said. 'We can't undo what we've done.' He surveyed the filing cabinets, the dark PC screens. 'That's what makes us real.'

Part III

What do you want for Christmas?

For a while, Michael stalled.

The project wound down. The results were conclusive. The learning process caused a range of chemical changes in nerve cells. The pathway of that chemical change through the brain was common. Some neural pathways for learning about light seemed to be pre-established, at least in chickens.

Michael began work on a small, publishable paper, for a respected scientific journal. He let Emilio go to his new job early. Shafiq was fine; he simply went back to his agency and a new post. Geoffrey Malterton at the Council found another project that could use their facility. He was pleased: he would end up being the lab's new Director, not Michael. It was left to Michael and Ebru to turn out the lights on the lab one last time, and share a quiet drink at the Pineapple.

Michael still had his teaching once a week, which was a living, not a calling. He explained the basics of neurology to students for whom it was not a calling either. It was a way of increasing their earning potential. They argued with him about each and every mark on their phase tests and worked out from their percentages so far whether or not getting an A on the final test would make any difference to their overall grade. If it wouldn't, then they would stop studying.

Christmas came, full of tinsel and loneliness. The students left for home, except the ones who had no home. They stayed on in student accommodation playing disconsolate dance music.

Michael went home for the holidays. His mother had gone back to Sheffield ten years ago and lived in a terrace house near where the city ended abruptly in green. She had her garden and her friends. She was 63, an age when it is still insulting to be described as spry.

His mother had come into her own. She made an effort. Her hair was dyed a believable shade of ash; you could see she had once been pretty and elegant, though there was also now something firm around her outlined eyes. She was good with a screwdriver and hard on building contractors. She was confident in life.

She greeted Michael without fuss, kissing him on the cheek and patting his arm. 'You've lost weight. It suits you.' She didn't get that stricken 'are you eating?' look. She just said, as she would to one of her mates, 'You fancy something to eat?'

'Yeah sure, a cheese sandwich or something. I can make it.'

'Go on then. You'll find all the things in the usual place. You can make me a cup of tea while you're at it.'

When he came back with the tray, she already had the Christmas cards out, ready for signing. She didn't believe in this nonsense of sending everything months in advance. You did your Christmas cards at Christmas.

'You forgot the spoons. It's all right, my turn.' She stood up and came back with spoons and a white envelope.

'You haven't been ringing me, and it turned out you even moved without telling me, you daft pillock. So I knew something was wrong that you weren't telling me, so I wrote you this.'

She put the letter next to the tray. 'Go on, have your tea. You can read it later, after the cards.'

There were fewer and fewer cards each year: one to their cousins in New Zealand; one to his mother's best friend Beryl now in Canada; one to the Blascos in San Diego. They were an isolated family. They only had each other.

'In the old days, people didn't move about so much, I suppose. There were more of you around it seemed. Are you on this e-mail? Because I was thinking it's probably a good way for me to keep in touch. Could you set me up on it?'

That would indeed be something good to do with the long and sometimes pointless days of Christmas. 'Sure could.'

In fact, it would be great fun, and it solved the problem of what to buy his Mum for Christmas instead of a scarf or chocolates.

They did the cards, and she brought out the roast chicken, with its clogged brand-name stuffing, and both of them ate hardly anything.

'So are you going to tell me what's wrong? You've broken up with Philip.'

'Broken up with everything. I um, forgot to apply for the grant, so the project ended.'

'So you're at a bit of a loose end. Shall I tell you what the letter says, save you reading it?'

'OK.'

'It goes like this. The worst things that happen to you in life turn out to be the best things. Like your father. He left me on my own and I thought, I'll never cope. But look at me now. And then I got that phone call from him telling me that you were gay and you'd done something *terrible*. But he wouldn't say what it was, except that he was plainly going to blame me. Well, that gave me the chance I'd been waiting for. I finally stood up to the man. I just told him. It isn't your fault; and it's not mine either so don't go putting all the blame on me. It's just who our Michael is, and what of it? I've known for ages, it's no news to me. And you should have known too, if you had your eyes open.'

Michael chuckled. 'What did he say?'

'Nothing he could say; it was all true. He said, You're right, Mavis. I felt sorry for him by the end of the conversation.'

'I sometimes think I killed him.'

Mavis wiped crumbs off her knee, sniffed and said, 'So what was it then? This *terrible* thing you did?'

Michael thought, then answered, 'I made a pass at him.'

His mother nodded once, downwards. 'People don't die from having a pass made at them, Michael.'

That tickled Michael and he chuckled. 'No, I guess not.'

'He didn't have himself sorted. He was all front.' Michael

359

saw his father's face, big and needy. 'I look at it this way. Because of all that, you knew that I knew. You didn't have to spend twenty years screwing up your courage to tell me. I could just ask you straight out if Phil was your boyfriend and make up the double bed. Speaking of which, have you found yourself someone a bit more down to earth now?'

'No. No one.'

'Sorry for prying. Mother's prerogative. Anyway, you'll be all right, Michael. You're smart. You work hard. You're a kind person. I've known you since you were born. You'll be fine, love.'

That was indeed what the letter said. That night in bed, Michael read the letter over and over. When he was young, his mother was always telling him to be careful. Now she was telling him to be brave.

How could I tell you, Mum, about the miracle? Could I say: I have the power to generate flesh from dream? Would you think I was crazy? Or am I just underestimating you again? What would you say?

Michael's head unconsciously adopted the slightly sideways bolshiness of her enquiring position, and his eyes took on her slow burn.

And he knew she would say: 'So how is all that any different from wanking?'

He thought and answered her: 'You can touch them. And they have minds of their own.'

'So how is it any different from the real thing?'

Michael thought again and said, 'It's safer.'

He saw Mavis chortle, just before she stood up to take out the tea things. 'You mean like trainer wheels on a bicycle. They'll have to come off sooner or later, love.'

Finally, Michael folded the letter away and snuggled down under the duvet that smelled of fabric conditioner. He felt safe and warm, like a child, which is what Christmas is for. He leaned across and snapped off the light. 'Goodnight, Mavis,' he said to her eternal and developing spirit. He slept.

Until something in the night stirred. There was a smell of talcum powder and liniment, and the sheets parted, and someone huge and smooth and naked slipped next to Michael. Biceps and forearms as big and wholesome as loaves of brown bread enveloped him. 'Hello, Mikey,' his father said, his voice low and hot and close to his ear.

'Jesus Christ!' hissed Michael in panic, and threw off the bedclothes and spidered backwards, away from him.

Street lights shone through the curtains. Michael saw his father's big and handsome face, and the light reflected in his eyes. The eyes shone with yearning.

'You know what this is, now, Mikey.' It was a statement. 'You know what this means.'

'Sssh!' Michael was frightened to shock his mother. Yes, he knew what this was. He had reached down into the darkness, and pulled something back like a plum.

What he had really wanted, outside time. All this time.

'So what's different?' his father asked, rumbling deep as if out of the springs of the bed.

What will be different is that this time you will want me. His father looked young now, almost like a teenager. He and his father were now nearly the same age. Their hands were the same size. Louis's hand enveloped his, and coaxed him back towards him.

'No,' said Michael. 'She'll hear.' Mum is real and you are not.

Michael pointedly rolled over and turned his back. The bulk of his father shifted closer to him. It was the smell that was the most powerful; indescribable and immediate, his smell, the smell of his body, still vaguely like honey, the smell of this breath tainted from too much exercise, a bit sharp, even vinegary. The smell of American soap, different from English.

Those ripped muscles, when pressed all around him, were soft and smooth and gentle, as if a giant baby were holding Michael. Not a 40-year-old Marine sergeant who could kill automatically on demand.

'Merry Christmas,' Sergeant Blasco murmured.

And Michael let himself be held. Yes, Dad, this is what I wanted, yes Dad, this is what I dreamed of, night after night, morning after morning.

But you know something, Dad? Big and beautiful as you are? I'm not sixteen now, and though it might be easy to slip into this, I'm not going to do it. I'm thirty-eight and it's been too long, and this is my mother's house.

Michael resisted. But Michael let himself be held. He settled into sleep.

He had a dream which mingled his father with Santa. He was a child and under the white fake beard, his saw his father's eyes.

Then Michael had to get up to pee. He stood up and rammed the front of his foot into his bookshelf. How could he forget the bookshelf? It was where all his records were kept. Outside, beyond the slatted Venetian blind, there was still the warm murmuring of the surf. Michael walked on towards the door, and walked into a wall. The door was on the left not the right. He fumbled through it, advising himself to remember: the stairs are just in front of this door.

There were no stairs. And the bathroom, instead of straight ahead along the landing, was right, and then left again.

And Michael's eyes started wide open, and he stared and saw: this was not his mother's house in Sheffield. This was the condo in Oceanside.

Michael looked down at his legs. They were thicker, and ice-blue in the light. He stroked them. They were hairless.

Michael was sixteen and smooth. There was no hair on his chest, and his nipples were sore and swollen from too much sunlight. He looked down at his own chest with desire and stroked it. Himself at sixteen. The dream was always of being someone else in a different situation. In the end, at root, all the fantasies had been this fantasy.

Michael's dick started to creep downwards. This situation was that he was young, only almost a man, and that his father in the last days of his sexual power wanted him.

This was no dream.

Michael was awestruck. I've really done it now.

He'd wrenched and pulled bodies out of nothingness, and now the need had wrenched round everything else. It had wrenched the whole universe around him.

This was the right miracle, now. This was the miracle he had really needed.

He had become someone else – Michael at sixteen again, back home, home in California. Without any Viagra at all, his dick was twice the size it had ever been, and it was slammed straight up against his stomach, reaching all the way to his belly button.

Michael was wide, wide awake, as wide awake as he would be if he were walking barefoot across broken glass. He remembered the flower of his self, the flower of cobwebs and light and areas of dark. It would not be thwarted, that flower. If even he himself blocked it, it could wrench other realities into this one. If thwarted sufficiently, it could, evidently, pull him, instead, into another reality. Into this one.

Michael at 38 could resist, but not Michael at sixteen. He felt the old white carpet under his bare feet, and he felt the lining of his stomach seethe. And Michael started to weep as he walked, out of relief and fear and joy. He knew he would do it now. It was really, finally going to happen.

Michael went to his father and hoisted up his smooth, thick legs, and he looked into his father's eyes, eyes that in this reality wanted him.

His father's pubic hair was a tight little purse over his pressed genitals. Like so many men about to fucked, he was not erect. Michael touched him. His father's ass was smooth, the crease between the cheeks was smooth, and the pucker of his sphincter was neat and tidy and hairless. To Michael at least, it still smelled of honey. Michael needed neither KY nor spittle to ease the passage; he was luminous with lubrication. He entered his father and looked into his father's eyes, and his father nodded and closed them as if to dream.

Michael saw his own young crouched thighs thick with muscle, his own belly, and his dick gently shifting in and out, lapping like little waves on the shore of a lake. My body isn't ugly, Michael told his father in his mind. My sex is not ugly, it's a gift, it's a gift I wanted to give to you. You didn't have to treat it like something dirty, you could have said no, no gently; no I don't want this. You could have been calm and wise and

363

said, no, you feel like that now because you don't know me, because we've been separated, because I am a man to you, and not your father. You could have continued to love me and care for me and hope I would find myself and someone my own age.

You didn't have to go and kill yourself slowly. You didn't have to try to kill me. You might even have let me do this once out of love, just once, so I could escape you.

Now we've gone and torn the real.

And I don't know if I can get back, and I don't even know if I want to.

Michael rocked back and forth, and felt as if he were moving through curtains. He saw his own body shift – when he blinked it had hair again. He was 38. He had accelerated from one reality to another. Then he flipped back: sixteen. He kept moving back and forth between the two, and that acceleration became part of the ride. We are fucking reality, Dad.

And that acceleration rose within himself, hurtling as if towards a brick wall. And there was a sudden, disintegrating crash, and part of him seemed to fragment and burst apart, scattering inside his father's body. He came in at least two different realities at once.

His father's eyes were round and brown, like a cartoon animal's. He looked trapped, cornered. Then the eyes crumpled into a smile. You really are the most beautiful man, Michael thought.

And Michael rolled away, and settled. This was still the room in California in some kind of 1970s. Michael was still sixteen. Cupped between his arms, his own smooth pectorals swelled. His fingers rippled over his own flat tummy and down his lean thighs. There was a kind of sparking in the nerve ends and suppleness in his joints. He could sense speed and reactivity there.

Michael held up the sheet and looked again at his own sixteen-year-old body. The thought of being in that body, and in this room, in this situation, made him rise again.

This time Michael turned and rolled over and presented. His father now was erect and reared over him, and settled on top of him, as heavy as the sky, as heavy as God, and the thought came: it could go on like this. I could stay here. I could start over again.

I could stay sixteen for ever.

'Oh, Michael,' his father breathed out, and shivered and went still.

They lolled in each other's presence as if they were warm waves. Michael had finally obtained his ends. He slept.

For a while. He woke up when the Oceanside train went past, at 2.30 AM.

His mind was clear. He touched his chest, and it was covered with hair. He looked down and saw the slightly greying fur and his plumper stomach. His father still slept beside him, only two years older than he was. Latin, big-dicked, as handsome as Brendan Fraser, and Michael did not want him in the least.

But this was still Oceanside in 1976.

Michael was terrified. He threw off the sheet and stood up, and looked out the window. There over the wall was the vacant lot next to the train tracks. The lot was now a multi-screen cinema, and there was a new train station.

My God, what have I done?

Michael still had to pee. He turned and walked out of the room and there was a sensation as if he were parting shower curtains. Reality billowed and separated and closed shut behind him.

In the dark, he felt his way straight along the landing, next to the stairs.

Michael pulled open the bathroom door in Sheffield. His mother had a 1960s colour sense and the walls were lavender and the door lintel was mauve. And on the toilet, naked, sat himself at sixteen. He was wiping his butt and looked up. His face was thicker and more obstreperous. He looked, curiously, more like his mother.

'Close the door, willya. Get the fuck outa here.' The accent was pure American. He was beefier; the strength concentrated in his shoulders and arms. He can throw, Michael thought. He plays football.

'We need to talk,' said Michael, his arms thinner, hairier, his stomach softer.

'I'll be with you in a second.'

'You're straight, aren't you?' Michael demanded.

'What's it got to do with you, fruit fly?'

Another self, another fantasy.

Michael sat on the edge of the bathtub.

'What happened?'

'Whatja mean?'

'To us. You were straight, what happened to you?'

This other self flushed the toilet. 'I dunno.'

'Go back to that moment in Oceanside when he pulls the car over and starts to cry because he's so happy you want to live with him for a while. So you go and study in San Diego. You play on the football team and you get your degree. What happens after that?'

This other self circled gum round and round in his mouth and looked confrontational, but curiously, he had Henry's puppy-dog eyes. He was bronzed and had a terrible seventies haircut: compromised Beatle with sideburns. He looked Latin.

'I met this girl, you know, in school. So we got married. I got my degree in veterinarian medicine, we moved north to Ventura, where her folks are.' This was still in his future but he knew his future because he was timeless.

'What happened to Dad?'

'He lost his job at forty-eight, but with an NCO's payoff and stuff. I'll help him set up in a window repair business. There's a real call for that in Oceanside. All that salt air on those aluminium French windows. He'll show up looking cool, and all those divorced women, man. He'll get a lot of ass.' This Michael chuckled.

'He doesn't drink?'

'Well, that Latin blood. He knows he suffers for it in the morning, so he'll take it easy.' His head jerked backwards; his face was impassive. This was how a tough guy laughed. 'Man, you look so English.'

'I am so English.'

'You really gay?'

'Yup.'

'What's that like?'

'No different from being straight . . . except you lead a different life.'

'Did you, like, really make a pass at Dad?'

'Yes.'

'Jeesh. You're really sick.' He was amused. Michael thought he was going to say something like Gross-out City. Instead he said, 'Do you like me too?'

'Up to a point.'

The teenager's grin was steady. 'Jeez. What don't you like about me?'

Michael stirred. 'Your attitude. I know what's inside and I know what you're hiding. Remember, I never saw Dad when we were kids. So, whenever I did see him, he didn't feel like my father. When I did see him, he was my ideal man.'

There was a glimmer of understanding. The voice went softer. 'Mine too. He sees my kids a lot. He comes up that driveway and they go running out. "Grandpa Blasco! Grandpa Blasco." 'Cause he always brings them little presents and stuff, you know.'

'Tell him I love him.'

Michael Blasco sighed. 'Where I am, you don't exist. And him and me, we don't have to tell each other that shit. We just know.'

'Cool,' said Michael, smiling.

'Cool,' agreed Michael the Angel. He looked around him at the walls and his face screwed up with distaste. 'Are all English bathrooms this colour?'

'Only Mum's.'

'I keep thinking I'll go and visit. I remember my English half too. Keep an eye open, you might even see me in London, England.'

They didn't really have much to say to each other. The other Michael narrowed his eyes. 'So. I guess I'll be on my way. It's been really . . . weird.'

'I'll go,' said Michael.

He stepped out of the bathroom. And looked down the corridor past both bedrooms to the sitting room. Somebody was watching the TV. He could hear sobbing music, and a breathy, posed woman's voice whisper a scripted lament. He padded down the corridor. The carpet and the walls were white.

In the Oceanside living room, another Michael was watching a movie at 3.00 AM. He was crying, and hugging and chewing a pillow at the same time. He was practically bald, with long hair in wisps, and just above the ears, a line of black scabs.

Michael sat down on the sofa next to him, gently, fearful of disturbing or even breaking him. 'Hiya,' he said gently.

'Hiya,' this Michael replied, miserable, and with a quick jab wiped his face.

'Howya doin'?'

'Oh,' this one sighed. 'Not so chipper.' He had lost even more weight than our Michael had.

'Where have you spent the last twenty years?'

This Michael didn't want to talk. He wanted to watch his movie. It was Gene Tierney. Who, these days, was a Gene Tierney fan?

'Are you gay?'

Long pause. 'Uh-huh.' An American yes.

'Did you marry Dad?'

Longer pause. 'I divorced him.' With a shiver of irritation, curdled anger, this Michael suddenly roused himself and snapped off the television from the remote control. He turned and faced Michael, looking like death. 'So what exactly do you want to know?'

'What happened?'

'What the hell do you think happened?'

Michael's voice went soothing. 'I don't know.'

'How long do you think you can stay married to your father?'

'Oh. I'd say until about six months after you graduate. And then everyone starts to ask when's Michael moving into a place of his own? People start to say: has Michael got a girlfriend? People start to say: Louis, are you seeing anybody? They start asking each other: have you ever seen Louis with a woman? Are you sure that's his son?'

The other Michael was looking at the TV as if the film were still showing. 'That's about it. Plus.'

'It's that plus I can't imagine.'

'Plus it fucks you up. Fucks you both up. You start saying to yourself every time you fuck and every time you don't fuck: this is my father. There is a word for this. The word is incest. It's supposed to be wrong.' This Michael punches the pillow. 'And you start to look at guys your own age. And he starts to think, it would be a lot healthier if you split up, if he found someone else too. He says that to you. You cry, because it's true. And because, goddammit, you don't want anyone else. Who could ever compete with your Dad?'

Michael asked, 'Did he start to drink?'

The other Michael just nodded. He sighed raggedly. 'And how.'

'Lose his job?'

Just a quick nod, yes. 'He had to have dental work.' Whatever that meant. 'He got all fat. You'd find him in the hall in the morning, and he'd shat himself. He'd get drunk and yell things. One day I just got in the car and started driving.'

'Bad scene.'

This Michael chuckled and shuddered at once.

'But you got out.'

A kind of cough. 'Not really, no. No, I wouldn't say that.'

'How come?'

'Let your father fuck you for seven years and find out.'

Michael coughed. 'I never did. I tried. I never did.'

Michael the Angel said, 'You end up in LA, you hit the bars and declare open season on your ass.' He shrugged. 'It was the 1980s. I got sick.'

'Michael, love. Is there somebody there?' It was his mother, calling from the spare bedroom.

Michael's heart stopped. He looked about the room. This was California; she shouldn't be there.

The other Michael answered, shouting towards the bedrooms. 'It's OK, Mom. I'm just talking to myself.' He leaned towards Michael. Michael could see the shape of his skull. 'She came over to take care of me. She's a nice lady.'

'She is,' murmured Michael. 'Look. I don't want her to see me.'

369

The patient's eyes said: she'd love to see you. You're healthy.

'See you around,' said Michael.

'You hope not,' said the other Michael. He flicked the film back on. Gene Tierney sat in a casino that was in circles like a circus.

'What year is it?' Michael asked.

'1995. Early.'

Before the three-drug treatment. Michael felt sick. He walked unsteadily back to the California bedroom.

His father was in bed waiting for him, but there were strands of muscle down his neck, and his pectorals sagged like an old woman's dugs and were thicketed with snow-white hair. His face had collapsed.

'Everything all right, Mikey?' he asked in a phlegmy, quavering voice.

'Sure Dad.'

'I love you, baby.' His father's age-spotted hand clasped his. 'I thought you'd gone away.' The voice trailed off with relief from panic.

And it could have been this too, me at 38 and him . . . how old? Michael started counting and got up to 70 and stopped.

There was nowhere else to go. Michael lay down next to him. His father smelled now of dentures and catheters and the ending up of things.

Get out; go away, Michael told the apparition. Leave me alone, we never would have ended up here, it would have been terrible, sick, sad.

Michael looked back.

And in the bed, there was himself. Himself at 38 now as he was.

'Welcome home,' his self said, and held open his arms.

Michael could see that he was beautiful, and he could see his body was beautiful.

The Angel smiled shyly and rolled up and over and pulled open his cheeks, and the fur crinkled apart to show the oddly innocent-looking croissant of an orifice. Michael leaned forward to kiss this lower mouth. It was like having a foot massage – an unloved part of the body responded with delight to unexpected tenderness. Michael both gave the kiss and felt it.

Michael was surprised how feminine his body looked with its hips spread wide, and the back arched. This only made him love it more, so he stretched forward and kissed the back of his own neck, which he had never really been able to see before. It was the youngest part of his body. It looked sixteen years old, even now.

His unreliable cock was now buoyant as if floating in salt water. Michael pushed forward but against anal resistance, it missed and swept up the crease between the buttocks.

Michael felt his own penis between his cheeks, and he felt his Angel feeling himself feeling that. He seemed to stand between two mirrors and feel himself reflected off into infinity.

Michael pushed forward again, and felt himself sheathed and entered at the same time. There was an enfolding tenderness and warmth, and superimposed on it, a sudden cramp as the valve of the anus was forced to work in the wrong direction. 'Relax, relax,' both of them whispered. The pain subsided.

The Angel settled down flat on the bed with Michael inside him and suddenly there arrived that most exciting moment of all, when a man welcomes you so deeply that his anus opens wide. The Angel turned around and Michael saw his own face flushed and happy. I'm beautiful, Michael thought.

After a time, the Angel said, 'I want to see you come.' They bounced their way around, slightly awkwardly on the bed, and the Angel nestled his face on Michael's tummy. Michael stroked himself and felt the familiar rise, like a voice heading for its high note.

But he came before it reached high C. There was a jet of semen that shot up onto his shoulder. And then the pitch was reached, and he shot outwards again, this time in lashings like cream over his other face.

'Oh,' said his other self, who felt it too, who was surprised as well. 'Oh, that's spectacular.' Michael kept on flowing like a fountain. It poured down over his hand, an opalescent sheen, as if it were liquid ice. He seemed to be settling back, the walls of his penis accordioning shut in wrinkles, when it suddenly tossed its head like a lion to roar one final time, taking Michael by surprise, one final flinging of come up in an arch over his body.

And both of them laughed, as if in relief. His other self swam his hand through a pool of semen, spreading it luxuriously up and over Michael's belly. For some reason it was funny. For some reason Michael laughed and laughed.

The joke was this.

He was a sexual being. He always had been. He had always been an especially sexual being, with especial sexual power. And that was why, paradoxically, he had been impotent.

It just struck him as funny, that's all. Both of them lay chuckling for a while. And they did it again.

What do I do next?

The next morning, there was no doubt at all which of his many selves Michael wanted to be.

It was Christmas Day and the air was full of the sound of 'Joy to the World', of breakfast sizzling downstairs, and of his mother humming along. The stairwell walls were lavender, the carpet a kind of ribboned purple-grey and white, the stair banisters a glossy orange. Britain in the 1990s, with thick grey bacon and eggs that had been fried in so much fat your mum tipped the pan so it would bubble over the yolks and cook them from above. There were baked beans and fried bread.

There is destiny. Destiny is how you shape your potential. Like fantasy, it's a kind of self. Here Michael was healthy, gay, still good-looking, and single, in Sheffield, in England at the age of 38.

'That looks great, Mum.'

'Don't be daft.' Michael kissed her cheek. 'You haven't shaved,' she complained. 'You're not washed.'

'After, Mum, after.' He sang along with the carol in a false and booming voice.

His mum sniffed. 'Roll over Pavarotti and tell Demis Roussos the news.' She held up food on thick white plates. 'You sit there. Go on, these plates are hot.'

'May the Lord make us truly thankful,' Michael said, finishing Grace before he had begun it. He tucked in.

After breakfast, looking in the bathroom mirror, Michael was satisfied. Dammit, I am good-looking. I really am. I look my age, that's all. It was as his Mum had said: intelligent, hardworking, kind. But also, he had to admit, kinda chewy, kinda chunky. Michael, just believe it. You're sexy, OK?

He looked back at his own flushed, still olive face, with its stubble and expression of slightly dazed delight. You're in the best place. You're in the best me.

They opened their presents. Mum's was a hand-written note. *This is a new PC and Internet connection*, it promised. She gave him new shirts and tie clips. 'Every time I see you, your tie's blown back over your shoulder,' Mum said.

They sipped sherry and ate Christmas cake, and about noon her friends called, all ladies of her age, all interested enough in Michael. He felt chipper. 'My last project's finished more or less,' he told them. 'I'll think of something else to do.'

On Boxing Day they went to PC World and he got a deal so good he was jealous of his mum: laptop, printer, Microsoft Office and five other bits of software including an encyclopaedia for eight hundred pounds. He took AOL because of its supposedly simpler operation, found its browser didn't let you increase the typesize easily and spent the day with his mother who tutted and felt stupid because she didn't get it. It was late at night when finally she sent an e-mail to his home address. 'And how do I send you an answer again? And how do I find it when I want it?'

He left the next day, a simple hug and a kiss.

She said, patting his shoulder, 'If you do move again, you know, change countries or the like, try to remember to let me know.'

'I will Mum, I promise.'

And not long afterwards, Michael found himself settled in on the train. The weather was changeable, turning between sun and rain. Outside the windows, the sky seemed lower and the world got smaller, lost in drizzle. It was a grey and indistinct world. Maybe that's why he felt fear and misgiving close in over him. He thought of the dirty Camden flat awaiting him, cold and dark. He thought of his project.

What, really, do I do next? The thought of going back to

teaching filled him with dismay. It's just daily life, Michael; it's like that for everybody. He would finish revising the article, and it would end like this: chicks don't make new pathways to see and interpret light. They are born with them.

And what did that mean?

Michael remembered the flower. It was moving and unmoving at the same time, like a bridge half built while its CADCAM model was whole and alive. That was him, that beautiful powerful thing. That was us all. Where was it?

It would be where there was no time. And where would that be?

Mathematics said there were eleven dimensions in all. Four of them existed only in time. The three dimensions of space were created by the big bang. They were expanding outwards. That expansion was simply time, flowing in one direction only: towards the future.

But.

That would mean there were seven dimensions outside time. They would be just as small as they were before the big bang. They would be a point. No height, width or depth. They would be like the smallest dot made by the sharpest pencil. But that dot would be everywhere. It would be at the core of everything around you. It would be in the core of you. You live there, but don't know it. Everything in your life flows in one direction only, into it.

A word came to him: neurophysics. The extension of the self into the universe.

He knew something was there. He had once stood in its presence or rather, had not stood. He had thought there, like someone hovering on the outside of a black hole, just escaping before being sucked into its powerful maw.

How would you research something like that? Was anyone else doing any work in it? Michael began to get restive. His hands, still in gloves, moved to assuage a sudden urge for movement in his gut. He wanted to get up and find out. He wanted a library, a bibliography, and a database to search.

How would anyone research something like that? Well, how do they do black holes? They do thought experiments, they work through the logic of the mathematical descriptions, and they model the maths on something else. It's mathematical metaphor, really. Like Einstein, proving atoms exist in a paper on molecules in tea. He just used the same maths that would describe ping-pong balls.

I said it was like standing on the edge of a black hole.

Heaven collapses into a point, where gravity can no longer work, because there is no space, and time cannot work because there is no expansion. Our eternal lives happen in something like a black hole. Mind you, only *like* a black hole.

Why not use the same mathematics to describe it and see what happens?

Michael went even more physically restive. He did a little jump in place. Does neurophysics exist? Did I just make that up, or did I read it somewhere? And if I did make it up, I could really be on to something, I mean I could, I could do that, I could take all that mathematical work, and just see what happens. And I wouldn't have to cut up any chickens to do it. I could just go ahead and do it, and if I was wrong, then that's great too, a negative result is still a result, we've still learned something.

Suddenly the train was too small and too slow. All he had to read was a John Grisham novel, and he wanted to throw it out of the train, or chuck it into the steam furnace like the boat in *Around the World in Eighty Days*. They burned everything on it for fuel. Get me home, get me to my computer, now!

And don't tell me it's not empirical. I've been there, buddy, I died to get there, and I saw it, and I'll know it when I see it again, described in numbers.

Michael settled back in his chair and slapped his own thigh. Outside, light rain was falling, like stars on grey farm outbuildings with tin roofs, pulled down by gravity, gravity which he had read in one paper could be described mathematically in the fifth dimension as electricity. The rain fell and dried and was exhaled as vapour. As a child he thought that was how the earth breathed. He loved the idea, the vapour going up like his own breath on a cold day, and turning into mountains of steam in the sky. The perfection of the system. It was perfect, the world was perfect, life was perfect, this rain and those farm buildings, ancient but with new roofs, were perfect.

Gravity twists reality out of nothingness, what physics calls quantum vacuum.

Is that what made his Angels?

If so, his mind, reaching into eternity, can twist his dead father back into being. What does it mean that he can twist those different selves so far that he can slip into another life? It means there are parallel universes. Universes you can stub your toe on and have a black toenail the next day. And parallel selves, with parallel flesh you can touch?

So gravity is thought? How can a black hole make anything?

And Michael jumped up yet again.

Well, because we know that matter going into black holes is ultimately ejected again as new creation, white holes.

So, I can take those equations too, for white holes, and see if they tell me how my real self can make Angels.

I can account for this, I know I can. I can account for the rain. I can account for the yearning between stars. Somewhere there in all that process is yearning between people as well.

Michael took a taxi from the station, an extravagance to slice through the rain, to get home. He ran up his stairs unwinding his scarf, and threw it and his coat onto the sofa, and took down his Stephen Hawking and his Daniel Dennett. He did a search on Amazon and ordered books. He began to think about how he could organize his days, teaching, marking papers, researching at night, like Einstein in the Patent Office. He would be invisible, unknown, effective. He felt fulfilled, abundant, forgiving. He had an answer to the question: What do I do next?

Michael made himself a cup of soup. Sipping it, he looked at his Picassos, which seemed to rise up in colours like a flock of parrots. The rain had stopped, and sunlight pierced the layers of skyscrapers to glow on his wall. And Michael felt a sudden sense of joy.

It could be of course that the miracle had been sent to teach him about the universe. It could be that it had come to help him understand God, or duplicate God's experience of creation.

But it seemed to him now that the miracle had simply come so he could finally learn to enjoy himself. That was what fun was: liking your destiny.

Over the next three days, Michael called back Mustapha the Afghani engineer and they made the love they should have made the first time. He remembered Rabindrath, who permed his hair and who worked in college administration. At one time Michael had been so drawn to him that he would deliberately walk into Rabindrath to feel the warmth of his body and the wiriness of his arms through his cotton shirt.

Michael remembered Stavros the Greek who delivered the post and lifted weights. In mid-winter he wore black T-shirts to show off his musculature. But it was his sweet, slightly dreamy smile that Michael had liked so much.

In fact Michael, who had once found difficulty thinking of someone he fancied, was suddenly shocked by how many beautiful people there were in the world. There were his students, whom university protocols said he must not touch. They rained down onto his bed, sweet and young and at their best, no longer calculating grades or hoping to avoid paying fees until they were sure of an A. In the magic space of the miracle, he and students became what they were in fact: equals. His beautiful body did its work and Michael did not even allow himself the thought: I'm cured. Everything had become light and easy and floating, as if they all had the bones of birds.

There was the boy behind the till at Tesco, whom Michael had once found almost unbearably beautiful. His beauty was not unbearable now because of that equality. Michael was up to it. The boy from Tesco liked being tickled and roared with delighted laughter on Michael's bed. He recombed Michael's hair with gel into a kind of cross between James Dean and Christian Bale. Michael combed it again to save it after the boy had gone, and realized he would comb it that way from now on.

Other kinds of fear disappeared. There was the brain-damaged boy Michael had met at a dinner party years before. His name was Robin. Robin had reached out to Michael and tried to take his hand and fumbled with it. 'I can't say things,' he said. 'I want to touch you.' Robin had offered up his hands that were helpless to hold. His slurry voice and his numb sideways lips had put off the younger Michael. Michael welcomed him now and was rewarded. In bed Robin was ruined, muscular, twisted, lithe.

Michael wanted to photograph them but knew that was futile. He wanted to sketch them but he couldn't draw.

Then Michael called up an actor who had once stayed in the same house during the Edinburgh Festival. They had gone to bed with each other, and it hadn't worked, and Michael had moped for weeks. Michael had him back now. His name was Stephen, and he began a dance around Michael's bed. It was an odd, looping thing he had learned in some other country, somewhere like Bulgaria. After Stephen was gone, Michael found he could imitate it. He could make his belly and heavy feet move like Stephen's.

Michael found he could recreate Stavros's dim smile and loping stride. He found he could light a cigarette one-handed like Nick. He could make his face and hands move like his brain-damaged lover. Among all his strengths, Michael's greatest talent would be of use only to him: he could remember people in his body. He would remember all of them.

A Christmas card came late from Philip. It was a photograph of one of his paintings, pasted on a white card.

It was a portrait of Henry and was resolutely free from technical innovation. It was just Henry, with hair in his eyes, looking sweet. His gaze was directly back at the viewer, appraising.

On the back was a note in Philip's newly elegant handwriting.

> And so I relax and become a traditionalist. It's more fun just getting on with the painting. Isn't Henry beautiful? We have decided to go our separate ways. We're still friends though.
>
> Would you come to a party? We're having one New Year's Eve, just a few friends. We were wondering if you wouldn't like to come early, say about 5.30 PM.

We need to have a chat, and there's someone we'd like you to meet.

Love,

Philip

The note produced a tumult of feelings. First was dismay; poor Philip, it couldn't have been an easy note to write. What on earth did they want to say to him? Whom did they want him to meet? It sounded a bit formal, even a bit intimidating.

Second was mystification. What did Philip know? Did he know Henry was an Angel? Was that why they were breaking up? And if so, what did Philip feel about it? Did he blame Michael?

And if they were breaking up? Well. Would Henry live with him? Michael wouldn't mind living with an Angel, he'd done that before. He could see himself so clearly living with Henry. Living here, with the Picassos and the unvarnished floors. Henry would like Camden Town; he'd like the market and its bookstores and its funky restaurants. But Michael wouldn't make the same mistakes. If Henry wanted to live in the country, then Michael would move. He would make sure this time that they both felt that the house was their home.

Hold on Michael, what if they're splitting up because Henry got tired of Philip? It wouldn't be surprising. Supposing Angel Henry had fallen in love with someone else? Michael's heart sank. In fact, that's the most likely scenario: Henry's younger, he's better-looking, and he isn't screwed up.

And what if Philip wanted to move back in with him? Michael felt embarrassment and dismay. Would he say, no, I'm waiting for Henry? What if Henry showed no signs of interest? Would Michael really turn down companionship, amity, kindness?

What if the end of the story was that he and Phil got back together? Would that be so awful?

In fact, Michael, you can calm down. Either way you win. You can't lose. There is nothing to worry about.

Even so, Michael went out and bought a new shirt. It was black, and he bought a fleece to go with it. He had a haircut.

The Christian Bale hairdo made him look ten years younger. No, it didn't, it just made him look less like a hippy. It made Michael look like himself.

He sat around the house for a full hour before it was time to catch the train. He checked out his hair, his new clothes. Oh for God's sake, Michael, they're not going to love you because you're wearing new clothes. You can't go there in a tizz. You'll say something daft. You have no idea what's going to happen today. Just calm down!

So he took the Northern Line down to the Central and from the Central to Docklands Light Railway at Bank. It was a long ride, on a sunny afternoon. He looked at London, gnawing on his thumbnail.

The old East End had been shouldered to one side by glossy new buildings that looked like Christmas presents wrapped up in green metallic paper. The crumbling hovels of the poor were now refurbished and had BMWs outside. Sparse art deco factories had been done up as flats and had flags and signs outside. They still looked like art deco factories.

Suddenly the train plunged into Canary Wharf. The train was all glass like eyes stretched wide open in wonder. It sighed to a halt surrounded by marble, dappled with the beautiful soft white light that comes when sunshine is filtered by a high glass roof. The doors opened, and there was a sound of a waterfall somewhere, and whispering music. The car sighed away and Michael saw to the right the new imperial buildings, huge with carvings and frontages of polished marble. There were fountains in squares with stone esplanades. There were no people.

My God, it was bleak. Michael tried to imagine living here. It would be like living in a new suburb of Topeka. The only thing you could do was go to the mall. The train hoisted up its skirts to stretch across dockland waterways. There were boats in quays. There were stranded new hotels with smoked glass and empty patios overlooking the river. The umbrellas over the white garden furniture waved in place of people.

Finally the train stopped at South Quay, and Michael got out.

The whole place smelled of drains. To be more specific, it smelled of sewage. Plainly all that new plumbing leaked. The pavements and the brickwork were new and gritty. Forgotten building timbers were piled in the parking lots beside the new buildings with TO LET signs in the windows. There was a news-agent, with an apartment over it. It was open, offering toffees and the National Lottery. Next to it was, of course, an estate agent. London property prices were booming, but not, apparently, here. There were plenty of studios for rent or pied-à-terres for eighty thousand pounds. *Would suit company needing to provide accommodation to visiting executives.*

The air was clear and freezing, as if the day were made of ice. The distances between buildings were Californian in scope. The roads didn't work like English roads; they melted away into huge parking lots, or twisted and turned around the canals like a dog trying to find a home in all this emptiness. Michael got lost, consulted his map and finally found an ochre-coloured brick building beside yet another canal. The doors and windows were new and half-sized.

He rang the buzzer, and stomped his feet because he was so cold.

'Is that Michael?' said a voice. Michael couldn't tell if it were Henry or Philip. 'Come on up. Top floor.'

The staircase boomed with the sound of Michael's feet. The plain white pine stairs shook as he trudged up them. There were scratches from furniture on the new brick walls. This was not a staircase for moving pianos.

'Come all the way up,' called a smooth dark voice from on high. At the top of the stairs one of them waited, standing in the doorway against the light. Michael thought at first it was Henry. No, no, there were acne scars on the cheeks: Philip. They did look just the slightest bit alike.

Philip exclaimed, 'Michael! Hello, how are you, how have you been?'

Every word was weighted because every word was meant. Michael was surprised by the surge of emotion he felt. The lower edge of his eyes seemed to shiver. It really was very good to see the old friendly face.

'I've been OK. How are you?' Michael meant, since the break-up.

Philip understood: 'It's OK. Really.' Philip kept his smile steady and kind. He had been lounging against the doorpost. He stepped back and Michael saw their apartment and Henry all at once.

Henry was standing in anticipation against a huge single window that looked out over the canal and a range of new buildings. Henry waited calmly in old jeans and an old sweater. 'Hello, Michael. It's good to see you.'

'It's good to see you both,' said Michael, and his look took them both in. He was relieved. This was going to work. This was in fact going to be delicious. He liked being with them both.

The apartment was a good place to be if you were poor and had to be stranded out in South Quay. Sunlight blazed through the huge single window so the flat was deliciously warm, even though the ceiling was rounded and high. At night it would be cold. The floors were echoey pine and the furniture was direct from IKEA: self-assembled blonde wood. The sofa was really a futon on stilts. There was a cheerfully coloured foldaway metal table. Around it were the six walnut chairs from Michael's old flat. They looked stodgy and out of place. The kitchen was tucked away in an alcove that was inserted beside the stairwell. Beside it was a doorway that led into the shower-toilet. In one corner were stacked in rows all of Philip's paintings.

'I want to see some of those later,' said Michael.

'Try and stop me. I want you to see them,' said Philip, sauntering into the kitchen. 'Darjeeling, rose hip, or camomile?'

'Um. Rose hip, I think. Vitamin C to make up for all that booze.'

Henry spoke, his soft voice echoing oddly off the hangar-shaped roof. 'The new work is really very good. You'll be proud of him.'

Michael felt a surge of longing towards both of them. This was a kind and calm household, and though Michael wanted both of them, he also felt sad. What could bring this beautiful way of life to a halt?

Philip was dropping the tea bags into the cups as if it were a game. He's different, Michael thought. He moves differently.

383

He used to shake and shiver all the time, and look angry, and dart about the place. As if sensing his thought, Philip said, 'Henry's taught me a lot.' And he looked at Henry with real affection. He looked back at Michael. 'Thank you,' he said. To Michael.

Michael pretended not to understand.

Philip was still looking at him. 'It was a very kind thing to do.'

'Whuh what was?'

Philip's eyes rolled slightly towards the ceiling. 'You know very well what.'

Henry stepped forward. 'He knows, Michael. I told him. I told him a long time ago. I have to keep telling him or he forgets. But that's good too.' He turned to look at Philip's face. 'It means we keep talking.'

Suddenly Michael felt awkward. 'I . . . it wasn't something I knew I was doing.'

Henry's voice was quiet. 'He knows that too.'

Philip stood in the sunlight, and his voice was as still as Henry's. 'It really is all right, Michael. Sit down.' He passed Michael his tea. 'Would you like some Christmas cake with that?'

Michael said yes, though his appetite had gone. He lowered himself rather shakily down onto the sofa. 'Is it why you broke up?'

Philip was slicing cake. 'Well, it's hardly a permanent solution, is it? But no, that's not the reason. Here you go.'

On the white rippled plate that Michael knew so well was the same old Christmas cake that Philip always cooked. Only now they didn't live with each other and had only the mildest, most friendly connection with each other. This felt like another reality as well.

Philip sat next to Henry, and the two of them hunkered down together on the futon sofa. 'Philip's found someone,' said Henry, smiling. He nearly pulled it off. He nearly did look entirely pleased, almost without a trace of wistfulness. He looked back towards Philip and his face seemed to open up like a rose. It was a look like a mother gives when she knows she has to let go. He's done it because he knows he won't be here for ever. 'Tell him about Lee,' said Henry.

'Well, you'll meet him later.' Philip was shy.

'Lee's lovely,' said Henry, regaining all his poise.

I'm not going to have either one of them, Michael realized. It was his turn for good behaviour. 'Tell me about him,' Michael asked.

A little smile of delight played around the corner of Philip's mouth. 'Well. Lee's from China. Communist China. Near Shanghai. He's over here to study computing. And he's . . . very handsome.'

'Very handsome indeed,' said Henry.

'And he says that after his course is over that it would be possible for me to live in China. And . . . I've said yes.' Philip chuckled at his own unexpected courage.

'I'll miss you,' said Michael.

Philip looked cheerful. 'Well, I won't be going for a few years yet.'

Henry was full of love for him, real love, the love that works to lose the thing it most wants. 'Phil's doing very well learning Chinese.'

'I figured it might take a while, so I might as well start now.'

Michael occupied himself pressing bits of Philip's cake together in order to eat it. Philip's Christmas cake was always too crumbly. Well, Michael, it never turns out the way you expect. You'd better start adjusting now. There's nothing else to do.

'Can I see the paintings now?' Michael asked.

They were very good portraits, done in a slightly impressionistic style. The paint was liberally applied, a little bit as if someone were making mud pies. They told you things about the people. There were several pictures of Henry. Then one dreamlike painting, all sunlight in this flat with a slim broad-shouldered man looking away. 'That's Lee,' said Philip.

The sun was lower. The light was golden, on the paintings, on the faces.

You can't go back, Michael. Like Time, love flows in one

direction only. You'll stay friends with Philip. You'll write e-mails. You might even visit him in China. And Henry?

Suddenly, there was the painting of Henry, the one on the card.

'What . . . what will happen when Henry goes?' Philip asked.

'I wonder that too,' said Michael. 'You'll have the painting. I don't know if you'll remember who it was. But,' he sighed, 'you won't feel any regret or loss. You won't be in the same reality. That's all.'

'Make up a nice story for me,' said Philip. 'How I came to paint this. About who he was. What he was like.' He looked back up at Michael, and his eyes had something of iron in them.

The other friends started to arrive about seven o'clock. The thought of them had caused Michael trepidation too, but these were different friends. There was no Jimmy Banter, no *Guardian* film critics, and no arts journalists.

One was a somewhat too precise, but sweetly quiet mathematician. Another was a small middle-aged guy with an earring, bald, with a calm kind manner and an East London accent. He was called Declan. He repaired cars in Limehouse. He apologized because Lorraine couldn't make it. Lorraine worked in computing. She was his girlfriend.

'Declan travels,' said Henry. It was true. Declan had no money but seemed to have spent his life going to Peru or the Andaman Isles.

Nice people.

The world is full of nice people.

Philip's new boyfriend arrived. Lee was tall and muscular and was as handsome as promised. Michael couldn't stop himself looking back at Philip: my God, Philip, you have done yourself proud.

Henry and Philip brought in the satay and sweet potatoes. People ate on their laps from paper plates, and drank tiny amounts of wine. It was a well-behaved gay conversation: everyone was involved, there was no splitting off into anxious, moody tête-à-têtes. People talked in turn, lightly, pleasantly, and they listened in turn. Henry told a story about barracking

386

a cat-breeding farm through a megaphone only to discover it was a nudist colony instead. Michael told the story about the time that he and Philip were both locked out of the flat. He didn't realize until halfway through that the story embodied the simple fact of their long marriage together. Lee laughed.

At one point, mysteriously, Henry said to Philip, 'He's not coming.'

At midnight, the fireworks went off over the river. The seven friends, a modest number, clustered around the one west-facing window. Synchronized flowers of light bloomed and sparkled, reflecting on the canal. To Michael they seemed to come erupting out the imagination, from the potential of the people who had designed them. He imagined them in their timeless aspect, forever a blurring of sequinned light, moving and still at the same moment. The fireworks looked like the self.

Someone, completely naturally, placed a hand on his shoulder and left it there. It was padded and hot. Michael turned around and it was Lee.

They toasted the New Year. They toasted absent friends: the mathematician had lost his partner two years before.

Michael liked them all. He hadn't known one of them, but before the end of the evening, he passed around his card, and got three in return, including Lee's. About one in the morning, the first guest stood up to go. Michael remembered the tubes, and was thinking about leaving as well, when the doorbell rang.

Philip and Henry each cocked an eyebrow. A voice barked up the answer phone. It sounded sinewy and smooth and reassuring. Philip looked back at Henry, his eyes wide and gleaming, and Philip nodded quickly, yes. He waited at the top of the stairs. 'Hello, hello!' he said.

'Sorry, but I had my sister's party to go to,' said a breathless voice, and Philip seized a hand and pulled in Henry.

Only this was Henry with slightly longer hair, wearing a brown sweater with a hole in it.

'This is him,' said Philip. 'Michael. Meet the real Henry. This is Stumpy.'

Stumpy perked up. 'So. You're the magic man,' he said. His

cheeks were redder than Henry's and the mushroom smell was stronger.

'Ah. Ah, yes.' Michael looked back at Henry, and all three of them – Henry, Philip and Stumpy – laughed.

'I told you once that Stumpy would love to know about this,' said Henry.

And Henry and Stumpy gazed at each other, grinning and slightly dazzled. Stumpy wobbled slightly in place and Henry had to catch him, and they were brotherly in each other's arms. And Philip cuddled Stumpy too, partly to keep him standing.

'I had a bit too much at my sister's,' Stumpy said, chuckling.

'He's staying with his sister. She lives in Camden Town too.'

'It's a long trip from Camden Town,' said Stumpy.

Michael asked, 'How did you get together?'

'Henry wrote me a note and said he was my long-lost twin, and sent me a photo of one of Philip's paintings of him.' Stumpy mimed amazement. 'So we met, and he told me all about you. How does it work?'

Michael heard himself say, 'The universe is twisted out of nothing by gravity. And I think I will be able to prove that thought and gravity are the same thing.'

'Wow!' Stumpy's eyes widened and he laughed with a kind of pleasure, while shaking his head. Michael realized he hadn't told Henry anything about his new research. He wanted Henry, particularly, to understand. 'I've got a new project. I think I can describe what has happened using equations.' Henry reached forward and gave Michael a kind of hug that turned into a shake of approbation. Michael looked at Stumpy and found he was embarrassed. 'I mean, I *think* I can do it. I don't know yet. I've still got to do the work.'

'It sounds fairly mind-blowing,' said Henry.

'I wish my head was a bit clearer,' said Stumpy.

'We've got other guests,' said Henry pointedly to Philip. When Philip didn't move, Henry pulled him away.

And for some reason Michael regained his old clarity. He had forgotten his talent for turning science into words. Michael sat with Stumpy on the futon sofa. He explained how he would apply the equations used to describe black and white holes. He explained that in the fifth dimension the equations that describe electricity also describe gravity. 'And thought is a matter of changing electrical charges.'

'Oh!' said Stumpy, and fell forward holding his head. He sat back up. 'If you did that, you might end up proving that God exists.'

'I might end up proving that He doesn't,' chuckled Michael.

Stumpy was younger than Henry. His smile was brighter, his enthusiasms more overbearing, his words more common and less distinct. Michael looked at Henry and pondered what that meant.

You're wiser than your original model, Henry. Of course, you're timeless. You are as wise as you will ever become. And does that mean you know what will happen? Or, rather what is likely to happen?

Michael looked back at this bright and cheerful, confident 24-year-old. It was like looking at old photographs of friends. You would need me more, Michael thought. I could even help you grow into becoming Henry.

It was nearly two o'clock. 'Well, I've really got to go,' Michael said. He kissed them all on the cheek, and hugged Henry and Phil together in a heap. 'Thank you, thank you, thank you!' he said. Stumpy looked a little wistful as he shook Michael's hand.

And suddenly Michael was back out in the night. Luck was with him: the evening seemed somehow warmer than the day and he did not have a long wait for the train. He heard it whining towards him, even as he climbed the station staircase.

The train doors whooshed open to show a car that was nearly empty. Past Canary Wharf, it began to fill with people. A gang of Indian lads in fleece jackets and trainers got on at West India Quay. They all had helium-filled balloons. The balloons were metallic, in the shape of dolphins. At the next stop, a merry black girl bounced in as lightly as the balloons, turning and laughing with her elegantly groomed friends. At Westferry two groups arrived, ebullient new City lads in modern fabrics who sang Abba songs against a competing group of what looked like nurses.

Michael was one of the oldest people there. He watched secure and detached from his early found seat, and settled into a kind of contented concentration.

He seemed to go on settling deeper and deeper. The settling almost made a sound. It would have been a sound like rain.

What were falling were impressions. The black girl had done her hair in perfect rows. The Aids-awareness ribbon on her coat was in fact an enamelled broach. Michael pondered the generosity that impelled her to take up permanently a cause that many people would think was someone else's. The Indian boys began shyly to offer people their balloons. They gave one to Michael.

Michael thought of his chicks. 'We ought to let them all go free,' he said to one of the lads.

'That'd be great. People'd look up and see all these dolphins up in the sky. They'd go like, oh wow, the sky is full of dolphins.'

It seemed to Michael that it was an inspired thing to say. 'I wouldn't let this one go if you don't want me to.'

'Do what you want, man. It's a party.'

Everyone, Michael included, got off at Bank to change onto the Central Line tube. There was a long, long wait for the train. A raucous bevy of young women stood near Michael. They were plump, pale and nearly nude, all in the common fashion of tight trousers, peel-off tops with little straps and shortish hair parted in the middle. They showed off pastures of perfect white shoulders, a sacrifice in winter. They had all written on pieces of paper, which they had taped to themselves. 'Innocent,' said one, 'till proven guilty!' Another said, 'Free to Good Home.' They were all more than a bit pissed and had done something extremely daring in either a pub or a party and couldn't stop talking about it.

When the train came, the girls all ran, though they didn't need to, the thick heels of their shoes clopping like horses' hooves. They swept themselves and Michael into the carriage on a gust of giggles.

Michael sat down and let everything rain around him.

A fat businessman with bags under his eyes like croissants

was gently going to sleep on the shoulder of a young man with slicked-up hair. The young man gently tapped him.

A girl was standing fast asleep against her boyfriend as if slow-dancing. She was thin and pale, almost translucent, with a slight contented smile. It was the smile she would wear lying next to him in their own bed.

And the settling seemed to stop, and Michael came to rest finally on the floor of the ocean, where it was deep and cool and calm and silent.

He loved them all. It had nothing to do with lust, or feeling safely superior, or being merely drunk. He was clear-headed, more clear-headed than he had been in a long time. He saw the girls wanted fun and friends and to be noticed and not to be dull before their time. Michael wished they would always be friends, and always go out, and never go sour from bitterness. He yearned for the sleeping man finally to find family or friends. The young man with the slicked hair had decided to let him go on sleeping, and that it did him no harm to leave him be. Michael wished that people would give the lad the same leeway, and that he would lose his slightly tense, pinched air.

In the quiet, in the peace, it seemed to him that he knew their stories and could guess how far they could go, and loved them like a father loves: from a distance, with best wishes.

It was promiscuous this love, it went beyond lust and romance and making families. Michael moved beyond biology.

The train pulled into the next station and Michael saw its notice slip past like someone trying to sidle unnoticed into the bathroom. He sat and waited for a while as the engine whirred, and he saw the sign partially obscured by the window frame: '. . . ourt Road'.

Jesus Christ, it's Tottenham Court Road! His stop. Just before the doors closed, Michael jumped off. It's 2.30 in the morning, Michael, you can't go missing your stop. He was tired and strolled towards the Northern Line. The balloon bobbed along after him, still tugging at his hand.

Just beyond the arch to the northbound platform, he heard

doors rumbling shut. Oh shit, he'd just missed the train. He jumped forward in time to see the grey and red train sigh away, moaning gently.

The platform was empty.

And there was a rush of wind as if another train were coming, and someone stepped out of the moving air. Michael's body knew the green gym uniform before his mind did. He jumped with recognition.

'Hello there,' said a familiar voice. 'You've stopped coming in for your workout.' It was the Cherub.

'No time, I'm afraid.'

'You've managed to lose some weight though. It suits you.'

'Thank you.'

The Cherub stirred, looking chagrined, and glanced about him. 'I'll try to keep my clothes on this time, shall I?'

It was good to see him. 'So, how is Tony?'

'Tony's fine,' said the Angel. 'Him and the girlfriend are going to move up North. She wants to open a restaurant. You might like to pop in and say goodbye to him. Since, you know, you liked him so much.'

'Thank you. Maybe I will.'

The Angel chuckled. 'Maybe you won't.'

Michael ventured, 'And how are *you*?'

The Angel looked pained. 'Me. I'm a bit different.'

Michael nodded. 'You become different.'

The Angel had a pleading look.

Michael felt love. 'Just ask me,' he whispered.

'I don't want my life to be just working in a restaurant, showing people to tables.'

Michael asked, 'Does that mean Tony doesn't want it either?'

The Angel shook his head. 'No! No way, he loves Jacqui, he wants a family. So, he makes sacrifices. But that doesn't mean that part of him . . . me, I guess . . . part of him wants adventure. He wants to go places, see things. And . . . and I thought I could go there for him. And he could see it, in his dreams, like when we made love, he saw that in his dreams.'

'He saw it for real.'

'Right. He saw it for real.' The Angel had passionate eyes. Need.

'Where,' Michael asked. 'Where do you want to go?' I can do this, Michael realized. My God, what a thing to be able to do.

The Angel's face was set. 'I want to go to Tibet. I want him to see one of those big monasteries. He wants to see Tibet, and, well, I know he never will. I can see all the way to the end you see.'

'Tibet . . .' agreed Michael. Lust pulls you out, pulls you into becoming someone else.

'Can I go now?' the Angel asked, glancing at his watch.

'Yes, now,' promised Michael. 'All you have to do is leave the platform, and when you turn left at the Way Out sign, you'll be in Tibet.'

'Brill!' said the Angel, and shook his hand. 'You're a star, mate. Thanks. Thanks a lot.'

'Say hello to Tony for me.'

'Sure,' the Angel promised. 'I'll make sure he sees it.' The Cherub looked anxiously at his watch and he turned, and broke into a half run. Michael watched his broad back retreat down the platform. The Cherub stopped and waved just outside the exit.

'Do you know why I called you up?' Michael shouted to him.

The Cherub nodded. 'Because you know it's not going to last much longer,' he called.

'Thanks,' said Michael, to the Cherub, to the miracle itself. Michael held a little hand up, a gentle sigh of a wave. He still held the dolphin balloon and it dipped in farewell.

The Cherub turned left and was gone.

Someone tapped Michael on the shoulder. He turned, and there was Henry, red-faced and panting. 'Gotcha,' Henry said, grinning.

Michael was expecting to see an Angel. This Henry's hair dangled differently and he wore a brown sweater with a hole in it. But there was no doubt in Michael's mind that he had called this one up too.

'You're Stumpy,' said Michael, and he found he was grinning.

'As much as anyone is,' replied the Angel. His cheeks glowed silver and sweaty, as if he had run to catch up with Michael. They both grinned and their grins latched as though their braces had locked.

'My God, you're pretty,' said Michael. He couldn't help himself. He took the Angel's hand and to his delight it squeezed back, and the Angel's cheeks glowed even brighter. Michael was a bit pissed and that allowed him to feel his own delight. He glanced up the platform. What the heck. There was no one there, and anyway, it was New Year's Eve. Without any doubt that the Angel would want him, Michael pulled Stumpy to him and kissed him. The Angel shuddered in surprise, and then his mouth worked.

Stumpy was delicious. He tasted of cinnamon. He tasted of celebration. Michael was slightly stunned. He had never kissed someone and felt taste as communication. He pulled back, and looked into Stumpy's beautiful nut-brown eyes.

'I'm embarrassed,' said Stumpy.

'I'm not,' said Michael.

'I didn't say I didn't like it.'

'I'm enraptured,' said Michael, and it was true. He laughed and pulled back and bounced the dolphin balloon up and down in his grasp.

There was answering laughter. Two men settled next to them on the platform and it took a moment for Michael to realize who they were. The Chinese Thai who had danced and grown up to run a plant nursery cradled Mustafa the Afghan. Michael laughed.

'These are Angels,' he announced to Stumpy. 'These are two more of my dear, dear Angels.' And he pulled them to him, and quickly kissed them both.

Stumpy's eyes widened. 'These are them. These are more of them?' He reached out to touch them, and the Thai seized his hand. 'Happy New Year!' the Thai said, syllable by memorized syllable, and dipped his head.

'It's love isn't it?' said Stumpy.

The train arrived but the Thai and the Afghan did not get on it. They waved as if at the departure of a ship, as if saying goodbye. The train pulled away, and they were dragged slowly past the window, and Michael's eyes were suddenly stung as if pricked by bees, and he could not think why.

'I think we must have caught the last train,' he said.

Stumpy smiled up at him. 'This is going to be a very nice New Year's.' He had to shout over the noise of the train. 'A miraculous New Year's.' His eyes were unbelieving and admiring and wondering.

They got off at Camden Town. At the foot of the escalator, the Angel enfolded himself under Michael's arm. The escalator lifted them up towards heaven like the machinery of an eighteenth-century opera.

Outside in the bracing air, the dolphin balloon grinned wide-eyed like a welcoming baby. Michael asked his Angel, who still stayed bleary within his arm, 'Shall we let him go?'

'Aw. Why?' protested Stumpy.

'Because if we let him go, we'll see him swim among the stars,' said Michael.

Stumpy smiled. 'Yes,' he said. 'Balloon liberation. Free all balloons now!'

Michael let the dolphin go. It bobbed for a moment, its eyes still on them as if reluctant, and then it turned away and began to rise.

A drunken man stopped beside them. He was a vicar in a dog collar. 'What a beautiful thing!' he fluted. They all watched together. The dolphin was silver and white and held the reflected light as if it carried candles. 'Fancy a swig?' the vicar asked, and held out a small hip flask of whisky. Both Stumpy and Michael drank. The dolphin gleamed until finally it was one of the stars themselves.

'Which one do you think he is?' Michael asked.

'All of them,' said Stumpy. 'He's become all of them. Or maybe all of them were dolphins all along.'

They walked north with the vicar, who was as pink as a rose, and they all began to sing 'Jerusalem'. 'And did those feet in ancient time?' They parted at the empty market street, waving goodbye.

Stumpy went all floppy, his hair lashing Michael's arms.

'I'm sorry. I don't usually drink,' he said.

'That's OK,' whispered Michael.

'I've never met anyone like you,' said the Angel, his eyes squiffy.

'Well, I've met Henry, who is like you.'

Stumpy nodded yes, a wide grin on his face. 'He's me when I'm older. He says I ought to become a politician. I think that's what he did. He even told me which Labour MP I should ask to work with.' This little Angel was very proud of himself. 'I'm going to do that.' He seemed to come into focus. 'The trouble with protests is that nothing happens. Nothing changes. That's not good enough.' His eyes had the hunger, the light that Michael had seen in Henry's eyes, to change things for the better.

Michael thought he had never seen anyone as beautiful. He said, 'That just happens to be my front door.'

They stumbled up the stairway and into the front room, and Michael switched on the light and the Picassos on the wall seemed to leap into life. Stumpy saw them and seemed to think the locale had painted them.

'I love Camden Town. It's like it could have been posh and rich, but it decided not to be. So it's full of good things and it's sleazy at the same time.' The Angel put his hand on Michael's breast. 'Like you.'

There was something in the Angel's eyes that had been given too quickly and too completely for Michael not to feel over-whelmed.

He found he chuckled and ducked. 'You're drunk. Let's get you to bed.'

And they thumped up the final staircase.

Stumpy undressed as Henry always did, slowly and methodi-cally in a way that meant all the clothes in the morning would look ironed. And that somehow cancelled out any doubt that he was anything other than what he said he was.

'I'm too sleepy for sex,' he said simply. 'Do you mind?'

'I don't think,' said Michael, 'that this is about sex.'

'It's about dolphins,' said Stumpy and grinned.

Stumpy slipped out of his trousers and his underwear and his skin all over was almost as silver as the dolphin's. He stumbled against the bed and then into it.

'Goodnight, my love,' said Michael. It was that quick and that simple and that unthinking.

Stumpy reached back over himself and took Michael's hand. Michael snapped off the light, and as heavy as curtains, sleep fell. In a dream, he looked up into the sky, and it was full of dolphins, and knew somehow it was a dawn sky.

Later, there was a movement in Michael's head. It was not entirely pleasant to feel the flesh inside his skull flex like a muscle. He woke up, and everything was dusky grey, in a different year. The blackbirds were singing their unexpectedly beautiful song, though they lived south in the Gardens next to Michael's old life.

Michael's mouth was dry from dehydration. Dreamily he stood up and padded out of his bed. And he felt the realities part again, as a series of curtains.

Dropping away.

He was padding down the corridor of the condo in California. He heard his father snore. Rest in peace, he murmured. I will always love you and you will always love me. Somewhere in eternity we are father and son running on that beach, and it doesn't matter what kind of love I feel for you.

And he moved past the little table with the telephone to turn left, leaving Philip behind him in their big Lancashire bed. He turned at the doorway, to see him asleep in their old flat. Well, what do you know, baby? We both finally grew up.

And he slipped downstairs towards the sitting room in the Camden flat and the expressionistic toilet. Who had left the lights on? He thumped down the steps and was only mildly surprised to see there was a party. It was all right, he realized. He had been having a New Year's party of his own.

'Hello, hello!' said James the Irish monk, merrily. He was wearing a lumberjack shirt now, instead of monk's robes, and a handsome moustached man in plus fours canoodled next to him. 'This is my George. I wanted you to meet him. He came to the monastery. He followed me all the way to California and I just went away with him to Big Sur.' They both had grey hair.

Michael smiled, pleased for them.

'Ah!' A voice. 'Ah, my old friend!' And Michael was suddenly enveloped in Picasso's arms. 'Look, look at what you made possible for me!' Picasso threw an arm up towards the wall of beautiful paintings. 'Here, here, did you see this?' He pushed a leaflet at him, glossy and in four colours. It was for an exhibition. 'MODERNIZING ART' it said, and showed a computer screen full of glowing colours. It was Michael's own mirror face.

Al pressed against him, and stepped back and was enfolded in the generous arms of Mark. 'We've just realized we should have met because of you,' said Mark. 'You and I would have become lovers for a while and afterwards Al and I would get together.'

'And then we'd both be alive,' said Al.

'Can you be together now?'

'We always were. That was the potential,' said Al. He seized Michael's hand hard. 'And that's as real as if it had actually happened.'

Someone put on music. The old Oceanside record player sang out *Cinderella*.

Bottles came dancing towards Michael, and took him up mischievously in her arms. She held her nose up in the air, miming Broadway posh.

Billie Holiday leaned next to the record player. She was older now, in the 1950s, and she was wearing a blue satin dress.

'Man,' Billie said, chuckling to herself. 'How can anybody sing that stuff? It sticks in your throat.'

She tried anyway. Billie sang Julie Andrews as if it were true in her rough old voice.

It was a sweet song about falling in love. Billie gave it uncertainty. Billie turned it into a song about last chances.

The old music swelled, and the two voices blended, hopeful, exhausted and innocent, exalted. The sweet long ended.

'Happy New Year,' growled Billie and held up an unsteady toast for them all.

398

And there was Henry.

Henry was weeping with joy. 'It's all right Michael,' he said, shaking. 'It really is all right. Everything will be fine. Really.' Michael hugged him, to soothe him.

'I love you,' said Michael.

'I love you too,' said Henry.

Michael said, 'You know who's upstairs?'

Henry nodded yes and smiled.

'You planned this!' exclaimed Michael, realizing.

Henry closed his eyes once and opened them. 'I can see all the way to the end,' he said. His eyes were as steady as car headlights. 'I am,' he said, 'there.' And he pointed far away, beyond. Michael knew what he meant: Always.

'I gotta pee,' explained Michael.

Michael stumbled out of his sitting room into the dark landing with the floor that would ram slivers into his feet. Parched, headachy and hungover, he slumped down on his own cold-seated toilet, and held his head in his hands.

He could feel a movement in the structured fat of his brain, a kind of kink, as if it had shifted gears. Abruptly the music was turned off.

Suddenly it was dawn for real, grey and quiet.

Michael wiped himself and padded out into his neglected sitting room. It was empty and quiet and dark. God, it was drab. It was like a hangover after a party was over. Why was it so dull suddenly? It wasn't just that the lights were off.

Then he saw why.

The walls were blank. All the Picassos were gone. So was the desk that was the only thing Picasso had directly carried up the steps himself.

And suddenly, eyes wide with terror, Michael knew what that meant. It's over. My God, it's over. And then he remembered Stumpy. He had not got the Angel's home address. And he couldn't ask Henry; Henry would be gone. Would the real Stumpy have any trace of memory of meeting Michael? What if he couldn't find Stumpy again?

Michael ran up the stairs and darted round the lintel of the doorway into the bedroom. And he saw the bed was full. A

399

pale, silver arm reached across the empty sheet for Michael.
Everything else had gone, but the real Stumpy was still there.
 Then Michael knew what that meant, too.